Gathering the Threads

Books by Cindy Woodsmall

The Amish of Summer Grove series

Ties That Bind

Fraying at the Edge

Gathering the Threads

Sisters of the Quilt series

When the Heart Cries

When the Morning Comes

When the Soul Mends

Ada's House series

The Hope of Refuge

The Bridge of Peace

The Harvest of Grace

Amish Vines and Orchards series

A Season for Tending

The Winnowing Season

For Every Season

Seasons of Tomorrow

Novellas

The Sound of Sleigh Bells

The Christmas Singing

The Dawn of Christmas

The Scent of Cherry Blossoms

Amish Christmas at North Star

The Angel of Forest Hill

Nonfiction

Plain Wisdom: An Invitation into an Amish Home and the Hearts of Two Women

CINDY WOODSMALL

New York Times and CBA Best-Selling Author

Gathering the Threads

THE AMISH *of* SUMMER GROVE, BOOK THREE

WATERBROOK

Gathering the Threads

Trade Paperback ISBN 978-1-60142-703-8
eBook ISBN 978-1-60142-704-5

Cover design and photography by Kelly L. Howard

Published in the United States by WaterBrook, an imprint of the Crown Publishing Group, a division of Penguin Random House LLC, New York.

Library of Congress Cataloging-in-Publication Data
Names: Woodsmall, Cindy, author.
Title: Gathering the threads / Cindy Woodsmall.
Description: First Edition. | New York : WaterBrook, 2017. | Series: The Amish of Summer Grove ; book 3
Identifiers: LCCN 2017019622| ISBN 9781601427038 (paperback) | ISBN 9781601427045 (electronic)
Subjects: | BISAC: FICTION / Romance / Contemporary. | FICTION / Christian / Romance. | GSAFD: Christian fiction.
Classification: LCC PS3623.O678 G38 2017 | DDC 813/.6—dc23
LC record available at https://lccn.loc.gov/2017019622

Printed in the United States of America
2017—First Edition

10 9 8 7 6 5 4 3 2 1

To Carol Bartley
with extreme gratitude,
fervent trust,
deep honor,
and an abiding hope for our future.
I'm indebted to you for editing every book I've written.

The Amish of Summer Grove series

The story so far . . .

Ties That Bind begins at an Amish birthing center, where a single, *Englisch* college student, Brandi Nash, gives birth to her daughter as a fire engulfs the building. A few minutes later an Amish woman, Lovina Brenneman, gives birth to twins, a girl and a boy. The midwife and Lovina's husband, Isaac, struggle to get the women and three babies to safety.

Chapter 2 moves forward twenty years, and Ariana Brenneman is trying to buy an abandoned café so she can help support her parents and siblings. She and her twin brother, Abram, have been working and saving for years to purchase it. As time is running out, Ariana's one-time friend Quill Schlabach offers to help her raise money by holding a benefit, but Ariana wants nothing to do with him. Five years ago he broke her heart when he left Summer Grove in the middle of the night, taking with him Frieda, Ariana's closest friend. Although Ariana has moved on and is seeing Rudy, a young man she cares for deeply, she resents how Quill and Frieda deceived and betrayed her.

Quill tries to win Ariana's trust, knowing that if she will act on his ideas, she will raise the money she needs. Although Quill continues to conceal why he left with Frieda, he longs for healing between Ariana and himself. But his main purpose for being in Summer Grove is to help an unhappy, disillusioned family—Ariana's eldest sister, Salome, and her family—leave the Amish.

Ariana lets down her guard and trusts Quill's guidance. Although Rudy has reservations, he backs her as she, Quill, and Abram hold a benefit, which raises the needed money.

While Ariana and Abram are focused on the café, their brother Mark sees a musical production in a nearby city and is struck by how much one performer looks like Salome. When Mark tells their *Mamm,* she seems concerned.

Lovina and Isaac ask Quill to investigate the background of this young woman, Skylar Nash. Quill obtains enough information to validate that she is probably Isaac and Lovina's biological daughter, which would mean Ariana is Brandi's daughter. Quill contacts Skylar's parents, Brandi Nash and Nicholas Jenkins, and a DNA test confirms that Skylar is not related to Brandi or Nicholas, and it also reveals that Skylar has drugs in her system.

Lovina struggles with the knowledge that her biological daughter seems so lost, and Nicholas, an atheist, is appalled that his daughter has been raised in an insulated religious society. When he learns that the midwife suspected the two girls might have been accidentally switched at birth and never did anything about it, he threatens to sue her unless Ariana spends a year with him and Brandi, cut off from the Amish community. And Nicholas gives Skylar a choice—time in rehab or time with her biological family—or he will cut off all financial support.

When Ariana learns that she's not a Brenneman and that Quill helped uncover the truth, she once again feels betrayed by him and asks him never to contact her again. Ariana leaves Summer Grove with Brandi and Nicholas to spend a year with them. And Quill picks up Skylar, confiscates the drugs she tries to hide, and drives her to the Brennemans' home.

Fraying at the Edge begins one day after Ariana meets her biological parents and leaves with them to live in their Englisch world. Brandi and Nicholas are married to other people, and the story opens with Ariana at Nicholas's home as her parents argue bitterly. She has three stepsiblings—two teen boys, who live with her dad, and one teen girl, who lives with her mom, Brandi.

Before she can adjust to the outside world and the loneliness of leaving her family and boyfriend, Rudy, behind, Nicholas gives her lists of things she *must* accomplish. His list includes removing her prayer *Kapp,* getting a new hairstyle, dressing Englisch, learning to drive, and being tutored in college-type courses on religion, history, and science. Nicholas appears determined to scrub the Amish ways from her mind and heart before she returns to Summer Grove.

Ariana's mom, Brandi, seems free spirited and easygoing, but despite that, she staunchly and loudly stands up to Nicholas. Ariana's parents' anger and contradictory expectations drain and confuse her in ways she's never experienced, and she feels herself coming undone.

During Ariana's time of exile from Summer Grove, Nicholas allows her to have contact with only one person from her past: Quill Schlabach. Since Quill left the Amish as a teen and never returned to join the faith, Nicholas believes he could be a helpful influence in opening Ariana's mind and heart to better ways of living than in the Amish society.

But Quill's singular desire is to help Ariana navigate this temporary upheaval and return to her beloved people and the Old Ways. Unfortunately, even though Ariana needs a friend in this strange setting, she refuses to reach out to Quill because twice he's hidden the truth from her and ripped her life apart.

Nicholas's expectations of Ariana and the pressure to adjust increase, and then Ariana learns that she is the result of an adulterous affair and that her parents were never married to each other. Desperate to talk to someone who understands her and the Old Ways, she finally calls Quill. Their encounter, which takes place at a bar, is far from smooth, but he gets her back to Nicholas's home safely.

Quill talks to Nicholas privately and makes him see that in his efforts to strip Ariana's mind of the Old Ways and religion, he is ripping *her* apart. Nicholas's viewpoint begins to change. His goal is still to broaden Ariana's mind, but his methods become gentler, and he begins to see the true Ariana—not a brainwashed girl, but a unique, fascinating, strong woman who is trying to do right by everyone.

After much angst and a few heated arguments, Ariana forms a bond with Nicholas, Brandi, her husband, Gabe, and his daughter, Cameron. Ariana develops a real thirst for knowledge because of Nicholas's influence. And her time with Quill becomes healing, helpful, and sometimes fun. He helps her get her feet under her, view God as bigger than she'd ever imagined possible, and learn when and how to stand up for herself.

With Ariana gone, her Mamm and *Daed* are struggling with guilt and fear for both girls—Ariana and Skylar—and all the changes to the family dynamics are taking a toll.

Abram, Susie, and Martha—three of the Brenneman siblings—work hard to get Ariana's new café on its feet. They want it to be a success when she returns, but they know nothing about running a café, and none of them can cook the items Ariana listed on the menu before she left.

Skylar is used to a comfy Englisch lifestyle, and her Amish dad, Isaac, quickly confronts her idle ways with the Amish work ethic and the need for accountability and contributing to the family. When pushed to help the family, she chooses to work at the café, knowing that is her best opportunity to see her forbidden boyfriend and get drugs from him.

Because Skylar knows a lot more about how to make a café appealing than Ariana's siblings do, she talks them into spending money Ariana set aside to pay the mortgage on the café in order to buy expensive coffee machines and a generator. But inside the Brenneman home, Skylar struggles with the endless lack of money and creature comforts. Without warning, Skylar's boyfriend stops bringing drugs to the café for her, and she has a physical and emotional crisis.

The Brennemans meet the challenges with Skylar, and she gets clean. Because of her Amish parents' tough love, she begins to bond with them and her siblings. But at the same time, she and Jax, a friend of Abram's and a former marine, have trouble navigating their emotions for each other. They are drawn to each other but are also distrustful of each other. Jax has good cause to hate drug use and distrust users, but he and Skylar manage a truce for the sake of the café and its workers.

Cilla Yoder, a friend of Abram's who works at the cafe, has dealt with cystic fibrosis throughout her life. When he witnesses one of her spells, he realizes she needs a better doctor. Jax, Skylar, Susie, and Martha work together to help Abram find one and pay for the medical expenses by dipping into the café's money.

Gradually Ariana develops a new understanding of God and every adult's right to stand against authority, including a father's. She uses this knowledge to talk Nicholas into letting her return to Summer Grove early.

Nicholas and Brandi set up a meeting with Skylar. They come to the café after hours and invite her to return home. Now that she's clean, they're willing to pay for her tuition and other perks again. Skylar shares her hurt and anger that they dumped her on the Brennemans and took off with Ariana without even looking back, and she refuses to leave Summer Grove.

Ariana has longed to return to her faith, family, and her cherished Rudy, but after she's pulled her hair into a bun and put on her Amish clothing, she stares into the mirror and feels unsure about who she really is. When Nicholas drives her home and she gets out of his car, she's thrilled to embrace her Amish family, but before the evening is finished, she feels a strong need to get away for several days to think.

For a list of main characters in the Amish of Summer Grove series, see the Main Characters list at the end of the book.

One

Summer Grove, Pennsylvania

Ariana's head roared with voices, those in the kitchen around her and others from far away, even from hundreds of years in the past. Voices of real people she'd talked to or had heard preach or teach, as well as the voices from the many books Nicholas had asked her to read. The voices grouped in clans, their murmurings growing fervent, insisting precisely what she needed to believe, who she needed to be, and why she needed to march to the beat of their drum.

Ariana needed to know herself well enough to pick a tribe she agreed with and shut down the rest with her own reasoning. But she couldn't parse what she believed, and they hounded without mercy.

Marred flatware jangled endlessly as her nine siblings, five of her fourteen nieces and nephews, her Mamm and Daed, and Skylar sat around the table in rickety chairs. The mid-January wind pushed against the house and seemed to come right through the walls.

An old galvanized bucket sat in the sink because the water pipe to the kitchen was broken again. If the pipes to the sink in the mudroom hadn't been working, getting breakfast on the table would've been a lot more work.

Rickety furniture, cold winds seeping in, and broken pipes didn't bother her. Money and work could easily fix those things. What nagged at her was much deeper. She was finally in the very home she'd pined for while away, and yet only a fragment of herself seemed to be here.

Her Daed worked really hard, but his income was too small for a family this size. Ariana couldn't remember a time when she didn't long to make life better for them. That was why she and Abram had spent years working to buy the café. She had been convinced it would bring in enough money to make life easier for Mamm and Daed.

The voices in her head grew louder. One group said money was evil and poverty was God's will, that it made people rely on Him more. Another group shouted louder than the first, saying that lack was from the Enemy. Still more voices said that being poor was due to a lack of education. A dozen more camps vied to be heard, and Ariana was powerless to sort them out.

"Ariana." Mamm pointed at her plate, sounding baffled, maybe even alarmed. "Is this not your favorite breakfast anymore?"

A stack of pancakes stared back at Ariana. Her stomach churned. "It is. *Denki,* Mamm." She used the edge of her fork to cut into the pancakes.

"You're not yourself." Susie passed her a plate of bacon. "That's more plain to see than your poorly pinned-up hair under your lopsided prayer Kapp."

Her bun was messy and her head covering was pinned askew? She should at least adjust the Kapp, but she simply nodded. "I'm a little out of sorts. That's all."

She didn't feel just a little out of sorts. She longed to scream at the voices in her head to shut up.

Salome smiled. "Anyone who'd been through what you have would be feeling strange. I imagine you feel as if you've been through the blades of a hay baler."

That depiction had a decent amount of accuracy, but to be more precise, her brain felt as if it had been rubbed with poison oak, and it screamed in discomfort, begging to be soothed with a poultice of clay, apple cider vinegar, and peppermint.

"A hay baler?" Daed smiled at her. "You'll be right as rain soon enough. A little time here at home with us and your Rudy, and you'll feel like yourself again. I guarantee it." He took a bite of food. "Forget what's behind you. Only look ahead."

"He's right." Mamm drew her mug toward her lips. "There's much to look forward to." She peered over her mug, smiling. "Your wedding for one."

Rudy must've told them they'd decided to marry. What else had he told them? When she'd arrived home last night, Rudy had seemed unusually connected to her parents, even asking Ariana to wait while he spoke privately to her Mamm. Ariana had been so involved in her own thoughts that the incident hadn't meant anything to her, but today it seemed a little curious.

Right now she didn't want to talk about a wedding, and she was pretty sure her parents knew it. She wanted to discuss her immediate future. Ariana forked a bite of pancakes, hoping she looked calm and natural. "Rather than my wedding, I'd like to discuss moving in with Berta."

When she'd mentioned the idea the night before, the reaction had been swift and negative. She'd defended Berta, leading to a respectful, soft-spoken disagreement with her parents as they tried to stuff her into the same thinking, the same role, the same box she'd been in before she left. It no longer fit. This morning as Ariana looked from her Daed to her Mamm, their facial expressions hadn't altered one bit. It was as if they hadn't heard her.

"A wedding and then"—Daed swept his arms open as if gesturing to a large crowd—"you'll be expecting your first little one by winter for sure. That's what you need to focus on, Ariana. It's what all our attention needs to be on."

"Okay," Skylar said, sounding offended, "the marrying-young part I get. They're in love, and they want to get busy."

"Skylar," Mamm chided, "we don't talk that way."

Mark chuckled. "What was the rest of your thought, Sky Blue?"

"Planning to have a baby that quickly after getting married is crazy. Completely crazy, especially in this day and age. If I understand right, they'll marry this fall. She'll barely be twenty-one. What about a little time for just her and Rudy?"

"That's not God's way, Skylar." Daed took a bite of bacon. "If people are mature enough to marry, they are ready to have children. Waiting is the Englisch way. Birth control and wanting the babies to come at a convenient time are worldly. God said that children are a blessing, and He commanded us to be fruitful and multiply."

Heat skittered across Ariana's skin. "He didn't *command* it," she mumbled.

"What?" Daed's voice deepened, and his brows furrowed.

She should've kept her mouth shut. "I just meant that we don't know it was a command."

"Of course we do." Daed's hands fisted as they rested on the table. "What are you saying, Ariana?"

Memories of living in the Englisch world and crying out to God to help her return home circled in her mind. She'd wanted to get back to her Amish roots as quickly as possible. She hadn't wanted to leave here in the first place, but she'd had no choice, and while she was on the outside, a different kind of life, a different way of thinking had been poured into her, purposefully and with diligence, for three months. Now it felt strange to sit at this table with her hair pinned up again and her Amish clothes on while science and philosophy books and Bible passages translated from the Hebrew text danced in her head.

She knew her Daed was waiting on an apology and a confession of belief that lined up with the church's teachings. But when she tried to say what was expected, the words disappeared. All eyes were on her, and every adult seemed unable to move. She had to respond.

"Daed, with respect, it seems we've been taught that God commanded things that aren't actually commands." She'd said enough, so she bit her tongue, but the rest of what came to mind shocked even her. *Even if God commanded people to multiply, that was thousands of years ago, long be-*

fore the planet had seven billion people. Is that what she believed, or were Nicholas's thoughts simply filling her head?

Daed seemed dumbfounded, but then anger grew hard in his eyes. He set his napkin on the table and pushed back. "If we're to be at church on time, we better get moving." He stood. "It seems one of us needs every moment of it she can get."

Ariana watched as he went into the living room. Her brothers walked toward the back door, and she knew they would put on their coats and go to the barn to hitch horses to enough carriages to get the throng to church.

Her sisters started clearing the table.

"Ari." Her youngest sister put her hands on her hips. "It's Daed's house, and you are his child. What are you thinking?"

"She's not property, Martha," Skylar corrected. "She has a right to think her own thoughts, speak them, and act on them."

Ariana had no idea what to say, so she stood and began stacking plates, wishing she didn't have to go to the Sunday meeting. It would mean listening to yet another voice telling her what she needed to think and who she needed to be.

"The Word says children are to obey," Mamm said. "And God didn't put an expiration date on that, although once she's married, her Daed will keep his opinions to himself."

"Well." Susie unloaded an armful of dirty glasses onto the counter near the sink. "Maybe God didn't give a cutoff date because He expected people to use common sense."

The voices of Mamm, her sisters, and Skylar moved inside Ariana's head to their respective tribes—the very conservative, the rational conservative, and the feminist—and joined the other chorus of voices.

Ariana longed for a moment of silence, where all voices let her think in peace. Maybe then she'd know who she was and what *she* thought.

Salome put her arm around Ariana's shoulders. "I'm glad you're home."

"Denki," Ariana mumbled.

Salome squeezed her. "We need time to talk, just sisters catching up, *ya*?"

"We do." But right now Ariana was busy thinking about a different woman in this room, the one she was watching. Skylar had on jeans and a tunic sweater. Since the three-hour service of songs, messages, and prayer would be in a language she didn't know, she wasn't required to go. Because she hadn't been born into this home, she wasn't required to wear the cape dress, apron, or prayer Kapp.

What about Ariana's rights?

"Salome"—Ariana held out the stack of dishes—"I need to talk to Daed. It might be a good idea to pray for me . . . or him."

Salome took the dishes, and Ariana went into the living room. Daed had a poker in his hand, banking the fire before they left the house for the next seven hours of travel, the service, a small meal, and expected fellowship.

"Daed, I . . . I know you won't understand this or agree with it, and I'm sorry about that, but I need a few days away to think. Out of town, at a hotel probably."

He stood. "Have you lost your mind, child?"

"Not yet, no."

He crouched again, shaking burning logs until hunks of embers fell into the heap. "We're so glad you're back. We've missed you, Ari." He remained crouched as he turned to look at her. "You really don't want to be here?"

He sounded so hurt.

"I do, Daed. Please trust me on that. I just need a few days away to think."

He focused on the fireplace again. "What you need is to be here, with us. To renew your mind to Christ's ways."

Christ renewing her mind would be lovely, but Christians wouldn't agree on exactly what that would mean or what she should think as proof that her mind had indeed been renewed by Christ and not by the world or heresy.

Sparks flew upward as Daed prodded the fiery embers. "Trust me to guide you, Ariana, and you'll be fine. You're feeling the pangs of transition, nothing more." He stood. "Transitions are always hard, but you just need to trust God."

"I do trust Him. But—"

"That's *gut.* We don't need to discuss anything else right now." He set the poker in its stand and picked up the shovel.

"*Nee,* Daed. I'm telling you that I need this."

He pushed ashes in a circle, making a crater of embers. "You're fine." His voice was calm, as if she were a five-year-old saying she wanted another ice cream.

She couldn't stand it. Of course he didn't understand. She didn't either, but it was every bit as unbearable as her first days adjusting to Englisch life, only then she believed it was her place to submit and obey. She needed to understand who she was so that no matter what happened in life, whether she was fully Amish or was stripped of it, poor or wealthy, single or married, she would know *this is who I am*—whatever *this* was.

Her thoughts meandered to her Englisch family. Her mom, Gabe, and Cameron were probably returning to their fancy home after a morning run. They would be dressed totally inappropriately, and without her there it might be a coin toss as to whether they went to church or not. Yet Ariana had come to love them and their unconventional ways of looking at faith. But learning to respect her Englisch mom, stepdad, and stepsister hadn't helped her know who she was and what she thought.

Her dad was probably in his recliner, reading some hard-to-understand book by a learned philosopher, cognitive scientist, or historian. She'd started out hating it when he'd shoved his beloved facts at her. A few weeks in, she began to find the knowledge fascinating. Part of her wished she could sit down with her Englisch dad and discuss the deep matters that were taboo in this home.

"Daed." Her voice sounded firm, but her insides were trembling. Was she really going to go against him?

He turned to face her.

"Out of respect for you and Mamm and a desire not to cause trouble with the preachers, I'll go to the Sunday meeting and stay with the family until we return midafternoon. But then I'll hire a driver to pick me up, and I'm going away for a few days."

His face mirrored disbelief, then fear, which quickly turned to anger. He walked over to her, his shoulders filling her view. "You came home only yesterday, and today you doubt whether you want to join the Amish or not?"

"What? No. That's not it at all, Daed. I suddenly have two million opinions zipping and zooming inside my head, and I need time to silence them. Time to sort them out. But most of all I need to understand who I am. I don't think I've ever really been clear on that."

"You're a child of God."

"I am."

"And you're Amish, today and always."

"Daed, *kumm* on, of course."

He relaxed a bit. "Then what else is there to figure out?"

"I don't know." Did she sound as torn and scattered as she felt? "Everything. Nothing. But at least something."

"That makes no sense."

"If you think that makes no sense, you should spend one minute inside my head. I need this, Daed. Please."

"Nee. A young Amish woman alone at a hotel? I can't allow that."

She had no desire to disrespect his needs while trying to address her own. "Then let Salome go with me."

The ministers and community were likely to discover she'd left for a few days. There wasn't really a way to hide something like that, but if Salome went with her, it would ease everyone's minds and keep it from sounding completely unbefitting. The community wouldn't have any trouble believing that after being in the world, she needed a few days with a good Amish woman, someone older and wiser, to help talk her through all she saw and experienced while *draus in da Welt.* Since no one outside the family, other than Quill, knew that Salome had planned to leave the Amish, her reputation was fully intact.

Fortunately for Ariana, Salome had good reason to understand Ariana's feelings of confusion and the opposing views being shoved at her. But how would Ariana pay for it?

Abram tapped on the door frame. "The carriages are ready, and the rest of the family is getting in them now."

She turned to the man she'd grown up believing was her twin. He looked so different, mature and more confident. What had happened to him these past three months?

"Abram, I'm sorry to ask this, but I could use a bit of money. Does the café have any discretionary cash left?"

Daed's face was pale now, and his shoulders seemed to quake. "I'm not agreeing to you going away."

She faced him, an eyebrow raised. "I understand, but I am going away."

Abram shrugged. "Maybe." He walked to a bookshelf and picked up three ledgers and an overstuffed manila envelope.

He'd said *maybe.* Her blood ran cold. "I . . . I thought the café was doing well."

"It is, and if you need a reasonable amount of cash, it's there. But be aware that no one has received a full paycheck yet."

"What?" Her head spun, and her knees suddenly felt like gelatin. "But when I closed on the café, there was enough money left over from the benefit to pay the bills on the café, so the day-to-day income should've covered paychecks, plus income for Mamm and Daed." The whole purpose of her years of trying to get the café was to make money so Mamm and Daed didn't live in poverty.

"I know that was the plan, but it hasn't worked out that way exactly. The largest portion of the money was used to help Cilla Yoder get a better doctor, new medical tests, and much better medication."

"Oh." Relief ran warm through Ariana, but just what kind of financial shape was the café in?

He passed her the books. "Everything you need to know is in there. I was going to wait until tomorrow to give them to you."

"But you've paid the mortgage each month, right?"

Abram looked at the ledgers. Was that doubt concerning what had and hadn't been paid?

Ariana's heart pounded. He and the others had sacrificed months of their lives to keep the café running until she returned, and here she stood, not only asking for money, but also planning to take a few days off when she had yet to work one! What was she thinking?

She set the ledgers back on the bookshelf. Right now she needed to put on her coat and go to church. Surely when the time came to focus on the ledgers, she could get the café finances straight. At least she hoped she could.

"Denki." She hugged Abram. "You did the right thing for Cilla and her family. That was the best possible way to use the money."

Daed dusted ashes off his hands. "The lack of money settles it, as it often does."

"Not this time, Daed."

He angled his head, looking at her as if she were an outsider. The issue was, she felt like a stranger even to herself. But a little time away would help that. She knew that as much as she knew her own name. A sense of peace rolled over her as she settled into the plan.

The need for money was only a speed bump. Nothing more.

Daed's eyes reflected confusion, and she felt sorry for him. She wished she could give him what he needed—the same obedient, naive Amish daughter who'd left here.

He pointed at her. "I forbid you to ask your siblings or brothers-in-law for money to do such a thing as this. While we're on the topic, that includes any other Amish person or someone related to the Amish, namely Quill. Do you understand?"

From the corner of her eye, Ariana saw someone enter the room. Based on the color scheme, she knew it had to be Skylar. It was a reminder that both of Ariana's Englisch parents had money. Nicholas could be a real pain about some things, but it would actually make him happy to give her money. Of course she would pay him back once she got the finances squared away on the café.

She glanced at Skylar.

"I'll be sure it doesn't come from anyone Amish."

Daed looked in the same direction Ariana had a moment earlier. His expression changed, as if he'd just remembered that Ariana had other resources.

What unfair challenges was she heaping on the man who'd raised her?

"Daed, I didn't do well during the transition from here to the Englisch world. I ended up in a bar, unknowingly drinking alcohol while some man who resembled Jesus tried to take advantage of me."

Daed fell backward into the closest chair. Concern etched deep within the wrinkles on his face. "Child . . ."

"Quill arrived, and he got me home safely. But I landed in that bar because I kept ignoring how splintered and confused I felt while I did what was expected of me." At least this time she knew herself well enough to realize she had to get away and think.

Daed nodded, but the grief in his eyes broke her heart.

Could she figure out anything within a few days that would make what she was doing to Daed and her family worthwhile?

Two

Skylar fisted her hands inside her coat pockets. *Just keep walking. Don't turn around.*

Dirty snow crunched under the soles of her boots. Her face smoldered as anger burned within her. Walking along the side of the road, she topped the stupid hill. Again.

Every time she got to this spot, she saw the phone shanty. Regardless of what she needed right now, Jax didn't want to hear from her. Not really. He was nice to her. Always. But that was because of who he was and how much he liked Abram and Susie, not because of how he felt about her.

"Just walk. Don't go home. Don't call *him*." Skylar squared her shoulders while mumbling to herself. But she'd come to this spot six or seven times over the last hour. Passing it by a quarter of a mile or so and then returning here, trying to trick herself into believing she could suffocate the craving on her own.

A daydream danced before her. She could see herself after taking a couple of pills—not too many, just enough to take the edge off—feeling chill and her mind freed of all the world's heartaches. That's all she needed.

She shivered as cold sweat ran down her back. All those empty Amish homes, families away having church . . . Could she find anything there?

If she could just talk to him . . . "Come on, Skylar. Have some guts, for Pete's sake. No drugs. No guys."

But it wasn't as if he would be drawn to her, and he wouldn't be rude either. And God was her witness that if she had anyone else to talk to about this, she would. Still, she walked away.

She stopped cold and turned to look at the shanty. Like a drowning girl trying to make her way to a life preserver, she headed for the phone. If she didn't reach out to someone, she wasn't sure what she would do. Something desperate.

After the Brennemans had left for church, she put on her coat and boots and started walking. Thank God for meeting Sundays! Those two days each month gave her time to do what she wanted without anyone there to answer to.

Usually she ate junk food, smoked cigarettes, and read *People* magazines—all of which she purchased with her tip money at a little gas station near the café. But today she'd been unable to go back to sleep or even sit still. Her emotions were taking her everywhere, but nowhere good, and the desire to ransack medicine cabinets and find a drug made her flee the house.

Once at the shanty she opened the door, which creaked as she went inside. An old phone sat on a handmade desk that was basically a long shelf. She picked up the receiver and dialed a number.

"Hello?" Jax sounded wide awake and upbeat, even though it wasn't yet ten on a Sunday morning. The background noise sounded different, as if her call was coming through the Bluetooth device in his vehicle. If it was, whatever she said would be on speaker. What if he wasn't alone?

Despite Skylar's ability to be brazenly outspoken, she couldn't find her voice.

"Is this an automated sales call on a Sunday?" he asked. "You have to the count of three to speak. One . . . two . . ."

"Don't hang up." She sounded pitiful and desperate, and she wished she'd just let him end the call.

"Uh, okay."

Silence hung in the air as Skylar wrangled with using him as a sounding board. Did he even know who was on this end of the call? Maybe she could hang up and he'd never realize who it was.

"Skylar, you still there?" Jax asked.

Too late. Since he already distrusted her, no matter what she said, he certainly couldn't think any less of her. More important, he had experience with addicts.

"Yeah." She drew a deep breath. "Look, I know you want to keep your distance from someone like me, and in theory I understand. I'm not the easiest person to be around. But I've been clean nine weeks and six days, and when tomorrow comes, I'd like to say I've been clean ten weeks. You know?"

"Okay. I get it. Tell me what you need."

"I have no idea!" She pulled the cigarettes from her coat pocket and lit one.

"You at the farm?"

"Yeah, like they have a phone, and I'm in my pj's all cozy by the fire while we talk."

"True. What phone—gas station or the community one?"

"I'm at the community one." She drew smoke into her lungs. "Sorry for snapping."

"Yeah, like you have to be calm and reserved or I can't handle it." He imitated her sarcasm, except he was being kind instead of bratty.

Silence filled the air again. She had no idea what to say, but he was nothing like she imagined a former marine would be. Kind, upbeat, and really honest. She was drawn to his honesty as much as he was cautious of her addiction.

"Don't go quiet, Skylar. You called with vinegar in your blood. Cut a vein and let it out."

"Ariana's back."

"Yeah, you've known for a few weeks now that she was coming, right?"

She inhaled the smoke, and the burning tobacco mimicked how she felt—a small, angry fire that left poisons in its wake, toxins she would pay for years down the road. "Knowing about a thing and it happening are entirely different."

"Very true."

"I met her yesterday."

"How'd that go?"

"She was really nice to me. It blew my mind. The family had killed the fatted calf, so to speak, and we had a feast last night. But the pleasant conversation turned sour. Lovina and Isaac want her to think and feel like she did before going away. I felt bad for them. I could hear my dad's influence in Ariana's answers, and yet everything she said was reasonable, and what she wants is perfectly normal for someone our age . . . who's not Amish." Skylar sat in the metal folding chair, and it sent a chill through her. "It caused so much friction her boyfriend took her outside to go for a walk." She told him about the breakfast conversation and how she ended up defending Ariana to her sisters. "But then . . ." Skylar trembled as anger crawled out of its hiding place. "Are you in your truck by yourself?"

"Of course. If I wasn't, I would've said so right after *hello*."

She should've known that. "Ariana is leaving again. Around four this afternoon. She told Isaac that she needed to go away, and she is going, against his wishes." Skylar opened the door to the shanty and flicked her cigarette into the snow. "I've been stuck in this hellhole working at *her* café for months, and she returns only to pack up and go to a hotel less than twenty-four hours later! But that's not the real kicker. She had no money—big surprise there. But I'm not stupid. She's going to call Mom or Dad to get the money."

"Sky—"

"No. I'm not listening to any kindhearted, rational empathy about this. They dumped me here, took every last cent I had, my car, *and* my phone, but I can guarantee you they'll give *her* whatever she wants! Here, Ariana, you want a car? How about a limitless credit card?" She paced, the cord twisting and stretching as she moved. "I'm shaking so hard I can't stand it, and all I want to do is ransack medicine cabinets."

"Come with me this morning. I'm headed your way. I turned around at the start of the conversation, and I can be there to get you in ten."

"You were on your way to church, weren't you? You're one of those, and it's why you're awake and moving this early on a Sunday. No way am I going to church. I'd rather overdose, thank you very much."

"But you won't overdose, will you? At least not for years to come. You'll just ease the daily pain while slowly becoming numb to all that matters, all the while falling deeper and deeper in love with the next fix. You'll undo the work you've done and who you could be and become someone you hate. Addicts who are using have the Midas touch, but everything they touch turns to ashes."

"Shut up, Jax." She hung up the phone and pressed the palm of her hand against her forehead, rubbing it until her skin hurt.

But he was right. They both knew it.

The phone sat there, silent and yet daring her to walk away. She could wait all day and he wouldn't call back. This was her battle. If she asked for help, he'd give it. If she sank into the miry pit of addiction, he'd let her. His mother had been an addict, but worse than that, she got her drugs by convincing doctors that Jax had ADHD. She'd mutilated his life in order to make him seem as if he had issues he didn't have. So it wasn't surprising he had no tolerance for anyone who used drugs.

Skylar put her hand on the receiver. But if, instead, she walked out of the shanty, she could go straight to someone's medicine cabinet for Xanax, pain pills, cough medicine with codeine.

She picked up the phone and called him. When she heard the soft static background, she knew he'd picked up. "I . . . I'm sorry. I've not been this out of sorts in a really long time. I don't know what to do. I'm an ocean of anger, Jax."

"Come with me. I'm not going to church . . . per se."

She didn't know what that meant, but she was afraid to ask, afraid his answer would cause her to yell at him and hang up. "But I've got on jeans."

"Good ones?"

"No. They're frayed and soiled."

"Even better. Go with me."

She couldn't continue discounting all faith while she wallowed in death-defying cynicism. "Yeah. Okay."

Three

Quill strode across the top of the rafters, unrolling coiled wires throughout the attic of the unfinished house. But his mind was on WEDV—Women Escaping Domestic Violence. A woman named Melanie from WEDV had called him last night, asking if he'd meet with her today. Her organization helped women in violent relationships get to safety when the local authorities couldn't protect them. She explained that she had Quill's contact info and knew of him because a former Amish person he'd once helped now worked for WEDV.

She'd been very professional throughout the conversation, but he heard a sense of urgency in her voice that made him think there might be a specific woman WEDV needed help getting to safety. It would be hard to turn down a volunteer position. The idea sounded good for several reasons. One was that he needed a distraction from thinking about Ariana—a loud distraction that might have to last a lifetime.

As grateful as he was for work and family, there was something deeply satisfying about helping those in need to get to the other side and begin life anew. Freedom was often hard to come by for some, but without it, life withered, causing hardships on the imprisoned and on future generations as well.

His phone vibrated, and Ariana's designated tone chirped. The surprise of it literally threw him off balance, and he grabbed a truss overhead. They'd texted briefly after she'd arrived home on Saturday, but he hadn't expected to hear from her again anytime soon, maybe for months. And it was only Wednesday. He dropped the remaining coil of wires on the rafters and insulation before pulling the phone from his jeans. The message was in a bubble across his screen.

Can we talk?

His heart picked up its pace, but that was the norm whenever Ariana was involved.

His Mamm called her the Thread Gatherer. Mamm believed life was like an heirloom quilt that life ripped at the seams, and gatherers were rare. But Ariana took the frayed pieces and worked with them until the quilt could fulfill its purpose once again. Quill had seen her do it. At least once she had done it for him, when he was eighteen and his Daed died of a heart attack.

Her text made him chuckle. Should he tease her? She was home and happy, with Rudy by her side, so he saw no reason to repress being himself.

Are we breaking up?
'Cause if we are, I'm busy.

We are.
But it's hard to make that official without a first date.
Dinner?

You buying?

What? Seriously, Quill Schlabach?

The text arrived, but the bubbles indicated she was still texting, so he waited.

I have to ask you out, buy dinner, and do the breaking up?

Your mama raised you better than that.

I was minding my own business, wiring a home, when you . . .

Fine! I get it. You're bored and need some drama.

I'll buy your dinner.

Do you think you could possibly drive to where I am?

Or do I also have to handle that part?

Do I get a dessert?

You're very needy for one so fiercely independent.

Not needy. HUNGRY.

Forget your lunch again?

No. It was planned.
I thought, you know what sounds like fun--going hungry!

See, this is why we have to break up.

Because I'm hungry?

Because you have a very warped idea of fun.

If there wasn't a great divide between them, they could have fun. Dinners. Movies. Roller-skating. Ice-skating. Sledding. Horseback riding. Bowling. But they had only fleeting moments of laughter over silly things or of gathering threads for the other before life reeled them back in.

You say warped. I say free food.

Sorry. It won't be free. You will pay. Dearly.
Just not money.
I'm with Salome at a place called Scarlet Oak B&B.
It's ninety minutes north of Summer Grove, off Hwy. 22.

What? He stared at the text for probably too long before responding. He'd thought they were completely teasing about having dinner, expecting that they'd have to meet somewhere odd like a barn, or he'd pick her up on a side road in town, and they'd talk in his car. Ariana was at a B&B? That was just weird, but it shouldn't be much more than thirty minutes from this job site.

He wasn't too concerned about what was going on. Ariana had passion and emotion to spare, and it got the best of her occasionally. But with a little time, she rallied and got her feet under her.

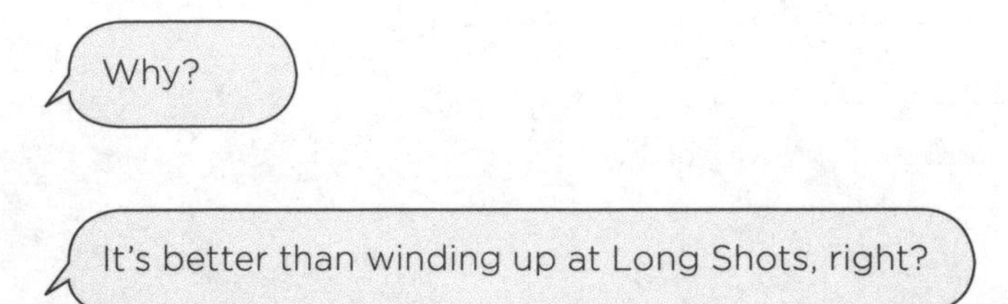

She'd received the most shocking news of her life that night, and she'd reluctantly called him because she needed to talk to someone, and he was the only one from her past that Nicholas hadn't banned from her life. The conversation went badly, and she hung up on him. Things didn't go much better once he found her inside the bar. But he got her home safely, and the next day she came to him to apologize. It was the beginning of rebuilding the friendship he'd destroyed five years earlier when he disappeared with her best friend, Frieda, leaving Ariana to believe for all those years that he and Frieda were married. He'd been twenty when he left with Frieda, and Ariana had been a child really, only fifteen, so he never allowed her to know how he felt. He'd intended to let her grow up before hinting at his feelings. But before that could happen, he needed to leave with Frieda, and he let Ariana believe the same lie everyone else in Summer Grove believed—that he and Frieda ran off to marry. He had different reasons for needing the community to believe that, but for Ariana it was his way of freeing her. She had a crush on him when he left, and he wanted her to build a life without holding on to any schoolgirl hope that he might return. Because he wouldn't, not in the way she needed. But then circumstances made him step out of the shadows and tell her the truth . . . or most of it anyway.

You okay?

Working on it.
Dinner?

For a moment he questioned whether he should cancel the meeting with WEDV. But that would be a complete overreaction, and it made no practical sense. He would aim to keep the appointment on track so he could be finished on time if not early. When the bubbles went away, he texted.

Absolutely.

The bubbles appeared again.

Salome's heading home in a few hours.
Could you come after that?

I'll be there by six.

Four

Ariana held sleeping five-month-old Katie Ann in the crook of one arm while she read to snuggling four-year-old Esther. The love seat that faced the glowing fire in the hearth was perfect on a bleary mid-January afternoon.

She glanced at Katie Ann's sweet face while turning pages. When Ariana was away, her arms had ached to hold her little nieces and nephews, and she'd looked forward to snowball fights with the older ones. Despite the roar of confusion in her head, she had no doubts about her feelings for her family.

She turned another page, read the few words, and waited while Esther ran her little fingers over the details of each illustration. Getting away had helped some, probably because no one here was preaching at her or feeling offended if she saw God's Word differently. Ariana turned the last page. "And the bunny had found his home."

Esther ran her little fingers across the silky page. "Again?"

Salome walked into the living room, carrying two cups of hot chocolate, one in a light blue mug and the other in a foam cup with a lid. "Look what I have." She nodded at her daughter as she raised the foam cup toward her. "But you'll need to sit at the table with the coloring books."

Esther smiled, and the scar that trailed down one side of her face contorted differently than the rest of the skin. *"Iss es heiss?"*

"Nee. It is *fehlerfrei.* Perfect." Salome grinned. "Kumm."

Esther put her arms around Ariana's neck, once again telling her in Pennsylvania Dutch that she'd had the best time ever. She kissed her aunt and hopped down.

It had been a good visit. Ariana and Salome had talked endlessly, and Salome had been a patient listener as Ariana shared what her life had been like the last three months and all she'd done. They'd laughed about a thousand things from their childhood and seemed to talk every waking hour.

After Salome helped Esther get settled, she returned and sat. "This place is sheer luxury."

Their time was drawing to a close. Salome's bags were packed and waiting in the foyer, and the driver was on his way. Two of her three boys were running a fever and needed their Mamm.

"*Luxury* would be an overstatement, but it's quaint with lots of comfortable space, and it's well-run."

"You're different, Ari. These days you ponder every word, weighing its merit."

"Do I?"

"Ya. It's not a bad thing, just different. You didn't used to think so deeply."

"I had only two categories—good or bad, right or wrong." Ariana leaned her head back and stared at the ceiling. "My mind was so closed. And now it's too open."

Salome patted Ariana's hand. "You'll figure it out. I know you will."

"I hope so." Her lack of peace scattered her.

"You must think Quill can help, right?"

"Maybe. When I left home, he knew how hard a time I was having before I knew it. That night at the bar I told you about? He knew I'd had alcohol, and he knew I was unaware of it. When I realized that the next day, it was the beginning of me saying 'enough!' I demand to know myself."

Salome giggled. "Ya, 'cause what's the use of drinking if you're not feeling it?"

Ariana laughed. "Exactly." She reached for Salome's hand. "There are no words to tell you how grateful and relieved I am that you and Emanuel are staying Amish."

"Me too. It was all too much for me to cope with—the severity of Esther's burns because of that stupid firepit, the pressure from the ministers and the community to treat the burns according to the Old Ways, the utter failure of the poultices to do what was promised, and the horrendous pain she endured—all to avoid using skin grafts and modern medicine." Salome looked up, as if looking heavenward, shaking her head as she sighed. "I still deal with anger over the whole agonizing situation," she confessed. "Anger with the ministers, the community, and Mamm and Daed, but most of all anger with our failure as parents by caving to the pressure."

Ariana had tried to be a supportive, helpful sister, but she'd fallen short by a lot and ended up not being much more than a baby-sitter who watched as Salome slipped deeper and deeper into depression. She and Emanuel eventually reached out to Quill to help them leave. Before they could follow through, the family learned that Ariana wasn't a Brenneman, and Ariana learned of Salome's plan. Salome promised her she would remain Amish until Ariana returned.

"But, dear sister,"—Salome squeezed Ariana's hand—"when you were jerked away from us, I realized how awful it would've been for Mamm and Daed if Emanuel and I and their grandchildren were to disappear during the night. The other side of that is I realized how much I need all of you." Salome sipped her hot chocolate, looking lost in thought. "Regardless how much pressure the ministers and the community put on us, no one stood in the doorway stopping us from getting skin grafts. Emanuel and I caved under the weight of expectations, but we've vowed never to do that again."

The remorse in Salome's eyes was almost more than Ariana could bear.

Salome glanced at the clock on the mantel. "I was hoping to see Quill before we left, but he's late. It's almost six twenty, and the driver will be here in a few minutes."

Ariana was sure Salome wanted to thank Quill for all he did to help them, from praying with them and gently trying to talk them out of leaving to paying out of his own pocket to rent them a home and get them a used vehicle.

"He's a busy man, and I only texted him a—" Ariana's breath caught in her throat. "Dad's here." She pointed at the check-in desk in the foyer. When had he decided to come? And why?

Salome turned. "Daed?"

"No, Nicholas."

"Oh." Salome sat up straight, checking on Esther. "*Daed* and *dad* sound very similar, and it's just so weird hearing you call Nicholas 'Dad.'"

"I don't always. It just slips out at times."

Nicholas had a pamphlet in hand, glancing at it and listening to a man pointing to things in the brochure. She didn't know what they were discussing, but that was very Nicholas-like. If he came across anything unfamiliar, he took the time to learn about it.

Ariana shifted the baby to Salome. "My two dads are similar in some ways, especially when it comes to believing what they believe and wanting me to believe exactly as they do."

"Then how on earth did you survive three months when he thinks so differently from the Amish? He doesn't believe in God, does he?"

Ariana stood, straightening the wrinkles from her cape dress and apron. "In a nutshell I fell apart, and he did a one-eighty. Now he encourages me to be painfully honest about how I feel."

"Ya, it makes sense that you like him. How else could you enjoy traveling the US with him the way you did?"

"Excuse me for a minute." Ariana left the living room and entered the wide foyer with its white wainscoting, antique chandelier, and hardwood floors. "Hey."

Nicholas turned. "There you are." He hugged her.

"When did you get here?"

"About twenty minutes ago. You didn't answer your phone, and I spotted a library and decided to make it useful. I found these." He held up a stack of books. "This fine young employee saw me wandering around in the library, and he joined me. He's been informing me about MAP. Apparently Scarlet Oak B&B is a sponsor."

Of MAP? Her heart jolted. The website she'd accessed on her phone when looking for places to stay hadn't mentioned anything about that. Mission to Amish People provided help to former Amish, usually older teens and young adults. It was founded in Ohio by an ex-Amish couple about sixteen years ago. If Daed or the church found out she'd stayed at a place that supported MAP, she would have to answer for it. What were the chances? It was bad luck, but she couldn't undo having stayed here.

"I . . . I didn't know you were coming."

He pulled a credit card out of his pocket and passed it to the young man. "You would have if you'd taken my calls. Where's your phone?"

She patted her hidden pocket and found it empty. "I'm sure it's in my room. I had it out earlier, using the calculator." She'd been studying the café's ledgers, receipts, deposits, and bank statements, but the numbers didn't add up.

"I won't stay long. I just needed to see you."

"I'm fine. I told you that when we talked Sunday, Monday, Tuesday, and earlier today."

"And yet I'm here, verifying those words."

"That's sweet, and thank you for paying for my stay."

"It's nothing. Seriously."

The man passed Nicholas a small piece of paper and a pen. He signed and passed them back. She thought he'd told her earlier in the week that he'd already paid for everything via the phone but apparently not.

"Ari," Salome whispered.

Ariana turned.

Salome had the baby in her arm and Esther by the hand. "I hate to interrupt, but my ride is here."

"You're a Brenneman," Nicholas said. "You're the one Skylar favors so much."

"Ya on both accounts."

Ariana made introductions.

"I'm glad we got to meet," Salome said. "And I apologize that I have to dash like this, but I have two boys with a fever at home, and my driver is here."

"Sure. No apologies," Nicholas said. "Do you need a hand?"

"The driver will get my bags. But thank you." Salome turned to Ariana. "I know Daed is expecting you to return with me. What do I tell him?"

"That I'll be home by Sunday evening at the latest. It will save him some angst if he doesn't know I have a cell phone, but tell him to call the B&B if he wants to talk to me." Ariana hugged her and Esther.

The driver stepped in and grabbed Salome's suitcases. As she was leaving, Quill walked in, and they stepped inside, getting out of the way of the foot traffic, and visited.

Nicholas examined Ariana. "You're not surprised Quill is here."

"I texted him, asking if we could talk."

"Then I'll go, but first . . ." Nicholas led her into the library. "I got this for you." He held out a plastic card. "It's a debit card."

"No." She held up both hands. "But thank you."

"I was afraid you'd feel that way. There's a thousand dollars in the account." He held it out again. "Please."

Temptation tugged at her. Even after she'd gone over a plastic grocery bag full of receipts for deposits and purchases made for the café, the account was still a mess. Between money spent and money missing, she'd yet to get the ledgers straight.

But accepting the card from him would be wrong. He carried a lot of guilt about his parenting of Skylar and her—or the lack of it—and she couldn't allow herself to profit from that. The frustrating part was she shouldn't need an outsider's help. Farming and small businesses usually thrived among the Amish, but not for her family.

"Just take it. If you have it in hand, you can use it or not, right?"

"Goodness, you're enough to drive me up a wall. Pushy on the one hand and so very generous on the other."

He held the card out to her again.

"The money would come in handy." She took the card. "Thank you."

"It works as a debit or credit card, and you can get cash out of any ATM. You remember how to use an ATM, right?"

"Ya."

He smiled. "I've missed that *ya* of yours."

"It's only been a few days since you dropped me off at my house."

"But you're here and not there. You should come back to my home or your mom's. If you're feeling oppressed, you should, and you need to—"

"Dad." Her whisper sounded harsh, and she hadn't meant for it to. She cleared her throat and started again. "I'm very grateful you paid for my stay here, and I appreciate the debit card, but you're projecting how you think I feel based on me being here, and please don't tell me what to feel or do."

He stared blank faced for a moment and then smiled. "Good for you, Ari." He kissed her cheek. "You call me if you need anything. Okay?"

"I'm an adult, and what I *need* is to pull myself together and not ask anything else of you."

"That's nonsense. You're my daughter, my only flesh and blood. Skylar is mine too, although she isn't claiming me."

Ariana could see the pain in his eyes as he paused.

He cleared his throat. "The PIN is 9874. I can text it to you." His eyes moved to the doorway. "Quill,"—Nicholas walked to him and shook his hand—"it's good to see you."

"Thanks. I'm surprised you're here."

"Ditto." Nicholas hooked his thumb toward the door. "I need to go. Good luck. As I understand it, you're here to talk, but she doesn't want any opinions. That should be quite a feat." Nicholas winked at Ariana. "I'm proud of you."

What was he proud of her for? Asking for money so she could stay here? Accepting a debit card? Pushing him to get her home, and then her being so overwhelmed she couldn't stay? There was nothing to be proud of. But being impolite would only add to her disappointment in herself.

She drew a breath. "Thank you . . . for everything."

Five

After a stilted greeting, Quill followed Ariana and the hostess to an out-of-the-way table in the dining room. Ariana flicked her fingertips across her thumb, one by one. When she wasn't doing that, she was fidgeting with something else. He'd teased her in the text, and she'd responded in like manner, but this face-to-face meeting was clearly uncomfortable for her.

She sat across from him. "I hate that I needed to text you."

Quill removed his coat and took a seat. "This is nice, and it has food."

She unwrapped her flatware and put the napkin across her lap. "Did you know Scarlet Oak supports MAP?"

"I didn't."

"Gut. When Daed asks Salome where we stayed, maybe he won't know either." She shifted the flatware and moved the vase with its fake flower several times.

He picked up the menu. "Any suggestions?"

"The filet mignon, roasted potatoes, and grilled asparagus are amazing. It's all covered in some package deal Nicholas got, so I'm not actually paying for it."

He studied the menu. "Then filet mignon it is."

A server brought water and unsliced bread on a cutting board with a knife and butter. They placed their order, and the server left.

"It was good of you to come, especially on short notice."

"Of course. My meeting ran a little later than I'd hoped." He'd gotten so involved in the plans Melanie wanted him to help carry out that he'd left fifteen minutes late and then got stuck in traffic.

"It feels odd sitting here, talking as if . . ."

"As if what, Ari? As if we're friends? As if we grew up together?" His awareness of being a phony formed a lump in his throat. They were friends, but he'd loved her too much and for too long. For both their sakes, they needed to put some distance between them. And soon.

"I should be here with Rudy."

Quill fiddled with his napkin. Could he really disagree with her? "I see it a little differently. I believe if Rudy was who *should* be here right now, you would've made sure he was here. But you apparently need to talk about something he can't help you with. That doesn't mean he's not everything to you. It only means you need a different perspective for maybe an hour before you return to him feeling better than when you left."

Her eyes glistened with unshed tears. "Denki. That was the perfect thing to say."

"Good. Mark it down"—he circled his index finger in midair—"that I said the right thing at least once tonight." He took a sip of water. "What's going on, Ari?"

She sliced a piece of bread and put it on the little plate in front of him. "I'm not really sure." She explained about the roar of conflicting opinions in her head, each group insisting on what she needed to believe and who she needed to be, and she confessed that she had no idea how to make them shut up or how to isolate which group of thoughts to believe.

"Is any of it complete nonsense?"

She grew quiet, apparently thinking, and their dinner arrived.

"Man, that looks great." He picked up his fork and knife.

"It tastes even better."

He cut the meat and took a bite. It seemed to melt while exploding with flavors. "Oh, my stars," he mumbled. "That's the best steak I've ever had."

"Good." She motioned at him, circling her index finger. "Mark that down as one thing I got right tonight."

He chuckled. "You have to bring Rudy here."

"I agree." She cut her steak.

He forked a potato. "What's the verdict? Is any of the roar complete nonsense?"

"Sure, but if something has no validity or value, I can toss it out like a piece of trash, and it's gone." She drew a deep breath, looking torn and tired. "But over the last few months, I've learned a lot that has substance and solid reasoning. Most of it collides with what I've been taught in church, and those teachings also have substance and solid reasoning. I'm like the wave of the sea in the book of James—'driven with the wind and tossed,' 'double minded,' and 'unstable.'"

"And your concern is God doesn't answer the prayers of the double minded?"

"I hadn't thought of that. What's bugging me is the dozens of different viewpoints inside of me on every single topic." She gestured at him. "When situations crop up in your life, you know what you believe and what you will and won't do."

"I only know the essential answers, Ari."

"What are those, and how do you get them?"

"We have a core value of who we are, right?"

"If that's true, mine is so muddled it's useless."

"I don't think so. Your thoughts and emotions are bewildered. But our core is our gift. Our way of making a difference. Our filter through which we see life."

"Uh, still confused."

"Push aside all you know of my beliefs and opinions, and tell me the lifeblood of who I am."

Her eyes bore into his as she pondered. "You're a protector."

He smiled. "Bingo, and on the first try." He took another drink. "It's like my personal North Star, navigating me through the important things. I mess up and make mistakes in all areas of life, of course. Too much and too often. But I don't ignore or discount that one thing I know about me."

"I know nothing about me." She set her fork down and leaned in. "The morning I was getting ready to return to my Amish home, I pinned up my hair and put on my cape dress, apron, and head covering. When I looked in the mirror, I had no idea who was looking back at me." She shook her head. "None, Quill."

He could see the aftermath of the earthquake that had shaken her. Her focus had been to get home, but once there, she discovered that her newfound knowledge railed against the Old Ways and vice versa.

"Are you having second thoughts?"

"No." She trembled as she took a drink of water. "This isn't about being Amish or not being Amish. I know with my whole heart that I could be in either world, and I would be equally bombarded and overwhelmed."

"You've done several vital things right. Can we take a moment for you to appreciate that about yourself."

"I've done nothing right—"

"You're aware of what's going on inside you, and you didn't repress it or assure yourself you were fine when you weren't. And you've taken time to get away to absorb and regroup." He knew she wouldn't have done either of those things before her time with Nicholas and Brandi.

"What's the next step?"

"I wish I knew, Ari. You want relief, and if I could give it to you, I would. But these things take time."

"It's normal?"

"I think so."

"You went from the simple life and limited knowledge to a chaotic world with too much information and too few answers. Did you feel like this?"

"Yeah. It was a mixture of information overload, grief, guilt, and who knows what else."

"It is, isn't it? I feel bad for leaving Nicholas and Brandi, and I feel bad for not being overjoyed to be home."

He'd carried so much guilt for hurting Ariana, and he'd grieved the loss of many friendships. It had been a hard adjustment, knowing everyone he cared about thought poorly of him. "Focusing on your purpose helps."

"You do get it. I knew you would." She pointed at him.

"I get it, so what's your purpose?" He knew the answer, but she needed to say it.

Her brows furrowed, and they both ate in silence for several minutes.

She pursed her lips. "All my life I've wanted to make things better for Mamm and Daed. But they're no better off, and the café's finances are in a mess."

He listened as she told him about the items Abram had purchased to make the café more successful and about Cilla's medical bills.

"Quill, the bank receipts and deposits from the café show a really good profit, except there's about five thousand dollars unaccounted for."

"What?"

"Ya. My reaction exactly. Sunday afternoon right before I left, Abram gave me everything concerning the finances of the café—checkbook, statements, receipts, deposit slips. I've spent a lot of time this week going over everything, and the café earned that money, but it's not in any account."

"Have you asked Abram?"

"No, and I won't. He and the others held down the fort for me. Without them I wouldn't have a café by this point. He's turned over everything, even the petty cash, so I'll either figure it out, or there's five thousand fewer dollars to work with."

"Well maybe at least ask. Any chance someone forgot to make a deposit?"

"For five thousand dollars? That's several weeks' worth of deposits, and Abram assured me they went to the bank each week."

"How big of a mess is it?"

"No one's received a full paycheck since the café opened. With the missing money and what's been spent on coffee machines and such for the café and medical bills for Cilla, I'm not sure there will be enough to pay next month's mortgage. Nicholas gave me a debit card with a thousand dollars on it, which is both generous and yet not nearly enough."

"It'll help, though, and I could—"

"You won't." She set her fork and knife on the plate with solid *clinks* and looked him in the eye.

He nodded.

She relaxed. "I'm not sure I'll even use the debit card Nicholas gave me. He's grieving over the situation with Skylar and me leaving and his countless mistakes. I can't take advantage of that." She looked exasperated. "What is it with us Brennemans and money? First the dairy farm and now this?"

"The café is a new small business. Those are notorious for being tough to keep afloat. You'll get the financials figured out."

"I'm beginning to think we're poor because we have no money skills."

"You know what happened that caused your farm to suffer, right?"

"Something happened?"

"I was eight. That would've made you three, so it makes sense you don't remember it. No one talks about it in your house?"

"I guess not."

"Your Daed had a milking herd, one of the best in the state is what my Daed said. Disease struck, and he lost half his herd."

"He didn't buy any new cattle to rebuild his herd?"

"The bishop said that it was God's will the cows died and that Isaac needed to accept it and rebuild the herd slowly."

"Not sure I agree with that thinking—although you should note that I have dozens of warring opinions coming at me from Scripture, Amish and non-Amish preachers, authors from times past and today. But moving on, cows have calves, and the cycle repeats continually. It's been *seventeen years,* Quill."

"His calves are often sold quickly because that provides instant money to pay bills. The loss of income meant your family had to borrow money to live on. I think maybe things snowballed from there."

"More like an avalanche." She sat back, seeming to stare through him. "If Daed had even ten more milking cows, he could make ends meet. What does that run a head?"

"Supreme milking cows—about two thousand dollars a head."

She coughed. "He'd need eighteen to twenty thousand dollars to buy enough cows to comfortably pay the bills. My brain is fuzzy and is still full of opinionated voices, but you've made my purpose clear again."

"Then being forced to eat this meal has been worth it."

Amusement glimmered in her eyes for a moment. "One last thing."

"Dessert?" he teased.

"I'd like to move in with your Mamm."

"She would love that."

"But Daed's not keen on it, and he says the bishop won't be either."

Quill knew what the bishop thought and why. The man was a tyrant with a Bible in his hand, preaching about love and forgiveness. "What's your Daed's hesitancy?"

"He seems to think her ways caused all her sons to leave, and he's concerned it'll rub off on me." She shrugged. "Sorry."

"Hey, I asked. You answered." Quill knew what the community thought of his Mamm. She'd been unjustly tried and found guilty, and her one bright spot in the district was Ariana. "Move in, Ari. I know my brothers would agree with me on that. Just don't grab a gun the next time you hear one of us sneaking in to visit."

Ariana sat up straighter, looking much better than when he'd arrived. "Tell them I'll try not to shoot any of you."

Quill laughed. "You'll *try* not to?"

Six

Lovina stood against the wall of her living room, unable to believe or stop what was happening. Ariana had arrived home from the B&B yesterday. The Saturday afternoon reunion had been better than Ariana's much-anticipated arrival from the Englisch world a week earlier. She seemed happy to be back, and until the last hours she'd been less outspoken about what she believed and wanted. But then . . .

"You will not bring the world into this home." From his tattered armchair, Isaac studied Ariana while holding out his hand, waiting for her to place her phone in it.

Rudy was on the couch behind Isaac and the bishop. The bishop had allowed Rudy to stay only *if* he remained quiet. He had been visiting Ariana when things blew up, but since the bishop arrived, he'd sat quietly on the couch. If the stress on his face was any indication, he didn't like what was happening.

Isaac had found the cell phone on the bathroom floor a couple of hours ago. It seemed odd that Ariana would've accidentally dropped it, knowing how taboo it was in this district to own one. Isaac's hands were trembling when he showed it to Lovina, and after he'd fiddled with it for a while, he uncovered numerous texts between Ariana and Quill from her time of living out in the world. Several of the texts had been sent while Ariana was at the B&B. Had Rudy been aware that Ariana was texting Quill during that week?

Ariana leaned toward her Daed, pouring fresh coffee from the percolator into his mug. She then filled the bishop's mug, but the phone she had taken back from her Daed an hour ago remained inside her apron pocket.

Earlier, while Isaac was trying to reason with her about giving up her phone, he had set it on the table and turned to get a drink of water. At that same time the bishop arrived, wanting to talk about someone who had called him and said certain things had occurred during Ariana's time at the B&B. With the bishop's watchful eye on her, she held her Daed's gaze as she eased the phone from the table. It wasn't as if she was trying to deceive them. It was her saying, *It's mine, and you didn't have my permission to take it.* She then put it into her apron pocket.

Ariana doing that in front of the bishop had embarrassed and angered Isaac, which wasn't a good combination for Isaac keeping a level head. When the bishop asked to question Ariana concerning what happened at the B&B, Isaac didn't hesitate to give his permission.

Rudy and Lovina suggested that Sunday wasn't the best day for this kind of discussion, hoping the bishop would decide to wait. That would allow time for Isaac to calm down and for Lovina to speak with him privately. But thus far the conversation had centered on the phone, not the B&B.

Ariana set the percolator on the coffee table and picked up a bowl of sugar. "I shouldn't have brought the cell phone inside. You're completely right." She held the bowl out toward her Daed, but he and the bishop shook their heads. Ariana's lips formed a tender smile. "This is your home." She set the bowl beside the percolator. "I'll take the cell elsewhere and won't bring it inside again. Not ever."

The bishop steadied his eyes on her while shaking his head. "My stance on cell phones has been clear throughout all my years as bishop. They are allowed under specific circumstances for work when I approve it, and even then it's *never* to be on in someone's home. It was on when your Daed found it. I want to look at your phone to see what you've been doing with it while under your Daed's roof."

Ariana sat in the tattered wingback chair across from them, eyes lowered. "I'm sorry. I won't allow it."

The bishop's face turned red. "She's been draus in da Welt, and now da Welt is in her."

Ariana's eyes moved to the bishop, and the gentleness on her face disappeared for a moment. She glanced at Rudy, and he held his hands out a bit from him and pressed them downward, signaling her to remain calm.

She inhaled, and all signs of frustration quickly vanished. "Of course I've been out in the world." She interlaced her fingers, looking as clean and pure as sunshine on newly fallen snow. "But not because I wanted to be there. Yielding to Nicholas's—my dad's—demands was important to the whole community, and he insisted I leave here. That was my only way of keeping the midwife from facing a judge and jail time. Daed, Mamm, and you, Bishop Noah, fully agreed with the decision."

It was so unlike Ariana to behave in this way. But Lovina held on tight to the fact that despite Ariana's atheist dad insisting she leave her Amish roots for a year, her girl had talked him into letting her return home after only three months. That was a victory to be celebrated, and Lovina was desperately trying to keep a grip on that triumph.

Ariana smoothed her apron, looking thoughtful. "But the world isn't inside of me. The proof of that is seen in how hard I fought to get back here. Surely you can see my heart through my efforts to return." She lifted the fabric on the shoulders of her dress and apron before running her hands over her prayer Kapp, reminding them of her faithfulness to the Old Ways. Rudy smiled, looking pleased with her response. It was probably a good thing Isaac and the bishop couldn't see him from where they sat.

"I disagree." Bishop Noah set his cup on the table beside him. "You hadn't been home twenty-four hours when you went away again, this time against your Daed's wishes."

"I needed some time to think."

"And time to text with Quill."

Ariana shook her head. "It wasn't like that."

"Your Daed saw the texts on your phone. They sound as if you and he are a couple. Are you calling your Daed a liar?"

"No. I'm not denying I texted him, but it wasn't like what you're saying."

"But Quill and Nicholas came to the B&B. Isn't it odd that you needed a break from your Amish family to think but you met with two worldly men while in seclusion?"

Ariana's shoulders drooped, and her eyes reflected a kind of sadness that stabbed Lovina's heart. If she was reading her girl right, she was holding her tongue because anything she said would make matters worse.

The bishop leaned back, looking pleased with himself. "Isn't it also interesting that the B&B sponsors MAP and that someone called me to say that Nicholas gave a substantial donation to them *after* talking to you? Are the reports true?"

She blinked, looking unsure. "If Nicholas donated to the cause, I don't think . . . I mean, I . . . wasn't aware of it."

"So he was there."

"For a few minutes, ya. But I didn't know the place supported MAP until I'd been there for days."

"Let's say that's true. When you found out, why did you stay?"

"If I explain it, you'll only find fault in it, but it was not my intent to disrespect the Amish by staying there. And I didn't conspire with anyone to support a cause that evangelizes against us."

"Then give up your phone," Noah said, "and we'll decide your innocence by your own texts, e-mails, pictures, and calls."

Isaac held out his palm toward her again, wanting her to relinquish her cell phone. "Where is your humility to submit to those God has put over you?"

"Daed, please. Nicholas asked me to keep the phone, and I told him I would. My sin is that since I knew you wouldn't approve of it, I should've put it elsewhere before entering your home. But he's my father too."

The hurt and confusion that ran through Isaac's eyes cut Lovina. Had Isaac not expected her to bond with her biological father? Or maybe he hadn't braced himself for exactly what that meant. Right now it meant Ariana was standing against the man who'd raised her in order to keep her word to the man who all but blackmailed her into leaving the community for a spell.

"You are not under his roof," the bishop said. "You are here with the people who taught you to obey."

Ariana wrapped her arms around her waist, rocking back and forth ever so slightly, and Lovina knew she was pondering her answer. Lovina could hardly breathe. The men were remaining calm, but they were coming down hard, unfairly so, and Lovina couldn't understand why. Did the bishop believe her answers to his questions? She'd avoided answering about Quill, but if he'd met her there, that was inappropriate, even if he'd been in good standing. But plenty of Amish had cell phones without the bishop's approval, including the youth who hadn't yet joined the church, and Ariana fell into that category. The problem was that Bishop Noah didn't like for anyone to have a cell phone unless he had personally given permission.

Isaac had begun this standoff with Ariana because he was deeply concerned he was losing her, but this was not the way to win her back. Besides, she was home now. She was in love with Rudy, and patience was the key to getting her to set aside worldly opinions and desires.

Would she yield to her Daed's wishes? Within the first moments of Isaac's confronting Ariana, he seemed to realize he no longer had the influence over her that he was used to. Rather than Ariana seeing her Daed's viewpoint, she apparently saw flaws in his reasoning and used her newfound understanding to hold her ground. But this standoff terrified Lovina. Ariana had people out there now, family who would welcome her return, give her a place to live and money. Isaac and Lovina already had proof of that. The only thing stopping Ariana from doing exactly that was how she felt about Rudy and her Amish family.

If Lovina were allowed to speak up with the bishop here, she would, but her appeals to Isaac to tread lightly would have to wait until the bishop went home. Could she do or say something that would draw this meeting to a close before the bond between Ariana and her Daed was worn too thin to repair?

Winter winds pushed against the old house, and Lovina moved to the window. Dusky light from the setting sun revealed barrenness and snow-covered land for as far as her eyes could see. Tonight was the third evening her two girls—Ariana, the sweet girl Lovina had raised, and Skylar, the feisty daughter Lovina had given birth to—were under the same roof.

Was it that wrong for Ariana to own a phone with messages on it that were no one else's business? Still, Isaac said it wasn't the phone or texts as much as what they stood for—Ariana being sneaky and headstrong.

When Ariana had awakened today, she had seemed determined to use the extra time of this "between Sunday" to melt the stiltedness between her and everyone under this roof, including Skylar. Lovina had started the day grateful there wasn't a church service. Even with what appeared to be everyone's best efforts to relate to Ariana the way they used to, her limited time here since returning had been emotionally exhausting. No magic cleanser could wipe away the residue of her being such a different person from the one who left here. Rudy had arrived after lunch, which seemed to help the others relate to Ariana a little easier, maybe because he was so comfortable with her even after moving back to Indiana and living in a very strict Old Order Amish community while Ariana was away. But with or without Rudy, Ariana had been making strides to reconnect with her family—until the phone was discovered.

Isaac shouldn't have been so quick to agree to the bishop questioning Ariana. Noah Stoltzfoos wouldn't admit it, but it seemed clear he didn't like the Schlabach family.

"Who is Quill to you?"

"Just a friend. There is nothing else between us."

That Lovina believed, but she didn't want any more worldly influences in her girl's life. Between Skylar and Ariana, this house felt saturated in the world's thinking. Both of them needed quiet time inside this God-fearing home and away from Nicholas.

God, lead them. Guide them. Open the eyes of their hearts.

Skylar's three months here seemed to have been good for her. But Lovina knew Skylar's decision to stay even after Ariana returned home had more to do with hurting the people who had raised her than anything else.

There was a world of choices spread in front of Ariana and Skylar. What would each one choose over the coming months?

The bishop set his mug on a nearby end table. "Quill sneaks into Amish districts at night and helps people leave. If you count someone like that as a friend, the world is in you."

"God made the world, and He sent His Son to die for the world. Maybe there is a different way of thinking about the world."

"You are using a different meaning of the word *world.* Is that what you have returned for—to try to confuse your people? Will you help Quill in his quest to tear apart the Amish community?"

"That is *not* his desire." Ariana fidgeted with her intertwined fingers. "He would be happiest if no one needed him, and he reaches out to no one. He pushes his beliefs on no one."

The back door opened, and three voices echoed through the house—her sons Abram and Mark and her son-in-law Emanuel. Even though Lovina couldn't see them from where she was, she knew they were returning from the evening milking. The rest of the family was scattered throughout the farmhouse doing whatever young people do at times like these. Mark and Abram came to the doorway. One glance at this room and their faces reflected the confusion and concern that seemed to be squeezing the breath out of Lovina. They had been in the barn milking cows when the phone was found and the bishop arrived.

Mark gestured toward Ariana. "Something wrong?"

Abram studied Ariana. *What must he be feeling?* He had grown up believing she was his twin. It hadn't been easy, but he and Skylar had formed a bond during her three-month stay.

"Nothing that concerns you." Isaac attempted to shoo them away, but neither moved, which was surprising. Abram, like Ariana, had been very compliant all his life.

Abram took a step into the room. "So it's just a friendly visit, Ari?"

Ariana rubbed her thumb against her palm and shrugged. "I'm fine. Denki."

But Abram didn't budge. His eyes narrowed on her for a moment before he turned to his Daed. "Is she in trouble for something?"

"She has a phone without permission for one"—the bishop zeroed his attention on Ariana—"and she should pass it to her Daed, as he told her to."

Abram seemed unsure what to say, but his face contorted as he turned to his older brother.

"Ah." Mark nodded, looking sincere. "Got it. Would you like us to make a sweep of the whole house and all the outbuildings, looking for other phones? With two families under the same roof, nine adults, a teen, and a couple of preteens, we are sure to find one or two cell phones. And if doing that sincerely feels right and important, we could do the same in the homes and outbuildings of your adult children, Bishop Noah." Mark's eyes were wide, and his body language said he was ready to embark on the task immediately. Although he appeared fully sincere in his offer to help out, Lovina knew he was challenging the man. Her usually jovial son was angry, but he hid it well. "I'm sure we can find the contraband."

The bishop angled his head, as if trying to decide whether Mark was sincere or questioning his authority. "She's exchanged texts with Quill Schlabach. It is rumored she met him at the B&B."

Abram took a step toward his Daed. "Just Ariana is being questioned for having contact with Quill?"

Lovina didn't know whether to be proud of her sons for taking up for Ariana or disappointed that they would question their Daed and the bishop. Either way, the conversation had made a sharp turn that could bring repercussions down on Lovina's and Isaac's heads.

The bishop sat up straight, his face taut. "Isaac, it sounds as if we should talk with all of your children to see if they've had contact with Quill."

Lovina's heart lurched, and Isaac's eyes met hers. Any questioning of Ariana or their other children about misconduct concerning Quill made them hypocrites.

Five months ago when they'd realized Ariana might not be their biological daughter, they had reached out to Quill for help, and he met with them secretly. Before Quill's investigation was over, Lovina and Isaac dressed like the Englisch in order to go unnoticed to a college play in which Skylar was performing, and Quill drove them. If the bishop knew any of those things, they could be shunned for a month, maybe two. But news of their deeds would tarnish their reputation for years, maybe decades. People didn't forget direct disobedience, especially from mature adults. But even now, Lovina couldn't imagine any other way to deal with what they'd been facing, and Quill had been wise, kind, and discreet.

Isaac opened his mouth several times as if he was trying to speak up. Was he going to confess their sin to the bishop?

Lovina had to do something before she and Isaac were shunned. No one ever fully recovered their reputation after a shunning. It was her worst fear, after the health and well-being of her family. She quickly made her way to the percolator. "Would you care for more coffee?" She held it out toward the bishop.

He shook his head.

"Noah,"—Isaac clasped his hands and looked at Lovina, a sure sign he was about to be brutally honest.

Lovina dropped the percolator, spilling coffee and grounds on her freshly cleaned rug and hardwood floors. Both men jumped to their feet.

"*Ach,* I'm so sorry." She was sorry she needed to resort to such trickery to put a stop to this meeting.

While the bishop studied the hem of his pants, Lovina nonchalantly elbowed Isaac and shook her head, hoping he would take her cue and draw this to a close. "Mark, grab some towels."

Isaac held out his hand for the bishop's mug. "I appreciate your time and wisdom, Noah."

Noah's face once again turned red. "You'll draw this to a close while she continues to defy you?"

"Ya. As my sons have pointed out, other Amish have cell phones, and I need some time to think. We wouldn't want to be hypocrites."

Mark passed the bishop a towel. The bishop gave Isaac his mug and wiped coffee from his pants. "You are letting your children lead you when it should be the other way around. This isn't about others having phones they shouldn't. Ariana is refusing to obey either of us, in part because she doesn't want us to see the evidence of why she went to that B&B in the first place." He handed the towel to Lovina. "But this is your home, and I will give you some time to sort out the problem on your own."

Isaac gestured toward the front door. "I appreciate how much the flock means to you."

"Ya, I think you need some time alone with Ariana. She needs to stay close. Very close. That's what she needs."

Isaac walked the bishop to the door, and they chatted about the weather as the man put on his coat. Ariana helped Lovina wipe up coffee and grounds, but no one in the living room spoke. Isaac waved as Noah left.

Isaac returned to the living room. "Ariana, tell Rudy good-bye, and all of you go upstairs, please. Ariana, we'll talk later."

She was on her knees, gathering up wet coffee grounds, when she lifted her head and studied her Daed, looking perturbed and hurt. If she had things she wanted to say, she held back. She put the grounds in a towel, wiped her hands thoroughly, and then got up and walked to the coatrack with Rudy.

Mark finished mopping up the coffee in his area and put the wet towel on a dry one. He stood. "Daed." He shook his head, looking appalled and confused by his Daed's actions.

His Daed held up one hand. "Go."

Mark and Abram took their muddy-looking towels, tossed them into the kitchen sink, and went upstairs.

Lovina stepped toward the kitchen so she could see the back door. Rudy had his arms around Ariana, his face close to hers. A moment later Ariana pulled away a bit and whispered to him. He looked angry as she started to walk away. Rudy grabbed her hand and said something. Ariana nodded, and Rudy leaned in and kissed her on the lips before she went upstairs.

After everyone had dispersed, Lovina turned to her husband. "Isaac," she whispered.

"I know." He had both hands clasped on his head. "I have no idea what to do or what to believe." He lowered his hands and started pacing. "I've been so worried about her for months, afraid she was accepting too much of the world's ways into her soul."

"I knew we had concerns, but this is the first time you've voiced your feelings. Have you been stuffing them deep?"

"I guess. When she confirmed my fears, I longed to set her straight, for her sake, to help her get her head and heart clear, but"—he sat and propped his head in his hands—"all I did was confuse everything by saying too much to the bishop. But if half of what the bishop said actually took place at the B&B, she's wrong, Lovina. Just wrong."

Lovina hurt for her husband. He wanted what was best for Ariana. "Isaac." She knelt in front of him. "We can't help her while being hypocrites."

"Hypocrites? We did what we had to in order to uncover the truth and find Skylar. Nothing more. Ariana took the phone off the table in front of the bishop and me and then refused to give it back, Lovina." His eyes filled with tears. "She's so different it scares me."

"Me too. But we knew she would return with new views and new opinions."

"We have to be able to put rules in place and her obey them, but I have no idea how to deal with this new-and-not-improved Ariana. I know this much: her first hour back home she spoke of wanting to move in with Berta, and that does not need to happen. I don't care how many available rooms Berta has."

"Isaac, please. She and Berta have been close for years. Berta is like a second mother and a good friend rolled into one. Even when everyone in the district distrusted that household, we never tried to curtail that relationship, and if we try now, it could backfire."

Isaac stood and gave her a hand, helping her stand. Then he went to the window and stared out.

Lovina understood him, from his jumbled reasoning to his outspoken zeal. The unnerving thing about young adults is they have the right to defy their parents and make their own decisions, and yet they don't understand enough about life to grasp the consequences.

"We made it work with Skylar." Isaac turned, looking less shaken now. "We stumbled, much like tonight. Now she's here because she wants to be, and she's free of drugs."

"But, Isaac, please hear me. Skylar had nowhere else to go. It was here, rehab, or live on the streets. She chose what she thought was the lesser of those evils. Ariana has choices, lots of them."

"Rudy is an anchor, even if I'm not."

Lovina thought about what she'd just seen. "You can't put all your hopes in that. Their relationship has been under a lot of stress for almost as long as they've been seeing each other."

This family had always needed Ariana. From a young age Ariana brought things to the table that no one else could.

But did she still need them?

Seven

Ariana stirred from her sleep. Where was she? Prying open her eyes, she saw mostly darkness, and she still couldn't place where she was. She spread her hands palms down, feeling a thick pallet of blankets. She reached farther and felt a cold floor. The familiar scent of sulfur hit her nostrils about the same time she saw hands with a lit match. She blinked. Why was a girl in blue jeans lighting a kerosene lamp?

"Ariana." The voice came from someone other than the lamp holder.

Understanding dawned as Ariana took several deep breaths. She was in her old bedroom, her Amish one, and Skylar, the girl in the jeans, was in her room. Or since Skylar was the true Brenneman twin, maybe this was *her* bedroom.

Every single question was one of ten million things Ariana no longer knew. Funny how very sure she used to be. But the feelings she had now were the same ones she'd struggled with when she was forced to leave home—loneliness and confusion.

Martha knelt beside her and held out a mug. "We've tried to wake you several times. Sorry to say it, but we're leaving for the café in twenty minutes."

"Denki." She sat up and took the coffee, grateful for some caffeine.

After Daed and the bishop questioned her last night and she and Rudy argued, she'd hardly slept at all. It was going to take several minutes to get going. But she couldn't wait to walk into the café. Her café. She had dreamed about it several times over the past few months.

Maybe there she could figure out why the end-of-the-day receipts didn't match the deposits.

Martha went to the line of hooks on the wall and grabbed an apron.

Skylar peered down at her while brushing her hair. "You look as bad as I felt my first few days here."

"Thanks." Ariana forced a smile. Skylar favored Salome as much as Ariana favored Brandi, the mom Skylar had grown up with.

Skylar pulled a sweater over her head. "Did I sprout horns or wings or something?"

Ariana startled, realizing she'd been staring, but it wasn't a good time to mention how much Skylar favored the Brennemans. Maybe Skylar didn't want to look like them. "How are you?"

"Yeah, sure—that's what you were thinking."

Martha angled her head at Skylar. "Be a little nicer, please." Martha then looked at Ariana. "Skylar's done some amazing things with the café. Remember that. It'll help you adjust to her brutal sarcasm." With that said, Martha left the room, closing the door behind her. So where was Susie?

"That *was* me being nice." Skylar shrugged. "You don't have to go with us today—this week even. I discovered there's a grace period."

Skylar had invited Ariana not to go to the café? It was Ariana's café! Feeling territorial was new to Ariana, and she wasn't sure what to do with it. She took a sip of her coffee, trying to think of the best way to respond. "I appreciate the heads-up, but I know how my parents do things, and I've already cut into my grace period."

Skylar pulled her hair into a ponytail. "*My* parents, actually."

Ariana couldn't believe her ears, and she had no response. With yesterday's argument with Daed and the bishop still spinning inside her, she had no idea what to think about anything. How had her phone ended up on the bathroom floor? She'd thought it was still tucked away in her suitcase. It must've been in the pocket of the apron she'd gotten out of her suitcase before getting a shower.

Even Rudy thought she should give up her phone. But the problem wasn't about the phone, although she had no desire to hand it over. She had the right to say no, and despite what the church said, she had the right to stay in contact with her biological family and Quill and anyone else. If Nicholas had taught her anything, it was not to be bullied by anyone for any reason—although he'd probably taught her that lesson unintentionally.

More important than the phone, she hoped the bishop was the only one who'd been told of the happenings at the B&B. It was possible a former Amish person working at the place told someone who was still Amish, maybe a cousin or a close friend who hadn't joined the church yet, and whoever they told had called the bishop. She hoped that was the case. At least that way the events, both true and misconstrued, weren't being spread throughout Summer Grove.

The bishop was exacting, but he wasn't a gossip.

Skylar tossed the hairbrush on the dresser. "I don't know why I said they're my parents. I don't even know why I'm still here. I didn't think Dad—I mean Nicholas—would let you return this soon."

"I was surprised by that too. And I fully relate to not understanding why I'm saying and doing certain things."

How had she entered the Englisch world knowing nothing, spent three months being purposefully educated by her dad and mom, and then returned to the Amish knowing less than she knew before?

She'd learned a lot about history, geography, philosophy, technology, and more. But when it came to the really important stuff, the kinds of things people built their lives on, she knew less than ever before.

Someone tapped on the door. "Skylar? Ariana?" Abram called.

"Kumm." Ariana hadn't yet budged from the pallet with her cup of coffee. Why was moving so hard this morning? Lack of sleep was one thing, but this felt more like the adjustment of coming back home was pressing down on her.

She had expected that to be gone after her week at the B&B. Being home was what she'd fought for the whole time she was draus in da Welt, so where was the joy and relief?

Abram eased open the door. He looked from Ariana to Skylar. "Morning." He smiled, but the tension among the three of them seemed to have sucked all the air out of the room. Skylar was his twin, and Ariana had been in her spot for too many years already. Abram's face betrayed the awkwardness he felt. "It's time to go."

"I'm ready." Skylar grabbed a coat off the line of hooks. "I think Ariana has decided to stay home."

"I'm going." Ariana spilled a few drops of coffee as she rushed to her feet. She might need to move out of her home to make room for Skylar, but she would not give up her place at the café. "I've just been moving slowly. Give me ten minutes. Okay?"

"I'll say it again, Ari. It's good to have you home." Abram smiled. "But five minutes would be better. We have a system, a good one."

The "we" didn't include Ariana, but it would, in time.

"We do." Skylar nodded at Abram as if the two were tight.

"Okay, I'll be ready in five."

Skylar walked out, and Abram closed the door, leaving Ariana alone. She peeled out of her nightgown and grabbed her pleated Amish dress. She'd put her apron on and pin it in place once she was in the carriage.

There were facts she had to accept with grace and understanding. *This* was Skylar's real home. Abram was Skylar's real twin. Mamm and Daed were Skylar's real parents.

Ariana had been naive to think that running back home would cause her life to be set right again. All she'd accomplished thus far was to unnerve Skylar by being here and to unnerve her parents with her newfound understanding of life, liberty, and the pursuit of happiness.

Once in her dress and with the apron slung over her shoulder, Ariana flung open the door and scurried out. Good thing she'd showered last night. All she needed to do was splash water on her face and brush her teeth. She could comb her hair and pin it up in the carriage.

Daed was on the landing, heading in her direction. *"Guder Marye."*

Uneasiness filled her. She used to trust him in every way possible, but that had been shattered, not so much by yesterday's events, but by Nicholas teaching her how to analyze people's stance by asking herself about their motives. Daed believed his motive was pure and protective, but she thought she saw a motivation based on fear—fear of her not being exactly who he thought she needed to be and fear of how the community would judge *him* if they learned she was stumbling around like a drunk as she tried to get her feet under her.

"Morning, Daed." She continued rushing toward the bathroom, in part because the others might already be waiting in the rig, and in part because she wasn't ready for another encounter that could go down the wrong path. Thankfully she would be gone most of today.

He stepped in front of her, smiling but appearing apprehensive.

"Sorry, Daed." She angled, sliding around him. "I'm in a hurry."

"You aren't, actually."

She stopped cold. "They're waiting on me."

"I think it'd be best if you stayed home today."

"But . . ." Instantly tears welled. "I . . . I've been dreaming of today for months. For years, if you count all the time Abram and I worked to save for—"

"You seemed fine about not going last week."

"I wasn't fine with it. I was taking care of me so I didn't fall apart weeks from now. I explained all that. And I spent a lot of time trying to get the books straight, so I was tending to the café while at the B&B."

"Still, not today, Ariana." Daed raised a brow, his face taut. "I sent the others on to the café. We—your Mamm, me, and you—need time. It would give us a chance to talk."

A familiar feeling washed over her, and she tried to place it. Images of her first days in Nicholas's home and the arguing between him and Brandi flooded back to her. She had felt trapped, out of place, and powerless.

Daed stepped to the side, allowing her to brush her teeth now that she understood the plans for today. "Perhaps after a week at home you'll feel more like yourself, and then not only will you be centered on obedience and humility, but you'll be able to meet with the bishop again and respond as any young woman should. But you can continue to work on the ledgers for the café, and you can see Rudy whenever it pleases you."

She stared at him, unable to find her voice. Was she a child whose Daed had just finished his list of what she couldn't do with a promise of ice cream and sprinkles?

How was her Daed's way of demanding she do as he wished any different than Nicholas insisting she do things his way?

While the café buzzed with dozens of customers, Skylar finished loading a bin with dirty plates, cups, and utensils. Three business days had passed, and Ariana hadn't been allowed to come to the café yet.

A bit of guilt hovered around Skylar like an annoying fly. So what if she had put Ariana's phone where Isaac would find it? Big deal. She smacked away that invisible guilt-fly, sending it off to harass someone else.

One night last week after Salome had returned from the B&B and while Lovina and Isaac were out of the house, Salome told the Brenneman siblings about what life had been like for Ariana while she was living with Brandi and Nicholas. Although Skylar wasn't in the room, she'd overheard all of it, and her insides had been on fire with rage ever since. While Skylar was getting up before dawn six days a week to earn *only* tips, and while she did the exhausting work of an immigrant laborer and used her skills to build a customer base for Brennemans' Perks, Ariana was in the lap of luxury, sleeping late, watching movies with Cameron, and traveling the US with Nicholas.

Skylar glanced at the register. Cilla was doing great taking orders and fixing people's coffee. Skylar had recently refilled drinks for everyone at a table, so she pushed the swinging door open and entered the kitchen.

"Hey." Martha glanced over her shoulder while remaining at the sink. "There she is!" Martha grinned. "Our own Sky Blue."

Susie and Abram spoke to Skylar too, sounding cheery in their Amish brogue. On the way to the café today, as darkness lifted and a bright blue sky shined through, Martha decided it was time they all started calling Skylar by the nickname she'd had for years.

Skylar thudded the tub on the sink, and it rattled. "Stop being all jolly and welcoming, and get to work."

Martha laughed. "Yes, ma'am."

Skylar tossed the paper products in the trash and scraped leftover food into the composting can. She enjoyed the sense of being welcomed and appreciated. Ariana's presence would taint that, but Skylar had at least bought herself a few days without Ariana here. Hopefully a full week. Maybe two.

Not only would Ariana be underfoot while learning to operate the coffee machines, but she would also start suggesting different ways of doing things, all the while inadvertently pushing Skylar to the side, just as she'd unintentionally pushed Skylar out of her former life and away from the parents Skylar had grown up with.

How long would Isaac keep Ariana away? Other than the phone thing, it wasn't Skylar's fault that all manner of accusations were hurtled against Ariana on Sunday afternoon. The bishop had brought up those concerns.

Skylar had tiptoed down the back staircase and sat on a step, listening as Ariana was questioned. It had sounded to her as if their bishop had a few scores of his own he wanted to settle with Ariana. But unlike Skylar he hadn't needed to plant evidence against her. Bishop Noah hid his agenda behind his pulpit position, or so it seemed. Skylar had seen it hundreds of times, maybe thousands, mostly through the news and history classes.

An idea came from nowhere. If she wanted to secure the Brenneman family's loyalty and love, she needed to lead the way for getting new plumbing into that old farmhouse. But she would have to act quickly so it would be evident the gift wasn't Ariana's idea. With the right timing

Lovina and Isaac would know Ariana hadn't been the one to work for that gift. Abram, Susie, Martha, and Skylar had.

"Hey, guys, I've been thinking." Skylar peered out the pass-through, making sure Cilla still had everything under control. "We know that Ariana mentioned she hoped to have the books squared away this week so we all would have a payday soon." Skylar put the dirty flatware into its soaking vat. "But maybe we should change our plans and do something for the whole family."

Was she really going to pretend her motives were in the right place in order to get the others to back her charade?

Martha slid more plates into the hot, sudsy water. "I'm ready to spend the money on myself, however I want. I think we all are."

Skylar poured the liquid from the cups down the empty side of the double sink. "Yeah, I hear you, but it just seems that the first thing we should do is . . ." How should she word this? ". . . get new plumbing into the house."

Susie, holding a stack of clean plates in her arms, stopped stock-still. "Oh, Mamm and Daed would love to have decent plumbing. That is such a great idea, Sky."

Abram studied Skylar. He was better at reading her than she was comfortable with. Could he see right through her?

Susie put the stack of clean plates in the open cabinet. "I have no idea what something like that would cost."

Since Skylar never saw the café's financials, their upcoming payday might not be all that substantial even if they pooled their money.

"Abram," Skylar asked, "you worked construction, right?"

"Ya, but I just did my job, which was roofing. We didn't have anything to do with the plumbing. Last Saturday Jax said he'd be in today. Is he here yet?"

She shook her head, her anxiety going up a notch. "Not yet."

"Well, when he gets here, ask him," Abram said. "He'll either know, or he'll know where we can get a reliable estimate."

"Will do."

After calling Jax and spending several hours with him the Sunday before last, she saw no reason to balk at asking him a simple question, even if they had been skirting each other before and since then. What did he think of her after their outing? Her mood had been all over the place. She'd started out extremely irritable, but once at their destination, she had been moved to awe and landed on speechless.

Skylar picked up a clean tub and left the kitchen. Three tables needed busing, and she began the simple task. Jax was a hard man to figure out. He reached out quickly, freely, and openly, but did he let others reach in?

They'd driven about thirty minutes south of Summer Grove to an impoverished town with a makeshift soup kitchen. Their task had been to take two large boxes of individually wrapped sausage biscuits and chicken biscuits and pass them out, along with blankets. That was it. No one preached, although Jax offered flyers that listed places to call for specific kinds of help. Most people took the biscuits and blankets and left, but some gathered in a group, and Jax talked with them once the food was gone.

But what shook Skylar out of her funk was when they returned to the soup kitchen. A keyboard was set up in a corner with a poor, unkempt woman hovering around it. She'd reach out for it and withdraw her hand before touching it. Skylar went to her. "You play?"

The woman jolted. "I didn't do nothing." Her fingernails were yellowed and her hands brown from grime. Skylar ignored the stench surrounding the woman. The thing that had Skylar's attention was the desire she saw in the woman's eyes. She clearly longed to play an instrument that Skylar hadn't cared about since being forced to leave college and move in with the Brennemans.

The bells on the front door jingled, pulling Skylar from her thoughts. Jax walked in. Skylar stood at a nearby table cleaning it, so he had no option but to notice her.

He nodded. "Hey, Skylar."

"Hi." She glanced at the register. Cilla wasn't there. Skylar picked up the tub and set it on her hip. "Would you like today's special?"

"Sure."

Skylar went behind the counter and to the pass-through. "Jax is here." She handed the tub to Martha. "He'd like the special, please."

Susie pointed her spatula at the skillet. "I know what I'm fixing for him. It's not the special." Susie grinned. "It'll be ready in just a few minutes."

Since Jax and Abram were former-coworkers-turned-friends, Jax ran a lot of errands for the café. It was easy for him to do in his truck and really difficult for them by means of a horse and buggy, so one of the ways Susie thanked him was free food.

Skylar washed her hands in the small sink before grabbing a plastic cup and filling it with ice and water. "Here you go." She set it in front of him, ready to get a clean, wet cloth and disappear cleaning counters.

He took his drink to a table.

This pattern of small talk and then going separate ways was the agreement they'd made since their heated argument before Thanksgiving. When he'd learned she was a recovering addict, he was disappointed not only in her but in himself for liking her, for being drawn to someone who was similar to his mother. Jax and Skylar agreed to speak, even to be friendly if others were around, but they also avoided each other in nonchalant ways so they didn't make the Brennemans aware or uncomfortable. They were remarkably good at it. They'd continued that even after their Sunday together. There was no reason not to. She'd needed some support. He gave it. Things had returned to normal, as they should've.

Several people entered, and Cilla came downstairs from the loft and returned to the register. "May I take your order?" she asked.

Skylar picked up pitchers of water and tea, ready to refill people's drinks.

"You know . . . ," Jax said as she passed his table.

She paused, listening.

"Since that Sunday I've been thinking a lot about that woman and the keyboard."

"Me too." Skylar topped off his water. "I was thinking about her when you walked in."

Watching the woman long to touch the keyboard, Skylar had decided she didn't care what the rules were. She plugged it in and turned it on. "It's okay," Skylar had told her. "It is." Skylar played the first chord of "A Thousand Years" by Christina Perri, and her heart went wild. Her fingers begged for more, and she played the whole song, her chest pounding like the beat of war drums.

She'd then backed up, feeling rather sheepish, and gestured for the woman to play. As the woman began playing "You Are My Sunshine," her face radiated with a kind of artistic joy that Skylar had forgotten existed.

"I wanted to know her story," Jax said. "How did someone so skilled at music end up homeless? There's always a long, painful story. What'd you think?"

"That I take too much for granted. The longing in her and her pleasure when she was playing . . . I'd forgotten how much music meant, you know?"

"Have you played since moving in with the Brennemans?"

"Other than that time, no." She shrugged.

"No easy way to be allowed to play an instrument in an Amish home, is there?"

"True." But more than that, she'd lost the stomach for it. Once her dad had started coming around to see her when she was a child, he had either taught her piano lessons or paid a very skilled person to give her lessons. After everything shook out the way it did, she had no interest in playing.

"I better get back to work." She started to walk off. "Oh, do you have any idea how much it would cost to put new plumbing in an old farmhouse?"

"The answer depends on lots of things—the type of pipes the person chooses and how much pipe there is to run and whether all of it needs replacing or just some of it. Why?"

"My Amish parents have the worst plumbing ever. You never know from one day to the next if there will be running water in the kitchen to cook or clean or if there will be water for a shower. It's ridiculous."

"It sounds as if the goal is to do it as economically as possible."

"That's a completely safe assumption."

"Does any area have plumbing that isn't an issue?"

"The plumbing that goes to the wringer washer has the fewest issues. The kitchen is the worst, followed by the only full bathroom in the house."

"It's been an adventure, then, right?"

Skylar sat. "Don't push your luck, Jackson Montgomery. I'm being polite. Make fun of my fight to get a hot shower in winter—or any shower for that matter—and I will not remain so." Would he know she was teasing?

"Sorry." He held up his hands, a wry smile on his lips. "I know a plumber." Jax pulled his cell from his pocket. "I'll ask if he could do it for cost."

"You can't ask that of someone."

"I can if it's my uncle who owes me several favors." His fingers flew across the screen of his cell. "I helped him roof his house a few months back and his son's house last summer—free labor."

She would never be this nice to anyone. She would, however, put a forbidden phone where it could be found by someone's parents.

"But he owes *you* a favor, Jackson, not strangers."

"I'll decide how to use the favor. But he would need an assistant, and it can't be me."

"Mark would be the best bet for helping out. He's sort of a jack-of-all-trades, and he has the most time on his hands right now."

He typed something else, but before he pressed Send, Skylar put her hand over the screen of his cell.

Jackson looked up. "Problem?"

"A couple. Maybe you're too nice, for one."

Frustration flickered through his dark-brown eyes. "You can rest your concern, but it's always a pleasure to offer help and then have your character questioned." He set the phone on the table. "I really like Abram, Susie, and Martha, so I go out of my way to help them, and I volunteer to work with the homeless only during winter, when they need it the most and construction work is extremely slow. I can put up boundaries, Skylar, and saying no is as easy as saying yes for me. You should know that."

She should. He'd had no problem telling her no and giving her strict boundaries. "You're right."

"But?"

"I didn't say anything."

"You didn't say it out loud. But you said it. I just didn't quite hear you."

"You reach out, but I've not yet seen you let anyone reach in."

"You have an example of something I did that gave you that idea?"

He was either very giving, as he was with the Brennemans, or he cordoned himself off, as he had with her. But then again, he had picked her up two Sundays ago when she needed him. "No, not really."

"Did you study this in college, or is it from the latest *Vogue*?"

She'd angered him, and she imagined that much of his reaction was because her addiction problem reminded him of his mother's, and maybe Skylar had sounded motherly while questioning him. Or maybe he simply didn't appreciate someone with a drug issue noticing some little issue he had. "I guess it's just as well that we usually avoid talking."

"It's looking that way." He picked up his phone. "Second thing?"

"I don't know that we can come up with the money. You might be wasting your time."

"I'll let him know that."

Skylar stood. "Thanks."

Nine

Cold winter air seeped into the barn as the cows lowed. Daed hummed as he worked. Mark cracked silly jokes here and there. If Abram were here instead of at the café, he would smile a lot, thinking plenty but saying very little.

Wonderful memories flooded Ariana, reminding her of why she loved this simple life. Cows were lined up and eating contentedly. The fresh hay and oats filled her senses.

Some of her earliest memories had taken place in this barn. She used to be her Daed's shadow, and he had allowed it, being patient and kind even when she made his workload harder day after day. Then, around six years old, she fell in love with baking and the challenge of helping Mamm get something good on the table when money was so sparse. So she stopped coming to the barn. Looking back, it seemed strange how skilled she was at knowing what could be paired to make something good for the family. She couldn't do any of it herself for several years, but she shared her ideas with her Mamm, and Mamm responded and often used the ideas, which made Ariana even more determined to come up with other recipes and dishes.

And yet, despite her and her family's best efforts, they were still poor.

"Hey, Ari," Mark called, a hose in hand as he rinsed the udders of another cow. "You have company."

He'd no more than said the words when she was nudged from behind. She stumbled, trying to stay upright. Mark's laughter echoed against the walls of the barn.

Daed came out of the milk house, an empty milk can in hand. "Daisy missed you while you were gone."

Her Daed was wrong about the phone and maybe the café, but they'd had a good few days, and neither seemed so angry or disappointed in the other.

Ariana turned to face the cow . . . again. She rubbed Daisy's forehead. "You need to stop this and go on out with the other cows that have been milked."

Daisy pressed her long hard head with its soft fur against Ariana's chest. "Ya. You're a good girl. Now go." Ariana backed up, waving her hands toward the door of the barn that led to the pasture. Daisy stepped forward and nudged hard.

Ariana fell, landing on her backside. Her right hand landed in the squishiness of manure. "Ewwww! Daisy!"

Mark roared with laughter as the cow moved in closer, breathing in Ariana's face and not giving her any room to get up. Ariana tried to push the cow away, which made Daisy try to nuzzle against her.

"Great. A little help, please!"

Daed put a rope around the cow's neck while Mark helped Ariana stand. "Denki."

Mark opened his mouth to say something, but all he did was laugh.

Daed pulled the cow a few feet away from her. "You have a nice aroma for the start of the day." He smiled. "You can go get a warm shower if you like."

This was the man she'd grown up loving. Kind, helpful, and thoughtful. He loved God, his family, and the Old Ways. Probably not in that order. Apparently the beliefs of the Amish church were more important to him than she had realized, and she'd known they meant joy and peace to him. What she hadn't known was that he allowed the rules, the laws—and fear—to think for him.

"I'm okay." She looked at her hand. "I'll use the sink in the milk house and wash up." She couldn't see one of the guys going into the house and getting a shower because they had gotten messy while milking the cows. Besides, the only reason she was out here was because Daed wanted her near him, mostly so he could talk to her and share his thoughts as they went through their day. He was so hopeful she would give up the phone and become the girl she was before she left. She wanted that for him, but she couldn't do it.

Daed nodded. "Ya. Gut idea."

She headed for the milk house.

"Hey, Ariana," Mark called. He pointed to the back of her coat.

Daed chuckled. "Washing your hands will do nothing for that."

She grabbed the back of her coat, trying to see how much muck was on it while Mark and Daed laughed. This sort of mess happened to them regularly, although not from falling. But she minded the yuck more, and they found her reaction funny.

She twisted, trying to examine her black coat, as if knowing how bad it was would solve anything. "Ya, well, apparently manure happens."

Mark returned to rinsing off udders. "You might be a farmer if . . ."

It was an old game, one she hadn't played in a long time. "You know cow pies aren't made with beef."

"Isaac."

Her breath halted in her lungs. She didn't have to look to know that the gravelly voice belonged to the bishop. Nonetheless, she turned around and smiled in an attempt to be polite. He didn't return the gesture.

"Ariana," Daed said, "why don't you go inside and get cleaned up."

The bishop was here to talk, and she'd been dismissed. That suited her fine, but she'd like to know if Daed was releasing her so he would have privacy to take up for her or to discuss what could be done about her rebellion.

Ten

From inside his small Kentucky home, Quill shoved clean, folded winter clothing for a woman and three young children into a good-size box.

"I don't like this plan at all." Frieda put an ice pack and individual yogurts into a cooler, along with sandwiches and fresh fruit.

He closed the corrugated box, folding the four flaps so the top would remain shut. "I know. Just breathe, find a distraction, and it'll be over in a few days." Even now as he stood on the brink of the most dangerous escape plan he'd ever been involved with, he couldn't erase Ariana's face from his mind. It was as if every one of her amazing traits was tattooed inside him. How could she be confused about who she was? It didn't make sense.

He'd met with Melanie from WEDV ten days ago. When he'd told Frieda a little about the society and that they were always in need of clothing for women, babies, and children, she started collecting the items.

Quill had come home a few days ago to tend to personal business and have uninterrupted time to plan an escape for someone named Gia and her three kids.

Frieda closed the cooler and began putting away all the sandwich fixings. "I don't understand why *you* need to be the one to do this. Isn't this the kind of stuff the police do? Or Child Protective Services? Some organization?"

"My understanding is the woman turned to two agencies for help at some point in the past, although I'm not sure which ones. All I know is it turned out really bad for her, and she won't trust them again. But I'm not the only one involved in this plan. There's a team." He hadn't chosen the team or even met them, so he had to trust each one was as good as Melanie said. The older woman had been involved in these kinds of escape plans for three decades, but this one had even her rattled. The ex-husband was well connected to violent criminals and had no aversion to killing anyone who got in his way. So why wasn't he still in prison? A legal technicality. And once he was out, how he had found some of his most vulnerable victims, also known as his ex-wife and children, no one knew. His abusive and controlling ways were well documented, and yet, ignoring all restraining orders, he had kidnapped them and moved to another state, violating his parole. They could call the police and have him arrested for breaking parole, but with his criminal connections he'd make one call, and his ex-wife, Gia Rice, would then be at the mercy of some other maniac until Rice was released. She needed a clean, untraceable getaway. Her fear was if she didn't escape soon, he would kill her.

Quill pulled his phone out of his pocket, making sure he had the addresses and contact numbers of everyone involved in the plan.

"You're the one escorting her and the children from the loading dock of the grocery store to your vehicle, Quill. You're the only one who won't be behind the scenes."

"That's not actually true. But if all goes well, Rice will think the others are mere bystanders. What do you want me to say?" He touched the Notes app and reread the plan one more time.

He'd devised the strategy himself, so he had it memorized, but he wanted to assure himself that he'd explained every detail very clearly in the e-mail he'd sent to the others. One weakness in the plan was that Gia had never seen Quill. When faced with putting her children into a vehicle with a strange man, could she make herself follow through? So far their only interactions had been through notes passed to her with her grocery receipts by the cashier, an older woman named Yvonne.

Quill's phone buzzed as a text came in. He clicked on it and read a construction-related message from his eldest brother. "Look, I've volunteered to do what I'm good at. Yvonne passed her the information about my plan and about me, without mentioning my name. Gia later returned a note to her that said she trusts my plan, but she'll only follow through if I'm the one carrying it out. Was there anyone else you would've agreed to leave with?" His fingers moved effortlessly across the screen as he responded to his brother.

"No," Frieda whispered. "Only you. But if we'd been caught, they'd have only used words to keep us from leaving, things about going to hell and such. At *no* time did we fear for our physical safety."

He lowered the phone and looked at the young woman who was like a sister to him. Because she had needed protection from her father and the church leaders, she'd had to walk away from her siblings, which broke her heart in ways she'd yet to recover from. The idea that something might happen to him, the one who'd made her escape possible and who was like a brother to her, was unbearable.

He slid his phone into his jeans pocket and gently clutched her shoulders. "I'll be fine."

Frieda slid her arms into her coat and grabbed the cooler of food. "You will text me every hour."

He picked up the box of winter clothes and headed out the front door. "Well, maybe not every hour. It's much more unsafe to text and drive than it is to steal a maniac's kids and former wife."

"Was that supposed to be funny?" She paused on the front steps while Quill locked his house.

"Yeah, it was. I guess it fell short." They went toward his car, snow underfoot. For the most part, Kentucky got less than half the snow Pennsylvania did, but every winter since he'd moved here three years ago, it had seemed more than ample.

He opened the car's back door and set the box inside before taking the cooler from Frieda. "You do know that if I text you every hour, I'll be sending messages while you're asleep."

"But that way the text will be there when I wake up, and it'll assure me everything is okay."

Quill suppressed a sigh. "Sure, I can do that."

"I'm a terrible person."

Quill knew where this was going without her saying anything else. "You're not. You had your life ripped apart, and you're healing."

"By leaving with me when you did, you gave up a life with Ariana."

"No one knows if that would've worked out. She was a fifteen-year-old kid with a crush on someone five years older. I'm just glad I never let her know how I felt. But seriously, what were the chances of that relationship actually working out?"

"Remarkable. You had a remarkable chance. I was her best friend, and I know."

"Okay, you're not helping."

"Sorry. I'm just trying to be honest with myself and you."

"Here's the bottom line. She will marry Rudy, and they'll make Mamm a grandmother at least seven times over."

"Berta isn't even related to Ariana."

Quill shrugged. "Family can be whoever you choose. Ariana and Mamm are bonded in ways that make them feel as if they're related, but—"

"But it's way past time for me to go see Berta face-to-face, and I think I'm ready. Ariana too, if she can meet me somewhere other than her house."

"Okay." He was glad to hear it but cautious. She'd made this kind of proclamation a few times over the last couple of months. Would she really follow through this time? "When you're ready, let me know. I think it's safe to say that Ari would gladly meet you at her café after hours and after dark."

"That's a good idea. Why didn't I think of that?"

"It takes genius-level thinking." He grinned and opened the front passenger door. "Let's get you to your place, and I'll be on my way."

Eleven

Pausing a moment before moving to the next table to be folded, Abram looked up and saw Cilla across his living room. The Brennemans were hosting the Sunday meeting this week, and their home was full with the community's Amish.

The window behind her bathed her in the dim mid-January light as the wind swirled the falling snow outside. He wanted to soak in the moment and appreciate how healthy and vibrant she looked these days. But he couldn't, because Saul Kurtz had moved in beside her. It wasn't Saul's first time to take an opportunity to sidle up near her and start whispering and joking about things.

Heat ran up the back of Abram's neck and inched up his face.

The service and the family-style meal were over. The current goal was to get as many benches and benches-turned-tables dismantled as possible and ready to slide onto the bench wagon so this small area had enough room for everyone to relax and visit.

Abram folded the legs of another bench table, and two men picked it up and took it toward the back door. He then moved to the next table to do the same. He flipped the bench over and reached to fold the legs, but they didn't move. He wiggled the hinge and shook the crisscrossed legs, but they didn't budge.

"Need a hand?"

Skylar's voice startled him. Last time he saw her, she was helping Mamm and the girls clean up the kitchen.

She crouched and ran her fingers over the table's hinge. "It's bent."

"Skylar," he whispered, "stand, please. You can't do that."

She pulled her hand back and slowly rose. This was Skylar's first time to attend church, and she was only here because it was taking place in their home and their parents told her it would be inappropriate for her not to come downstairs and join the meeting. He couldn't imagine how boring three hours of church in a language she couldn't understand must have been.

She rubbed her fingers together. "Why? Is there some type of oil or residue on it that's harmful?"

"No. All work is divided by gender, and you can't step in to help the men. It's how things are done."

"Seriously?"

He nodded. "Can we talk about this later?"

Skylar huffed at him. "The men pitch in to help the women."

"You mean to carry boxed dishes and such? That's because the items are heavy."

She stared as if he had slipped into Pennsylvania Dutch. She had on a dress, but it wasn't an Amish cape dress. It was something she'd picked up at a secondhand store. *Vintage* is what she called it. When she came downstairs this morning in the dress, their parents told her how great she looked, probably because it was the first time they'd seen her in anything except blue jeans. Blue jeans were forbidden at all times for the Amish, men and women. How Skylar had gotten away with wearing them for three months was a bit of a mystery to him.

"So am I allowed to stand here and talk to you?" Skylar asked.

"Ya, sure. It might be frowned on if I wasn't your brother. The Sabbath is intended to honor God. It is not for selfish desires like flirting."

Abram glanced over at Cilla and Saul. If they were talking and laughing now when it was frowned on, how much were they doing that at other times? He wouldn't feel so jealous about her talking to Saul except Susie had told him a few days ago about a couple of funny incidents that happened between Cilla and Saul. He could discount a single funny event, but two or three? Were the two spending time together?

Only a few weeks ago, after Cilla received a miraculous doctor's report, she'd told Abram that she longed for them to go out and that she dared to dream that love and marriage might follow. But along with her elation over the great report, she was distressed because the doctor told her that a woman with cystic fibrosis and her particular issues shouldn't have children. Her health was fragile, and having children would be life threatening.

Abram couldn't hold her responsible for that outpouring of emotion. They'd been on the sidewalk outside the doctor's office at the time. Now, with a new lease on life and new medications making her feel and look better, she seemed to feel differently toward Abram.

"What about singings?" Skylar asked. "Those have to involve some flirting since they're all about singles gathering."

"Okay, I should've clarified." Abram pressed his foot against the crisscrossed pieces of wood that served as legs for the bench. "The first part of Sunday, especially church Sundays, is for focusing on God. The men and women, whether married or single, stay divided during church, mealtimes, and for a while afterward. The rules relax as the day proceeds, but even singings are divided—girls on one side and boys on the other."

"Really? Did I know that?"

"I'm not sure, but if you attended, it would be imprinted on your brain, and you might see how well it works."

"No one wants me there, although from what I've heard of the Amish singing, you people could use someone who knows music to point out a few helpful tips."

"Skylar, sh." Abram glanced around, hoping no one had heard her. "The youth would like the help, and they could teach it to their parents. But I doubt the adults would go for it. The men lead all the songs."

She rolled her eyes, but she didn't say anything. "When can I retreat to the bedroom?"

He wanted to ask if she had seen Ariana but second-guessed himself. There had been tension, lots of it, between Skylar and Ariana this past week.

"In an hour or so, I imagine. It's a little different with the visiting church group here. But people will begin to thin out soon, and the expectations will continue to relax as the afternoon wears on."

Hopefully he could locate Ariana in a few minutes and talk her into rejoining the church crowd. If she didn't, it would only make things worse for her. Nothing had gone well with or for her since she'd returned home last weekend from the B&B.

Today was the first time Cilla's district had joined Abram's for church. There was a visiting preacher from Maryland here for just this one Sunday, so the districts combined. During the service the bishop, preacher, and deacon had each given a short message, as they did every church Sunday, but all three sermons zeroed in on Ariana. They railed against those who left the community and returned willful and disobedient, but more than that, they preached against specific things that had happened in Ariana's life. At least the visiting minister's sermon hadn't been directed at Ariana.

How had she remained on the bench with the other single girls while the men preached a sermon that was clearly aimed at her and the Brenneman family? He'd expected her to dart from the house at any time, but she hadn't. When the service was over, she helped get the food on the tables, doing as the women instructed, while too many men and women whispered every time she turned her back.

He'd thought she returned to Summer Grove looking a lot different than when she left, but today, after the three preachers spoke directly about certain things in her life, she looked nothing like herself, which meant she felt nothing like herself. The bishop had agreed to her leaving the community, even encouraged it in order to avoid legal trouble with Nicholas.

Now he protested the changes—even perceived changes—that happened to Ariana while she was out there. Was he that misinformed or just a hypocrite?

Unfortunately there was no freeing themselves of him. The church lines of each district were clearly drawn, and no one could leave one church to become a member of another. Being under the authority of any bishop, preacher, or deacon had to be accepted as God's will, and the only correct response to God's will was to submit.

"So . . . ,"—Skylar gestured toward Cilla and Saul—"if you don't mind me asking, what's the deal?"

Saul put his hand on Cilla's arm as she laughed about something.

A thousand tiny daggers of anger stung Abram as if he were walking in a sleet storm. "Not sure."

Cilla's eyes met Abram's, and she offered a faint smile along with a shrug and a shake of her head, all while continuing the conversation with Saul.

Abram had managed to whisper to her about fifteen minutes ago, asking where Ariana had gone. Cilla had whispered back that she would look for her.

Apparently she hadn't found his sister.

His brother-in-law grabbed one end of the bench, and they walked to the back door and stacked it near the others. With enough of them collected, he and Emanuel put on their coats, preparing to haul the benches to the bench wagon. It was more their job than the other men's because that's the way it worked when it was a family's time to have the church meeting in their home.

Cilla worked her way through the seventy-plus people inside the home and came toward them. Cold winter days like this caused everyone to remain inside after the meal.

She nodded toward the washhouse, which, as Skylar had pointed out weeks ago, wasn't a house at all but simply their laundry room.

Emanuel grinned. "Go," he whispered. "I'll cover for you."

His brother-in-law seemed to understand there are times when you just need to talk to a girl, even on a Sunday before all the church benches are put away. But rather than using this time to talk about where Ariana had slipped off to, they could have a few minutes to talk about what was going on between her and Saul.

They walked down the short hall leading to the washroom, and when they entered it, he realized another young couple had chosen this quiet room to talk. When he recognized Rudy's back and saw that he was standing directly in front of a young woman, relief eased the tightness in his muscles.

"Gut. You're here," Abram said.

Rudy turned, and Susie peered out from around him.

"Where's Ariana?"

"She went to the café. I gave her my key." Susie's eyes held undeniable anger. "I can't believe what is happening. Someone needs to explain this to me. The ministers purposefully picked her out and said things that would embarrass her. It's not fair." Susie fisted her hands. "None of it."

"I agree." Rudy looked like a simmering pot with a tight lid as he leaned against the wringer washer. His movements looked smooth and calm, but Abram didn't buy it.

"I was telling Rudy that Ariana needed time alone to think, maybe to call Nicholas or Brandi. I suggested she go to the café."

"You *suggested* that? Why?" Abram asked.

"Because it's ridiculous that she hasn't been allowed to go to *her* café for the whole week."

"That was a dangerous thing to suggest," Abram said. "You told her to disobey Daed. She's doing enough of that on her own, and it's not helping her fit in very well."

"Maybe she's not fitting in because the ministers don't want her to fit in."

"Who walked out during the service?" Cilla asked. "I only saw the back of her head as she was leaving."

Abram wished this whole thing wasn't happening.

"Berta." His head began to pound. "The ministers had to see her leave, and because of it, she'll have them on her doorstep later today or first thing tomorrow."

"Ya, well, I wanted to go with her," Susie snapped. "And if I hadn't been afraid of making things worse for Ariana, I would have. But Ari stayed put, so I stayed put."

"You've always had fire in your gut, Susie, and you need to douse it, not add to the flame."

"Douse your own fire, Abram." Susie twirled a prayer Kapp string around her index finger, jerking it as she did.

"Again, maybe she just needs to do what's being asked," Abram said.

"Nee." Susie released the string to her prayer Kapp. "Nothing they have an issue with is strictly forbidden, and Ariana knows it. I'm with her—hands down. Is that your life plan, Abram? If a minister puts a bull's-eye on your back, are you just going to hand over your will to him?"

Giving in to the leaders seemed like the right thing for Ariana, but Abram had been pondering a far more disobedient thing. Since Cilla's appointment with the doctor, he'd been thinking that if they were to marry, he and Cilla would use some form of permanent birth control. From his days in construction work, he knew such a thing existed. Some of the married Englisch guys with kids joked about how they'd been "fixed." But he wasn't sure he and Cilla would inform the ministers.

Abram shook his head. "Nee."

"Gut." Susie drew a breath. "I'm glad to hear it. Because there are good ministers throughout Amish country, but ours aren't requiring the same lines to be toed by everyone under their authority."

"Hallo?" Daed called from the doorway of the washhouse.

The room fell silent.

"Anyone know where I can find Ariana?" he asked.

No one answered. Daed eased forward and looked each one in the face. "Either you are refusing to answer me, or you don't know. Which is it?"

Abram's head pounded. Was he right to disobey his Daed? He didn't know, and he refused to sell out Ariana while he tried to figure it out. "I know. But I can't answer you. I'm sorry."

Susie nodded. "Same here." She skirted past her Daed, but before going into the main house, she paused and turned back. "Just because people think they're right doesn't actually make them right, and that's true whether they are a minister or a Daed. What about Judas? Jesus chose him, and Judas was following the letter of the law when he betrayed Him. Jesus knew who Judas was from the start, and yet He chose him for specific reasons. It seems to me Judas wasn't put in that position because Jesus expected him to be wise and holy in his authority. He was there for other reasons. Maybe the ministers are not over us for all that's wise and holy and you're giving them free rein to hurt your daughter, a person you *know* to be good and loving."

Daed stared at Susie's back as she left. He then turned and faced the rest of them, looking as confused and hurt as Ariana had during the church service.

Twelve

Tears continued to well, threatening to spill down Ariana's face. Her hands trembled as she held on tightly to the reins while driving through historic Summer Grove toward her café. The streetlights gave off a warm glow, powering through the gloom of winter and dancing snow. She swallowed hard. She should bask in the beauty of this quaint town she loved so dearly, but instead of joy surging, her heart wept.

How could the ministers have said those things about her and in front of everyone? The bishop, preacher, and deacon hadn't called her out by name, but they used her incidents with the cell phone, her going to the B&B, and her meeting with two worldly men as indications of rebellion. If the listeners weren't clear who the ministers were alluding to, the deacon said it was the same girl who, at fifteen years old, refused to hand over a letter she'd been given from a young man who'd left the Amish, taking a teen girl with him.

Everyone then knew he was talking about her. Quill had put the letter in her hand five and a half years ago on the day he left the Amish, taking Frieda with him. His goal had been to share enough about what was happening that Ariana wouldn't grieve as hard or as long over losing her two dearest friends. She had run home before reading it, hoping her Daed could explain what was happening. The deacon happened to be at her house and insisted she give him the letter. Fearing Quill had divulged something, such as an address, that would cause problems for him and Frieda, Ariana tore it up and held the remnants under the faucet.

When it was the bishop's turn to preach, he said the fruit of such rebellion caused that same girl to be with a worldly man as he gave a large donation to MAP. His captive audience gasped when they learned that. He used her unwillingness to submit to her Daed about the phone as a demonstration of how anyone who spent time in the world would return more rebellious. And he warned that if the willfulness didn't stop, such a person would be in jeopardy of going to hell.

More rebellious?

The desire to look the bishop in the eyes and tell him what she really thought made her heart race. She hadn't been rebellious in her young years. Never. Not at all. The ministers could convince themselves and the community otherwise, but they could not convince her.

Her cell phone buzzed. She had retrieved it from the hayloft before getting into the buggy. It'd been in the loft a week, and the cold had drained the batteries, so how did it have enough energy to ring? She dug it out of her coat pocket and read "Dad" on the screen. She swallowed hard, not wanting to talk to anyone, not wanting anyone to hear her voice quiver and crack as she tried to control her emotions. But when she'd grabbed her phone from its hiding place, she realized he'd tried to reach her seventeen times since she'd returned home from the B&B eight days ago.

She swiped a cold finger across the screen and hoped she could force happiness into her voice. "Hey, how are you?" Her voice cracked, and tears threatened once again, but she forged ahead, hoping to avoid his asking too many questions. "I'm in a rig, driving, and it's really cold." Would that excuse cover why she sounded so weird?

"That was more words than you used the entire first week you were here."

"Really?"

"Yeah. You were even more quiet during driving lessons, and I . . ." He continued talking, but her mind couldn't focus on small talk, so his voice faded.

She had sinned. She would never deny that the ministers were right about that. Often she thought too highly of herself, convinced she could do anything set before her and much more. But when faced with the stress of action, she fell apart instead of being strong and having rock-solid faith. Unfortunately that same character deficit was trying to take over again. Or maybe it wasn't a lack of character. Maybe it was just being human—her way and the wiring of her humanness.

She turned onto the small street that led to the lot behind her café, drove onto the snow-covered area, and stopped the rig. The ministers blamed her for what was happening, saying that keeping bad company corrupted good morals and that if one's biological parent is worldly, the child must follow Jesus and choose to let the dead bury their dead, choose to forsake family to follow Christ.

The verbal assault was every bit as painful and humiliating as taking a physical beating. She hurt for her family and for Rudy. They deserved to be honored, not humiliated.

Tears worked free, drizzling down her cheeks. The salty warmness turned frigid, burning her cheeks. Wind and snow swirled, threatening to freeze any tears, even inside the rig.

"Ariana?"

What had he been saying?

"Ya, I'm here," she whispered, unable to speak any louder because of the emotions pounding her.

"Is everything okay?"

"How are Brandi, Gabe, and Cameron?" She'd exchanged a few lighthearted texts with her mom, stepdad, and stepsister while at the B&B without revealing her state of mind or where she was. But she hadn't spoken to them since leaving their house two weeks ago. It wouldn't help them deal with her absence if they discovered she'd been home only one night before she needed to get away for a week. It would hurt and worry her mom most of all.

"Fine. They're ready to get more texts from you, and I know that because they texted me to see if I'd heard from you. I told them only during your first week away, just as they did."

"You didn't tell them about the B&B, did you?"

"Not a word."

"Thanks."

She missed them. Cameron would definitely have some choice quips about the bishop and lots of humor to get Ariana through this grief-filled saga. Brandi would take her out to the movies and to dinner and shopping. Spending money was the upper-middle-class Englisch answer for a lot of emotional upsets. "You won't believe where I am. I've just pulled up to my café."

"Ari, you don't sound good."

His concern flooded her, and thoughts of fun with Cameron and Brandi disappeared. "I . . . I'm fine." She brushed away a tear. "You know, cold but just fine."

The windows of the rig were frosty, impairing her view of the café. Her hands trembled harder as she got out of the carriage. Were the ministers *trying* to run her off?

She needed to keep talking. It was the stops and starts that allowed her emotions to overwhelm her. "The café looks so different from when I left here, even from behind."

There was a permanent lean-to in place to protect the horses of the café workers from bad weather. Horse blankets hung over a rail in the lean-to, and there were feed and water troughs. All those things had been on her to-do list, but they hadn't ranked high enough to get done in the short time between purchasing the café and having to leave home.

But there was one thing that hadn't been on her to-do list: an ugly generator. It sat against the back of the café under another lean-to. "There is a generator outside the back door of the café."

Abram had said it was absolutely necessary for running the café successfully. Apparently the many types of coffee served were part of the success that only Skylar knew how to pull off.

She took the key out of her coat pocket and went to the weatherworn wooden back door of the café.

"Ah, but how well does the generator work?"

"Great . . ." She jiggled the key until it turned. "Or so I've been told." Why would she say that?

"That's what you've been told? You don't know?"

Her vision blurred with tears. "This is my first time to be in the café. I've been grounded since coming home." Why couldn't she just shut up? Two sobs escaped her before she gained control. "It's such a mess. I'm right where I want to be, but the ministers are so angry with me, and it's not just me they are taking it out on. They found a way to embarrass Mamm, Daed, my family, and Rudy." She leaned her head against the door. "I don't know what to do to make it better. And Daed . . ." She felt so bad for him, and yet he was being as difficult as the bishop. The difference was she knew Daed's heart was in the right place, even if his understanding wasn't.

"What about him?"

"Daed found my phone. Long story short, I took it back and refused to turn it over when he demanded. I think that more than anything else is why I'm grounded."

"Has he lost his mind?" Nicholas growled.

"You're going to judge him for jostling my life? He's being no worse than you were when I first arrived there, and his fears are the same—that I'm going to ruin my life by not seeing the truth."

Nicholas sighed and said nothing for nearly a minute. "You're right. I see that. You could give him the phone. I'll get you another, and—"

"I've thought of that, but no. Step into my shoes for a minute. Imagine being me, raised like me, poor and with Amish rules, and the phone is the first gift your real dad gave you."

"I see what you mean, and your description means a lot." His voice was soft, as if her words had truly moved him. "Sort of ironic that you didn't feel that way at all when I gave it to you, and two weeks ago as you were getting out of my car to go back to your Amish world, I had to beg you to keep it."

"I know. Since then, and maybe not fully until the last few days, I've realized that I've grown to like it, just like we grew to get along and understand each other." Her mind cleared as she defended her right to hold on to the phone. It had every text she'd sent or received. It had the first pictures she'd ever taken. It testified to her first contact with Frieda in five years. It had the images she'd seen firsthand as she and Nicholas crisscrossed the country. "After a lifetime of walking to a community phone to make a call, I can't explain how this phone makes me feel. It was my first taste of having any information I wanted at my fingertips. Information is power. You know that. This tiny device means I don't have to rely on what I'm told. I can Google anything, read, and think. The GPS guided me while I drove. Somewhere in the past two weeks, I realized this device represents the Englisch side of me, and I'm not giving it up."

"You sure you're not wavering on this topic?" Nicholas teased.

Ariana's whispery laugh was a mixture of tears and relief. "Apparently I'm suddenly positive of one thing about myself, and interestingly enough that piece of understanding is wrapped in the word *no*."

No, she wasn't giving up her phone. No, she wasn't yielding to what Daed or the church said she needed to do. No.

A feeling of foolishness skittered through her. She sounded like a toddler. But then passages in First Corinthians about love came to mind. Scripture was clear on what love is, deliciously clear and encouraging. In the list that defined love, the first two items described what it is, and that was followed by eight things it isn't. After that, the list returned to what love is, but the list of what it *isn't* helped to clarify what it *is*.

When she and Nicholas ended this call, she should look up that passage on her phone.

"Ari, is your cell the only problem? I ask because maybe we could come up with some other solution that would appease people and smooth things over."

"No, there's more but nothing fixable."

"Indulge me, please."

She hesitated.

"Ariana, if you're surviving the thick of battle, I assure you I can handle hearing about it."

"You won't like it, but word got back to the bishop that I saw you and Quill while at the B&B and that you made a donation to MAP."

"I'm so sorry, Ari. I didn't think . . ."

"You meant no harm." One of the things whipping her emotions into an unbearable state dawned on her. "I really resent the bishop telling me that I'll go to hell if I don't do as Daed and he want."

Nicholas cursed. "He said that to you?"

"In his own way—indirect directness—ya." Ariana drew a deep breath. "Before I left here, before you shoved academia at me, I would've believed him, and now, even though it's possible he's right, I'm angry that he's using it to try to manipulate and control me."

"He's not right, Ari, and you should begrudge it." A beeping sound came through the line, as if he was turning on his computer. "Listen, you need to leave there. I'll come get you. We'll buy a new café elsewhere. You can't let these people use you to confirm they have the answers when they don't."

What? "Walking away would never, ever be the answer. You think I should walk away while Daed and I are at odds like this? Do you know what that would do to him?"

"I don't care! He's dead wrong. He's not only hurting you, but he's also allowing the ministers and the community to pile on you, and—"

"Whoa!" She paced around the café. "No. Just no." There was that word again, defining who she was on another topic. "That man you're so very willing to criticize is the only reason I'm alive, the only reason my mom is alive. If she'd died, where would I be? Or maybe the question is where would Skylar be? With you?"

The very hour that she, Skylar, and Abram were born, a fire swept through the clinic, burning it to the ground. Her Daed, the man who raised her and was overwhelmed with fear concerning the direction of her life, could've easily chosen to rescue only his wife, Mamm, and their newborn twins—Abram and Skylar. If it hadn't been for Daed's heroism and effort, Ariana's real mom, Brandi, would've died before an ambulance could get to her. If Ariana had survived the fire and been paired with the right mom, where would she be now? Nicholas wouldn't have raised her. When she was born, he'd been married to someone else, and he'd wanted Brandi to end the pregnancy. Ariana could've been put up for adoption.

"The possibilities of who would be where today are overwhelming to think about." But empathy for who Nicholas was now caused her to reel in her emotions. He regretted being that man, and he couldn't undo it. "Dad, all I'm trying to say is people clearly mishandle situations because their understanding and motivations are wrong. I'm not walking out on my Daed and the Brenneman family. That's about all I know right now, but look at how differently you and I see life, politics, and faith today compared to four months ago."

"You're right. I see those things vastly different. But, Ari, I've never known anyone who looks at things the way you do." His contrition was clear, and she wished it were as easy to change the minds and hearts of Amish men.

"I'm not as clear headed as I sounded just then. I only know that Daed deserves time and respect and that I feel a bit like a traitor."

"Why?"

"You were the bad guy in all our minds only a few months ago, and everything you stood for was evil. Now I'm on the phone with you, talking about them as if I've switched sides."

"Could we find middle ground?"

That was a really good question. Was there any middle ground? If so, could she find it? "I used to think the same way as the congregation did this morning—that people need to be either fully in or get out, way out, as in no contact. And there are some scriptures that back that kind of thinking."

"I imagine we could find scriptures that also give balance to those verses. Would you like us to try that?"

"Maybe later." Who would've thought that Nicholas Jenkins would be someone she could be brutally honest with *and* confide in? She was grateful he encouraged her to speak out. When she did, her mind cleared a bit. Maybe that's why the world was so quick to grab an opinion. Whether the view was right or wrong, it brought a measure of clarity to the confusion.

She stared at the exquisite old wood floors. A fresh ache mixed with the new joy of finally being inside her café again.

"The café is charming."

He cleared his throat. "So walk me through it and tell me all about it."

The kindness in his voice strengthened her. Her breath was frosty, but there was no potbelly stove installed as she had intended. She walked down the small hall, looking into the kitchen area, noticing how well organized and spotless it was. "The kitchen is endearing with hanging pots, open shelves filled with clean dishes, a huge double sink, and an old refrigerator. Everything is spotless and is either powered by natural gas or the generator. But something has a funny-sounding squeal to it."

As she searched for the noise, she paused a few steps from the ordering counter and looked out at the tables filling the dining area. "Behind the ordering bar is a long countertop that is now filled with shiny silver coffeemakers and gadgets of all types. I have no idea how to operate those."

"Sounds as if Skylar may need to walk you through that."

Ariana couldn't imagine Skylar showing her anything except the front door. Ariana would be glad to go out the front door, but she couldn't right now. If she moved in with Berta, it would put her under suspicion of helping Ariana remain rebellious. The café had a good loft, but if Ariana lived here, it would hurt her Daed and embarrass him in front of the community. Besides, if he refused to let her move here and she did so anyway, he could insist Abram, Susie, Martha, and Skylar not come here to help out. Maybe they would come anyway, at least some of them, but it would cause a rift, and she wouldn't be a part of that.

She decided to change the subject. "Abram was right. It is all very quaint and nice, despite the Englisch technology."

"Will you try your hand at making coffee?"

"Abram said they've taken the percolator home, and they now have no way to make coffee other than with the machines Skylar got them to order, ones that are powered by the generator."

"Ha, you're caught," Nicholas teased, "if you want coffee."

She had no choice. If she wanted to get the hang of running this place—or at least working here in a skilled manner—she needed to start the generator and figure out these machines.

The phone beeped, letting her know the battery was running low. "I better go. If I can get the generator started, I'll recharge my phone and text you and the others later."

"One thing first. I've been online, looking through Scripture as we've talked. Do you recall the verses about not loving the world or anything in the world?"

"By heart since before I was born, I think. It's First John 2:15."

"I thought you'd know that one well. So you're also familiar with the part that says all of you know the truth?"

"I don't recall that one." Her heart felt a little lighter just knowing he, a nonbeliever, was trying to find answers in the only way that would help her. "What's it talking about?" It was a perk that this meant he was still reading the Word even though she was gone. Seemed funny that his sole purpose in reading the Word when she first went to his home was to prove to her how ridiculous it was. Now he read it to be of benefit to her. That was really sweet.

"It's just a few verses later, and there are lots of versions, but paraphrasing, it basically says you don't need anyone to teach you right from wrong because the same anointing that was in Christ is in you and teaches you all things about truth and it is no lie." Nicholas paused. "I know you'll want to study that for yourself, but, Ari, it sounds to me as if the Bible itself is saying you have the right to discern between truth and a lie because of your faith in Christ."

"You don't believe any of that."

"But it's your handbook of life and liberty. Isn't it odd that you know the verses just above it and don't recall these at all? Are you allowing that bishop to take verses out of context and convince you that the ministers have more rights before God than your own handbook?"

"Who's it written to?"

"What do you mean?"

"Is it talking to men? If it is, that helps me not at all."

"Oh. No, it seems to be talking to everyone. I'm just skimming, but the writer uses the words 'dear children' several times and 'dear friends' at least once. It's a beautiful chapter, even *I* can see—"

Her phone beeped and then fell completely silent. She looked at it while pushing buttons. It was dead, but at least Nicholas knew that might happen.

Silence engulfed her, as did his paraphrased words from the Bible. *You don't need anyone to teach you right from wrong because the same anointing that was in Christ is in you and teaches you all things about truth.*

Was that possible? Did she have the same anointing that was in Christ? What an amazing thought. She'd settle for a little dusting of that anointing. *Dear God, even a dusting of it.*

It would be nice if her phone had power so she could look up the verses herself. But she was finally here, in her café, and the most immediate need was to get her phone recharged and the power going to the café. So she headed out the door to the generator. Once she had it running, she needed to learn how to use the coffee machines. She looked heavenward, seeing low-hanging clouds and flurries. In some ways her life felt as cold as this long, harsh winter and her spiritual understanding was being blown like the snow.

The squeaking noise returned, and she listened closely, trying to determine where it was coming from. With her head tilted and listening carefully, she followed the sound.

Then the noise of a rig and horses caught her attention, and Rudy pulled a carriage in behind hers and got out. "Hey."

Rudy's admiration of her and his sense of humor used to fill all the spaces between them, but now she felt his disappointment and rumbles of anger.

"Hi." They stood looking at each other in the cold as winter's wind pushed and pulled at them. The sound of squeaking continued to tug at her, but she knew better than to put something else ahead of Rudy.

He held the horse's bridle. "I know you came here to be alone, so I won't stay long. But I talked to the bishop and deacon privately and asked what we could do to set things right again."

She went to him, staring up and longing for a hug. "I'm sorry, Rudy."

She wanted to marry him and to raise their babies while bringing him honor, not disgrace. She longed to be in good standing with her Daed, the community, and the ministers. But how did she get there from here?

"I want to believe that, Ari." He brushed his fingers down her cheek. "But this bedlam that has followed you around since you learned you weren't a Brenneman has to end. I love you. I want to marry you. Those two things have not changed. They will not change."

"Denki."

"I've spent this week thinking, and I believe what you've told me about your feelings and Quill."

"Gut."

"If you were interested in him, why would you relentlessly push Nicholas to allow you to return to Summer Grove, to your roots, to your family, to me?"

"Ya. That's the right conclusion, Rudy."

"But . . . if there is no romance with him, and if it is as you say about Nicholas—that he chose to support MAP on his own without your influence—then do as the bishop and deacon want. Repair at least some of the damage, because right now I look and feel like an idiot. Everyone knows you asked Quill to the B&B, not me."

"It's exactly as I told you. He's navigated both worlds and lived to tell about it. That's all." The squeaking noise tugged at her again. "Do you hear that?" She took Rudy's hand and started toward the sound.

He pulled back, stopping her. "Ari, could you focus on us for five minutes, please?"

She glanced toward the sound before facing Rudy. "Ya. Of course." His exhaustion seemed to spill over on her, and she just wanted peace . . . for everyone. "What do they require?"

"It's simple really. They want you to repent of your contact with Quill and Nicholas and for you to give your word that you won't see either one of them again without a minister present."

"That's a lot."

"It's the bare minimum."

"I've agreed with you about Quill." She wouldn't want Rudy seeing or texting a young, single woman. "But Dad? Because of me, he's reading the Bible, and—"

"No one will have all that they want, but I've worked out something about your phone that I think everyone can live with. You don't have to turn it over to the ministers or your Daed."

"That sounds promising." But it was disappointing that he wouldn't even let her finish her sentence about Nicholas. Although she understood Nicholas and had forgiven his faults and appreciated his strengths, all he was to Rudy was a stubborn man who'd changed the harmony and dynamics between Ariana and him.

"It's very agreeable," Rudy said. "You'll turn it off and give it to me. After we're married, the bishop will approve the phone as part of your needs for the business, and you can have it back."

"That is a good compromise on their part. How did you manage it?"

"I talked and reasoned and bargained. The ministers take no pleasure in what's going on."

"They targeted me in their lengthy sermons about rebellion and hell."

"Gossip was going to inform everyone anyway. It's out in the open. They've cooled off and expressed regret for saying as much as they did."

She cupped Rudy's clean-shaven face. "You are a peacemaker." She lowered her hands. "But to leave my phone turned off until we're married?"

"Instruction begins this spring. We can marry by mid-September. That's less than eight months." He smiled. "It'll take longer than that to carry a child one day. This will bring peace to the district and respect back to your Daed and Mamm."

Her powerful defense to Nicholas for keeping the phone seemed to taunt her as it faded on the wind. "I . . . I'll think about it."

Rudy nodded and kissed her cheek. "Choose us, Ari. Above your Englisch family, your phone, and Quill, choose us."

When he put it that way, she longed to nod her head and fall into his arms. "But my family?"

"It's horrible luck to discover you have Englisch family, and not just any Englisch family, but, well, you know what yours are like. But we will build a new family—you, me, and our children. And the Brennemans are every bit as much your family as they were before all this."

"I never doubted that." The squeal faded to almost nothing, and despite it not making sense, she wanted to search for the source. "Kumm." She tugged on his hand, hoping to direct him toward the noise.

"Nee." Anger flashed in his eyes. "I was hoping for a more favorable response. Is that too much to ask?"

Memories of the laughter and fun they used to have whirled in her head. He'd been so patient. If he'd embarrassed her in front of everyone with news of meeting a young woman at a B&B, she wasn't sure she'd stand near him, calmly holding out solutions.

"I want to do it for you, Rudy. I do."

"And?"

"I . . . I need to think about it. I promised Mom and Cameron they could be in my life once you and I were married. I'm an only child for Brandi and Nicholas. At the very least they'll want a few days each year with their grandchildren, and I was hoping they could come to the wedding. You can understand that, right?"

"I understand how you feel, Ari, but our reality is we have to choose what we believe over what we long for."

"That may be easy for you to say." He wasn't talking about cutting his mom and dad out of his life. And beyond her parents, she had other relatives in the Englisch world who mattered too. "I'll have to cut off part of who I am, and it's not as if they won't feel that cut for the rest of their lives."

"It wasn't easy to convince the ministers to find ground where a compromise was possible."

"Kumm." They needed to change the subject and get out of the cold. "I'll put some coffee on for you while I see what that strange noise is."

"Nee. Denki. I'm worn out from the disarray and resentment I've handled today, and I'm going home." He kissed her on the lips. "And apparently you need to think."

"I love you, Rudy."

He smiled and kissed her cheek. "As God is my witness, I hope so, Ariana." He winked and got in his carriage.

She waved good-bye before marching through the snow. The cold, white flakes fell inside her ankle-high black boots, and as she waded through the damp coldness, the squeaking noise grew louder. Whatever it was, it wasn't coming from inside the café. The farther she walked into the field, the louder it got.

In the middle of a field of thick snow, she noticed a spot where the white covering was moving. She reached down and poked it. A puppy yelped.

"Ach, du liewi Bobbeli!" She dusted the snow off of it. It was a little thing, maybe no more than a month old. "Liewi, what are you doing draus here?" She tucked it inside her coat, amazed she'd heard it at all and sorry she hadn't arrived sooner. "Let's get you inside and give you some warm milk, ya?"

Thirteen

Quill's head pounded. How could his careful planning to get Gia and her children out go so terribly wrong? And the things that went wrong were on him. He should've taken everything into account. Would he get another chance, or would he read in the newspaper that her ex-husband had killed her and taken the children?

He'd talked to Melanie and another contact, Constance. They both assured him he had done everything right, but he knew better. If he had, Gia and her children would be with him. But Melanie and Constance told him there was nothing that could be done right now. Gia had made her decision, and all they could do was wait to hear from her, which might not happen until her next trip to the grocery store.

He turned off the car lights, slowly exited the snowy main road, and pulled onto the narrow path on his Mamm's property. Although the barn was closer to the house and a straight line from it to the main road was the easiest route, Mamm often drove her horse and carriage down this same path to keep it serviceable for her sons year round. In the winter she hitched the horse to an Amish snow scraper. The trail was hidden by a patch of woods that led to the double-wide doors of the old shed. He stopped the vehicle in front of the familiar dilapidated building. He hoped the roof was sturdy enough not to collapse under the thick snow. He wouldn't mind shoring up the old structure, but doing any work on the building would be a dead giveaway that it wasn't abandoned. That was not a message his Mamm could afford to send to the community. He put the car in Park and jumped out, leaving the vehicle running as he unlocked and opened the shed doors. He returned to the car and drove inside. After turning off the car, he closed the double-wide doors from the inside and exited through a side door. He eased along the shadows of outbuildings until he was on the porch outside his bedroom window. Using his key, he tapped on the window three times. The sound was faint enough that anyone visiting his Mamm would think the noise was just the old farmhouse, but his Mamm would hear it. She always heard it. A moment later he saw light from a kerosene lantern floating his way.

He opened the window and began to crawl through the small space. "All clear?" he whispered.

She smiled. "I don't know when I've been so glad to see you."

"Glad to hear that . . . I think."

The moment he stood up straight, she embraced him, holding tight. This wasn't normal. His Mamm gave hugs and was very open about her love, but this time she clung to him as if she were drowning, and since he felt as if he were drowning too, he held on tight. He kissed the top of her head. "You okay?"

She jerked a ragged breath into her lungs. "I've been thinking." She pointed at the rug under their feet. "You picked this out about ten years ago, and you loved this rug. How about if you roll it up and take it with you for your home?"

"Strange welcome." He looked down at the sturdy, colorful rug with the bits of melting snow that had fallen off his boots. "But I really like the plan." He took off his coat and tossed it on the bed.

Mamm was unique. He knew no one else like her. She was steel wrapped in fleece. Maybe that was her nature, or maybe that was who she'd become since giving birth to five strong-willed sons and burying the love of her life. Sometimes he didn't understand her actions and reactions, but he knew she'd just used a diversionary tactic to avoid answering his question about her well-being. Something was seriously out of kilter.

She raised the lantern toward his face. "You're pale."

He nodded. "It's been a bad twenty-four hours. I . . . I planned poorly, and it could cost a victim of domestic violence and her three children their freedom. Maybe even their lives."

Her eyes stayed on his. "I'm so sorry."

"Denki." Quill hugged her again.

"Have you heard from the woman?"

"No. Last night after she changed her mind about leaving with me, I stayed at a hotel close to her house just in case she made contact with someone and wanted me to get her." He had been up all night, pacing the floor and talking to people in the organization who knew Gia. But he'd been told this afternoon that he needed to leave Camp Hill. He couldn't live in a hotel room without getting out some, and they couldn't afford for him to be spotted. One of the children might recognize him and blurt out that he was the man from the grocery store who tried to get their mommy to leave with him. So he came here since it was only thirty minutes from Camp Hill.

When his Mamm released him, she motioned for him to follow her. "Clearly we both need hot tea and a long conversation."

He hovered in the dark hallway while Mamm lowered the blinds in the living room and kitchen. Then he moved to the table, and they chatted as she peeled potatoes and cooked hash browns.

After giving some details of the failed rescue and Gia's fear of going with him, Quill was ready to change the topic. "Enough about me. How are you?"

"Today"—she stabbed a knife into the cutting board—"the ministers were taking turns preaching about different dangers of being willful, and all of it was aimed at Ariana. I walked out."

Quill couldn't believe his ears. "Mamm . . ."

"I know." She pointed a shaky hand at him. "That was my reaction."

"If you left in the middle of the meeting, you're likely to get a visit tonight."

"Ya. The doors are locked, but if someone knocks, you'll have to move fast."

He nodded.

She jerked the knife free and started cutting the potatoes again. "They never mentioned anyone's name, but let me tell you what was said . . ." Mamm rattled on about the letter he'd given Ariana and how she'd destroyed it in front of the deacon when he'd told her to hand it over. Mamm told him about the preachers mentioning texts between him and Ariana and his meeting her at the B&B. As the list went on, Quill was tempted to grab the knife and threaten the bishop with it.

"How's Ariana?"

"I haven't seen her since I left the meeting. Did you know she's not been allowed to go to *her* café all week?"

"Why?"

As Mamm was explaining, someone knocked on the door, and Quill disappeared down the hallway and into his room.

The ministers would have a lot of questions about his Mamm leaving the service, and he didn't imagine she had any measured, polite responses right now, so it could be a very long visit.

Could he get out the window without being heard? He really didn't want to hide in this house for endless hours, and he feared he might come out of hiding and tell them what he really thought.

Fourteen

Ariana stomped her feet, trying to knock as much snow off her boots as possible. She knocked again. Where was her key to Berta's house anyway?

The lock clicked, and slowly the door opened an inch. The chain caught. Berta gasped. "Ariana!" She peered behind her. "Are you alone?"

"Ya."

The door slammed, the chain rattled, and then the door flew open. "Ach, Ari." Berta hugged her and ushered her inside. "Are you okay?"

"Better, actually." Ariana closed the door. "But I'm not as alone as I said." Ariana pulled the pup out from under her coat. "Look what I found." The puppy wriggled and whimpered, clearly preferring to snuggle and sleep than to be showcased. "Is she welcome to come in too?"

Berta laughed. "Ya."

"We need to be a little bit careful because she hasn't gone potty since I found her four hours ago."

Berta lifted the puppy from Ariana. "I know what you need. Kumm." Berta put a towel on the woodstove, and Ariana knew in just a minute she'd wrap the puppy in it and feed her something tasty.

Ariana unbuttoned her coat. "She was half-frozen in the middle of the lot behind the café. I don't know how she got there, and I can't believe I heard her whimpering and was able to spot her under a layer of snow."

Berta stroked the puppy. "You went to the café?"

"I did." Ariana hung her coat on the back of a kitchen chair. "I snuck out after the fellowship meal and . . ."

Chills ran up the back of Ariana's neck. But it was different from feeling cold. The feeling was a familiar one. "I'll be back in a minute."

"Sure." Berta never looked up. "I think I lit the lamp in the bathroom, but if not, I put a fresh lighter in the right-hand drawer under the sink."

Ariana stepped to the edge of the hallway and peered down the dark corridor, looking at the closed door of Quill's bedroom. If Quill was here, Berta wouldn't volunteer that information. It would be up to him to make himself known or not. But if he was here, why would he hide from her? Maybe he hadn't realized she was the person who came to his Mamm's door. "Quill?"

The bedroom door opened, and moonlight shone around him as if he were a dark cloud outlined by a shimmering silver lining. He said nothing. Didn't even move.

Relationships of all kinds are odd, each one unique to the two people in it. Apparently, based on the last five or so years of her life, they were also complex and really hard.

A memory of the two of them in this exact spot five months ago washed over her. At the time, all that was between them was the darkness of a stormy night and the silence of brokenness. But now, even in the evening shadows, she could feel a tremor in him and knew something was wrong, something cataclysmic.

She brushed a strand of hair from her face, wondering how much had fallen from her prayer Kapp since daylight. "I didn't expect you to be here." And hadn't she promised Rudy she wouldn't see him anymore?

"I heard you've had it rough," he whispered as he came toward her. He stopped mere inches away.

"Ya, but right now I'm asking about you."

He drew a deep breath, and she waited for his answer, but none came. Then he gestured toward the kitchen. "I'm good. No worries."

"Fine." She didn't believe him. "Of course you are. You always are. It's no problem if I'm a wreck, if I need to vent and cry and talk about my issues without a filter. But it's entirely too much for you to stop protecting me for three minutes and just tell it like it is."

Quill gestured toward the kitchen again. "How bad is the damage from what's going on with the ministers?"

"That's it? That's your response? Because that's the kind of diversion and withholding of information that adults use on children."

"You have a lot going on right now—"

"Everyone on the planet has a lot going on right now." Why was she prodding him to talk to her when she was supposed to avoid him? It just seemed wrong that he carried too much and shared so little.

A loud knock made them both jump.

Berta hurried down the hallway with the puppy. "It's the ministers." She pushed the puppy into Ariana's arms. "You both should go. It won't help Ariana to be seen here," she whispered.

"Berta." Ariana put a hand on her shoulder. "I'm not going anywhere. Calm." She said the word slowly. "I'll stay back here as an excuse for any noises Quill makes as he goes out his bedroom window, and I'll join you momentarily."

"Ach, gut. Ya." Berta took a deep breath, returning to her usual calm.

"Go." Ariana pointed at Quill's bedroom door.

They heard the front door open and the minister enter.

"Ari," Quill whispered, "I didn't mean—"

She covered his mouth with her hand. "Sh."

They went into his room, and Ari closed the door. "You most certainly did mean it, every single word you didn't say." She picked up his leather coat and thrust it at him.

"But . . ."

Footfalls in the hallway caused both of them to hush. The bathroom door closed. Without another word Quill eased the window open.

The ministers could be here for hours, and Quill needed to leave while he could. She put the puppy on the rug to close the window behind him.

"She'll use my rug," he whispered as he stepped out the window and onto the wraparound porch.

Through the moonlit darkness, she grasped the window to close it. "Good."

Fifteen

Skylar stood behind the counter of the café, disinfecting the smudged keys of the cash register. How many people who'd come in today had a cold? Or worse.

The Saturday crowd had simmered down to a dull murmur of coffee-sipping regulars. Apparently the ridiculous amount of snow lately had caused cabin fever, and this café was a hot spot to go to.

When the bell on the door jangled, her heart sped up, expecting to see Jax lumbering toward her. After their last encounter they needed to clear the air a bit. Because of the sunlight, she saw only the silhouette of a man, but it clearly wasn't Jax, and her heart seemed to drop a few inches.

It was reasonable for him to have pulled back. She was the pot calling the kettle black to question his issues. He had served his country, was good to his friends, and reached out to help those less fortunate. That was a far cry from how she spent her days.

But Jax would be here soon. He came every Saturday around closing time, bringing whatever supplies Susie had ordered.

The man came to a halt in front of the register, interrupting her thoughts. She didn't recognize him for a moment, but then his handsome face brought it all back.

"What?" Skylar tossed the cleaning cloth to the side. "Have you uncovered another long-lost biological family member of mine and are here to rip apart my life again?"

Quill seemed unfazed by her sarcasm. "I suppose I deserve that."

"You think?" She looked at an imaginary watch on her arm. "Oh, look. You dropped me off here almost four months ago." She tapped her wrist and held it to her ear as if the pretend watch was broken. "And never looked back." She lowered her arm. "I'm sorry to disappoint you, but Ariana isn't here. Just me." She shooed him. "So off you go. No need to linger."

But instead of backing away, Quill leaned in, propping his hands on the counter. "You're right, and I'm sorry. I got completely caught up in work and being there for Ariana, and I should've made time to come by here."

"Shoulda, coulda, woulda. It's the story of my life."

"Mine too, I think. But I knew you were in good hands with the Brennemans."

Skylar's insides relaxed, as if she'd stepped into a warm shower. "You're right about the Brennemans. I mean, they are bat-crazy religious, and if I ever forget that part, Isaac lowers his iron fist on someone and quickly reminds me. Thankfully I fall into a different category, so as long as I carry my share of the workload, he doesn't put his iron-fist expectations on me. But the religious part aside, they are real and kind in ways that . . ." She shrugged, unwilling to be vulnerable with him. But she'd desperately needed the type of kindness and authenticity that defined the Brenneman family. "Anyway, I'm clean. Can you believe that?"

He smiled, and his blue eyes lit up with pleasure. "I believe it. And words can't convey how glad I am, for your sake. But you're right, so I'll say it again, I should've made time to come by sooner. You deserved at least that."

"You're really good at apologies."

"Glad to hear it. I need to be." He looked toward the kitchen. "Where is she?"

"Grounded."

"Still?"

"Yup." Apparently when Skylar did something sneaky and underhanded, she did a great job of it.

Quill drummed his fingers on the counter and sighed. "All the same I'll have a coffee."

Skylar grabbed a mug and filled it. "My guess is you've tried to reach her via texts or phone calls."

"I have." Quill sat at the counter directly in front of Skylar. "How are you?"

Skylar put the mug in front of him. "Drink your coffee. I was nice to you once, and you used the information against me."

Quill put out his hands pleadingly. "I thought you just accepted my *good* apology."

Skylar enjoyed being passive-aggressive. "That was for dropping me here and not checking on me. Now I'm focusing on your flirting with me to get info."

"I did do that, didn't I?" He shook his head. "Can't apologize for it. It was necessary to uncover what I needed to know, and based on this conversation, you'd only find something else you'd want an apology for."

"Maybe. Four months has given me a long time to think."

Quill bounced his palm against the rim of the mug. "Any idea how Rudy is handling all of this?"

Skylar shrugged. "He seems good. A bit quiet when the bishop says to be, but I haven't seen him do anything but support her, whether he's by her side or winking at her from across the room during church service."

"That's good. I'm glad to hear it."

"Are you?" Had he forgotten that when he first "happened" to meet her and was trying to break the ice, he'd told her how he felt about Ariana?

"Yes. Very."

"Okay." Skylar refilled his mug. "Just wondering."

"Any idea how much longer she'll be grounded?"

"None." Skylar returned the carafe to its burner. "You're a weird guy, you know that?"

"How so?"

"You displace my entire life and then sit in front of me, sipping coffee like we're old friends."

Quill didn't react. "Yup."

"Is that it?"

He didn't break eye contact or blink. "Yup."

She propped her folded arms on the counter in front of him. "Really? You actually think the scraps you just threw me were plenty?"

"Apparently smart women don't like brevity very much."

Skylar suppressed a giggle. "Ah, have we stumbled on why you're here and need to be good at apologies?"

"They say silence is golden, but it clearly also gets under people's skin."

The door jingled, but she ignored it. "I'll tell you this much. Ariana has more pluck than I imagined."

He barely smiled as he stared into his mug. "Pluck to spare of late."

She laughed, grabbed a dish towel, and threw it at his face. He didn't react, but when it fell over his coffee, he removed it.

"You're too calm, Quill. Just too calm." She glanced up to see Jax hanging back, a folder in one hand and flowers in the other. "Hey, Jax." Since their uncomfortable conversation more than a week ago, they'd simply spoken when necessary and danced awkwardly around each other. She gestured between the two men. "Jax, meet Quill, a.k.a. the life ruiner." She picked up the cloth and smacked Quill's arm with it.

Quill stood and shook Jax's hand. "Life ruiner isn't my official title."

Jax's usual smile was barely visible.

Skylar leaned over the counter. "Oh, my. Look at those flowers, and here it is stark winter, no floral color peeking through anywhere. Those had to cost you a pretty penny, and Susie will love them. Do you want a vase?"

"Uh . . ." He looked from the flowers to Skylar. "Nah." He held up the folder. "I brought the estimates to show you."

Skylar pointed toward the pass-through. "The people to talk to about all of that are in the back." She shooed him. "Go."

Jax left, and Quill took a five-dollar bill out of his wallet and held it toward her.

She shook her head. "You're good."

He held on to the money as he put away his wallet. "In my opinion he didn't bring in the estimates to talk to the others about them." He tossed the money on the counter. "And the flowers weren't for Susie."

"What?" She looked beyond the pass-through, trying to see Jax. "You think . . . me?"

"Yup." Quill rapped his knuckles on the counter. "If you like that guy at all, it was a bad call not to tell him we barely know each other." Quill briefly lifted both brows, a smile tugging on his lips. "But it's a fixable situation . . . if you care to." Quill walked toward the front door.

He was known for being savvy, but he had to be dead wrong about this.

Abram rushed out of the kitchen, causing the swinging door to flop to and fro with fury. "Quill."

Quill stopped and turned. When the two men were close, Abram spoke softly and pulled what appeared to be a folded piece of paper from his pocket. The two talked for maybe a minute before Abram handed it to Quill, and then Quill left.

As Abram passed her to return to the kitchen, she squirted the counter and wiped it down, pretending she hadn't seen the interaction. But they both knew she had.

It was easy to understand Quill coming to the café if he wanted to speak to Ariana. It wasn't as if he could stop by the house. But Skylar liked that, regardless of how taboo contact with Quill was supposed to be, her quiet, hardworking brother had just talked to and passed a note to him. Skylar was sure the note was from Ariana. It was fascinating to watch how a kindhearted group of siblings, who were innocents in many ways, could band together to defy the Old Ways, the ministers, and their parents in the name of love and loyalty.

Jax's voice rumbled through the café as he laughed about something, causing different questions to come to mind. If he had brought those flowers for her, was he ready to get past the uncomfortable conversation they'd had last week? Thus far they'd swept it under the rug and kept things cordial.

Had she just trampled his effort to smooth things over between them?

Sixteen

Ariana opened the door to the phone shanty and went inside. She had turned off her cell and put it away in order to be fair to Rudy, at least while she pondered what to do. He was pleased she'd turned off the phone but frustrated she hadn't given it to him.

He didn't approve of her coming here to call her dad either, and he'd be angry if he knew why she was calling him. Was she wrong?

Maybe.

Maybe *very* wrong, but she didn't know what else to do. If the café went under, she'd never be able to help her parents buy one new cow, let alone several.

To that end she'd made a decision, and she lifted the phone from its cradle and dialed. Nicholas didn't answer, so she left a message and hung up. She doubted if he'd recognize this number. When he got her voice mail, he'd call her.

Her heart was bruised and battered. With the exception of some of her siblings, everyone seemed displeased with her, and a majority of them were furious. Too many acted as if she needed to be stoned—not to death, mind you. That would be wrong. But stoned until their anger and fear subsided and she was willing to submit.

The phone rang, and Nicholas's number showed up on caller ID. She grabbed the receiver. "Hey."

"Hi, Ari. Where are you?"

"Phone shanty. I turned off my cell for a bit, as a compromise for Rudy."

"Sounds like the Ariana I've come to know and love—may not agree but knows how to sacrifice for the betterment of others. How are you holding up?"

"Confused, mostly. Unsure where to give in. Unsure where right ends and wrong begins."

"And your young man. Is he confused too?"

Thoughts of Rudy grieved her. She loved him, and he loved her, but he didn't understand how she felt or why. He understood how the ministers, her Daed, and the community felt.

"He's confused by me and sure about everything else. I don't blame him. I get where he's coming from and why. I wrestle with concrete issues, like the finances of the café, and abstract issues of where the lines are concerning moral behavior. But Rudy's interest lies solely in us talking about getting married." Of late she felt like she was a cow and he had a prodder, trying to rush her into the corral that led straight to the altar. "If I'm still unclear who I am by spring, how can I begin instruction?"

Nicholas was silent.

"Sorry." Ariana rolled her eyes, so weary of these new thoughts. "There isn't anyone I can talk to about this."

"Needing someone to talk to is why people usually end up in groups with others who are like-minded."

"I don't have a group. I'm not sure a group exists that I'd fit with anymore. And I feel like a deceiver, never really being honest and never really lying."

" 'This above all—to thine own self be true, and it must follow, as the night the day, thou canst not then be false to any man.' William Shakespeare."

The beauty and insight of the words grabbed her heart. "Say that again." She tore a page out of an old spiral notebook that was left there for anyone to use. She picked up a pen and wrote it down as he repeated it slowly.

To thine own self be true . . .

Whenever she thought she knew something about herself that was true, she faced such a backlash that she melted into a puddle of confusion.

"I didn't mean to get into all of that and be warm and friendly, because the truth is that I called to ask a mammoth favor."

Nicholas chuckled. "I like you, kiddo. I really do. What's up?"

"I need to borrow money. Just a loan."

"How much?"

"A lot. There are four full-time employees who've worked six days a week and a lot of overtime and two part-time employees. None have received a full paycheck. It seems they decided to donate their pay to cover the medical bills of a young woman with cystic fibrosis and let me figure out the rest when I got here."

"How much do you owe them?"

"If I deduct two thousand from each person's pay to cover the medical bills, I owe thirty thousand in back pay, plus taxes. And that's if I stick to paying minimum wage." She rubbed her forehead. "I need twenty thousand dollars."

"I'd spend far more than that in a year if you were in a major university, so that's not an issue."

"I'm sorry."

"You're a twenty-year-old business owner. Nothing is as hard to get on its feet as a small business, and you weren't there to pour time and energy into it."

"The café is bringing in good money, and I know it can do even better if we expand our menu and the hours. Not being allowed to go there has given me time to research and set goals. If we start serving desserts, selling cake by the slice, and some other things, I think we could clear about fifty thousand next year after overhead and taxes."

"Seriously?"

"Ya, the customer base is there, and I know we can build on it."

"You'll have to hire more people."

"Definitely. There's no shortage of Amish teen girls needing a job between graduating from the eighth grade and getting married five to seven years later. We'll do shifts, and those who've been working can manage those coming in and make more money for doing so. In a year I could start buying cattle for Daed."

"That's your goal, to buy cows?"

She explained.

"But why would you want to?"

"Because love gives." She didn't know how to explain better than that. Since she was a little girl, her heart had longed to give her Daed a financial boost. But she was no saint. Not only was she talking to Nicholas against everyone's wishes, but she would go to the café to pass out paychecks and have a meeting. Daed would just have to deal with it. "I can pay three hundred a month until the loan is covered."

"Ari, I'm not keen on this being a loan. If love gives, then let me give this."

"Three hundred a month until it's paid."

"Could we shelve that part of the deal until later, please?"

She would be in so much trouble if the ministers found out what she was doing. At least if it were a loan, it might be acceptable. "I guess I could add it to my long list of things to think about. But I also need financial and business-meeting advice."

"I'll try to answer your questions, and if I don't know, I'll check with my financial advisor."

Ariana asked a dozen questions about the finances of the café and how to handle various situations. She took notes, snatching more paper from the notebook, but most of his counsel would easily stick with her. "Thank you."

"You're actually quite good at this. I can tell by your questions and your answers to my questions. If you have your account number, I'll move the money there now."

Abram and Susie had given up their jobs to get the café running while she was gone. Everyone who'd worked at the café shouldn't have to go one more week without full pay. With five thousand in cash missing, there wasn't enough money to pay the bills over the next few months if she didn't get a loan.

"Skylar, with all her ideas and her push for coffee machines and a generator, was a godsend . . . as far as the café goes. I wouldn't have thought of or known how to do all she suggested."

"Good. She's smart as a whip, always has been."

"If the church ministers learn I'm asking you for money, I'll be in even worse trouble."

"Did you know that the word *Protestant* comes from the word *protest*? Starting in the sixteenth century, people were protesting the Catholic church. The Protestants felt it was their God-given right to follow their hearts as God directed rather than having to do as the church dictated. The Catholic church would excommunicate people and condemn them to hell. I find it interesting that the Amish fled Europe in great part due to the persecution of the Catholic church, only to resettle in a free country and create new restrictions that keep people from being able to follow their hearts for fear of excommunication."

"Nicholas."

"Yeah?"

"Have you tried researching all the good that's been done by those same faiths?"

"Some. Anyway, moving on. I'd be glad to help Skylar in a similar way . . . when she's no longer at risk of using it for drugs."

"She'll have money once I pay her, about nine thousand dollars after taxes."

"That's a little scary, but she's a working adult. All we can do is hope for the best."

"Thanks. I really appreciate this. I need to go. Okay?" She felt like a selfish teen, asking for money and then saying good-bye. "We'll talk soon."

She understood the need to put space between Quill and her. Rudy needed that of her, and she would give it. But was it fair for anyone to tell her she had to give up contact with her Englisch family?

Seventeen

Abram waved as the final pair of customers exited Brennemans' Perks. "Thank you for coming. Have a good day!"

"You too." The young man closed the door behind him and went down the sidewalk talking to his female companion.

Abram flipped the sign on the front door to Closed. While he'd been cleaning tables for the two o'clock Saturday closing, he couldn't help but notice how the couple's words had flowed easily between them, punctuated by laughter and demure looks over their coffee mugs.

He wanted that. Maybe he shouldn't, since quiet awkwardness had defined most of his life, but he did. Not with just anyone, though. With Cilla. Over the last five months as he'd come to know her better and leaned on her for advice, he'd discovered he could open up with her in ways he'd never imagined doing with anyone except the person he'd believed was his twin, the one he'd grown up with. Strangely, it was the predicament of learning Ariana had been swapped at birth that caused Abram to begin going to Cilla's house to talk.

Abram took the bin with its few dirty dishes into the kitchen.

"Whatcha got there?" Susie was putting on her coat.

"Two mugs, one plate, and two spoons."

"It was a hectic Saturday, and I'm beat. Just fill the bin with hot, sudsy water, and I'll wash them first thing Monday."

That plan sounded good.

The back door swung open. "Hallo?" Ariana called.

"She's here in *her* café!" Susie screamed. *"Wilkum!"*

Susie and Martha about knocked her over, book bag and all, and Abram steadied his sisters before wrapping them in a group hug.

"Great," Skylar said. "Another Amish tradition I'm not familiar with. Who knew the Amish did their own version of huddle and squeal?"

Abram stood straight, and his sisters peeled outward, like a flower opening.

Skylar saw Ariana, and her eyebrows furrowed a bit. "Oh. Makes sense now. Carry on." Skylar went behind the counter near the register, carrying the box of gourmet coffee beans she'd found in the loft after thirty minutes of searching for it.

"I come bearing good news." Ariana smiled and held up the old book bag. "I have an envelope with a check for each of you, back pay for all your work. But could we sit and talk first?"

"Sure." Susie beamed. "You're here."

Ariana grinned and went toward the dining area. Abram helped her scoot several tables together. She sat and pulled out the ledgers, papers, and a stack of envelopes. Abram, Susie, and Martha took a spot at the table.

Cilla remained standing. "I'm glad you're finally here, Ari."

"Denki. And I'm very grateful you and your sister helped out as much as you did."

"We were glad to do it. I should go now so you guys can talk."

"Could you stay for a few minutes? I have a couple of questions." She peered around Cilla. "Skylar, you too, please."

Skylar shoved the box aside, looking annoyed, but she came from behind the counter and took a seat.

Ariana picked up the envelopes and tapped the edge of the stack on the table. "This money can't begin to cover all I owe you. My gratitude runs deep." She set down the envelopes. "It took me a while to get the books straight."

Susie laughed. "I bet. We made and spent money and kept shoving the receipts in a pile for you to figure out."

"That was fine. It's given me something to work on since I got home. But there is a bit of money still unaccounted for. We have several weeks of receipts tallied for the café, but no deposit was made. It's not a big deal, but I thought maybe we could brainstorm what might have happened to it. Is there a safety box with petty cash?"

Cilla pressed her hands down her apron. "Money was spent for me. Could it be that?"

"All of that balances, Cilla, and it was money well spent. The only thing anyone in this room wishes is that it had been done for you sooner."

Cilla relaxed against her chair. "Denki."

Abram stood. "I don't think it's possible to still have a deposit here, let alone several." He went into the kitchen.

"He's looking in the crisper," Susie said. "We put the money in a bank bag and keep it there."

Ariana chuckled. "Gives new meaning to cold, hard cash, doesn't it?"

"Nothing is there," Abram called out and returned to the table. "We made one deposit each week before noon on Saturday."

"Sounds like a good system. You said *we.*"

"We took turns. Whoever had time carried the deposit to the bank."

"Does anyone remember anything unusual happening?"

"Did you talk to the bank?" Skylar asked.

"I did. We went over everything."

"You're being supernice," Skylar said. "And I can hear Dad's—sorry, Nicholas's—words and voice in yours. But the bottom line is you think someone stole it. And by *someone,* I mean me."

"That's not true," Ariana said. "I think money is missing, and it would help if we could figure out what happened to it so we can put it in the bank."

"How much is missing?" Martha asked.

"It doesn't matter. I'm not here to—"

"Oh, I think you are," Skylar snapped. "You just don't want anyone to realize what you're actually saying."

Ariana separated the envelopes, placing each on the table and never looking up. "I hear Nicholas's words and voice in yours, projecting your thoughts on me as if they're mine. I can assure you that wasn't how I felt, but since your conscience is so quick to accuse me of accusing you, I do wonder why that is."

"Take it back." Skylar stood up fast, sounding like an angry school kid. "Or I'll drag you out of *your* café by that silky blond hair of yours."

Abram started to speak to Skylar, but Ariana raised her hand slightly.

Seeming as calm as a sleeping baby, Ariana looked at Skylar. "You have no idea how much I appreciate your hard work and inventive ideas. I see you as an asset."

"I didn't do any of it for you."

"Of that, I'm sure. But you worked hard, and you showed the others what needed to be bought, things we wouldn't have without you. Almost half of all profit made since the machines arrived has been through the sale of coffee. So I prefer you knock the chip off your shoulder and sit down. But if you wish to drag me out of here by my hair, I promise you it's a fight I won't lose."

"You are so full of it—from your fake gratitude to your 'it's a fight I won't lose.' "

Ariana's face grew taut. "While you had a lifetime of Mom chauffeuring you from one cushy event to the next, going to movies, eating out, and taking every artsy lesson that suited you, I was working every muscle in my body helping to put food on the table. And since you really don't want to be here . . ." Ariana slid an envelope with Skylar's name on it across the tables to rest in front of her, and then Ariana turned her attention to Susie, Martha, and Abram. "Any ideas?"

Skylar folded her arms. "You can't come into this café for the first time in months and tell me to leave." She sat.

Despite Skylar's words Abram saw the anger drain from her. She seemed in the midst of a revelation of some type, but he didn't think it was the fact that Ariana would fight her and win in short order. Something else, something puzzling, registered in Skylar's eyes.

The conversation about the money started again, but no one had any ideas about what could've happened.

Cilla tapped the table. "I need to go."

"Sure." Ariana pushed an envelope toward her. "If you think of anything, even something silly that might have happened, let us know, okay?"

"I don't feel right about taking this. I told Abram I was volunteering my time. Then Abram—all of you—paid for my medical bills."

"What's in there is yours," Ariana said. "It's less than the others because you worked fewer hours, and I deducted accordingly for medical things."

Ariana did what? Abram didn't want her medical bills deducted.

Cilla grinned. "Denki." She grabbed her coat and went out the back door.

"How much did you deduct from her pay?" Abram asked.

"'Accordingly,'" Skylar said. "Didn't you take note of the angel's smoothness?"

"She's right," Ariana said. "That was the gloss-over word, not fully honest, not dishonest. I kept a portion from everyone's paycheck based on the agreement made when you began looking for a doctor, but I kept more from hers, just enough that she'll feel as if she paid for her own medical bills. But she didn't."

"But she deserves to have all she worked for," Martha said. "We did the medical bills as a gift."

"This way frees her, Martha. She will no longer feel as if she owes any of us."

Abram pointed at Ariana. "Welcome back."

Ariana dipped her head as if bowing. "I knew you'd like that plan." She cleared her throat and handed out the other envelopes. "The sums in the envelopes aren't the same even though you basically all worked the same number of hours. I used an Englisch formula to arrive at the pay grade. If you disagree with what I've done, let's talk about it."

Skylar tapped her envelope on the table. "Anyone want to guess who made the least?"

Ariana raised an eyebrow. "I'd rather you didn't. It's best not to discuss wages. I'd like that to be the policy, no talking about it."

"Isn't that just great for you."

Ariana slammed her hands on the table. "What is your problem, Skylar?" Ariana closed her eyes, regaining control. "You didn't earn the least. You were paid based on your personal contribution, which was quite significant, not just for the last few months, but for years to come because you knew how important various coffees are to people, types of coffee I hadn't even heard of until I was in your world. I'm grateful for what you've done, and I did not let your mouthy attitude toward me get in the way of the math."

"My mouthy attitude? I've hardly said a word to you in weeks."

"But you've made yourself heard, haven't you?"

"Finally the queen speaks an ounce of truth. Admit it: you really don't want me in *your* home."

"If it's truth you want, I suggest you stop looking at me or Brandi or Nicholas as the source of the sour milk inside you and look in the mirror. They love you, Skylar. I am grateful to you beyond words. But you never look over the fence into our lives and see the bounty of the garden we'd like to share with you. You only see the weeds."

Abram saw both sides to the emotions being displayed, but Ariana was trying to be fair and kind, and Skylar was clearly trying to ruffle feathers. Was Skylar looking for an excuse to quit the café and walk away from the Brennemans?

Cilla walked back in. "I'm sorry to interrupt, but something's wrong with the rigging again."

As much as Abram had hoped to avoid time alone with Cilla, he was grateful for an excuse to get away from this escalating rivalry.

He rose. "I'll tend to it. You stay inside where it's warm until I have it fixed." He put on his coat and went outside.

Cilla followed him. "It's really exciting about the money, isn't it?"

"Ya." Abram inspected the rigging.

"Any fun plans?"

"Nee." He continued following the leather lines.

"I know what I want. I want ice cream." Her teeth chattered as she jumped up and down to stay warm. She was teasing, and he refused to get pulled into it.

"The breeching near the tug needs repair." Abram went to his rig and pulled out the repair box. He toted it to her carriage and set it in the snow. He had repaired this same spot once before. "You used the wrong rigging again."

"Nee." Cilla removed her gloves and tugged on the tattered leather. "I was paying attention this time, but the good ones were taken, and my only choice was to use this or stay home."

"It'll take me a bit to fix it. You should go back inside where it's warm."

"You sound as if you're concerned, but I think you're just trying to get rid of me. You've hardly said a word to me all week, and it's not my imagination, Abram."

Most of his life he'd been too awkward, too weird, too quiet to have a connection with a girl he liked—until he got to know Cilla. But now her situation had changed, and his current goal was the same as it'd been all week: get her in the rig and gone with as little interaction between the two of them as he could get away with.

"Abram . . . what's going on with you?" Her soft voice seemed to fill him. "I thought maybe you were worried about Ariana. But she seems to be faring better than we are."

He couldn't think of anything to say.

"You can talk to me about anything. If you doubt that, just look at all we've been through over the last five months."

His mind reeled with memories. She was a good listener, a hard worker, and a lot of fun to be around. He opened the repair box and searched for the right leather strips. "I'm sure I have what's needed."

"So either I can drop it or continue to beg you to let me in. Is that it?" Her voice shook a little at the end of her sentence, and he knew he would have to come clean or he'd hurt her even worse.

"I don't know how to say it. I may say things wrong and hurt you." He found several of the straps he was looking for and turned around to face her.

"Just try, please. For me."

Abram looked at the ground. There was no easy way to say what was on his mind. "Now that you're better, you've got other men interested in you. Problem is, you're interested right back. That's fine. You should be."

Cilla looked as if his words were hot pokers. "I wasn't . . . I would never . . ." She took a breath, closed her eyes, and seemed to be trying to refocus her thoughts. "Abram, sick or well, I like being with you." She took the leather strips from his hands and threw them on the ground. "I've been very clear how I feel, how I've always felt. You're the one who asked me to slow things down. You!" She stormed off, heading for the café.

Her words washed over him. Had he let jealousy and insecurity cause him to see things that didn't exist? New guys were interested. He hadn't imagined that part. "Wait." He hurried to catch up with her. "Please."

She stopped, and he moved in front of her, facing her.

Her beautiful hazel eyes had tears. "Abram, how could you not talk to me about this?"

"I didn't know how to begin, what to say."

All traces of anger disappeared. "Oh. This is my fault. I should've—"

"Saul?"

"He can be funny." She peered at the door, as if making sure no one was there to hear her. "But that's his only quality. I would trust a rabid dog more, and since he dated my sister, I've got my reasons for knowing things about him."

"Gut." Relief surged through him.

She walked back toward the rig and picked up the straps she'd tossed into the snow. "I know how hard it is for you to speak your mind, and I should've prodded you when I noticed something was different."

Was that who he was, a man unable to speak his mind? He didn't like that description at all.

She smiled. "I'm sorry, Abram. I—"

He silenced any more apologies with a kiss. Her lips were soft and warm, thawing parts of his soul that he hadn't realized were chilled.

Eighteen

Ariana rinsed a roasting pan and passed it to Rudy while his aunt's voice droned on, touting the virtues of women submitting to and obeying the men in their lives. Betsy's words were honest, and Ariana understood the value, but a little silence would be nice.

Outside Betsy's kitchen window, the late-afternoon sun glimmered against the snow. Coming here today was supposed to provide a safe haven, a break from all the tension in the Brenneman home, but strain had filled the house from the moment Ariana entered hours ago. Apparently Rudy had misjudged his aunt's and uncle's empathy for the position Ariana was in with the ministers.

She tuned out the woman's preaching and sank into the reprieve of the beauty outside the window. Light refracted off the snow, sparkling with what appeared to be gold and silver. She needed God's light to reflect off her.

Last Sunday the preachers had railed against her, she'd found the puppy, and then she'd argued with Quill for being so clammed up about his life. The visit from the ministers at Berta's house had been long and boring, but she wasn't leaving Berta to deal with the men on her own. Rumors were flying about her, and she hadn't found the missing money. But she had balanced the café ledgers, and with the loan from Nicholas, she had paid everyone.

What a week it'd been, filled with too many emotions she still didn't know what to do with. When it was time for Rudy and her to meet with Quill, she hoped her overwrought emotions didn't spill over on him again.

The aroma from the chocolate-chip cookies Ariana was baking filled the air. Some were for Quill, for the meeting they would have soon. She needed a peace offering. If he never wanted to share a personal thing with her, he had that right. Moreover, she'd been wrong to ask. On the rare occasions that she and Quill would see each other from here forward, she needed to keep her distance, physically and emotionally. Rudy had been very clear about that, and she understood. But if his aunt and uncle knew that some of those cookies were for Quill or that she and Rudy would meet with him, they'd be furious with her *and* Rudy.

"I just don't understand you, Ariana." Betsy sounded as if she was at a counter behind Ariana, probably helping her clean up. "I've known you all my life, and even though I feared Quill Schlabach would eventually try to sway your thinking, I always believed you had a good head on your shoulders. But while you were draus in da world, you let him influence you. That's what the bishop says, and I think—"

"*Aenti* Betsy." Rudy's tone was respectful, but there was no denying he was asking her to stop.

"Well," Betsy huffed, "I'll leave you two alone now." She put something in the fridge and clomped up the stairway.

"Sorry," Rudy whispered.

Ariana bit back disappointment and managed a nod. If Rudy's aunt and uncle felt this way, his parents did too, only they lived too far away to complain to her in person.

It seemed so strange to think that a few months ago she would've felt the same as Rudy's aunt toward any girl behaving as Ariana was. But something was wrong inside this community. Maybe it was her. Maybe it wasn't. Either way, she couldn't commit to becoming a part of it until she knew.

Rudy held the pan in front of her, between her and the window, clearly aiming to pull her attention back to the room. He rubbed the dry towel over it vigorously. "You do know this dishwashing help is only a dating ritual." Rudy grinned, staring down at her as he moved in closer. "Right?"

Apparently he wanted to change the subject and lighten the mood. Ariana stared up at him, trying to play along as his eyes bore into hers. "Salome has somewhat informed me of this phenomenon, ya."

"Big sisters are useful for something after all, I suppose."

"So you consider it useful that she's said men only help in the kitchen while dating?"

"Ya, it kept me from having to explain it to you, didn't it?" The grin on his adorable face did lighten her mood, and it was just playfulness. Emanuel had continued to help Salome with dishes throughout the first few years of marriage, but then his workload became such that dishes just weren't on his list.

Rudy seemed to be trying to ignore the tension that now filled every house she entered. It was really the only power anyone who cared about her had—to behave as if everything were normal. At least his aunt and uncle had put effort into making small talk during the Sunday lunch. But once the meal was over, his aunt and uncle had shared their opinions, and then he had retired to sit next to the fireplace and read.

"True." She ran the scrubby back and forth against the last pan. "Would it have been so hard to explain it to me?"

"Maybe." His dark-brown eyes reflected amusement. "Depends on who I was talking to—the old you or the newer, distracted you."

"Hey." She brought her hand out of the dishwater and flicked suds at him. "Watch it."

He laughed and grabbed her by the wrist. After glancing to the various doorways that led to the kitchen, he pulled her close and put one hand on the small of her back. "Of course, as we both know, you could talk me into helping you with anything. That won't change after we're married."

"Gut. I like that answer." She played with the collar of his shirt.

"We can make this work, Ari. You can go without a phone until we're married. I'm going with you to see Quill. It's a tad of inconvenience in order for you to make things right with the ministers."

She pulled away and took a sheet of cookies out of the oven, inspecting the color and glossiness. "I didn't make things wrong with them." She glanced at him.

Playfulness disappeared from his face, and anger filled his eyes. "It's been a week, and they are ready for you to commit to the offer. I don't understand your hesitancy, especially since you turned off your phone and you're taking me with you to see Quill. Clearly you're willing to compromise."

"I did those things for you, for us, not for them. They raked me over the coals in front of everyone, and because of your remarkable peacemaking skills, they've agreed to be reasonable. Will there be a public apology? An effort to undo the damage to my reputation? We both know there won't be."

"Your reputation will heal on its own once we're married."

Tempering a loud sigh, she nodded. He was right, but it wasn't fair, and she was tired of their marriage being talked about as a way to set everything right. Weddings were meant to be a union created out of love and blessed by God, not an insurance policy that covered cleaning up past messes. Besides, she hadn't made this mess. The ministers had. She'd handled a few things wrong, and they magnified them beyond reason.

"The bishop dropped by the shop, and I asked if it would help if we married sooner, and he's considering letting us marry before couples are published."

Anxiety balled in her chest. "That's . . . interesting."

"I thought so."

Rudy was ever so agreeable. She knew of no other man who would accompany her on a cold winter night just so she could talk to a man she wasn't supposed to have any contact with. Still, she wished Rudy would stop using a cattle prod to herd her along. She would get there, but she needed to do it in her own time.

"But I don't understand the bishop's rush to extract an agreement from me. The damage to my standing in this community is done. And he did it. Why do I need to hurry up and agree to the terms of peace?"

"So healing can begin."

She turned. His anger seemed gone again, and she was glad of it. He was weary of the whole ridiculous mess, and his patience was thin, but they both kept trying to be the person the other one needed.

"Why is the bishop so much more agreeable about me when you talk to him?"

"He believes you need a good, strong husband to bring things back into place in your life."

She began moving cookies from the tray to a cooling rack. A question that had circled in her mind all week returned once again. "If pressure from ministers and husbands was removed, if fear of going to hell was removed, what would life look like for women?"

"You can't remove the fear of going to hell, Ariana. Only God can do that."

"But if it was removed—just for the sake of conversation—what would any of us do and think? Do we even know?"

"I'm not sure I'd want to know."

"Why? We all have traits that are both inspiring and destructive. You think talking honestly would cause us to take a wrong path?"

"How would the answer to your question help you or change anything that's going on?" Rudy went to a cabinet, pulled out a glass, and held it up, silently asking if she wanted a drink too. She shook her head, and he went to the fridge. "What you have to focus on, Ariana, is not the women. Not answers to questions you shouldn't ask. Think about the consequences of your response to the ministers. That's all."

Ariana melted into a chair.

Rudy poured milk into his glass. "And don't give any more thought to all you learned while away."

She rested her cheek against her fist, thinking. While the clock ticked off the minutes, her thoughts tugged in every direction, like a dog walker taking a dozen pups to the park. "I'm just not sure that kind of agreement would be right."

Rudy sat adjacent to her. "What's so wrong with giving in, Ariana? I'm sorry, but I don't understand. I live without a phone because it's expected of me since I have no business need for one. Not having contact with Quill and Nicholas without someone else being with you? Those are no-brainers. If I lived in Indiana right now, we'd be cutting ice and storing it, because the Amish in our area don't believe in using propane to cool a refrigerator. We yield to the authority above us—men *and* women. I do so because it makes no sense to try to build a life somewhere while fighting the authority on every hand."

"Ya, but—"

"We could say *but* to a hundred things a day. Submission to our parents and church leaders is the same as submitting to God."

Ariana's heart sank. "Rudy." She put both hands over his. "Something is off," she whispered and tapped her chest. "I don't know what exactly, but—"

"Rudy?" Betsy's footfalls were loud as she hurried down the stairs. "You and Sim can't put off removing the snow from the roof for one more day."

His uncle Sim came into the room, a Bible in hand. "What's going on?"

"I was resting in our bedroom when I heard a deep moaning, the kind I told you I've been hearing for a week, and you said it was just normal sounds for winter. This time I followed the noise, which led me to the attic. The beams are moaning, one appears to have fractured, and the roof is sagging."

Sim put the Bible on the kitchen table. "We were planning to get to it on Thursday, but I'll take a look." He went toward the stairway.

"I know it's Sunday, but I don't think it can wait until tomorrow. The roof could cave in while we sleep." Betsy followed him up the stairs.

Rudy turned to Ariana. "She's not one to exaggerate. Uncle Sim will return, confirming we need to remove the snow today. I need to be the one up there, not Uncle Sim."

Ariana nodded. "I agree. Is there anything I can do to help?"

"Let me get the snow removal started, assuring them I'm doing the task, and then I'll take you to the campsite to meet Quill. I can finish the job when I get back."

"Nee. Sim might get on the roof while you're gone."

Rudy glanced toward the stairs, and his shoulders slumped. "True. But I don't want you going without me."

"If that's how you feel, I won't stay to talk." Ariana opened the Tupperware she'd brought with her and slid cookies into it. "But I need to let him know something. Otherwise he'll think we were delayed, and he'll stay there in the cold, waiting for hours."

"Is that so bad?" Rudy grinned. "Maybe if he gets a little frostbite, it will do me some good."

"You're awful. You know that, right?"

"I do. It's you who have no clue." He winked and took a bite of a cookie.

"You stay here. Despite the winter wonderland obscuring landmarks, I know how to navigate to that campsite." She slid the container of cookies and the thermos of coffee into her oversize purse and put it on her shoulder.

"You're handing him those things and telling him there can't be any more texting, calls, or visits. Then you're leaving, right?"

"Ya. I promise."

He kissed her forehead.

"Listen." She cradled his face with her hands. "Tie a rope to the chimney and to you, making sure it's a strong rope, okay?"

He kissed her lips. "I'll be careful."

Ariana slid her arms into her coat. "I'll take your rig since you picked me up."

"Good thinking. I won't need it tomorrow, and I'll get someone to drop me off at your place later this week." He kissed her cheek. "You make it quick. Don't let him keep you there with excuses of any kind."

He had no idea who Quill was. Quill would rush her away the moment she said she couldn't stay even though she wished they could sit down one last time and talk the way they had at the B&B. But those days were behind them. "Okay."

Nineteen

Quill turned the knob on the Coleman heater, raising the output of heat.

He pulled his phone from his pocket and checked the time. Four fifteen. She was running a few minutes late. The old campsite carried laughter and voices of yesteryear. When Ariana was younger, she tagged along with her brother Mark.

Mark.

He was another casualty, another loss. Mark and Quill used to be good friends. Before life fell apart. Quill had been powerless to alter the path of his own life, but he would do all he could to keep Ariana's life on course.

Quill was inside an alcove. A path between two boulders connected unused pastureland to this campsite, and inside this area there was flat ground between the rocks and the creek and an alcove where three boulders fit together, blocking the howling wind from those taking refuge in it. He'd removed snow from the rocks and the ground and had set out three folding chairs, old ones from the years when Ariana and Frieda used to go camping.

A rumble echoed. The earth beneath his feet shook, and the familiar sound of branches breaking vibrated the air. He left the alcove and studied the barren patch of woods across the frozen creek. An eerie silence replaced the grumble.

"Quill!"

Ariana's voice sent millions of goose bumps over him. "Ariana?" He ran down the small path between the two boulders, searching for signs of

Rudy and Ariana. His horse whinnied, pawing the ground, but he saw no sign of Ariana.

"Quill, come back!" Her scream sent his mind reeling.

He turned, ready to run back to where he'd been, but that made no sense. He commanded his emotions to calm so he could think. As his mind slowed a bit, he realized which direction her voice had come from. He quickly freed the horse's reins, tugged them, and ran in the direction of Ariana's voice.

Another faint yell caused the hair on the back of his neck to rise as if he were a dog with hackles. He cupped his hands around his mouth. "Ariana!"

He listened. Had he imagined she was calling to him? It wouldn't be the first time, but he'd never answered before. In the past he'd always known it was his conscience, his dreams, his soul calling to him.

He hurried down the path, looking for signs of her. Through the barren woods he saw a horse and carriage where she would've left it to go on foot through the woods to the old campsite. He headed that way, leading the horse and moving quickly. "Ariana!"

As he walked among the trees, he saw where her footprints veered off the trail. He followed them and saw a dead tree that had broken under the weight of the snow. Limbs were scattered over the ground. He continued following the footprints until he saw her about fifty yards away. Why was she walking that way? She knew these woods, this area, as well as he did.

"Ariana!"

Rays of light surrounded her. She had a leather satchel slung across her body and a black winter bonnet covering her head. The brim of her winter bonnet was wide and followed the curve of her face, limiting her peripheral vision. But it was Ariana bundled under that coat and bonnet.

When he took another step, he sank into snow that came up to his knees. "Ariana." He pulled himself onto the horse.

Why was she still walking deeper into the woods? Quill dug his heels into the horse's sides, clicking his tongue. Soon he was within feet of her. "Ari."

She turned, looking confused. "It wasn't you?"

"No. Did you see someone?" He dismounted. In all their years of coming here, he hadn't seen another person in this area.

"I . . . I thought it was you. He . . . he called to me, and I . . . I . . ." She held her head as if it hurt.

"A dead tree fell near some of your footprints. Were you hit by a falling limb?"

"Nee."

He moved in closer. "Take off your bonnet."

When she ignored him, he untied and removed it. She had on her white prayer Kapp, straight pins keeping it neatly in place. She had smudges of blood on her forehead, but he saw no gash or cuts. "I need to check your head, okay?"

Again she said nothing.

He ran his fingers lightly over her head, feeling for bumps or cuts. "Do you recall being hit when the tree broke?"

She pulled away. "The man . . ."

Quill looked across the ground nearby and saw only her footprints. Added to that, he didn't like how shaken she seemed to be. "Where's Rudy?"

"He couldn't come."

He tugged on the reins, bringing the horse closer to her. But Ariana just stood there, staring into the woods.

He tilted her chin, gazing into her eyes. "Ari, do you know what day it is?"

"I . . ." She looked behind her. "It wasn't you?"

He shook his head and pressed his fingers against her face so she would look at him. "What day is it?"

She stared at him, her scattered emotions seeming to settle a bit. "It's the first Sunday in February, a between-church day, and I've been back in Summer Grove three weeks, and yet I've managed to anger and alienate half of the community, including my Daed." She rattled off the list, and her eyes filled with tears.

He wanted to pull her into his arms and assure her it would all blow over soon. Maybe it wasn't traces of blood on her face. Maybe it was dirt from under some thin patch of snow.

She shivered, but all she'd shared seemed to indicate she didn't have a concussion. Maybe stress and cold were causing her to see things. "Let's go to Mamm's, or maybe you should go home." He couldn't take her all the way to her house, because if she was seen with him, it would cause far more trouble for her. But he could get her close and watch until she was inside.

"A man was right there." She pointed deeper into the woods. "Evidently it wasn't you, but he needed me to follow him. He needed my help." She rubbed her shoulder.

"Did something hit your shoulder?"

"Maybe." She tilted her head. "We're not supposed to see each other anymore. I wasn't supposed to stay. Rudy's patience with everything . . . with me is thin."

He swallowed hard. "Sure."

She gazed into the woods. "But you need me, don't you?"

"No, Ari."

She sounded only slightly coherent. The snow was up to her bare knees under her dress and had to be in her boots. Did hypothermia make people see things? Regardless, he needed to stop looking for a stranger and get Ariana someplace warm.

"But . . . you said . . . he said . . ." Her breath was raspy, and her shivering increased as she pointed into the woods. "You did."

Quill had no idea what was going on, but being practical seemed the best way to move forward. "He's not the man you'll need to answer to." He grabbed the horse's reins again. "Kumm." He interlaced his fingers for her to use as a step.

"You don't believe me."

He wanted her warm for sure and maybe to see a doctor. "You thought it was me, and it wasn't. So, please, come on." He motioned for her again, but she stayed put. "Now, Ari," he growled.

She looked into the woods, obviously trying to catch a glimpse of the man. "Could you please stop ordering me around?" She sounded more preoccupied than annoyed.

"Gladly. Just as soon as you stop being difficult. When did you become like this?"

She turned, gazing up at him, disappointment seemingly mixed with disbelief in her hauntingly beautiful eyes. "So that's how you see me? Difficult? I'm the problem?"

"At this moment? Yes." He pointed. "Get on the horse, and when you get warm and dry, get to a doctor."

She stared at him, disbelief showing more clearly on her face.

He removed his coat and put it around her shoulders. "If you don't get on the horse, I'm going to put you on it. Are we clear?"

"It's clear." But other than trembling she didn't budge. "I'm not the problem."

He bent and lifted her at the waist with his shoulder as if he were carrying a sack of feed.

"Quill, you're not hearing me."

He sat her on the horse, both legs on one side, but he knew she'd have to straddle it or chance falling off. She intertwined her fingers with the horse's mane.

"Yeah, well, apparently neither one of us is capable of hearing the other one."

"You're being just like Daed and the bishop."

He could have ripped out his hair in frustration. Her words cut, and it wasn't true, but right now as her lips were turning blue and she began shivering harder, he didn't care. "Now that you've got that clear, go home."

He slapped the horse's rear, and it took off toward the path and then headed out of the woods.

With this much snow, he could safely let the Coleman burn itself out. He strode through the woods toward her rig, determined to follow her and make sure she got home safely. Despite the trees between them, he saw her come to a stop near the carriage, get off his horse, and get into the rig.

His pulse beat against his temples as he assured himself it was time to walk away. She didn't need him, and Rudy was no longer fine with their relationship. He'd known this day was coming. But he'd expected to be able to say a reasonable good-bye.

Twenty

Colored streamers hung across the ceiling, and balloons were tied to the kitchen chairs as Skylar spread chocolate frosting across the top of the huge cake. Her siblings had ushered Lovina and Isaac into their bedroom a couple of hours ago, and then they helped decorate this room in a way it'd never been decorated before.

Other than the party frills, it was another Sunday afternoon that felt like something from a hundred years ago. The living room was teeming with siblings, spouses, nieces, and nephews, all wearing old-fashioned clothes. A roaring fire was keeping the winter chill out, and the aroma of fresh-baked goods filled the air. The house hummed with life, and none of it was artificial—no earphones plugged into a device, no electronic games, no voices coming from a TV.

This way of life had some powerful, soul-strengthening aspects that had helped her get clean and start thinking about life differently. But she couldn't discount the other parts of living Amish. The overzealous authority of her Amish dad. The lack of musical instruments, which she would remedy now that she had some money, but where would she be allowed to play? Her Amish mom and siblings accepting that Ariana wasn't allowed to return to work at the café. Not that Skylar minded that part, but it was odd that everyone remained calm and passive about Ariana's new misfortune, as if she deserved what was going on. Skylar could come clean about the phone, but apparently that wasn't much of an issue any longer. Ariana had turned it off and put it away.

Martha came to the counter and covertly slid a card toward Skylar. "All of us have signed except Ariana."

"She's been gone since we started pulling this together before lunch."

Martha held up a pen. "I could sign it for her. It won't matter as long as she's here in time for cake."

Skylar nodded, weary of feeling like a cat facing a dog when it came to Ariana. She put a few candles on the cake. It wasn't anyone's birthday, but what was a surprise without someone having to blow out candles.

"Hey." Salome walked into the kitchen with her husband and their brood behind her. "I thought Ariana was going to be back by now. I've held off the gang about as long as I can, and I'm sure Mamm and Daed are ready to be released from their room. The cake ready?"

"Ya." Martha gestured toward it as if she were Vanna White showcasing the letter board.

Even Skylar's married siblings who didn't live in this house were here—Malinda, Abner, Ivan, and their respective spouses and broods. The children were restless, ready to spring the surprise on their grandparents and have cake.

Skylar set the cake in the center of the table. "Maybe we should—"

"*Grossmammi!* Kumm!" Ten-year-old Andrew hollered up the stairs, drowning out Skylar's suggestion that they wait for Ariana.

John, the youngest Brenneman sibling and barely more than a year older than his nephew, ran toward the stairs. "Mamm! Daed!"

"Is Ari here?" Mark asked.

Martha shook her head, but the older grandchildren, all twelve of them, had raced after John, hurrying up the stairs, whooping and squealing with delight. There was no stopping the party at this point.

Abram, Susie, and Mark joined the adults around the dining room table. The house had thirty people in it. Maybe Ariana would arrive before Isaac and Lovina realized she wasn't there.

Lovina and Isaac floated down the steps, laughing while talking to the grandchildren. The children sang a few lines of a slow song, but its rhythm was faster than anything Skylar had heard at church. Of course she recognized very few words, but the adults joined in, and when it ended, no one clapped, only stood, all smiles and calmness.

Isaac scanned his adult children. *"Was iss geh uff?"*

Martha picked up the envelope from the table and passed it to them.

After Isaac and Lovina studied the card and the handwritten gift card, their faces lit up—a mixture of joy and humility radiating from them.

"New plumbing?" Lovina burst into tears. Isaac's eyes twinkled as if he had a few tears in his own eyes. They hugged their children, laughing and clearly proud of their family, seemingly unaware Ariana was absent.

Skylar lit the candles.

Salome gestured. "Kumm. Out the light." Salome winked at Skylar, and Skylar was sure it was an Amish saying.

The room erupted in laughter and chatter. After Isaac and Lovina blew out the candles as a team, they hugged their children and grandchildren. Susie began cutting the cake and doling it out judiciously to the grandchildren.

Something near the doorway caught Skylar's attention.

Ariana.

The part of her dress that hung below her coat appeared to be wet and stiff, and her face was pale. But more than that, she appeared frazzled, as if she was on the verge of a meltdown. Who could blame her?

She closed the door, and the room slowly grew quiet as each person noticed her. John rushed to her with a plate of cake. "Mamm and Daed are getting new plumbing. No more sopping up water from broken pipes or hauling water from the well."

Ariana's smile was faint. "That's great." Her voice was hoarse, as if she'd been crying.

"Ya." John pushed the plate toward her, as enthusiastic as any eleven-year-old boy with cake. "It's a party. Skylar did it."

If Skylar had wanted to exclude Ariana and make it clear to Lovina and Isaac that Ariana had no part in this, she'd accomplished her goal. But the victory sliced a gash in Skylar's soul.

Ariana looked at her family, tears welling as she nodded. "That's so wonderful." She hugged John as if her emotions were from excitement, but if any of the adults believed that, Skylar wasn't one of them. Ariana's eyes met Abram's, and in that moment an entire conversation seemed to take place. They were the real twins, and no amount of manipulation from Skylar would change that.

Ariana walked toward Skylar, and Skylar's first reaction was to run. Ariana clutched her hand and nodded. "Good party in every way, Skylar."

As crazy as it seemed, Ariana seemed to mean it. Why was her hand so very cold? She turned to her Mamm and Daed and said, "Congratulations." When she removed her leather satchel and coat, it was evident her dress was wet and parts were frozen. "I'll be down in a bit. I need to change."

Lovina took the coat and satchel from Ariana. "What happened, child?"

Ariana's eyes swam in tears. "It doesn't matter," she whispered. "I'm fine." She cleared her throat and looked at her youngest brother. "You guys leave me a piece of that cake." She went up the stairs.

Skylar hadn't been able to put the brakes on the very thing she'd set in motion. She had everything she'd wanted: Ariana pushed out of her own café and a huge gift for Lovina and Isaac without Ariana being any part of it.

Skylar couldn't remember a time when she felt more defeated.

Twenty-One

The kerosene lantern flickered and steam drifted through the bathroom as Ariana filled a tub and slid out of her clothes. Her tears wouldn't stop. He'd listened to her as a confidant for months, both in the Englisch world and here. He'd calmed her and advised, but through it all, he believed she was the problem? He hadn't even cared that tonight had been their last real opportunity to talk. She pulled a towel off the rack and dried her face. The crying had to cease.

She dropped the towel on the floor beside the tub and stepped in. The warm water against her legs hurt, and she had to clench her teeth to keep from crying out as she eased to a sitting position. She leaned back, drawing a deep breath and trying to relax her aching body. Hopefully she would stop shaking fairly soon.

What had she seen?

God, what's happening?

She closed her eyes and prayed, focusing on the weird thing that had occurred when she was walking through the woods. The sequence of events was blurry, maybe disordered in her mind. She relaxed against the tub and let her mind ponder.

As she'd walked through the woods, a loud sound cracked through the air and startled her. Maybe the ground shook, but whatever happened, she'd fallen hard. She remembered rolling over, face down and covering her head as a tree fell near her.

Pulling away from her thoughts, she looked at the backs of her hands. She had scrapes, cuts, and a gash. Looking at her forearms, she realized the tops of each had red patches that were swollen and bruised. That gave her a little evidence to go along with her memory.

She remembered being unable to breathe, as if something had smacked her in the back and knocked the air right out of her. Gasping for oxygen, she'd pulled herself to her knees. When she looked up, she thought she saw Quill. He was blurry and still as a tree trunk. Maybe that's what she saw, a dark tree the height of a man. It had fallen pieces all around it, all around her. Then the wavery figure turned and walked off, telling her he needed her. In that moment she'd been positive it was Quill.

Her head spun with confusion, but it was her heart that was as splintered as that broken tree.

Someone tapped on the door. "Ariana, *kann Ich kumm rei*?" Salome asked.

Normally Ariana would say yes. Any sister could enter and talk while Ariana was in a tub or shower or getting dressed. But Ariana felt too naked in front of everyone of late, even when fully clothed, so she picked up the towel she'd dropped beside the tub and pulled it into the water with her. "Ya."

Salome came in, carrying a steamy mug, and closed the door behind her. "Hot chocolate just the way you like it."

"Denki." Ariana took the cup. The two women sat in silence as Ariana slowly drank the goodness from the mug. He thought she was the problem? Her emotions got the best of her, but she'd been confident she was level headed and fair minded, even obedient to a fault at times.

Salome leaned her backside against the sink. "What happened that you returned without Rudy and with half of your dress wet?"

Ariana didn't want to talk about that. "I'm sorry, Salome." Tears fell again. "I'm sorry I didn't understand how bad the pressure can get when your family, ministers, and community disagree with your decisions. I'm sorry I fought with you when you wanted Quill to help you leave. I'm sorry

I made you promise to stay until I returned when I should've set you free to do as you needed."

Salome knelt beside the tub and wrapped her hand over Ariana's arm. "Honey, we've talked about this, and you're painting yourself as the one who was wrong. Are you okay?"

"Not at the moment, but I will be. I promise."

"Is it Rudy?"

"Nee." Ariana shrugged. "Maybe. But Quill . . ." When she'd thought he was calling to her, she'd been ready to help, and like a lot of dreams, it felt good, as if she had something of value to give to a friend who'd helped her time and again. But when the confusion faded, she realized he felt the same about her as Daed and the ministers did—that she was the problem. Tears came again. "Salome, could we talk tomorrow?"

"Sure thing." Salome passed her a dry towel and took the empty mug. "I'll be back with some fresh clothes and my warmest housecoat. A girl could get a chill in your old housecoat."

"Denki." Ariana closed her eyes, thinking of the vision in the woods.

One thing seemed rather clear. Answers to life did not come easily, and they didn't come without challenges and emotional turmoil. It was past time she accepted that. Every issue had numerous facets to it, and every person had a multitude of opinions. She was responsible for figuring out for herself what she believed and how she would respond to circumstances. She'd spent twenty years thinking her Daed, the bishop, and the other ministers had the answers.

They didn't.

Would she learn to navigate this new Amish world of hers, the one where she was supposed to submit to people who thought they had the right answers for her but didn't?

Twenty-Two

Quill leaned against the side of the barn, waiting for the owners of the three carriages to leave the Brenneman home. If he was positive the rigs belonged to family members, he'd go to the door now and knock. He used to know who every horse and rig belonged to, but he'd been away too long, and people had traded horses and bought new rigs.

As the winds howled and the temperature dropped, he wondered if he'd get a chance to speak with Ariana before he had to leave Summer Grove tonight. Remorse pressed in as he stared into the vast beauty of the dark sky and its sparkling stars. She'd wanted to talk, to have a final, decent good-bye, and he'd lied to her, making her believe the problems crashing in on her were her fault. He'd needed her to get to warmth, to get home, where she could be checked out, maybe seen by a doctor. But he couldn't leave things like this. He'd done that five years ago, and he could *not* do it again.

A clatter echoed from the barn, and Quill assumed Mark was finishing the last milking of the day. Mark's brother-in-law Emanuel had been helping him for a while, but he'd gone inside about thirty minutes ago.

Maybe Ariana and he could be at odds on a colder, more miserable night, but he doubted it. He was reasonably skilled at remaining calm and in control of what he said. But, good grief, she got under his skin like no one else.

Her voice echoed in his mind, and his body grew tense. *You need me, don't you?* What was he supposed to do with a question like that other than deny it?

The door to the Brenneman house opened, and he recognized three of her married siblings and spouses. They were surrounded by seven or eight children and carrying two little ones. He couldn't tell through the thick coats, but he guessed at least one of the three women was expecting again.

Quill was looking at Ariana's future. He wanted that for her—the dream she'd always had of a good man, an Amish wedding, and a houseful of children. But he was tired of thinking about it.

The siblings waved and bid one another good night, and soon they were in their carriages and pulling out of the driveway.

Quill hurried across the snowy yard. He climbed the wooden porch steps, knocked on her door, and waited.

Isaac opened the door, and apparently he was speechless.

"I know you don't want me here, but I need to see Ariana. I won't take but a minute."

"Nee. *Du kannscht.*" Isaac started to close the door.

Quill stuck his foot in the way. "I'm sorry, Isaac. I mean no disrespect, but I can't leave here until I see her."

For a long minute Isaac stared at him. "Wait here." He left, and through the window Quill saw the busyness cease as the other siblings disappeared, probably being shooed upstairs to their rooms and told to stay there. It wasn't likely Isaac told them why he was clearing the downstairs.

About five minutes later Isaac opened the door. Quill stepped inside and closed it behind him.

Isaac picked up a kerosene lantern. "I'll get her. You can wait here."

By *here,* Isaac meant for Quill to stand at the back door, ready to speak his piece, and then leave. Isaac wasn't being intentionally rude. He had asked for Quill's help in September because he didn't have anyone else to turn to. Even then, there had been an unspoken expectation that Quill would disappear from the Brennemans' lives once his investigation of the daughters being swapped was completed. For a multitude of reasons, it hadn't yet worked that way.

Mark came inside, and in the middle of taking off his coat, he spotted Quill. "Schlabach? What are you doing here?"

"Hi." Quill saw no reason to avoid the question. "I'm waiting to speak to Ariana."

"So you just traipse in and out of Amish homes at will these days?"

"No, of course not." The Brennemans had approved Quill picking up Skylar in October and dropping her off here. Should he remind Mark of that? He'd made himself available to this family whenever they asked. Tonight he needed them.

Mark removed his boots and winter hat and went to the mudroom. A moment later Quill heard water running in the sink. He knew this routine well. Mark returned, rubbing his face on a threadbare towel. The two had been close at one time, but that friendship had been another casualty of Quill's decision to leave the Amish.

Isaac returned. "She'll be down in a minute."

The three men stood there, awkwardly trying to make small talk about the harsh winter and being ready for spring.

Quill decided to say something worthwhile. "Skylar seems to be doing well."

Isaac smiled, looking pleased. "She is. Now if I can get Ariana's attitude straightened out, both girls are looking at bright futures."

"Yeah, we often want people straightened out by our standards. I'm guilty of it too."

"God's standards, not mine."

"Maybe." Quill shrugged.

Soft footfalls echoed off the stairway. "Daed?"

"Here. By the back door."

Ariana came around the corner, looking like something from his dreams as the glow of the kerosene lamp in her hands surrounded her. Her hair was only half pinned up, the blond tresses damp, water still dripping from some of them. An off-white dress peeked out from a thick housecoat, and her feet were bare.

When she saw Quill, she stopped cold. The look in her eyes made it clear that her Daed had not told her he was here.

Quill's heart moved to his throat. "I'm sorry."

She didn't budge or speak, but the kerosene lantern trembled.

Isaac took the lantern from her. "Can you forgive him of whatever it is and let him be on his way?"

She stared at Quill, no hint of forgiveness on her face. "You're not supposed to join the ever-growing crowd in Summer Grove who believe I'm the problem. Not you too."

"My temper flared. Still, as a friend, I never should've—"

"A friend?" Mark asked. "Are you friends again?"

Ariana grabbed a handful of hair and twisted it in a knot, tucking it up somehow without a hairpin. "The only way I survived the Englisch world at first was because Quill came every single time I needed him." She looked at Quill. "But apparently throughout every trial, there and here, he thinks I'm the problem, which is . . . very insightful." Her eyes searched his, as if she was trying to see if he'd been lying to her all this time.

"Could you be reasonable here, Ari? I was saying—"

"You should be thrilled." She turned to her Daed. "He agrees with you and the ministers. Apparently I'm a problem in both worlds."

"That's not what I was—" Quill began again.

"No? Because the words seemed clear to me," Ariana said.

Isaac's head moved back and forth between Quill and Ariana. "You can't have a foot in both worlds. You'll love one and hate the other."

Quill blinked. How did that fit into this conversation?

"I *am* of both worlds, Daed." Ariana held out her hands, palms up. "You can't discipline or humiliate that out of me."

"Humiliate?"

"You've stripped me of the right to work at my own café. The ministers stood in this home, my home, and preached against me, feeling no concern that you would be offended. And you weren't. You agreed with them." Her voice trembled. "We both know the news of it has spread like wildfire among the Amish, crossing state borders."

Isaac's face reflected remorse. "It has gotten out of hand. I never meant . . ."

When Isaac let the sentence drop, Quill tried to veer the conversation back to its point. "Ari, I don't agree that you're the problem. Not at all. Not for a minute. But you were thigh deep in snow and addled, and yet you refused to get on the horse. I would have said anything to get you headed toward home."

"Her refusal to do what's best continues to grow," Isaac said. "The ministers offered reasonable solutions, and she's refused them."

"Reasonable for whom? Would you have considered it reasonable if Nicholas had refused to let me return here?"

"Nee. That's absurd."

"Is it? Your grounds for wanting me to cut off all contact with him are religious. His grounds would be to stop the inflow of religious teachings. I hate to upset the apple cart, but both viewpoints have merit, and I will not end either relationship."

"Nor turn over your phone to me. Or even Rudy, as I understand it."

"Oh, the phone. Good grief, you'd think it was a golden idol. I will not cave to bullying."

"Ariana," Isaac whispered, clearly struck immobile for several long seconds. "You stand in my house and call my decisions, my appropriate discipline, bullying?"

"Discipline is used to protect someone or to turn a person's heart toward God. Bullying is using one's power to force another to do what he wants."

"But disobedience to your father isn't of God."

"Daed, there are lots of things going on here that aren't in obedience to our heavenly Father. Things are being twisted. Arguments are being made against me as if obeying God is the issue, but it isn't. Opinions of who God is and what He wants is all I've defied. The Word doesn't mention cell phones. It doesn't approve using Quill when needed but not befriending him, and it certainly doesn't say I need to forsake Dad because he's not yet a believer." Ariana brushed drops of water off her neck. "I need to talk to Quill."

"What?" Isaac looked from one to the other. "Alone? No."

"How is it that you connected with Skylar?" Ariana asked.

"That was different. We were parents looking for our child, and . . ." He sighed. "Fine. But I could be shunned for allowing this." He shooed them toward the living room and put on his coat. "I sent everyone to their rooms earlier, and I'll be in the barn. If someone shows up unannounced, I hope I can distract them in conversation until they decide to leave."

Ariana went to the living room, and Quill trailed behind, with Mark following him. She sat in the chair next to the fireplace and curled her feet to the side where they could absorb the warmth from the hearth.

Quill sat across from her. He wanted to ask about the man she saw and find out what she thought now that a few hours had passed, but since he wasn't sure how she would feel about that topic with Mark listening, he didn't mention it.

She grabbed a pillow and pulled it to her stomach. "Mark, do you know what Mamm did with the satchel?"

"Ya." He left.

Quill stood and removed his coat. "I know me being here is awkward, but I had to see you. I couldn't leave things as they were. If this is good-bye, let's do it right, okay? But for the sake of everyone in this house, I need to leave as soon as possible." He sat again.

Mark returned with the satchel.

"Denki." She pulled out the container of cookies and the thermos. "Are you going to join us or stare at a distance and eavesdrop?"

"I'd just as soon keep my distance." Yet Mark stood there, neither leaving nor sitting.

"Mark, five years ago Quill had no choice but to leave as he did, without warning. I doubt any Amish since coming to America have paid a higher price for doing what they believe in."

Quill knew she wouldn't see it that way if they hadn't been forced together while she was living Englisch. They'd worked through five years of damage while she was on the outside. Now if he could just keep from damaging that while he said good-bye.

She passed Quill the thermos.

He opened it, poured the liquid into the cup, and passed it to her. Mark tossed a log onto the fire.

She sipped the coffee before holding it out to Quill.

He took the cup, wondering why they were sticking to the thermos as if they were at the campsite.

She tucked her hair into the bun again. "You need my help."

"No."

She picked up the container, opened it, and held it toward him.

He didn't want to take a cookie and sip coffee as if they were working through things the way they had when she was living Englisch. He wanted her to accept his apology, to truly believe he hadn't meant what he'd said, and for them to say good-bye without dragging it out any longer. He and Rudy agreed on a couple of things. They both loved Ariana, and Quill needed to put space between himself and her. But he took a cookie.

She picked up one too and held the container toward the fireplace, where Mark stood. Mark got a cookie, and she set the container on the couch next to her.

Quill fidgeted with the cookie. "How does Rudy feel about all this turmoil going on with you?"

"He's not jumping up and down for joy, but he's a sweetheart, and we're doing really well."

"That's good." Quill was relieved. "Look, Ari, you've seen what Mamm's life has been like. The ministers have marked her because every son left. In most people's eyes she's barely short of being shunned, and the condition feels contagious to them, so most avoid her. You, on the other hand, can keep yourself from being branded. There's still time. Think of Rudy and your future."

Mark moved to the couch and sat beside Ariana. "He makes some good points."

"He always does." She took a bite of the cookie. "I know what happened in the woods. After getting out of the rig to walk through the woods to the campsite, I fell. When I heard a rumble, I instinctively rolled onto my stomach and covered my head with my arms and hands." She showed him the back of her hands. "Some of the limbs from the tree must have hit me."

"The whole thing is starting to make sense, isn't it?" He leaned in and held her fingertips, inspecting the backs of her hands. He pushed the sleeves of her housecoat back. "Those are deep bruises. Are you sure nothing is broken?"

"Pretty sure. The breath was knocked out of me, so I think I was hit in the back too. I rose to my feet, fighting to breathe again. My vision blurred, but in the quiet afterward, with my hands on my knees, I looked up, and I saw you. I *heard* you—the one you keep hidden."

Was it possible? He hoped not, although she'd spent months trying to learn how to pick up on what wasn't being said by others and even within herself. How would he explain himself if she saw even a tiny bit of what he tried so hard to hide from her?

"You need my help."

"Come again?"

"In the woods you stood, motioning for me to follow you. You said, 'I need you.' I've been putting it together, and you were rattled at your Mamm's house a week ago. Something somewhere was going wrong. In the woods, while my senses were dulled or maybe more alert, your hidden man told me the truth. Am I wrong?"

He glanced at Mark, trying to think of something he could say. If she heard Quill's heart say that, it wasn't for one specific area of need. But given the choice, he'd rather admit that he needed her for one thing rather than the truth—that he needed her for all time. As much as he didn't want her involved with Gia, maybe it was his out to avoid admitting anything else.

"Maybe I could use your help, but I'm not taking it."

She lifted an eyebrow. "You left here with Frieda at twenty. I'd like the kind of moxie you had to steal away at twenty with a sickly girl and make it on your own—knowing I would learn to hate you for it—and take care of her in every way."

Was she still a bit addled? "I'm not sure I'm following your thinking, but was it necessary to hate me for it?"

She laughed. "Mark, tell him that a woman scorned does not dabble in being slightly frustrated."

Mark said nothing.

Quill lifted the thermos and refilled its plastic lid. "I'm not sure a fifteen-year-old girl can be considered a woman, and we never talked about dating, so you weren't scorned."

"A quote from *Moonstruck*: 'What you don't know about women is a lot.'"

He held out the cup to her. "Thanks."

"You're welcome." She took it. "Let me help you this one time with whatever it is. It's my gesture to thank you for all you've done for me. Then we can say our good-byes, and our only contact will be through your Mamm."

"I can't, Ari."

"The voice, your voice calling to me, said otherwise."

He was caught. She was convinced of what she'd heard, and she'd heard right. His only salvation was that she thought it pointed to one event.

"Besides, the oddity of everything—Rudy not coming at the last minute, the tree, the insight—I'm thinking it could be God intervening. Who's Gia?"

Quill now had the breath knocked out of him. He closed his eyes, taking a moment to regroup. "Why do you ask?"

"Your Mamm let the name slip. She's the one you're trying to help, right?"

He said nothing.

"If I have to track you to Kentucky or Mingo or wherever Gia is, I will. You know I can. I think I'm meant to help you, Quill. Why else would that message be so clear?"

What was God doing?

Quill thought of an out. "How would Rudy feel about this?"

The stairs creaked, and when they looked that way, four-year-old Esther was at the foot of the stairs, rubbing her eyes.

"I've got this." Mark strode in that direction. "Hey, sweet girl. Let me guess. You're thirsty, right?"

Esther nodded and held out her arms. Mark scooped her up, and Ariana returned her attention to Quill. "So when a twenty-year-old *guy* tells you that he believes he's supposed to do something to help a friend, that he believes God has opened doors to him that he's supposed to go through, you respond by continually asking how his girlfriend feels about it?"

Quill slouched. "It's different where you're concerned."

"I get that. You're more invested when it's me."

He glanced toward the kitchen where Mark had Esther in one arm while he filled a glass with water. Quill turned to her. "That's part of it." He wasn't sure if he was right to share this or not. "I don't know how to best explain myself, but I can handle disappointment and heartache as long as you are okay."

"I'm confused."

"Yeah, I guess so." He was in too deep to stop now. "Leaving Summer Grove was really, really hard, but I did it in a way that didn't disrupt your finding the right guy and making everything you wanted come true. I can't sit here now and make a plan that could jeopardize you and Rudy."

"Ya. But you also can't tell me no simply because I'm a female with a beau when you wouldn't tell a man no simply because he had a fiancée. That would be a double standard, and that's not you. Is it?"

"My sanity for five years has come from knowing I'd done nothing to ruin your dreams."

Ariana building the life she wanted had been his only solace in the heartbreak of losing her. There was an initial heartbreak on her part too. He knew that, but then two years after he left, she started dating, going long distances in search of the right guy.

She leaned in. "I'm learning how to know me. It's a huge step. We both know it is. You want me to ignore the whisper on the wind, Quill? You want me to have worked through all the layers of how to follow God even though that may be outside the *Ordnung* and then tell me no because of a guy?"

"Not just any guy. Rudy. My understanding is you dated half of the eligible Amish men in three states to find him."

She laughed. "True. Well, not nearly half, but other than that, true." She leaned in. "Here's the funny part. Rudy lived in Indiana, in an area I would've never come close to visiting because the Brennemans have no relatives there. And yet he came to Summer Grove. I hadn't needed to do all the searching after all."

He knew her message: trust God and stop fighting this.

Could he keep her safe while getting Gia and three children to safety?

Maybe he could devise something for her to do that kept her far removed from the activity.

"So here's what's going on . . ." He explained the situation as well as his plan. "Gia's ex-husband takes her grocery shopping in Camp Hill at the same store on Saturday afternoon once every four weeks."

"I've heard of Camp Hill."

"It's about fifty miles northeast of here, but it's just a few miles outside of Harrisburg, so it has lots of roads and highways. The time Gia shops is anywhere from noon to closing, but the place and the day of the week stay the same. The other good thing is, because she goes only once a month, he expects her to be in the store a really long time."

"I bet. A month's worth of groceries is a lot."

"That works in our favor. He doesn't leave the parking lot, but he gets glued to his phone, or he naps. The difficult part is that Gia is skittish. She's desperate to get out but afraid to take a step in that direction."

"She's probably afraid it's a setup."

"I've been wondering the same thing."

"Why are you taking a plane with her? If she doesn't trust you, wouldn't it make sense to get her to the airport and you leave?"

"Someone somewhere along the line seems to know her. The word is that she panics in new places, so bad she can't think, which makes everything worse. If I go, all the stress of how and where to go is on me. Plus, a mom with three young children needs an extra pair of hands."

"You're right about that."

"I'm not sure she won't have the same fears rule her again."

"Have you seen this angelic face?" Ariana propped a hand under her chin and gave a smile that said she was teasing.

He didn't like the idea of involving Ariana, but Gia was more likely to respond to an innocent-looking woman than him. "Maybe it could be our key to success," Quill said. "Harrisburg is the closest airport, but the goal is to get her out of the area. We'll go to BWI in Baltimore. It's busier and harder to spot someone, but if he's going to check public transportation, he'll start at the closest and easiest ones to get to."

She tucked fallen hair under her prayer Kapp again. "Just to clarify, I'm going with you to help this woman escape to somewhere safe, right?"

His heart pounded with anxiety. Again, what was God doing? "Apparently so."

Twenty-Three

The snow crunched under Abram's feet as he sprinkled salt on the three steps that led to the café's back door. He blinked and then opened his eyes wide in the cold air to wake himself up. Getting up before sunrise was never easy, no matter how many times he did it. The world was finally getting lighter around him, although the sun hadn't risen yet. He had already been to the café, back home, and returned to the café this morning. Sidewalks were salted, and baked goods were in the gas oven. But the generator was out, so all of Skylar's beloved coffee machines were down. He could use some of the coffee Skylar was currently making by a pour-over method.

"I'm really hoping this won't take too long. Denki for coming, Daed."

Daed had a Phillips screwdriver in hand, removing the cover to the generator. He'd already tried all the tricks of starting a generator. "Glad to help. If I can't figure it out, Mark will be along in a few minutes. He knows more about these gas generators than I do, but he and Emanuel are fixing something on the milk-cooling tank first. Machines get finicky in cold weather."

A horse-drawn rig pulled up behind the café and headed down the snow-covered gravel path toward the hitching post. Abram set the bag of salt beside the steps. "I'll be back." He went toward the carriage, and when it stopped, he opened the door.

Cilla grinned. "Morning, Abram." Her sweet voice shook out some of his sleepiness, as if her smile was a strong shot of caffeine.

"Guder Marye, Cilla." His eyes met hers, and he saw the possibilities of his future unfold before him. As he helped her down, he wondered if she was thinking about the same thing he was, that tomorrow was Valentine's Day *and* their first official date night. Part of the reason he was so tired was because he couldn't sleep for thinking about it and the kiss they'd shared last week.

He was as bad as a kid at Christmas. They would drive to the Sunday evening singing and then leave together, making their burgeoning relationship public, at least to the other singles and chaperones.

Aware of his Daed being not more than fifteen feet away, Abram tried to keep the conversation sparse. "The generator is acting up. Daed came by to take a look at it. Mark will be joining him soon."

"Ah." She began removing the rigging from the horse. "That means Skylar is probably having to be creative with making coffee." She led the horse to a small pasture while Abram lowered the staves of the carriage to the ground. She patted the horse, peering around it. "How about I bring you each a hot cup in a few minutes?"

"That sounds great." Abram couldn't look at her without smiling and daydreaming, not just about their first date, but about what life would be like if they proved to be as connected as it seemed they were.

"Gut." She gave a little wave as she entered the café.

"Abram, ready?" Daed's voice interrupted his thoughts, and Abram realized he had been staring at Cilla for a moment longer than was socially acceptable.

He shook himself out of the reverie. "Ya, let's see if we can figure out what's going on."

Daed had the cover removed, and he looked the machine up and down. Abram was a roofer and apparently a bit of a chef, but he had no idea where to begin looking for a problem on an engine. He wasn't sure Daed did either.

After a few moments Daed took a step back. "I think we'll have to wait until Mark gets here. I don't see anything obvious."

"Ya, I've got nothing."

Daed leaned against the brick wall of the building, looking at his feet. "You and Cilla?"

"Ya. Well, sort of. Our first date is tomorrow."

Daed pursed his lips and nodded. "After working together all these months, I guess you two know each other pretty well."

Something was on Daed's mind. "I think so, at least far more than most who are going on a first date, right?"

"Are you two sort of set on a path?"

"Unless something unexpected derails us, ya."

Daed released a long sigh through pursed lips. "Listen, Son, marriage is a serious commitment, a much more difficult and complex relationship than any single person can understand. Marrying someone with a serious illness will make you appreciate the good times more, but it'll also make the hard times heavier."

"You disapprove?"

"Nee. I'm just asking you to think. Look at how difficult things get with your married siblings and your Mamm and me. Imagine the excitement and the fever pitch of wanting her don't exist. Imagine she's done the unthinkable or you have—like what your Mamm and I did that caused Skylar and Ariana to grow up in the wrong homes. Stop romanticizing your life and be real. That will take some effort, and you won't really come even close, but try. Spend weeks trying, and when you see the relationship without those things, when you can imagine living year in and year out with each other's weaknesses, if you still believe a relationship with her is worth it, then stay on that path. But if you have doubts, end it."

"Way to ruin the fun first date, Daed."

"Ya, well, it's all fun and games until the real pressures of life hit. I'd marry your Mamm again. I think she'd say the same, but I've seen a lot of bad marriages in my day. There were red flags before they were married, but everyone was too smitten to pay heed. I'm begging you to pay heed."

"Did you have this same conversation with Salome, Malinda, Abner, and Ivan?"

"I did."

"Ariana?"

"Not yet. I'm not sure I need to have it. Her relationship with Rudy is being tried in the fire already."

A soft cough made them both look up. Mark was standing nearby, and it seemed neither of them had noticed his arrival. "Sorry. I parked around front and walked. I didn't mean to eavesdrop."

"I'm glad you're here, because we can't figure out what's wrong," Abram said.

"I agree about Ariana and Rudy's relationship being tried in the fire," Mark said. "Unfortunately, Daed, it's sort of a flame you started even though you didn't mean to. I don't know whether you can put it out at this point, but you should try."

"I love Ariana." Daed's brows furrowed. "And I'm trying to get her in line with the very things she used to respect."

Mark crouched, looking at the motor of the generator. "But you keep at her, and you've let others keep at her, and yet when you discovered Salome and Emanuel were going to break their oath and leave during the night, taking their five children with them, you didn't say or do anything to them. You just swept it under the rug and behaved as if none of it ever happened."

"I was plenty upset about that, but Salome is a grown woman. Ariana is still under my protection as an unmarried child." Daed looked from Mark to Abram.

Mark stood, wiping his hands on his pants. "Daed, do you think Bishop Noah is holding himself to as high of a standard as you are expecting of Ariana?"

"I see it differently. When you have a daughter you're trying to safeguard, we'll talk about this."

"I'm all for safeguarding *her,*" Mark said, "but it seems you slipped into safeguarding other things, and it's being done at her expense."

Daed's eyes were wide. "Have you forgotten all she's done wrong?"

"No one will ever forget, Daed. It's a story that will be passed down to her children and grandchildren, much like the story of the clinic burning down the day she, Abram, and Skylar were born. Only one of those two stories should've been made public. Only one."

Daed stepped nearer to his older son. "Bishop Noah is our leader, appointed by God to keep our community on the right path. I'm following his lead."

Mark shook his head and looked at his father. "Daed, I've overheard the bishop talking to you in years gone by. I won't mention anything specific, but how can you have such unwavering support for a man who clearly thinks himself better than you—and at the cost of dividing your family?"

Daed paced, looking heavenward. He turned to face them. "I . . . I don't know. All I know is I'm trying my best to be loyal to our ways. The situation is impossible."

"Daed,"—Abram stepped forward—"if you don't know the answer, stop pushing your children to accept your answer."

Twenty-Four

The house was pin-drop quiet as Skylar finished washing the breakfast dishes. Church Sunday, and everyone was still gone. At least seven hours passed on meeting days from the time they left until they returned. Isaac had requested she start going with them. It made absolutely no sense for her to sit on a hard, backless pew to hear words in a language she didn't understand. So she told him that.

The sound of carriages caught her attention. They were home, and just in time, because Jax would be here soon to pick her up, and she needed to get permission. Back home she wouldn't have sought anyone's approval to leave when and with whom she wanted. She was twenty, for Pete's sake. But simply forewarning Lovina or Isaac could have dire consequences on her living situation, and she wasn't ready to leave yet.

Only God knew why she wanted to stay—if there was a God. Skylar pushed all thoughts of God aside, an increasingly hard topic to ignore in a home such as this.

After everyone had left this morning, she walked to the community phone and called Jax. Her plan was to nonchalantly assure him who Quill was, and maybe she'd called because she needed to tell someone what she'd done to Ariana. But Jax told her about helping with a community outreach program for children today because it was Valentine's Day. He asked if she was busy.

She'd quipped, *"My social life looks like Arendelle after Elsa lost all control of her superpower, so of course I want to go."*

Jax's laughter still had her smiling. He asked about Quill, and she clarified that he was a friend of Ariana's.

Loud clatter and people talking drew Skylar from her thoughts.

The Brenneman women started flooding through the door. The men would put the carriages away, and with so many hands they would make short work of milking the cows.

Lovina spotted her and smiled. "This is not at all the condition we left this kitchen in. Thank you."

"Not a problem."

The family had gotten out the door late this morning, and the usual cleaning had not happened. The Amish had a few things right. Quietness mixed with hard work was good for the soul. Digging in the dirt and harvesting food for so many from a small plot of land was amazing, although she doubted she would be very inspired by it if she'd had to work the garden during the heat of the summer. Following her arrival last October, she had sat outside on church Sundays and watched the leaves change from green to red and orange and gold.

While Lovina removed her coat and winter bonnet, Skylar moved in closer and waited. Susie, Martha, Salome, and Ariana were busy hanging up their coats and bonnets and those belonging to the younger children. Skylar liked this part also. The chaos, the laughter, the constant sharing of tidbits of wisdom from the older generation to the younger one. Things like different ways to respond to an annoying sibling or why they shouldn't play in their Sunday best.

But this life wasn't for her. Those were the positives she'd uncovered while trying not to share her disrespect for the negative parts. This kind of family life was too simplistic. She felt children should be better educated. If they had a talent in sports or music or academia, they should be encouraged and supported in pursuing it. Her Englisch parents would fully agree with her on that. Then again, Skylar and all her peers had lived that go-for-it life, and it hadn't worked out too well for her or many others. So maybe the Amish weren't as wrong as she thought. What did she know? Seriously.

There was something clean and honest about staying focused on the inner person, accepting an old-fashioned job as a worthy goal, and valuing love over striving for the ever-elusive, ego-stroking self-fulfillment.

After her coat was removed, Salome cradled six-month-old Katie Ann in the nook of her arm, ready to nurse her. Ariana picked up a whiny Esther, cooing to her and kissing the top of her head while carrying her up the stairs.

Lovina put the last pair of winter gloves in the cubbyhole. "Is something on your mind?"

"Yeah, Jax will be here shortly to pick me up."

Lovina's eyes widened. "Jax?"

"You remember, the Englisch guy Abram roofed houses with. He picks up the groceries that Susie orders and delivers them to the café. Susie and Abram have mentioned him a lot."

"Ach, ya, I remember now. You have a date?"

"No. We're just going somewhere"

Lovina looked amused. "And on Valentine's Day, but it's not a date. Amish men usually avoid taking a girl even for a simple buggy ride home on Valentine's Day unless the relationship means something. Is it different for the Englisch?"

"No. The same, I think, but I called him this morning and . . ." Skylar would never get used to answering so pointedly about simple matters.

"You walked to the community phone on a Sunday morning?" Lovina frowned, her stern-mother look in place as she put her hands on her hips. "Skylar."

"How is that any different than me sleeping in or cleaning up the kitchen?"

"Sleeping is justified because the Sabbath is for resting. Dishes are allowed because we eat. But Sunday morning is God's time."

"Yeah, I can see that, because the guy with no beginning or ending is very particular about how those nanoseconds on His radar are spent by a girl He forgot to get to the right parents for twenty years. Makes perfect sense."

Lovina's face etched with hurt.

Skylar wanted to crawl under the piles of snow and not be seen until the spring thaw. "Sorry. It comes natural to dismantle what seem to be silly stances of faith, and statements like that make it easy, but it was rude, and I'm sorry."

Lovina reached into the closet and gently removed Skylar's coat. "Forgiven." She smiled. "Maybe while you're out with Jax, you should ask 'the guy' how you should spend your nanoseconds on this planet." She held out the coat to her. "Because you holding a grudge about your raw deal in life is a waste of precious time."

Different words but the same message Ariana had given her last week. Had the two been discussing Skylar? It sure sounded like it. She started to respond, but someone knocked, and she knew Jax was here. About twenty minutes early.

She stuffed down her sarcastic reply and opened the door. "Hi." As she slid into her coat, Jax peered around her.

He waved, and Skylar took a step back to let him in. He held out his hand to Lovina. "Jackson Montgomery. You must be the mom."

Lovina shook his hand. "Lovina, and, ya, I am. You're the boy who's friends with Abram."

"Yes, ma'am."

"Lovina," Skylar chided, "he's not a boy. He's served in the military, for crying out loud."

Lovina's face flushed pink, and she laughed. "Sorry, I just meant—"

"It's okay." Jax chuckled. "I wear Marvel Comics pj's and have a room dedicated to model trains."

Skylar hadn't known either of those things.

"Hello?" Isaac had walked up behind Jax. "Can I help you?"

"Hi." Jax held out his hand, looking friendly and unperturbed. "Jackson Montgomery."

Isaac closed the door behind him. "And you're here why?"

"Jax?" Susie called as footsteps clomped loudly on the stairs. "Is that you?" She rounded the corner, smiling. "I didn't know you were coming."

"Hey. Me either until Skylar called this morning. We're going to that community service event I was telling you about."

"Gut." She nodded. "Sorry, I meant *good.*"

Jax grinned. "After all these months I know what *gut* means."

"Daed,"—Susie took his coat—"this is the man who's been delivering supplies to the café for the cost of a meal. I don't know that Brennemans' Perks would have survived without his help and Skylar's know-how. He and Abram were friends before the café opened."

"Ach, ya, good to meet you."

"Same here. Is Abram around?"

"In the barn."

"Well, I'll see him tomorrow then. Skylar, you ready?"

"You're going where?" Isaac asked.

"To a community benefit to give homeless children a little bit of a special Valentine's Day. Their parents will be there too, but it's geared toward the kids."

"What will you do?" Isaac asked.

"Well . . ." Jax seemed to be searching for the right words. "We'll serve food with a Valentine's Day theme. The children will sing a few songs to their parents. We'll play some games, and since for some reason the schools didn't have their class parties last week, we'll make sure the kids have those inexpensive Valentine's Day cards to take to school, at least for those who go to school. Lots of them don't, due to a lack of basic needs, like being able to bathe and such."

Isaac stood straight, using each foot to remove a boot from the other. "Sounds kind, but can I ask why Valentine's Day even matters?"

"Most kids enjoy observances of special days. They get excited and look forward to whatever is going on—Halloween, Valentine's Day, Christmas. But when they're homeless, they just feel left out and hurt." Jax shrugged. "So a group of former marines and their families are trying to make a difference for some of the homeless in our area."

Isaac seemed confused by the notion. Unfortunately, Skylar also wondered why it mattered. Seemed like a silly holiday. No one was even off for it. Just another day.

Isaac set his boots to the side. "You're in the military?"

"I was."

Isaac stood straight, looking at Jax. "We don't believe in war or fighting, but we know we're safe because other people do believe in it. Thank you."

Skylar couldn't believe her ears.

Jackson nodded. "You're welcome."

"Do you have time to sit?" Susie asked.

"Maybe another time," Jax said. "Skylar, we should probably go."

Skylar told her family bye, and they left. After walking across the snow, he opened the door for her, and she climbed into his truck, noticing his cell in the console along with loose change, a receipt, and a bottle of red Gatorade. The seat was warm, and she assumed it had a heating device. She relaxed into it, realizing how much she missed having a vehicle. He went around and got in.

"You up for this?" He started his truck, pressed the clutch, and put it into gear.

"Sure. My dad does this kind of thing sometimes, helping out the less fortunate. I've lent a hand, often begrudgingly, to a few functions over the years, so I think I can be helpful."

"Begrudgingly." He chuckled. "Who admits to that, Skylar?"

"Just keeping it real." If she had to repress every bit of who she was, she'd explode.

"I like that about you." He shifted gears. "And I'm sorry for the overreaction to your question a couple of weeks back."

"I know. Me too."

"What you said was true, and I've been working on it for a while now. I just wasn't ready for you to notice it."

"If there's one thing I'm particularly good at, it's knowing what needs improvement in someone else's life. I've only recently come to realize it, but I'm working on it. Air clear now?"

He nodded. "I'm surprised you called."

"Yeah, well, I haven't kept things quite as real as you might think, and I need to talk to someone about it. There's a house full of people and no one I can tell this to until I'm braced for the apocalypse."

"Wow. Sounds serious." He picked up his cell phone from the console. "Choose your favorite song or list."

Didn't he want to know what she'd done? She took the phone and was struck by how odd it felt to hold one again. She didn't miss having a phone nearly as much as she'd thought she would. It was annoying and inconvenient not to have one, but she liked not being connected.

"It's locked," Jax said. "Needs six digits: 102715."

She pressed the numbers, and his world unfolded in her hands. The screen had a background with the marine emblem and rows of icons, including apps for games, Amazon, a calculator, a camera, and e-mail. "Whoa, you have two thousand and fifty-two unopened e-mails and eight unanswered texts."

"I ignore most e-mails, but I keep up with texts, so those probably came in while I was at your house. Could you read them to me?"

"You don't mind?"

He snatched the phone. His quick motion startled her, and she burst into laughter. He gaped at her. "How dare you think of reading my personal stuff." He mocked indignation.

"You're very animated for a former marine."

"Oh, just because in the ads on billboards and television we are straight faced and serious about our job, you think that defines who we are in social situations?"

"I guess I did."

He held the phone toward her again. "Have you heard the Jeff Foxworthy bit about 'here's your sign'?"

"Who?" She looked through his favorite songs and was impressed. They liked a lot of the same music.

"Oh, tell me you did not just ask me who Jeff Foxworthy is. He's a comedian, part of the Comedy Roundup channel on SiriusXM."

"Okay, I won't tell you, but we both know the answer."

"You need some serious educating, Skylar. He has this bit he does about people saying stupid things, and then he says, 'Here's your sign.' An example is this story he told about having the inside of his house repainted, and he had a grand piano in the corner, and the painter said, 'Is that y'all's piano?' And Jeff said, 'No, that's our coffee table; it just has buckteeth. Here's your sign.'"

Skylar chuckled. "Okay, I get it. You're passing me an imaginary sign because you asked me to read the texts, and I asked if you minded if I read them."

"Exactly." His laughter filled the cab, and when he finally stopped chuckling, he glanced at her and started laughing again.

"I'm going to remember this, and it's not going to be pretty, trust me." She pressed "Same Ol' Mistakes" by Rihanna. The familiar beat moved through her veins, and she felt a bit of the old Skylar again, which was fun. And scary. Was fear the only reason she continued to give up all rights to her car, phone, and music while going with the flow of staying with the Brennemans?

Jax turned on a blinker. "Read the texts, Sky Blue. I've got nothing to hide."

"Oh. Sorry. I was distracted by your song list." She pressed the Home button. "But everybody has something to hide."

"True. Everybody has personal stuff, and some of it's really embarrassing. Not everyone feels a need to hide it from friends and family."

"When I had to leave my phone at home, I made it so password protected that my parents would have needed the FBI to open it."

"I'm sure some of that was drug related. Some of it is being twenty and not wanting your parents in your business."

It was sort of nice to ride down the road with someone who knew the real her and accepted it without wanting to capitalize on it or make a big deal of it. It seemed as if she'd been the queen of picking guys who wanted to take advantage of her secret life, and her mom and dad made a big deal of drug use and bad boys, which was beginning to make sense.

She touched the icon for his texts. "The eight texts all appear to be from one person. Someone named Trixie."

"She's the leader for today's event."

Skylar touched the text, and it opened. She skimmed the lengthy messages and decided to summarize. "She sent apologies, hearts, smiley kisses, and promises to make it up to you, but she's got the flu and is running a fever of 103 and can't make it today."

"She's not going to be there?"

Skylar lowered the phone. "Here's your sign."

Jax laughed. "I deserved that, but you're missing the gravity of this information. This isn't good. At all. Not only does she run the whole program, but she's been working with the children for a few weeks on the songs they're going to sing to their parents. Do you have any idea how hard it is to coordinate practices for homeless children?"

"No, but we wouldn't want all those practices to have been for nothing. Do you have a list of the songs they've been working on?"

"Yeah, somewhere in those two thousand unopened e-mails."

"I'm sure I can do whatever is needed."

"Really?"

"Your skepticism is disconcerting. You heard me play at the soup kitchen."

"Knowing a song or two only means you know a song or two."

"I grew up taking music and voice." She touched the e-mail icon and began searching for messages from Trixie. "My dad is a professor of music, and if I hadn't let boys and drugs throw me off track, I'd be well on my way to having a degree from Carnegie Mellon, so, yeah, I definitely know enough to work with children on the spur of the moment."

She was ready to do anything with music. But she hadn't bought a keyboard yet. Since instruments were forbidden in the house, it would be problematic for the younger ones.

"Jackpot." Skylar waved the phone near him. "One e-mail with two attachments: today's agenda and the song list."

"That's good, right?"

"Oh, yeah." She put her finger under some of the text in the e-mail. "It sounds as if the food is all taken care of except for serving it."

"I hope so."

"Trixie not coming has you a bit spooked, doesn't it?"

"Yeah, I know my limits when it comes to volunteer work and children. I'm a helper, not a planner or a leader."

"I'm not a leader either, unless it's being the lead in musicals, but I know we can do this. Worst-case scenario we'll make a food run and pick up hot dogs and chips." She read over the song list. "Hey, Jax?"

He turned the volume down. "Yeah."

"I doubt you'll understand this since you're a really nice guy, but the reason I called you is because I needed to tell you something."

He looked from the road to her several times. "New or old news?"

"A few weeks old."

"Then there's no rush to share it now, and if it's going to be something that's likely to frustrate me, I'd rather wait. We have a long, busy afternoon ahead, and I'd like to enjoy and appreciate that your helping, not look at you and seethe."

"I haven't used drugs, if that's what you're thinking."

"Good. It helps to know that. Still—"

"I got it. You don't want fresh reasons to avoid me while we have to work together."

"That's what I was thinking. Change of subject. I stayed late at work the other day, and the boss walks in and says, 'You're still here?' I said, 'Nope, I left ten minutes ago. Here's your sign.' "

She laughed, but what really struck her was that he was a giver, whether that was running errands for Brennemans' Perks, helping with this homeless group, or trying to lift people's moods.

What did she give unless backed into a corner?

Twenty-Five

Ariana's stomach tingled with butterflies as the tall roof of Rudy's workshop came into sight. He was an easygoing man for the most part, which had probably been the saving grace in this relationship since her life over the last six months had been one long, wearying storm. He'd lost his temper only once, but that was because she decided to allow Quill to help her get the money to buy the café. A couple of days after her accident, she'd told Rudy what had happened to her in the woods and about Quill coming to the house and her planning to help him with a rescue.

He hadn't been pleased.

Who could blame him? But it'd been nearly three weeks since the accident, and she could still feel the intensity inside her from those moments of seeing and hearing what wasn't real. Well, it was real. It just wasn't Quill's actual voice. She'd been knocked loopy, and she heard what Quill would never say. Or maybe God was saying it for him. She'd had plenty of time to think about what happened, and the longer she thought, the more it felt as if God was directing her path.

Rudy didn't want her to go, especially with Quill. He'd asked her to reconsider, and she had. But she needed to do this one last thing, and she needed Rudy to understand it. He could go too. She'd been very clear about that. But his work was overwhelming right now, and she didn't think he had any interest in doing something the ministers would frown upon if they found out.

Afternoon sunlight glinted off the murky, dirty snow. Odd how something so clean and pretty as it fell from heaven and covered the earth turned ugly after resting on this planet only a little while.

She slowed the carriage and tugged on the reins, turning onto the driveway in front of the workshop. The aroma of the meal she'd made for him filled the carriage, and she hoped this gesture would help him take her decision in stride.

Taking the picnic basket with her, she got out, tethered the horse to the hitching post, and tapped on the workshop door.

"Kumm," Rudy groaned.

She slipped inside, grateful to see he was alone. He was on a ladder, hammering on what looked to be the skeletal walls of a new shed. His brows were knit as he whacked the hammer with determination.

He and his uncle built backyard sheds, usually on the person's property, but they had received a huge order for a local garden shop, and they were doing as much prefab work as possible.

When he stopped hammering, he looked her way, and a tender smile replaced his studious look. "Hallo. *Des iss* a surprise."

"Ya. *Iss es allrecht?*"

"Very all right." He grinned while climbing down. "Gut timing. *Ich bin hungerich.*"

"Ach." She pulled the picnic basket to her side, away from him. "You may be hungry, but it's not for you," she teased.

"Good luck keeping it from me." He reached for it.

She hurried toward the door. He came up behind her and lifted her a few inches off the floor so that she was running with no traction, laughing.

"Say it again, Ariana Brenneman."

"It's yours. All of it."

He set her feet on the floor. "That's more like it." He peered down at her, smiling. "Hi." Without any doubt he'd like a kiss, but she placed the basket between them.

"Kumm." She moved to a workbench, pulled a clean cloth from the basket, and spread it over the sawdust and dirt.

"When I said I couldn't get away for a date tonight, I didn't expect this."

"I'm full of surprises."

"I'd say that's accurate, ya."

She quickly put the shepherd's pie, green beans, and rolls she'd made today on a plate and passed him a fork. Rudy dug in without pausing to pray. He *was* hungry. She retrieved fresh milk from the container of ice and poured it into a glass.

"You're not eating?" He reached for the milk.

"Not right now." She was too nervous to be hungry. "How many sheds do you have to build for that garden place?"

"Twelve of various sizes, and they need them by March eleventh."

"Can you have that many done in two weeks?"

"Ya, it'll just take effort because that's not the only order." He took a few more bites. "Without knowing it, we built a shed for the brother of an owner of garden shops in Pennsylvania, and when the owner went in his brother's shed last week and saw our work, he compared what we charged to what the factory charged, and he wants us to offer his customers a choice."

"That's really good."

"Ya, for us too."

She meandered around the shop while he ate. Memories of her years with Quill in his Daed's cooperage filled her mind. They'd worked and laughed, and she'd adored him. Any girl who'd been around Quill would've fallen for him. He was smart, fearless, and endlessly patient—a lot like his Daed, and Eli had been a good man. His early death had left a huge hole in Berta's and Quill's hearts. Hers too. He'd been like a second Daed, and if he were here, he'd have one of his quiet talks with her Daed about letting her return to the café. The district lost a solid voice of reason when Eli passed, a role Quill could've taken if he hadn't felt compelled to get Frieda out. What had happened that Frieda needed medical help and the ministers balked? They didn't usually meddle when it came to a person's health. Although they had opposed Salome getting skin grafts for Esther because they felt their poultice method was tried and true. Poultices for burns were part of the Old Ways. But Frieda hadn't been burned. Whatever the reason, Quill felt it was too personal to tell Ariana the whole story, and despite the numerous texts she and Frieda had shared while Ariana was living Englisch, Frieda never told her.

She saw Rudy gazing into the picnic basket. "Something on your mind?" she teased.

"I smell something sweet."

"You do." She returned to the basket and pulled out a plate of fresh-baked chocolate croissants. Removing the cloth, she said, "Voilà."

He took one and bit into it. *"As gut."*

"I'm glad you like them."

He'd told her earlier in the week he wouldn't be able to go out tonight, and she hadn't come here to be a needy girlfriend who couldn't be away from him on a date night, so she should tell him her decision and let him get back to work.

She poured him some more milk as he took another bite of the croissant. "I've decided to help Gia and her children."

Rudy's hand was halfway to his mouth when he stopped cold. He stared at her. "What?" It wasn't as much a question as an outcry of anger. "I thought this dinner was your way of saying you wouldn't go. That you'd chosen to do as *I* wanted."

"I know this isn't what you were hoping for, but it's only for one specific thing, not an ongoing issue."

He tossed the croissant onto the workbench. "What could Quill possibly need your help with?"

"I told you. There's an Englisch woman with three children in Camp Hill, and they're caught in a really volatile situation."

"He's helping a woman leave her husband?"

Ariana had talked to him about all this weeks ago. Apparently he'd been more preoccupied with work than she'd realized.

"An ex-husband who isn't allowed to have unsupervised visits, and yet he's moved in with her against her will. He keeps her moving from rental to rental, which keeps him from getting caught and arrested. It's very complicated, and all of it is worse because she's afraid to turn him in. If he kills her, the children will be raised in fear and violence, moving constantly to keep him from getting caught. Or if he leaves them behind, they'll be raised by the state. I don't understand all the intricacies, but I know he only lets her out of his sight once every four weeks while she gets groceries and he waits for her in the car outside the store."

"He doesn't work? No other time she could slip away from him?"

Ariana shrugged. "My understanding, which could be very different from the facts, is when he leaves the house, he has a brother watch her, making sure she doesn't leave. I don't know if that's true, but it probably doesn't have to be. She's terrified of trying to get away, which is where Quill and I come in."

"Not the words I ever wanted to hear from you again once you returned home: 'Quill and I.'"

"I know, but—"

"This is absurd. I don't know how to make you see that. It's dangerous, and I don't want you to be a part of it."

"I understand."

"And yet you're going anyway." Rudy crossed his arms, studying her. "Is he still baby clothes to you?"

"What?"

"Last fall when you accepted his help in figuring out a way to earn money to buy the café, I objected, and you said he was baby clothes—things people pull out of storage and feel nostalgic about but they would never want to return to that time. You said Quill was like baby clothes to you. And you said you could never be drawn to a man who was in staunch rebellion to the Old Ways."

She wasn't sure how to respond. Since that time she'd slowly changed her staunch, uncompromising belief system. It had broadened but strengthened. During her time with the Englisch, she'd come to see life and Quill very differently. In the past she had to work to cope with their differences, but now they felt and thought similarly in many areas.

Stand in front of Rudy, take him by the hands, and tell him what he means to you. But she didn't. Instead she put the dirty dishes back in the basket. "It was rude to call him baby clothes. But this trip isn't about any personal feelings toward Quill. I know I'm supposed to help him get that woman and her children out."

"This situation you're talking about is ridiculous. I don't want you involved in it in any way, especially not with him."

"It sounds dangerous. But the man will never see me, and I'll only need maybe ten minutes with the woman. Once she agrees for her and the children to go with us, we'll go out the back of the store, where the loading docks are, leave in a rented vehicle, and head for the airport. I'll drop them off and go to my dad's house for the night." She was leaving out a lot of details, including that taking them to the airport wouldn't work if the woman didn't have her ID and her children's.

"Nicholas's house?" Rudy's voice got louder every time he spoke.

"Ya. I'll park the rental in his garage. He'll bring me home in his car, and Monday afternoon he'll return the rental."

"How did you work out all of this since meeting Quill that Sunday evening?"

"My phone."

His face matched his reddish-brown hair, and anger flashed from his eyes. "I didn't sign up for this, Ariana."

"I know, and I'm sorry."

"Are you serious?" He picked up his hammer and flung it across the room. "That's it? You're sorry?"

Other than the one time he'd lost his temper with her, he'd supported her in every way and through every single thing. She prayed God would help them once again. The outbursts didn't bother her. She cried when upset and could talk the hind legs off a mule while working through things. Rudy yelled, pounded one fist into the other, and apparently threw hammers across the room.

"Maybe I should repeat what I told you when I explained all of this. I feel God is asking this of me. I could be wrong. Who can know the mind of God? But I have to follow what I think He wants. I know this is hard on you, Rudy, and you're right to be weary of the constant challenges to our usual quiet way of life, but my world, my dreams, are here with you. It's just that I have to do this one thing that's really outside of normal. If you think about it, the Amish do outreach like this from time to time."

"Not without the blessing of the bishop and never alongside someone who's left the Order. Why you? Why would Quill be willing to put you in this predicament?"

"Because I asked. I need to do this. When it's over, I'll leave Quill at the airport with Gia and the children, and I'll tell him good-bye. After I return to Summer Grove, you have my commitment that I will have very limited contact with Quill. And to be fair, you did sort of sign up for this, ya?"

He frowned and sighed, but a few moments later a hint of a smile came through. "I knew the moment I saw you that you weren't like any other woman I'd ever met, Englisch or Amish. I was right, and I'm glad. I really am."

"Gut. Because right now that not-like-any-other woman really feels a deep need to do this. And Quill has a good plan."

"No secure, detailed plan of Quill's will keep you out of trouble with the bishop if any of the ministers find out. There will be no coming back from it. Forget regaining your reputation."

Her heart pounded in her ears, and her chest hurt for all she was putting Rudy through, but she was confident she was supposed to do this, whether for Quill or God or herself she wasn't sure. "I think it's the right thing to do, Rudy."

He slumped onto a barstool. "I have no argument for that."

She went across the room, picked up his hammer, and held it out to him. "Just keep working. I'll be back Sunday."

"It's a church Sunday."

"I know. Nicholas said he can have me home in time."

"And if he can't have you here in time, what then? Are we supposed to lie and say that you're sick?"

"No. I . . . I'll be back in time." She nodded. "I will."

Twenty-Six

Sitting on her side of the bed, Lovina sewed a button on Isaac's shirt. The kerosene lamp burned bright. He was next to her, restless and looking through his Bible for answers. Even though it was a Friday night, their offspring were home and getting ready for bed. The café opened early, although that didn't explain why Ariana and Rudy weren't out tonight. Lovina glanced at her husband, praying a conversation could open between them.

Isaac tapped the open Bible. "It clearly says that we need to submit to the authority over us. And the bishop and other ministers feel strongly that we've done the right thing by applying pressure about her phone and keeping her here instead of allowing her to go to the café."

Her fingers trembled as she worked the needle through the hole in the button. She wanted to stand up and scream how wrong she thought he was. "The bishop doesn't have to live with the fallout, does he?"

"What do you mean?"

"Umpteen years ago the bishop told you it was God's will for disease to take so many head of cattle that we couldn't make ends meet. When his son lost cattle five years ago, he said it was God's will that people pull together and give him more than he had before the disease struck."

"Lovina, tread lightly."

"There are many good bishops among the Amish. Most, even. But this one makes decrees that aren't fair, maybe because he doesn't have to live with the fallout. But we do. You and Ariana were as tight as any Daed and daughter I've ever known. There was a special bond, no?"

"I thought so."

"Will the bishop lose anything by demanding she give up what he would never demand his own children to give up?"

"His two oldest have phones for business, but we don't know that the others do."

"We know. We saw it on the bishop's face when Mark offered to gather all the cell phones in the community."

"There is no proof, Lovina." Rubbing his whiskers, he closed his eyes. "It's not enough that Ariana has defied me to my face? You are against me too?"

"When I was unbearably distressed about my negligence concerning the girls and then rushing to make them switch places, you comforted and encouraged and forgave me. I want to be there for you in that same way. But my mistakes had already happened. We are in the middle of this, and perhaps we could change the course of things if we talk honestly before more horrid mistakes are made."

"Then talk."

"When Ariana returned, I think maybe you weren't braced for all the weird, overwhelming feelings that were a part of adjusting to her being so different, to her having a mom and dad out there that she also listens to. It's like we were in a carriage going downhill too fast, and when we ran off the road, we overcorrected the horse's movements. And now we could lose all control if we don't relax the reins."

Isaac fidgeted with the thin pages of his Bible. "Ya, I fear the same."

Lovina was grateful to know he was rethinking his position. He'd been so quiet about everything since Ariana returned. She stuck the needle into the shirt and reached out to hold his hand. "Your goal concerning her is God centered, but it's not working. Actually, it may be working in reverse. She's calmly accepted her lot in not going to the café, as if she's settled in, ready to wait you out. She clearly met Quill privately somewhere before he arrived here asking to speak with her."

"Am I to free her to have contact with her godless parents and whoever else she met while draus in da Welt?"

"She is free. Out of love and respect for you, she's staying where you've told her. She hasn't moved in with Berta. She's not going to her café. But she's an adult. She has money and regular income. She has two Englisch parents who would welcome her back. She has a biological dad and could easily say, 'God has made him my head, not you.' But she hasn't. Not yet."

He pulled free of Lovina's hand and clutched his head. "We sent her out there. And then I held her accountable for getting the dust of the world on her feet. But I thought with a bit of pressure from me, she would shake it off, as Jesus said to."

"This *world* you refer to is her family. She returned to us, ready to be true to a life she wasn't born into, but that wasn't enough. Why?"

"I thought it was my duty to bring her back in line. Still do."

"Something's not right about how well she's accepted your refusal to let her go to the café, and that scares me. Ariana said she and Brandi had gone to lots of cafés while she was with them. They gathered recipes and practiced them in Brandi's kitchen, all in preparation for Ariana coming home to *her* café. You take it from her, and she hardly says a word?"

Isaac nodded. "I'm aware."

"Are you? When Quill learned she might not be our biological child, he said nothing to her about it, but he did reach out to her to help her buy the café. I've pondered this, and I'm convinced that his goal was twofold: to give her a constant source of encouragement when she was on the outside and to give her an anchor to this community. And you've taken it."

"How do you know this?"

"How do you not?"

"What happened to our family, Lovina? Last summer Ariana loved me. She went out of her way to talk with me, and what I said and wanted mattered."

"That's gone, Isaac, just as her loving me as her only Mamm is gone. But we don't have to lose her more than we already have. There's still time to change the direction things are going in. Let her go to her café. Help her get approval to use the phone as part of her business. The ministers aren't likely to give it, but your word matters in our community. You have the power to help her regain her reputation as an obedient, sweet girl before more damage is done than can be undone."

"How can I? The phone was a symptom of a greater issue. I knew it was. It's why I did everything in my power to get her to let it go. As you said, she met with Quill in secret, and then he came here and refused to leave until I let him talk to her. She'd turned her phone off for about a week, but yesterday I stumbled on her in the barn with the phone in her hand. She looked right at me, said she was texting Nicholas, and then she tucked the phone in her coat pocket."

Someone knocked on the door. "Kumm," Isaac said.

Ariana poked her head in. "I need to tell you something."

"Tomorrow night, okay?" Isaac asked.

Lovina couldn't believe Isaac was shutting the door on Ariana's offer to talk. Was he that wrung out and tired?

"I won't be here tomorrow night."

Lovina's heart pounded. "Why?"

Ariana stepped inside, closed the door, and began talking about helping Quill get a woman and her children to safety. Lovina tried to follow what she was saying, but alarms were ringing in her head.

"You will not leave this house tomorrow." Isaac pointed at her, talking in a way he'd never done before.

"A woman needs help, and Quill needs help. If I stay here, she could be killed by someone I could help her get away from."

Isaac pressed his index finger on the Bible. "It is forbidden for anyone in good standing with the church to accept a ride from someone who's left."

Lovina cringed as memories of their being in the car with Quill returned, and their hypocrisy reared its ugly head again.

"Daed, that's not in the Bible. Nothing even close to that is in the Bible. That's from the Ordnung. Man decided that was important because it helps hold our society together. What *is* in the Word is not to withhold good from those to whom it is due if it is in your power to do it." She glanced at his Bible. "I believe this woman is past due for someone to do good for her, and I also believe it is in my hand to help."

"You believe it? Why? Is it in the Bible?"

"More so than the belief that I'm forbidden to ride in a vehicle with someone who's left the Amish. The Bible says the same anointing that was in Christ is in you and teaches you all things about truth and it is no lie."

"Ariana," Isaac gasped, "that is the bishop's place."

"And yours and Mamm's and mine. I believe I'm supposed to be there. Maybe I'm wrong. But it'll be a fresh wrong from trying to follow God's leading, not a stale wrong from old lines held up as if they were God's Word. That's all I know."

"Do you realize the bridges you're burning?"

"None, I hope." Ariana's face seemed to reflect that she understood the gravity of her plans. "It would be helpful and possibly safer if this news didn't leave this room. Rudy knows and now you."

Lovina had known for weeks that something was up. "Ari, honey, why even tell us?"

"I know I could have told you I was spending the night with one of my siblings and asked them to cover for me, but I don't want to deceive you. It's not my intention to disrespect you in any way. What I'm doing may be against the Ordnung, but it's not against God. I see no justification for me needing to tell the bishop, but you will have to follow your conscience on the matter. I'll leave here tomorrow around ten, and I'll be back Sunday morning before church."

Isaac got out of bed and put on his housecoat. "You can't stay out all night with any man, especially Quill."

"I won't. I'll drop off him, the woman, and her children at an airport, and I'll drive back to Nicholas's."

Isaac looked frozen, as if he weren't even breathing.

"Daed, it's a good thing to help this woman. My plans are not against God's Word. If I need to go against my conscience in order to be in good standing with the church, something is wrong." Ariana blew them kisses, the way she used to do when she was a little girl. Then she left.

Lovina went to her husband and shook his shoulder. "Breathe."

He inhaled sharply. "I . . . I was so sure she was infected with the ways of the world. What are we doing, Lovina? Me? The ministers? Her unbelieving Englisch dad will help her follow what she believes is God's leading while we fight her over disobediences that aren't mentioned in the Word?"

Her husband had a good point, maybe the most important point. But it was often odd what two people in the same room heard. Lovina's heart trembled at the thought of Ariana and Quill working together, being alone together, and aiming for a common goal.

Twenty-Seven

Quill waited for Ariana in his car behind an abandoned building several miles from Summer Grove. There was no good place for them to meet. Anywhere they went, they could be seen, but at least it wasn't *likely* they'd be seen here. Was he right to let her go with him?

He saw her round a corner, bundled in her coat and a winter bonnet, walking fast and toting a box. Could she stick out any more to passersby? If she'd worn something of Skylar's, like a hoodie and jeans, no Amish person would think anything about her getting into a car. Fortunately there weren't any Amish rigs in sight right now.

He started the car and eased across the broken concrete lot.

She waved and picked up her pace. When she reached the car, she hopped in and settled the box on her lap. "Guder Marye."

"Hey." His car filled with her scent and her bubbly energy. "Here." He held out a baseball cap. "Remove the bonnet. If you can tuck enough of the prayer Kapp under the cap, you can keep it on."

"No thanks."

"Ari, please." He shook the ball cap gently in front of her. "Just until we're out of Amish country."

"Fine." She did as he asked. "Sorry I'm late. After pulling everything together, I had my overnight bag in hand and told Salome I was going to your Mamm's, which was true. She didn't believe that was the full plan, but I told her to stick to the story, and she agreed." Ariana lifted the box and got on her knees facing the backseat. She put the box down but got a leather satchel and a brown grocery bag out of it. She turned around and fastened the seat belt. "I told my parents the truth about where I was going, so I fibbed as little as possible. It's really hard to want to be honest and up-front but know you can't be. Your Mamm drove me most of the way here because if someone in the district saw me walking, they'd stop and offer me a ride. Plus she drove me because I had a lot to carry." Ariana reached into her leather satchel and pulled out the puppy.

Did she understand the gravity of what they were doing? "Why did you bring that?"

"She's not a *that,* although she is still nameless."

"Ari, today is a serious situation. I need you to have your head on straight and your thinking cap on."

"Are you going to speak in idioms the whole time?"

Quill brought the car to a standstill at a four-way stop. "You're not hearing me."

"Quill." She startled him when she cupped his chin and turned his face toward her. "Today will go as smooth as us skating on the back pond. Okay?"

A decade of memories washed over him. No one was supposed to skate there, but they did and never got caught. He cherished those memories. Stress drained from him—most of it anyway. "Promise?"

"I promise. Now relax. And drive." She nodded at a car approaching the four-way.

He pressed the accelerator.

She pulled her phone out and plugged it in to charge and turned on music. "It will be our last great adventure together, and what was it you used to tell me?"

He remembered it well. "You can't soak in the good if you're dreading the what-ifs."

"Exactly."

"Ya, but when I used to say that, you were anxious that everything was crossing a boundary."

"And you liked attaching rockets to your foot scooter and sailing right past all boundaries as if they didn't exist."

He chuckled, feeling better by the minute. His interest hadn't been in going outside the boundaries. He'd just thirsted for boyish adventures. And he'd liked impressing Ariana with his daring ways. "The crazy thing is, after us being that opposite, we're both inside this car, working as a team, and you're the calm one."

"Wonders never cease." Ariana brought the puppy's nose to her own. "You're just too sweet."

"Thank you."

Ariana lowered the pup to her lap. "Not you." She elongated the word and pulled something out of the brown bag. "Food, because of all the things I know about today, one is that you haven't eaten yet."

"True."

She opened the cloth napkin, revealing a thick sandwich cut in half. "I also brought coffee and cupcakes."

"Should we stop and spread a blanket on the snow for a picnic?" He picked up half of the sandwich and took a bite. He didn't know what was in it, but it was really good.

"Go ahead. I'll wait inside the warm car." She opened the thermos. "Did sneaking in and out of your Mamm's place all those years bother you?"

"Sometimes. Today has me more addled than usual."

"Because I'm involved." It wasn't a question. She knew him. After pouring the liquid into a to-go cup, she put the lid back on it.

He turned down the heat. "Since, if Gia leaves, she'll have only the clothes on her back, I put some outfits for her in the trunk. I think we should go to a rest stop so you can change out of your Amish clothing."

"Nee. I'm good. It's who I am." She jiggled the bill of her cap. "I mean, I understand about needing a little bit of disguise until we're in the city, for my parents' and Berta's sakes. I have absolutely no desire to get anyone else in trouble. But, Quill, my clothing goes with my angelic face and will help Gia trust me." She held out her arms. "Ta-da."

Some of her fast talk and vigor was Ariana in determination mode. Some of it was nerves, probably from disobeying her parents' wishes. He sighed. "High energy, clumsy, and becoming fearlessly headstrong."

She wrinkled her nose. "That last description is worrisome. Amish and Englisch alike seem to have too many who are headstrong."

"It's impossible to hold on to a way of life without being headstrong." He took another bite of his sandwich. He didn't like that she wouldn't change her clothes, but she'd been on a long journey to become her own person, and he would respect it. "How did your parents take the news?"

"Shocked. Hurt. Disappointed." She passed the cup to him. "But they remained calm, and there were no threats." She wiped one cheek. "I never expected to hurt them or disappoint them like this."

Was she crying?

She put the puppy on the floorboard and slid out of her coat. "You've got clothes for the whole family?"

"Yeah." He took a swig of coffee. "In suitcases in the trunk."

"What are the chances she'll have the necessary ID with her to board the plane?"

"Good, I think. If not, I'll take them by car. But she shouldn't need any ID for the children, just herself."

"Minors don't need an ID to fly?"

"Not domestically."

"I didn't know that. I just assumed they'd need it too. Ever been on a plane?"

"No." He turned on a blinker and merged onto a ramp, and soon they were on the turnpike. "As it turns out, you've traveled a lot more than me."

"Years ago who could've guessed that one?"

"God?" he asked. "Certainly not either one of us."

"It's been a year of upheavals and surprises." The puppy whined, and she picked it back up. "This little nameless one is my secret clout. I have a picture of her on my phone, and I'll show it to Gia first, and if she approves, we'll share it with the children and tell them she needs food, cuddling, and a name."

Snow began to fall, swirling gently. Quill had hoped the snow would hold off until tomorrow, but maybe they would only have flurries, as the weatherman had said. "What's the clout when it comes to Gia?"

"Woman-to-woman honesty. Offering her safe passage to a new life, and assuring her you are the most trustworthy man she'll ever meet."

"I thought you just said you were going to be honest."

"I am. Let's just hope she doesn't question whether I also consider you difficult, secretive, and bossy." She leaned against the headrest and closed her eyes.

"Well,"—Quill turned on the wipers—"we can't all be as easy to work with as you."

Her whispery laugh filled him in ways no one else could. "Touché, my friend."

While he finished his sandwich and coffee, she rode with her eyes closed and began softly singing along with the music. He loved listening to her sing. Was there anything about her he didn't love? For five years, when he was waiting in a shed or the barn to visit his Mamm, he would hear her singing as she hung or gathered his Mamm's laundry or worked in her garden. It didn't matter how bad times were, when she sang, he felt renewed.

"Any chance you'd sing 'Amazing Grace' for me?"

She stopped the songs on her playlist. "If you'll sing the chorus with me."

That caught him off guard. He wasn't thrilled at the prospect, but he nodded. And once they sang the song, he thought they sounded really good together. They sang several more songs where he joined in on the chorus. Between songs, they reminisced and laughed about dozens of little things. She did the same as always—worked her way deeper into his heart without knowing it.

There was no way to ignore what she did to him. All he could do was cope with it. Maybe talking about Rudy would help him keep his subconscious rooted in reality. It was worth a shot. "Was it fun being the dating queen of numerous districts far and wide for a while?"

"It was necessary. I blame you."

He wasn't expecting that answer. "Me?"

"You'd been gone two years, and I was sick of thinking about you, so I began searching for a distraction." She raised both brows and nibbled on her bottom lip, looking far too charming for her own good. "I found distractions. The problem was each guy had only so much ability to distract me before it was time to date someone else. But in my quest I found one guy from another state who lasted a few months, and then at a singing in Summer Grove, there was this new guy from another state, and when my eyes met his,"—her balled fists slowly opened and expanded outward—"boom! Fireworks."

"What attracted you to him?"

"I just told you—chemistry. It could be felt across the barn at first glance."

He laughed. "Okay, but after that."

"He seemed to think I was amazing."

"There's no way that was a first."

"But the real me, the one who takes on debt to buy a café when all the other single young women are earning money to fill their hope chests. He was witty, and from the start he was supportive of my goals. Not many Amish men would get behind a young single woman with dreams that could interrupt the traditional stance of not working outside the home for the first few years of marriage."

"All sounds very . . . something. I'm not sure what the word is I'm looking for."

"Romantic?"

"Dull."

She laughed. "Thanks."

"But clearly you and Rudy have more than the thrill of romantic fireworks and his being supportive of your dreams. You have unity on all the major aspects of life?"

She started to nod as if agreeing, but the merriment slowly dimmed from her eyes. She turned to look out the window. "We used to agree on everything about life, love, and faith."

Quill's insides knotted, and he was sorry he'd begun this conversation. "I read a quote one time by Ruth Bell Graham. It was something along the lines of 'If two people agree on everything, one of them is unnecessary.' "

The nuances on her beautiful face hinted at thoughts he wasn't privy to. She shifted. "How about you? Date much?"

"I don't answer personal questions. You know that." Would teasing bring back the sense of adventure he'd managed to douse? Despite his teasing remark, they both knew it was basically true. But he kept precious little from her these days.

"So twenty girls—less or more?"

"Less."

"Ten?"

"I don't like this game."

"Less than ten? Okay, how about five?"

"Let's just get this over with already. I've dated one person."

"One person is enough."

"I agree. Fully."

"Still seeing her?"

"I thought we just agreed that one date was enough."

She laughed. "Sorry, I didn't realize that's what we were agreeing to. When this thing with Gia is over, Frieda needs to work on fixing you up."

"This may come as a shock to you, but I'm not all that easy to get along with."

"There is someone for everyone, isn't there?"

"Sure. You get Frieda working on that."

"Will do. Favorite season?" she asked.

"All of them since I now have electricity and can flip a button and shut out the heat. You?"

They bantered and even sang a few more songs. In no time they were at a stranger's house, parking Quill's vehicle in the open garage and moving their things into the rented van.

Overcoming obstacles felt easy with her beside him, but as they left that driveway in the van with its three secured child car seats, he felt the reality of the next few hours press in on him.

Twenty-Eight

Ariana sat across the table from Quill with a chessboard between them. She knew nothing about chess, but it gave them a legitimate reason to be in no hurry to eat and leave. They talked quietly while he kept his eye on the convex security mirror that showed a distorted view of every person who walked into the store. The deli café inside the grocery store amounted to three wobbly tables, each with four chairs. They had food, drinks, and a rest room, which was good, because they'd been here four hours, waiting for Gia to appear.

The white van, which looked like any number of work vehicles, was parked in a space on the side of the building. Without knowing when Gia might come, they couldn't park near the loading docks because that would draw attention. But Yvonne, the cashier who was connected to the organization trying to help Gia get away, had left no stone unturned today. She had discreetly reserved a parking space for them and even taken the puppy out of the van to go potty several times. She suggested Quill and Ariana get something to eat, buy a lot of groceries and leave them in the cart near the café, and buy a little something from the bakery. It would be easier for people not to think anything about their being here if they were buying things and looking as if they were on an outing, wasting time, maybe waiting to meet with someone.

A store worker passed by and did a double take of Ariana. "I should've listened to you about changing clothes." She hadn't thought what the workers might think or report if she and Quill had to stay in the store this long.

Quill pulled his attention from the security mirror to her and smiled. "This has been nice. You being you in all your honest Amishness, and me being fully me in my not Amishness."

She knew what he meant. They were their authentic selves with each other, nothing left to hide.

He shifted his attention back to the mirror. "Besides how much can an Amish person stick out when we're in Pennsylvania?"

"With me dressed like this and you like that, we look as if we're seeing each other behind my parents' back."

"And I'm teaching you chess." He smiled, looking calm as ever.

She hoped Gia arrived soon with all three children, but Ariana was fairly sure that if she and Quill had to camp out in the store for a week, they would never run out of things to talk about.

As she watched Quill study the security mirror for the fourth hour, calmly keeping a conversation going with her, never seeming to miss a beat about anything she said, taking note of the surroundings and what needed to be done, she was . . . impressed. Every time she thought she understood all the facets that made up this unusual man, she discovered something else about him. In a world of self-centered people with short attention spans and an unwillingness to reach out to help their neighbors or family, let alone a stranger, Quill stood way above the fray.

"I'm glad you left."

His eyes fixed on hers, silently probing for understanding.

"You needed to be free to help people, to use your strange set of skills to do as God needs."

A faint smile tugged at his lips, but she saw something sad reflected in his eyes. "Denki." He looked to the security mirror again.

But that look in his eyes lingered with her. She'd seen it before. The first time was after his Daed died. He left the Amish two years later, but that morning, as he gave her the letter and told her good-bye, she saw it then too. Five years after that, when he slipped out of hiding, she saw it again. In that moment she knew what it was. "It gets lonely, though, doesn't it? I mean, despite having family and friends."

He flinched ever so slightly, as if her words had hit closer to home than he was braced for. "It does. The former Amish talk about it from time to time. There is no letting go of our childhood, of the people who loved us and we loved and left behind. It was an idyllic childhood for my brothers and me, and there's no freedom from the remorse or pain of having to uproot from everyone and sneak around to see Mamm. I had to learn to live with it, and Mamm has had to learn to live with all her sons leaving."

"I don't know that I'll ever get to move in with your Mamm. Rudy's pretty set against the idea, feeling you and I would bump into each other too much."

His glance at her was fleeting, but she saw disappointment flicker in his eyes. "I know Mamm would've loved that, but from Rudy's point of view, I get it." His gaze seemed to pierce the air, and his brows furrowed as he stared at the mirror. "She's here." He rose.

Ariana grabbed his hand, pulling downward. "Stay out of sight." She stood and took hold of the cart with its two dozen items. "The woman in the shiny blue coat?"

"Yeah."

"She's limping."

"She wasn't last time."

"Better plan on her moving very slowly." Ariana squeezed the handle of the cart. "Move the van close to the loading dock, and then come back in. When it's time for her to see you, I'll text you the number of the aisle we're on. She seems nervous, so stay as far away as you can."

He studied Ariana, seeming to filter a hundred thoughts per second. "Okay. But you pay attention to all incoming texts. Yvonne has both our numbers and a text saying 'he's in the store' already written, waiting for her to press Send. If you get that text, you go out the back way. Immediately."

He looked sorry he'd allowed her to be here.

Feeling some of that herself, she drew a breath and watched the woman put the youngest child, probably eighteen months old, in the cart. "It'll be another story for us to add to our list. Not quite as brave as you releasing that illegally caged bobcat in the middle of the night or us cracking the case of your grandmother's missing medications, but it'll do."

"Be alert, Ari." His barely audible voice rang loudly with warning.

She nodded and pushed the cart toward the bakery on the first aisle. That was the most likely spot for Gia to begin her shopping. Ariana wouldn't engage her there. She'd speak to the kids first. Then she'd make eye contact with Gia, giving a reassuring *I'm an approving person* message, which should lower Gia's guard just a bit. Then on another aisle, as they passed again, she would say a few encouraging words to Gia about her precious children. Having sisters and nieces and nephews seemed to give her a clear advantage in knowing what she would say. She was totally comfortable with women Gia's age and their children. It made Ariana feel creepy and manipulative, but the real sickening part was that a violent man Gia didn't want near her had moved into her house and wouldn't leave.

Ariana's heart beat fast, but she felt surprisingly confident as she passed Gia and spoke to her kids. When she smiled at Gia on the second aisle, Gia responded well.

On the next aisle Ariana waited until Gia was right behind her to turn toward her, holding up a store-brand oatmeal. "Do you know if this cooks up as nicely as Quaker oatmeal?"

"I . . . I don't. Sorry."

Ariana lowered the container. "I'm Ariana." She nodded, keeping eye contact. "And I'm here to help you and your children l-e-a-v-e." Ariana spelled the word so she didn't alarm the children, causing them to ask questions their mom wasn't ready to answer. "I'll be with you for the next couple of hours, all of us together until it's time to board a p-l-a-n-e. The plan is to take you to another state to a woman's summer condo. You and the children can stay there rent-free for four months, during which time someone will help you get a job and find a place to rent. Do you want to go?"

"I . . . I do. I really do, but that's too much. I could never accept that much."

"Take it. Pay it forward to someone else ten years from now. Apparently that's what is taking place today." She typed "3" into her phone, letting Quill know what aisle to come to. "And Quill, the guy who was here four weeks ago, is a good friend of mine. I've known him my whole life, and I promise, you could not be in better hands."

"Are you Amish?"

"I am. He used to be, until he left to help people caught in difficult situations. We good so far?"

"Yes." Gia nodded. "He's done this before?"

"Helped people? Ya, and I'll be glad to answer every question I can, but if you're on board with the plan, we really need to go, Gia."

Gia looked toward the entry. "There's not time. He's drinking his beers, and he'll be in to pee and check on us shortly."

Quill came to the end of the aisle and waited.

Ariana put her hand on one of the children's heads. "Be brave, Gia, for their sake. Trust us with this first step." She pulled up a picture of her puppy. "I have a puppy in the van." She showed it to Gia.

Gia took her cue. "Hey, guys, want to see a puppy?"

Gia showed her children the picture, and they oohed and aahed.

Gia looked behind her. "He'll see us."

"Let's move quickly and now." Ariana rested her hand on the oldest child's head and smiled. The girl must've been five, and Ariana hurt for all she'd seen in her short days. "You should see her tail wag when she's excited, and if you rub her belly, she'll snuggle against you and sleep."

"Okay," Gia whispered, nodding. "You'll go too?" She lifted the youngest child out of the cart and set his feet on the floor.

"For now. I can't continue on the journey."

Gia looked at Quill. "Your whole life?"

"He helped me when I was in a really tough situation too. Kind. Thinks through every move. Knows what he's doing like no one else can." Ariana received a text. She drew her phone closer and read it.

He's in the store.

Quill had his phone out, reading the same message. He motioned for her.

Ariana pressed the Home button. Gia had no need to see that right now. "The clock is ticking."

"Okay," Gia repeated. "Let's do this." But it was going to take time for her to limp down the aisle and out the back of the store.

Ariana covered her lips with her finger. "Sh." She looked at each child and repeated. "Sh. Let's go find the puppy, but be very, very quiet." The last thing they needed was the abusive dad to hear the children squealing about a puppy. "See that man." She pointed at Quill. "He'll take you straight to the puppy."

The kids looked at their mom. She put her finger over her lips. "Sh." She shooed them. "Go."

They scampered toward Quill. He gestured for her and Gia. Ariana nodded and shooed him. He needed to get the kids in the van.

Gia leaned into the cart, shuffling in the direction her children had just gone out of sight. Ariana received another text.

Walking, looking down each aisle.

She prayed Gia could move faster or that he wouldn't see them even if he looked down this aisle. As they walked into the open area where dairy products lined the walls, she glanced behind her and saw a huge man at the far end of the aisle. But Gia was in front of the endcap, where he couldn't see her. But in a moment when he was looking down the next aisle as they cut toward the back exit, he would spot them. Should they stay behind the endcap? Would that maneuver buy them time? A huge trolley of some type, loaded with boxes of food, slid across the end of the next aisle, and she heard Yvonne whisper, "Go. Don't look back."

Ariana and Gia went through the Employees Only doors and stepped onto the loading dock. Quill and Ariana flanked Gia and half carried her to the vehicle. They piled in, and Quill had the vehicle in Drive by the time Ariana closed her door. He drove slowly, not drawing any attention, while Ariana and Gia buckled the children in.

"Where are we going, Mama?" the little boy, maybe three years old, asked.

"Somewhere new."

The older girl broke into tears. "Are we free, Mama?"

"Yeah, honey." Gia peered out the window while snapping the safety belt on one of the car seats. "I think we are."

Quill and Ariana received texts simultaneously. Ariana climbed over the console and into the front seat. She buckled in and read the texts. "She says, 'Still in store looking for them. Getting agitated he can't find them. Seems clueless they're missing. Deleting all texts now.'"

Quill stopped at the sign and turned out of the parking lot. "That's good news. Yvonne and I talked about this. If he dares to ask to see security footage, he would be denied. He's not legally allowed to have any contact with them, so the store would inform him the police have to be notified before he could see any footage. He'll leave."

Gia and her older daughter broke into sobs. Relief had never sounded so good.

Ariana relaxed against the car seat. "We did it."

"I think so." Quill drove, regularly glancing at the rearview mirror. "You have plane tickets to purchase." Quill passed her his phone.

"I do." She texted the next link in the chain of people working to get

Gia to safety. While Gia talked to her two older children, explaining what was going on, Ariana kept checking Quill's e-mail. The youngest child was about eighteen months old, so he couldn't understand much more than Mama was happy and there was a puppy. And the puppy was excited to be cuddled and played with.

"He didn't start out a horrible man." Gia talked softly to her daughters. "I saw some anger issues before we got married, but nothing like what he became."

"It's okay, Mama. I'd never be mad at you."

Quill's watchful eye on the rearview mirror was less intense as they put distance between them and Camp Hill. Thirty minutes into the drive, he drew a deep breath. "Hey." He leaned across the console. "We did it," he whispered. His grin said it all. They talked with Gia some, but at first she only wanted to soothe her children and talk about their future.

Ariana and Quill talked, and as the ride continued, Gia seemed to be eavesdropping, probably to reassure herself that Quill was the man Ariana said he was.

"Where did you say we're going?" Gia asked.

"Panama City Beach, Florida, to a condo on the beach," Quill said. "One of the people helping has offered her second home and is paying for the tickets. It'll give you time to regroup, find work, and start anew."

"I can't do this on my own. I'll get lost, and I don't have a clue how to—"

"I'm going with you," Quill assured her. "I'll get you acclimated to the new surroundings in as stress-free a manner as possible. We'll figure out how you can get to a grocery store, pharmacy, doctor, and anything else you'll need."

"Who would do this?"

Quill shrugged. "I don't know."

"I have a stepsister. She and her husband have money, but when my ex first got out of prison, he threatened her and her family if they came near me, and they disappeared from my life."

"I have no idea if she's involved, but on the chance she is, don't call her. Don't write. If she's doing this, she's trying to stay hidden, and she'll reach out to you when the time is right."

Quill's phone received five e-mails from Delta, each called a flight receipt. "Tickets." Ariana looked at the flight times. "Uh, you don't leave for quite a while."

"Yeah, but we're leaving—me, Gia, and the kiddos." He grinned.

"You might feel a little less happy by six tomorrow morning."

"Nah, it'll be five in a blink, and we'll eat supper. Then roam the airport. Shop. Waste some time. Settle down around ten and doze until morning. And then, to use your word, ta-da."

"This is you when you're relieved. I've seen it before, and I like it."

"Oddly enough, me too," he teased. "I know kids. I've been raising them since I was five."

"Hey," she scolded. "I was born when you were five. You're talking about me, aren't you?"

"Could be." He raised a brow, smiling. "Kidding aside, this delay will allow me to keep my phone turned on so that if you need anything, I can be reached. And you text me as soon as you're safe inside Nicholas's house."

"You still think there could be a problem?"

"Other than your driving on slick roads in the dark? No."

She laughed.

He did too. "I'll never forget your first time to drive a car in the snow. You came to our temp home in Mingo to fix my brothers and me a meal. But before you arrived, you'd slid off the road twice. Later the tow-truck guy texted you, 'Are you in for the evening? My wife would like me to come home for supper.' "

Ariana laughed. Had only two months passed since she drove there to tell Quill the good news that Nicholas was going to let her return to Summer Grove early? She'd been so excited, but until tonight nothing had held the pleasure or sense of reward she'd expected it to. "You're using my secrets against me."

"Never. I'm just enjoying that I know some of them." He pulled off the highway, and soon they were driving into a parking deck where car rentals were returned. She assumed he'd chosen this area because of its seclusion. And because it had no traffic, it would be less chaotic for Gia and the children as they coped with the trauma of what was happening. "Set your GPS for Nicholas's place." He unbuckled. "You'll loop around that way." He pointed. "Turn left as you leave the parking area, and make a right at the end of that road. Your GPS will pick up where you are at that point and get you to Nicholas's. Go straight there, and park in his garage."

The ninety-minute ride to BWI seemed to have taken only fifteen minutes.

"Got it." She hopped out and helped with the kids and luggage. When he paused, looking at her, she hugged him, and he held her tight, as if he didn't want to let go.

Twenty-Nine

Isaac paced the living room. "We can't keep waiting for her." He glanced at the clock. "We'll be late."

Lovina knew the time. She'd been aware of it since waking before sunrise. She knew Isaac wouldn't like hearing the question pressing in on her, but she'd held it back for as long as she could. "What if the thing she was involved in was more dangerous than Quill expected?"

"She's perfectly fine. If she wasn't, Nicholas would've come here and informed us," Isaac groused.

"I didn't think of that." Relief worked its way through her, and she wished she'd dared to ask that question earlier.

Isaac popped his knuckles, pacing. "She got to his place safely. I will not lie to the ministers to cover for her. But even so, she's backed me into a corner. I'm responsible for her, and I'll have to answer for why I allowed her to get in the car with Quill and go"—he waved his arm through the air—"wherever it is she went." He shook his head. "Here I was thinking maybe I'd been too hard on her, but the truth is, Ariana returned home determined to embarrass me in front of the whole community. She's angry. That's what this is about. It's her way of dealing with it."

"Nee, not Ari." Lovina wouldn't listen to him assign to Ariana the very thing he was guilty of. "That's how you've dealt with your anger." Lovina realized something she hadn't thought of before. "You were pleased she was coming home nine months early, but when she and Nicholas got out of his car, she hugged him good-bye. A sweet hug. Your little girl hugging her Englisch dad. A few minutes later, as we all sat around the dinner table, you began to realize just how different she was from the little girl you raised. Ariana isn't the one masking her anger and hurt through unpredictable responses."

Isaac closed the gap between them. "Could you try to understand what's going on from my perspective?"

She nodded and went to the foot of the steps. "It's time to go."

The next ten minutes were a blur of activity as everyone found their good coats and got them on. When she stepped outside, a vehicle was in her driveway, and she hoped it was Ariana, home at last. Isaac spoke with the driver, pointing down the road as if he was giving directions. It was then that Lovina saw car after car pass. Her knees trembled.

This back road was a detour artery that only had this much traffic when there was an accident on the nearby highway.

Salome put her hand under Lovina's elbow. "I know what you're thinking—that there's been an accident." She helped Lovina walk down the few steps. "But Ariana's simply late because she's caught behind all this traffic. That's all."

Lovina's heart slowed a bit. "Denki. You're right. That's all."

As the vehicle left the driveway, Isaac stared up the road at the oncoming traffic. When he turned back, he appeared agitated. He then motioned. "We need to go."

Lovina crossed the snowy driveway. "Are you okay?"

He didn't lift his eyes. "I'm fine. Let's go."

But he wasn't okay, and she knew it. She got in the carriage, and they drove five miles to the Millers' home. Berta was there, getting out of her rig. It dawned on Lovina how remarkable she was. Her sons had left the faith, and as a widow she was completely alone, but she had not let fear or bitterness take over her life. She was a quiet woman who sold eggs, produce, clothes, and quilts to earn money.

The ministers were hard on her, but despite the physical separation, she had not allowed any religious opinions or doctrines to put up walls around her heart, keeping out her children or causing strife with them. She didn't get to see her sons often, but they adored her, and as Lovina and the rest of the community learned while Ariana was living Englisch, Berta's sons went through misery to sneak in visits.

Isaac brought the rig to a halt and got out. Lovina hopped down, and while the others got out, she went to the hitching post, where Isaac was tethering the horse.

"Lovina," he whispered, "is it truly God causing a separation between us and Ariana? Could it be only our notion of what God wants of us?" He stared down the road as if hoping Ariana would magically step out of one of the slow-moving cars.

It was bad timing for him to get to this place of questioning right before a three-hour service began. The ministers would preach the virtues of submission—ministers to God, men to ministers and God, women to ministers, fathers, husbands, and God.

And Isaac would have the fires stoked against Ariana once again.

They spoke quietly to people and made their way to their respective sides of the Miller-living-room-turned-meetinghouse. She sat on her row, next to other women her age, and Isaac moved to a bench that was mostly empty. Watching him, she soon figured out why he'd sat there. He could see the road through the front windows and could watch for signs of Ariana coming in either direction.

Did he recall what Nicholas's car looked like? She didn't, other than it was black, maybe, and had four wheels. When the congregation sang and knelt, Isaac did so, but his attention constantly returned to the windows. While the bishop was preaching, Isaac stood and walked out.

Lovina waited for him to return, but when five minutes passed and he was still gone, she slipped out too. She looked around the farm, searching for signs of him, and finally found him on the other side of the barn, near the road. She hurried that way. He'd chosen a place where he could watch for Ariana but not be seen by those inside. "Isaac, *bischt du allrecht*?"

"Nee. I . . . may never be all right again. Where is she?"

"She got caught behind the traffic."

"Look!" He gestured at the empty road. "More than three hours have passed since that man pulled into our driveway, asking for directions, and told me about the wreck. The roads cleared two hours ago. The preaching and praying will end soon, and she's still not here."

"Maybe she went home instead of coming here."

He shook his head. "I told Skylar to have Ariana at least pass by this home in a rig after she got home. She was in that wreck, and that driver said people died." He rapped his fist against the center of his chest. "She was in it. I know it." Despite his words he gazed down the long road, searching for his girl. "I rescued all three babies from the fire that day. They are all mine in one way or another. But Ariana . . . I walked the floors with her when she had ear infections. No one could calm her except me, not when sick or when throwing a tantrum at two and three. I was the one she ran home to when Quill left with Frieda and broke her heart. Me. What happened to that man? The one she trusted to understand her and help her."

His certainty that Ariana was in the wreck made Lovina want to sink to her knees in the mucky snow and curl into a ball, wailing. But Isaac needed her right now, as she'd needed him time and again after discovering the girls had been swapped at birth. Ariana had to be fine. She had to be!

Isaac made a fist. "She's mine and I'm hers, but I've been so afraid of losing her that I've pushed her away. That makes no sense, and yet I've done it." He drew a ragged breath and refocused on the road. "In the meeting while we were kneeling in prayer, a question hit me so clearly it was as if someone was talking to me, and it shook the foundations of all I've lived by."

Lovina waited.

His eyes moved from the road and met hers. "How much of my life and my relationship with my children is molded by fear"—he pointed at the Millers' home—"of what everyone in that house might think?" Isaac looked down the road one way and then the other. "What if the last thing between me and that sweet girl was my coming down hard on her as I've done ever since she returned home?" His eyes misted. "Dear God." He grabbed a fistful of hair. "I need another chance. I'll listen to You more than anyone else." He pointed at the Miller home. "Please." His voice shook.

Lovina stepped closer. "Isaac." She put her cold hands on his cheeks and tugged until his eyes were on hers. "Even if the worst thing possible happened, she knows you. If she's gone from this planet, she left able to see your heart, your love." She held his face gently, keeping his full attention, and she saw him return to himself. "But she's not gone, and you will get the chance to set things right. Okay?"

He nodded and pulled her close. "Denki."

She held him tight. Relationships were hard, so very hard and so very worth fighting for. Surely Ariana hadn't gone through all she had this year to die before the people who'd raised her and loved her as their own could get their bearings and support her as she deserved.

Thirty

Ariana's hands were still trembling as she watched through the car window, unsure what to tell her dad to do. Her head throbbed. She had a lot to be grateful for right now, and one was the fact that Quill texted her at five thirty that morning to say they were boarding the plane and asked how she was. She'd responded enthusiastically, assuring him everything was fine.

She wasn't so great now, and she was glad he didn't plan to text her again until he and his wards were settled in the condo. She'd be home by then and could respond "home and safe," leaving out the incident that had happened between the morning and evening messages.

Nicholas glanced at her. "I'll say it again. You're to take it easy for three weeks. A concussion is nothing to brush off."

She nodded. The doctor didn't give her anything for her nerves because of the concussion. He said the shaking was from the release of adrenaline. The first accident, which involved three other vehicles, had happened seconds ahead of them, and there were fatalities. But a car had simply ricocheted into them, pinning them against a highway wall. The air bags had deployed, bruising one side of her face. She'd been examined at a nearby hospital while Nicholas rented a car. One thing about her dad was that he wasted no time. Things that should take hours, he could accomplish within minutes.

"Maybe you should just take me home." Ariana's voice trembled. "No sense in disrupting the meeting by arriving this late."

"I will if that's what you want, but I have a different thought on the matter."

"Why am I not surprised?"

Despite not arriving at Nicholas's until nearly ten last night, she'd had a really nice visit. Her mom, Gabe, and Cameron were there too, waiting to see her. Even now Ariana could recall the most wonderful feeling of being in her mom's arms. And her stepsister was full of barbs and wit, and all of them visited and talked and laughed until nearly sunrise before they parted ways to get some sleep. Cameron had fallen in love with the puppy, and with Brandi's and Gabe's permission, Ariana gave it to her. Cameron said the puppy would always remind them of Ariana—all bright eyed and excited about life but kind of clueless. Even thinking back on it, Ariana smiled. That was Cameron, simultaneously insulting and endearing.

This morning she saw her stepbrothers and stepmom. But she wasn't close to them. The boys were Nicholas's wife's children, and she got along with them just fine, but Cameron felt like a blood sister. Ariana's biological mom had raised Cameron since she was five, and their bond was really strong.

"Sorry, kiddo," Nicholas said. "But Isaac and Lovina are sure to be worried. You go to church. Slip in and take a seat. Spare them hours of worry."

"You think seeing this face is going to bring them relief?" She angled her face, giving him a good look at the swelling and bruises.

Nicholas cringed. "Well." He elongated the word in a perfect high pitch. "It's better than what they're thinking now."

"You're sure?"

"I am."

"Okay, turn right at the next two-way stop sign." She squirmed in her seat. "I feel so bad about—"

He raised a hand. "Covered. Talked about. I wouldn't have been on that highway if it weren't for you. But that's life, sweetheart. It's how it works. We do our thing and keep moving until death catches up with us."

"A bit apathetic, isn't it?"

"It sounds that way. What are my options? To be more afraid than necessary? To blame you? Did you plan that accident, Ariana? Are you holding out on me?"

She put her hand up. "Point made." His car was totaled, and it wouldn't be if it weren't for her. But his acceptance of the event worked past her overwhelming guilt, and a peace about it settled over her.

"Besides, Ariana, I would give up far more than a car or paying a few medical bills if it helps you help others, especially women and children. I spent a lot of years having no respect or understanding of either. I can't undo that, but being a part of this with you and Quill feels a bit redemptive."

Whatever flaws her dad had, she appreciated his willingness to be upfront about who he was . . . and who he had been.

Despite her pounding head, she seemed to have weeks, maybe months, of scattered thoughts weaving together like threads on a loom. She closed her eyes. "Lately as I look at women inside the Amish culture, it feels as if I should do . . . something to add insight to their views."

"How so?"

"I'm not sure, but it's a patriarchal society with some heavy-handed ways of molding girls to accept who we're told we are. There's no teaching that girls can be anything. No self-discovery into the uniqueness of who God made us to be. We're to fill the role we're taught. No questions asked. And any deviation from the plan is met with backlash. Maybe sadder than that, I see an attitude—not among all the men but too many of them—where women are viewed more as sinners and more prone to sin simply because of our gender."

"You're up to the task of helping young women. I know you are. Lucy Stone, Julia Ward Howe, Susan B. Anthony, and Harriet Tubman. Do you know what all those women had in common?"

"They fought for the rights of the oppressed."

"Exactly."

"But I don't want to stir up trouble. I don't think I'm supposed to." She had information and understanding that could provide balance to the rules of the Ordnung. That could be some help. People needed to know the difference between the Ordnung and the Bible, and they needed to hear other Bible verses that would help balance the ones that had been taught over and over. The men wouldn't listen to her, but how many women would? A lot less since her reputation had been damaged. Maybe only a few to begin with, but if she helped only her sisters and her nieces, that would be amazing.

"You know what else those women have in common? They were all born in the early eighteen hundreds, which is pretty close to how the Amish live." He was trying to add levity to the moment.

"Very funny."

"My mom, your Gammie—"

"Gammie? As in rhymes with *whammy*?"

"Skylar named her that because she couldn't say *grandma*. Anyway, starting a decade before I was born, she marched in and organized protests during the civil rights movement. She saw Martin Luther King Jr. speak. Twice. She believed nonviolence was the way to influence change, but she went to jail twice for participating and was ostracized by all the good women in her community. I think time is the true judge of how we lived. Not people's opinions or fads, but time. It's judged me on more things than I can count, and I've been found guilty. Was your grandma wrong?"

"No." But Ariana wasn't a protester or an activist. Still, it was encouraging to know she had Gammie's blood in her veins. "How did she die?"

"Mountain biking."

"Like a motorcycle bike?"

"No, it's a pedal bike, but mountain biking can be very rugged and sometimes dangerous. Her death rocked my world like nothing else had to that point. You look like your mom, but I see my mom's peaceful warrior spirit in you. Just remember that any good trait can become a bad one if you forget to listen to reason. You know that. You've seen me be so ridiculous in my stand that I was breaking your heart when my intention was to free your heart."

"I don't think listening to reason is a problem I'll have, but I'll keep what you said in mind." She pointed. "The Millers' house is a few hundred feet up ahead. Just stop here, and I'll walk. If a car pulls onto the driveway and I get out, it'll cause unnecessary disruption."

He checked his rearview mirror, waited until he was at the top of a knoll, and stopped the car. There was too much snow piled up on the shoulders for him to pull over and let her out. "I'm grateful you felt comfortable enough to reach out to me. You do it again."

"I will." She pressed the Unlock button. "Daed's going to be so angry I'm walking into the Sunday meeting late."

"Is that your purpose on this planet—to keep people from being angry with you?"

It seemed as if it used to be. "It's not my purpose, but it would be really nice if it was a perk of trying to do the right thing."

"I can't argue with that." Nicholas smiled.

"You? Unable to argue?"

"It's rare, but it happens."

She reached for his hand and squeezed it. "I'll text you later in the week." She wasn't going to turn off her phone for long periods again. She wasn't giving it to Rudy to keep until they were married. If it was acceptable for her to have one after she married, it was acceptable for her to have one before.

"Good." He frowned, looking baffled. "Is that an Amish man running toward us?"

She looked out the window. "Daed." Was something wrong? Her pulse quickened as she started to get out.

Nicholas grabbed her wrist. "No running. You're to take it easy and rest for three weeks."

"Okay." She got out and strode toward him, too stiff and sore from the accident to do more than a fast walk even without Nicholas's warning. Her Mamm was trailing behind, hurrying but not running. The road was a slushy mess with soot-covered melting snow.

"Ariana!" Daed continued to run, his face hopeful. "Bischt du allrecht?" he yelled, frost forming as he spoke. "Bischt du allrecht?" His hat flew off, but he took no notice of it.

"Daed, I'm gut." She hoped her words would slow him, but his face reddened as he hurried toward her.

His breathless body engulfed her. "Bischt du allrecht?" he asked again, holding her tight.

"Ya, I'm gut. I'm gut, Daed."

He laughed. "Ya?" He backed away and gasped. "You *were* in an accident."

"Ya. I was."

"I'm so sorry, Ariana." He cupped her shoulders with his hands. "It won't be like it was. We'll talk. We'll reason together, and I'll hear you. Okay?"

Was she really here, and was Daed actually saying that? Or was she somewhere else and unconscious from the accident and dreaming it? "You'll hear me?"

He cupped his ear. "Eh?" He laughed, eyes twinkling with joy. "Ya, ya, I'll listen."

"Sell iss wunderbaar, Daed."

He patted her shoulders, beaming. "Wonderful. That's right." He hugged her gently. "I will not let the church come between me and you," he whispered. "I won't."

Her heart pounded as she rested her head on his chest. *"Ach, Daed, Ich lieb du."*

"I love you too, honey."

Mamm arrived out of breath. She took one glance at Ariana's face. "Ach, my girl." She hugged her tight, sobbing.

"I'm gut, Mamm." She pulled away and clutched Mamm's hands. "I am."

Mamm nodded.

Ariana looked behind her, and Nicholas was still there, his hazard lights on as the three of them stood in the road.

She longed to invite him to stay, and he looked as if he wasn't ready to go, but they waved, and he drove off.

Thirty-One

Skylar plunged her hands into the soapy dishwater for what had to be the fiftieth time that evening, but scrubbing dishes or clothes or countertops either here or at the café did nothing to cleanse her conscience. She washed another cup, rinsed the bubbles from it, and set it on the rack. Ariana continuously dried the dishes and put them away. She had volunteered to wash the dishes from dinner, but before Skylar could stop herself, she had offered to do them herself.

Guilt was an unruly beast.

She had to do it. She had to come clean to Ariana. Confiding in Jax wasn't the same. It didn't offer solace to the one person who deserved it. On the other hand, clearly Ariana and her Daed had been getting along much better lately. Still . . . *Just do it. Rip the Band-Aid off.*

"Ariana." Second thoughts about confessing hit hard, and she longed to say something on a totally different topic. Maybe mention how quickly the bruises on her face were healing.

"Hmm?" Ariana stacked plates in the cabinet.

"Man, this is hard. And it shouldn't be, because you already know I'm not the most moral person." Skylar dried her hands on a dishtowel hanging on a rack, took a deep breath, and faced Ariana directly.

The blond young woman resembled Mom in so many ways, even in some of her mannerisms and gestures and definitely that kind-but-determined, dig-her-heels-in way. Concern flickered through Ariana's eyes. "What's wrong?"

"I . . ." *Spit it out, Skylar.* "I took your cell phone out of the suitcase and put it on the bathroom floor, knowing your folks would find it and you would be in trouble. I'm so sorry." She rested her gaze on the wood floor, afraid to see the hurt that would be in Ariana's eyes.

"Why?"

"I don't know. I just thought it would knock you down a few notches in everyone's eyes and make me look better. I didn't understand a thing about your family. *Our* family. I didn't understand the consequences." She looked up, braving a glance at Ariana's face. But instead of finding pain, anger, or condemnation, she was greeted by an expression of softness.

"I knew right away that you weren't comfortable with me being back. I'd hoped you would come around, and I'd hoped to move in with Berta."

"I'm sorry."

"And I forgive you."

It was as if someone had slapped Skylar on the back really hard. "What?" She coughed. "Just like that? With all the trouble I caused you? Don't you want to yell at me?"

"A little, but mostly no." Ariana shrugged.

"Geez, the cultural divide still baffles me at times. Normal American family members would yell and argue, maybe for hours or days, over a confession like this. And I deserve it."

Ariana shook her head. "The falling out was going to happen. You just made it happen sooner and for a different reason." She sighed and looked out the kitchen window above the sink. "I didn't want my time in the world to change me, but it did. I came back too different, and Daed didn't know what to do with it. But I'm curious. Are you sorry you were raised by Brandi and, to whatever degree Nicholas was involved, him too?"

It seemed all the oxygen in the room was suddenly gone, and Skylar couldn't catch her breath. She wanted to scream *yes!* But that wouldn't be honest. It would be her lashing out, because believing Mom and Dad were the problem came naturally. She'd behaved like a brat most of her life, but her mom—or rather Brandi—loved her like Lovina loved Ariana. Maybe

Nicholas loved her the way Isaac loved Ariana. The love was real even if the demonstration of it needed a lot of improvement.

Still, Skylar had been allowed to pursue her love of drama and music. Rather than repressing or refusing those desires, which would've happened if she'd lived in this house, the parents she called Mom and Dad had encouraged her and paid for more than a decade of acting and music lessons. Had come to her performances. Had helped her practice for auditions so she had the best chance of getting a part.

Skylar lifted her eyes. "I . . . I'm actually glad I was raised by your mom and dad. But the truth is, I needed my real parents too. Seems as if they swooped in at the right time. Maybe saved my life, definitely changed the course of it. Living here, despite the overbearing strictness, it's hard not to learn what real love is." Skylar gripped the kitchen towel on each end and gave it slack and then tugged, over and over again. "Mom loved me like that too, but I ruined those feelings by holding on to hurt and anger with Dad. He ignored me when I was young. Then when he did start coming around, he undermined Mom, and I took advantage of it. On my sixteenth birthday, he took me out, had too much to drink, and told me he was married to someone else when I was con—" What was she telling Ariana?

Ariana got a glass and filled it with tap water. "I know how *I* was conceived." She took a few sips of the water. "And I didn't react well to that news."

"It's hard, isn't it? It's like Dad was saying, 'I don't really like you, and here's why.' "

"He didn't intend to hurt us. He's outspoken, so suppressing the truth may have been impossible for him. But he has regrets. A lot of them. In some ways I needed time with him and Mom like you did with Mamm and Daed." Ariana set her glass on the counter and took Skylar by the shoulders. "We're going to be okay. Now you have to forgive yourself.

That's probably much harder than coming clean to me." Ariana lowered her hands.

"I'm indulgent, at least that's what a middle school teacher told Mom, and it fit. If I wanted something, I was going to get my way or make others pay. Mom tried to talk to me about that character flaw, but I whined that the teacher just didn't like me."

"Basically in this world-swapping thing we had to do, we discovered that Nicholas and Brandi were more right than you thought, and Mamm and Daed were more wrong than I thought."

Skylar laughed. "Seems like it."

"Can I give you a hug?" Ariana offered her arms.

Skylar stepped forward and embraced her sister-by-circumstance. Heavy weights lifted off her shoulders. "Thank you."

Ariana squeezed. *"Gern gschehne."*

"Did you just tell me to go milk cows or something?"

Ariana giggled and released her.

They made short work of the remaining kitchen duties.

"You know what surprises me the most about the Amish?" Skylar rinsed suds down the drain. "I keep expecting there to be these huge gaps between what I know, with my education and experience, and the Amish, who grew up with limited education and limited experiences. But the gap just isn't there. People's ability to understand and navigate their own minds and emotions are the same either way. Neither side is better at it than the other—just different."

Ariana looked amused. "Spoken like a true college-educated girl."

"As if you returned speaking Plain like your family."

"*Our* dad." Ariana mocked total frustration, sighing and rolling her eyes. "Vocabulary lists and mandatory studying on every possible topic."

Skylar laughed. "Tell me about it. Forget this *our* stuff. *Your* dad is so stubborn."

"Oh, and *your* Daed isn't?" Ariana mocked. "And we never push any boundaries that are problematic for them, so what's the deal?"

"Parents." Skylar sighed before she rinsed a washrag and began wiping the counters. But she liked how Ariana helped put things in perspective. She was good at compartmentalizing. Skylar tended to resent the whole person if she had reason to resent anything about them. Ariana's viewpoint was definitely healthier, and maybe it was time Skylar called her parents. "Has the trouble between you and the ministers died down?"

She shrugged. "Some. A lot of people believe the exaggerated, gossipy tales of my sins, and that's not going away anytime soon. But it's calm enough that I can ignore it and go about my life."

"You're just a little weird. You know that, right?"

"That's what you and Cameron tell me. Personally, I don't see it."

"You talk about the gossip as if it's a given and you don't care."

"I care, just not enough to rearrange my life in order to stop it."

"Mom's like that, except if people crossed a line—you know, about her lifestyle—she'd unload until their opinion was dust in the wind."

"Ya, I saw some of that. I thought she was going to end Nicholas in my first forty-eight hours of being there. I'd never seen a woman scream at a man like that. She got in his face, going toe to toe and yelling." Ariana laughed softly. "And Gabe remained observant and thoughtful, trying to calm her."

As Ariana's easygoing forgiveness filled Skylar's mind and heart, she longed to reach out with that type of kindness to those much more deserving of it than she was.

"Mom wasn't the only good parent. Gabe has been a good stepdad," Skylar said. "Cameron and I would fight like cats and dogs, and he was a 'peacemaking funmaker,' as Cam and I used to call him. Having a fight? Let's make ice cream!" She laughed.

Skylar regretted taking their love—Mom's, Dad's, Gabe's, and even

Cameron's—for granted. Selfish or shortsighted people did that, and she didn't want to fall into either of those categories.

Ariana moved the soaking cookware to the sink. "Speaking of Cameron . . . you should call her sometime. Extend an olive branch."

"She'd take it and beat me with it."

Ariana shrugged. "So take the beating and then hold it out again."

"Who would do that?"

"A big sister who knows she was wrong too, maybe more wrong than she's been willing to admit."

Skylar liked to believe the issues between Cameron and her were Cameron's fault, but it was time to be realistic. She didn't remember doing Cameron wrong. Based on Skylar's memory, Cameron sabotaged her willfully and purposefully. But even if that was true, would Skylar hold a grudge about it for the rest of her life?

"Honestly"—and for some weird reason Skylar longed to be very frank with herself—"I need to call all three parents and Cameron. Could I borrow your cell phone rather than walk to the phone shanty or the gas station?"

"Sure. It's recharging in the cooperage at Berta's. Tomorrow?"

"Thanks."

"You go, Skylar. I'll finish up."

"You don't have to offer twice." Contentment hummed a tune inside Skylar, making her feel as she did after getting through a difficult college exam. She walked into the living room and picked up her novel from the lower ledge of the coffee table. It was a "clean," Christian novel, borrowed from Susie, and not something she could have imagined herself reading a year ago. She hadn't expected to enjoy the book but was surprised by its likable characters and a plot line that twisted when least expected. She flipped to the page she had dog-eared and sat by the fire, leaning sideways in the recliner and crossing her legs at the ankles.

After she was a few pages further into the story, she noticed Isaac joining her near the hearth on the adjacent couch. She glanced up to see him open his own book. She smiled and gave him a little nod. They both sat in silence, save the crackling of the fire, for several minutes. This was another one of those things that Skylar knew the Amish had right: time to sit and read without the pull of technology and overscheduled lives.

Ariana walked through the living room, chuckling softly.

Skylar lowered her book. "What?"

Ariana pointed from Skylar to Isaac. "You both were sitting in the exact same position with your ankles crossed while reading your books, with the exact same look of concentration on your faces. Maybe it's genetic."

Isaac studied Skylar, nodding as Ariana smiled and continued on her way.

He put his book down and turned to Skylar. "I couldn't have overheard you if I'd tried, and I wasn't trying, but I saw you and Ariana hugging in the kitchen." He smiled. "Can't tell you how that does my heart good, Skylar. In fact, you seem a bit different lately. You've gained a peace, ya?"

Skylar nodded, thinking about what she wanted to share with this man. He had times of being open and supportive with his family and times of being inflexible and rigid. Right now, in the living room, sitting by the fire with him, she almost felt as if their relationship went as far back as her first memories.

Isaac sat more upright and leaned in. "Does it have to do with Jax?"

"Yes, but not in the way you probably mean it." Skylar fidgeted with the pages of the book. Maybe one day she would have her life together enough to be able to have a functional romantic relationship, and maybe Jax would be interested, but she wasn't ready. "I think I know what I want to do with my life."

Isaac looked a little surprised. "And what is that?"

Skylar wanted to be honest and yet gracious. It seemed to be a Brenneman trademark. "I hope it's not too big of a disappointment to you, but I can't be Amish. If I had been raised in your community, maybe I would feel differently."

"I know." Isaac nodded slowly.

"I can't stay living Plain, not with the plans I have. I need to study music, and since instruments aren't allowed, it wouldn't be a good influence for my nieces and nephews."

She'd felt sorry for them when she first moved in here, but this life had so much to offer that couldn't be easily seen. Perhaps some of her nieces and nephews, many of whom weren't yet born, wouldn't end up staying Amish when they were adults, but she did *not* want to be the cause of them pulling away. What had looking into the eyes of those homeless children and their parents done to her? The children just wanted to be loved and to give love, but the parents looked so weary, and their eyes held grief and a sense of powerlessness that had broken Skylar's hardened shell.

"But I don't want to lose my connection to you all either."

"Good." He looked relieved and unsure. "Your Mamm and I have been hoping you'd feel that way. I was concerned I'd blown that by showing how difficult I can be at times."

"Parents." Skylar huffed, smiling at him. "What can I say? You guys try. I can definitely say that."

Isaac grinned. "Thank you. Do you have a plan?"

"Maybe. Something stirred in me when I went to the charity event with Jax last month. I realized I'm not the only person who matters, and what I considered an unfair shake was actually quite fair. I want to help others who are in the thick of a truly difficult childhood, and apparently I have a knack for it." She couldn't explain all that had happened to her that day with the homeless families, but she saw everything differently now.

"This sounds good." Isaac tapped the book against his leg. "Really good."

"Yeah. I think so too. On Valentine's Day I worked with children, leading them to perform some simple songs for their parents. We practiced a little bit before they performed, and I connected with them in a way I didn't know was possible, encouraging them and using humor to motivate them not to be nervous. After the performance several of them hugged me and thanked me. These kids have zero resources to get their parents anything for a holiday like Valentine's Day, not even a card. But I helped them give the gift of music." Deep emotions stirred at the memory.

"Interesting. I think I finally understand a little better why Valentine's Day and days like it matter so much to people."

"Me too," Skylar confessed. "I want to go back to school and become a music teacher. I'm not exactly sure where I want to teach or at what level, but I want to help children like that all the time, not just at special events."

Isaac nodded, and she hoped it was an approving gesture, not just an admission that he was hearing her.

"I'll need to take out some student loans, but I could start this May. I'd do the Maymester and summer semesters. I'd need to change my major, which was music, to education with a minor in music. I'll probably lose a lot of credits if I change schools, but . . ."

"Ya? I'm sort of lost on most of what you just said. But where will you go to school?"

"I was thinking of applying to Shippensburg University."

"The school's not more than fifteen miles from here."

"Yeah. They have a forgiveness program for bad semesters like the one I walked away from. I'll also need to get an apartment, a car, and a phone. The school would be in easy driving distance of the café. So if it's okay with everyone, I could continue to work there while I'm taking classes. But would that be allowed?"

"I'll allow it, and under these circumstances I don't think it'll be a problem with the ministers. If it is, I'll deal with it. You're not the only one who's seen a need for change. I saw it in myself quite clearly, and I'm standing my ground with the ministers on Ariana's behalf too."

"But she's not back at the café yet."

"After the accident she needed rest and no stress or strain. What's the plan with Brandi and Nicholas?"

"I don't have one, other than apologizing. Since I came here a wreck, you probably think it's their fault, and maybe I wanted you to think that. I've blamed them time and again when it was solely my fault for getting off course."

"Sometimes"—Isaac stroked his beard, looking thoughtful—"we get off the right track and it's no one's fault. Maybe I did judge your parents at first, but then I saw that my children are better than I deserve. So maybe parents don't plant the seeds for all the things that are harvested—good and bad—in their offspring's lives. But I know it's never too late to get back on the right track, not for either of us."

What kind of patching up had happened between Ariana and him? She wouldn't pry, but she was glad to see this accepting man in place of the hardened rule enforcer.

"Skylar,"—Isaac set the book on the coffee table—"what would you think about living above the café in the loft?"

"I've heard Susie talk about it."

"Ya. That's what she thought she wanted, but since Ariana is going to hire additional crews, she'll have days off. She said the other day she doesn't want to be in that noisy loft during her days off, especially on her mornings to sleep in."

"People are allowed to sleep in? In this family? On a day that's not Sunday?"

"If they have a full-time job, they are."

"Wonders never cease."

"Would the loft work for you since you'll be in school five days a week? You could do what you need to with your music but not move away."

Skylar's heart leaped. It was perfect for what she needed. Perfect. A solid connection to her Amish family while she had the resources she needed to succeed in her new plan for the future.

Thirty-Two

Abram carried an armful of boxes of coffee beans down the loft stairs and into the storage room behind the kitchen.

Susie shifted another box and slapped a handmade label on it. "Put that there, please." She pointed.

It had taken time and considerable effort to clean out the loft while changing two main-floor closets into storage rooms.

"We're running out of space. How much more is there?" Susie eyed the supply of coffee.

"Help," Skylar yelped.

Abram turned and grabbed two boxes from Skylar's hand.

"Thanks, Bro." Skylar winked.

"Bro?" Abram tried to pass the boxes back to her.

She laughed, raising both hands. "Denki, *liewer Brudder.* Better?"

"Depends, I guess." Abram held the boxes, waiting on Susie to find the right spot. "What were you trying to say?"

"Hey." Skylar rapped her knuckles on a box. "That was clearly, 'Thank you, dear brother.'" She peered around him at Susie. "Right?"

"They were certainly words from some language in this world . . . I guess." Susie took the top box from Abram and set it on a shelf.

"That bad?" Skylar asked.

"Nee." Abram patted Skylar on the head. *"Ich denk du bischt verhuddelt. Du schwetze wunnerlich."*

"I have no idea what that means."

He scooted past her, getting in a position to leave fast. "It means, 'I think you are confused and you talk strange.'" He walked away.

"*I* talk strange?" she called after him.

Abram chuckled and headed back to the stairs. Everyone was upbeat and staying faithful to their tasks as they neared the end of at least this portion of the project. Martha was cleaning the floors after the boxes were removed from an area and also cleaning where the boxes were being moved to. They still needed a plumber to add a shower to the bathroom in the loft, which would make the tiny room even tighter. Then there was the process of moving in a bed and Skylar's few belongings.

When he topped the stairs, he found Ariana on her knees, reaching into a crawl space. "Was there any spot in the loft where you guys didn't store things?"

"No." Abram walked over to her and removed the boxes near her as she emptied the crawl space. "We pretty much scouted out the loft, looking for spots that would be particularly hard on you to empty." He held out his hand. "Now get out of that space."

"What?"

"You were in a car wreck a little more than two weeks ago. You're supposed to be the supervisor. We're the worker bees. Right, Martha?"

Martha stepped out from behind a wall, a mop in hand. "Ya. Sorry, I didn't know she was doing that."

"Two weeks is plenty." Ariana took his hand, and he pulled until she was on her feet.

"I saw the care instructions that came home with you from the hospital, and it clearly stated *at least* three weeks." He passed her a clipboard. "This is the most you're to lift."

She looked over it. "So nothing in these last three stacks of boxes has been counted?"

"Not yet." He snapped his fingers at her.

She smiled and moved to the first stack of boxes.

Skylar bounded up the stairs. "What's next?"

Abram gestured. "Ariana will point, and you will move these boxes into the correct pile. Each stack is going to a separate area downstairs. She'll take inventory before they leave the loft."

"Got it." Skylar turned to Ariana. "Direct me, oh, wise one. Your wish is my command."

"Don't tempt me to give you all my chores for the next year." Ariana lifted a brow. "Just move these boxes to group one."

Skylar began shifting the boxes as Susie entered the loft. "For the record, I can't believe everyone is spending so much time on a place for me."

Abram knelt and reached into the cubby. "Well, you may find it surprising, but we *do* like you." He turned and smiled at his birth twin. "We get that you can't stay in our house while studying music, but we're glad you chose to stick close."

Susie crouched and opened a box to inspect its contents. "Oh, my! Oh, my goodness! I think . . ." She grabbed something out of the box. "Look!" She waved a bank bag in the air. "Money!"

Exclamations of shock filled the loft, and everyone huddled around Susie. "This box has two bank bags." Skylar laughed. "Who put the deposits in a half-used box of coffee beans?"

Martha peered into the box, her eyes wide. "I . . . I think I did. I hadn't thought about it until now."

Everyone except Martha laughed.

"Guys,"—Martha looked at each of them—"I'm so sorry. I was unloading supplies in the kitchen a few times, and I needed space in the crisper, so I took out the money bags and tossed them into the coffee bean box sitting between the fridge and the counter."

Susie chuckled. "I saw a box sitting there several times and told Skylar I was going to bean her with a bag of coffee beans if she didn't keep them out of that spot, because I needed it for fresh produce."

"Yeah,"—Skylar raised a brow—"because onions and cucumbers are *so* much more important to customers than coffee."

Abram had often heard these two sass and tease each other.

"I moved the boxes upstairs whenever Susie complained, but they were always closed," Skylar said. "I even remember hearing a funny noise once, which apparently was change jingling, but I never took the time to check it out."

"And when I saw the boxes sitting in the loft, I shoved them to the very back of the attic storage"—Abram knelt, looking into the tiny cubbyhole leading to the storage space—"to make room for other boxes."

"I ordered more of those coffee beans because I couldn't find the boxes with half-full bags of beans." Skylar laughed, covering her mouth. "I thought maybe we'd used all of them when Cilla was manning the machines."

"Didn't anyone realize they were having to get new bank bags from the bank rather than reusing the same ones?" Ariana asked.

"Cilla mentioned the need to get more bags," Abram said. "We just thought sometimes whoever took the bags to the bank left the bags there."

Skylar continued to giggle. "Sorry, Ariana. I know it's not funny, but . . . it is."

Chuckling, Ariana pointed at herself. "That makes me the only innocent person in the missing-money scandal."

Susie narrowed her eyes in a fake glare, given away by the smile she couldn't quite suppress. "Ya. Let's peddle that 'I'm innocent' jargon to the ministers and see if it gets you anywhere."

Ariana laughed. "You!" She shooed her toward the opening. "Go pull out any other boxes in the cubby. The rest of you thieving rascals look through the boxes. According to the ledgers, we have two more missing deposits."

Skylar scooted a box with her foot to the second stack. "Apparently the skill you have with numbers, Ari, doesn't help when it comes to using 'fancy' coffeemakers."

Ariana pinched the bodice of her apron and flapped it. "I'm wearing more steamed milk than Skylar's ever sold. I think it was a plot. Skylar thought, 'I'm going to talk everyone into getting fancy coffee machines so I can soak Ariana in various forms of foamy milk and espresso when she returns. And to top it off, she won't even know the names of the coffee I make, let alone how to make them.'"

Skylar opened another box, looking for the missing bank bags. "And the plan worked so much better than I ever dreamed. Can you say *caffe breve* with me?"

"I've seen the receipts, so I know it sells beyond belief, but who would've thought that people in rural Pennsylvania would come to this café and want that?" Ariana asked.

"You needed me in this café, just like I needed to be here. People love the coffees served here . . . at least until I'm in school and they taste *your* caffe breve."

"I'll get the hang of it. I will." Ariana rubbed her forehead, and Abram knew her head was aching again. Since the wreck her mind hadn't been as clear as it typically was, and he wondered if that was slowing her down when it came to learning new things.

"I'm just kidding," Skylar said. "You could make coffee with mud, and it'd taste better than Susie's and Martha's best attempts at croissants."

"Keep it up, Sky Blue," Susie said. "You think you're insulting us, but I hear it as an invitation to come to the café, also known as your apartment, to practice baking before the rooster's up."

Martha resurfaced and banged the handle of the mop against the wall. "And we're loud when we practice." She banged it harder. "Really loud."

"I'll join her and work on making coffee," Ariana piped in, "and on Sundays too."

Skylar stood and massaged her lower back. "Did I tell you girls that your coffee and croissants are the best I've ever had anywhere?"

Ariana, Susie, and Martha looked at each other, a bit of a victory smile on their lips. "No," Susie said, "you didn't."

Skylar picked up two boxes and headed for the steps. "Good. Because it'd be a lie." She scampered downstairs, and they broke into laughter.

"And voilà!" Abram held up two more bags of money.

Skylar came back up to the loft. "Would anyone like me to make us some coffee?"

"It's five-thirty in the afternoon. It'll be dark in an hour, and you want coffee?" Abram's brows knit.

Skylar shrugged. "Why not, lightweight? We are in the business of caffeine after all."

"*I* want coffee." Susie's voice came from behind one of the stacks of boxes. Apparently she had opened another container and was looking through it.

Ariana pointed to a stack. "Those can go."

Skylar picked up two boxes. "Okay, real coffee for the girls and wimpy decaf for Abram. Got it." Skylar went to the top of the steps and paused. "You know, Abram, you're right. There is a time and place for decaf." She went down a few steps. "Never, and in the trash."

Ariana laughed and cupped her hands around her mouth. "I was the nicer twin, Abram."

"I heard that," Skylar quipped.

Abram chuckled. "The café is doing great. Your dream to buy it was spot-on. Skylar's ability to know how to bring in as many customers as possible was also spot-on."

"It wouldn't have survived my absence without you guys, and I'll never forget that. But, Abram, if you want to return to construction . . ."

"I'd like that. I could work here whenever construction is slow."

"Perfect plan." Ariana nodded. "In a few years, when we're on our feet a little better, I'd love to see if we could buy the building next door and knock out a wall. Brandi took me to a place a little similar to ours, except they had a huge section with couches and love seats and big coffee tables."

"Couches? Whatever for?"

"Women gather to chat for hours, buying lunches, coffees, and desserts. Writers use it as a home away from home or a place to gather with other writers and brainstorm. Oh, and it had a small area in a corner with a half wall and a gate for children. It had cushy building blocks, books, and some toys. The kids would play, and the parents would sit at nearby tables. The place was open from eight in the morning to nine at night every day, and I never saw it with less than twenty people."

"That's a really cool idea, and I know you could make the expansion work, but you'll have babies by then, and Rudy . . ." Susie let the sentence drop.

"Ya, you're right," Ariana agreed. Rudy would want her home, managing from afar as much as possible.

"Okay, here comes some liquid salvation from exhaustion." Skylar held a tray of coffee mugs. "Oh wait." She set the tray on top of a box. "Abram, here's your brown water." She held out a pink mug to him that had a kitten on the front.

He eyed it before he took it, suppressing a smile and refusing to acknowledge her teasing.

"Thanks, Skylar." Ariana lifted a traditional café mug off the tray. "And thanks for the lesson on the espresso machine and steamer earlier. Sorry about your shirt."

Skylar waved away her apology. "It's no big deal. That machine has sprayed me on multiple occasions. At least it happened when we were closed this time."

"There will be multiple perks for Skylar once she's living here," Susie said. "She can make her usual mess brewing coffee, and then she can take a shower up here."

"Watch it, or I'll aim my messes in your direction."

Susie laughed and picked up a cup from the tray. "You're not allowed to smoke up here either, you know?"

"A newborn knows that. I'm in the process of quitting. Parents are right—Amish or Englisch. It's counterproductive to indulge in something that will begin to steal my health before I'm middle age. Besides, how can I in good conscience have a habit I wouldn't want my students to pick up?"

"I used to smoke," Abram said. "Ask Skylar."

"What?" Martha looked seriously stressed.

Skylar nodded. "He did. He took two puffs of a cigarette while trying to get me off his back. You know, back in the day when I was difficult."

"Yesterday?" Ariana asked.

"You're a troublemaker in sheep's clothing," Skylar said. "I like that!"

They chuckled, enjoying the lack of stress and newly strengthened bonds.

"So tell me about Cilla." Ariana raised an eyebrow as she sipped her coffee. She had known Cilla as well as Abram had before all the turmoil pushed him and Cilla together. "Inquiring minds want to know, Abram."

Picturing Cilla's face made Abram feel as if he was stepping out of winter and into spring sunshine. Imagining her sweet laughter had him longing to be with her again. "She's great."

"Well, there you have it," Skylar said. "I would make fun of him for using so few words, but I think the look on his face says it all."

"Ya, it does." Ariana nodded. "She's a much better match for you than Barbie."

"You were interested in *Barbie*?" Skylar made a face. "She's nice and all, but I can't see you really connecting with anyone else like you do with Cilla."

"Sometimes we have to take the wrong path to find the truth," Abram said.

His sisters, four of them anyway, stared at him.

"That's what Cilla told me to say if this ever came up."

The women broke into laughter.

"You're making that up." Ariana shook a finger at him. "Cilla said no such thing."

"Is he?" Skylar asked.

Abram nodded. A knock on the door echoed through the loft, and Abram went downstairs.

He opened the door to find an Englisch man with a slight build, probably in his early forties, staring back at him.

He dipped his head in a quick greeting. "Good evening. I'm Detective Blake Torres. I'm looking for an Isaac Brenneman, and I noticed your sign said Brennemans' Perks. Any chance you know Isaac?"

"Ya. He's my father."

"Good. That's a start."

"You're a detective?"

"Yeah." The man pulled a badge off his belt. "No worries. He's not in trouble. I'm doing some preliminary work on an old complaint, but so far I've hit only dead ends. I couldn't find a Summer Grove residence listing for Mr. Isaac Brenneman. Could you tell me the address?"

"Sure." Abram gave him the address. "The house may be in my grandfather's name or maybe in my uncle's name. It's been passed down."

"Mr. Brenneman called us, and he mentioned an Eli Schlabach."

His Daed called the police station? Abram could hardly believe it, but his Daed had changed a lot. Maybe he was sick of the ministers running roughshod over the flock, or maybe he wanted to push for justice for Berta Schlabach.

The detective clipped his badge back on his belt. "I have Eli Schlabach's address, but public records show he died about seven years ago."

"Ya. His widow still lives at the same address, though."

"Okay. I'll check again. I went by there, but no one answered, and I wasn't sure anyone lived there."

"Maybe you should talk to my sister Ari. She goes by there at least once a day."

"It sounds as if I caught a break by knocking on your door."

"Maybe." Abram went to the foot of the stairs. "Ari?"

All four girls came down the stairs, carrying boxes. "Ya?" Ariana answered, unable to see them for the boxes. Abram went up a few steps and took them from her. "There's a detective here with some questions."

Ariana walked over to the man and extended her hand. "Ariana Brenneman. What can I help you with?"

"I need to speak to Mrs. Eli Schlabach. Any idea when she might be home?"

"I assume she's there now."

"I was just there, and no one answered. I'm in an unmarked car, so maybe she just didn't come to the door."

"Can I ask what this is about?"

"I'm looking into a complaint filed by Eli Schlabach."

"By Eli? Why would you ask about that now?"

"Typically I wouldn't answer that. But the Amish community tends to be very closed to working with the police." He shifted, offering a smile. "If I answer your questions, could you surprise me by answering mine?"

Ariana sighed. "You know the Amish well, Detective."

"Enough to be familiar with the code of silence." He pulled a small pad and pen out of his pocket. "In answer to your question, Mr. Brenneman called the station and asked why we never followed through on Mr. Schlabach's complaint. I couldn't even find the case file, and we're still looking for it. But we know two things: the detective assigned to the case had to leave his job abruptly and move to another state due to a family tragedy, and we were in the process of changing the computer systems at the time. So a lot of files were redirected or corrupted. There's a main database that saves everything, and we're trying to locate the complaint. In the meantime I'm doing some prelim legwork."

Ariana looked grieved. "So the detective assigned to the case left, the file was lost, and Eli died. I have to tell you that's a lot of bad things happening at the same time."

"It is, which is why I'm trying to unravel some of it before I go home tonight."

Ari gestured toward a chair. "Reopening this case now is going to be hard on Berta. She's sort of put everything in a box, tied it with a ribbon, and is waiting for heaven so God can unravel the confusion and take the hurt."

"I can't drop this, if that's what you're asking."

Ariana nodded. "She has five sons, and not one of them would want her by herself when you discuss this."

"Okay. Fair enough. It'll probably take a few more days for IT to find the original complaint. Something about searching through corrupted backup files. Do you think she knows much about the report her husband filed?"

"I do. She and her youngest son, Quill, know more than anyone."

He nodded. "I apologize for how out of touch I sound, but I don't have a file to refer to. All I'm going by right now is the call Mr. Brenneman made to the station and the research I've done in public records based on that call. Mr. Brenneman mentioned that a girl had been poisoned, a Frieda Miller. But he wasn't able to confirm if she was still alive."

"She is. I only text with her, but Quill sees her regularly."

He rubbed his forehead, sighing. "I can't tell you how relieved I am to hear that. Any idea of the whereabouts of John Miller, the girl's father?"

"No. I was told he took off when he heard Eli went to the police with the information."

"Was she an only child?"

"No, one of seven. But it's believed she was the only one he poisoned."

"Do you have an address for the Miller family?"

"I don't. But I can text Quill and ask for it."

"That would be great. Thank you. And let him know I'll go by his mother's house Saturday around three."

Ariana pulled her phone from her pocket, and her fingers flew across the screen. After a few seconds the device made a *boing* sound that Abram had learned meant an incoming message. Ariana read it, typed a response, and quickly received an answer. "I have an address for you, and he'll be at his Mamm's house Saturday."

Thirty-Three

Ariana struggled to breathe as Rudy drove the carriage down the paved road.

He tapped the reins against the horse's back. "Why?" he whispered. "I keep trying to understand your actions and decisions, and I just don't."

"I needed money to get the café's finances in shape. I'll pay him back."

"You just don't stop, do you, Ari?"

"Meaning?"

"You always have to get your way. You wanted to go to the B&B, and you went. You wanted to keep your phone, and despite the ministers' displeasure, you still have it. You wanted your Daed to lift the ban on the café without you giving any concession in return, and he did. And now you're telling me that more than a month ago—more than a *month,* Ari—you borrowed money from *the man* who gave money to MAP. Do you realize you've linked yourself, your café, and your Amish family to an atheist?"

"First, the *man* is my father. Second, he's seeking, and seekers find. Remember? Third, I will be his daughter for the rest of my life. Should I shun him because he's not exactly where you think he should be? I certainly hope not, because I'm not where I think I should be either. Are you? We're made worthy by grace, Rudy. Not judgment or expectations from the church, but by God's grace."

His brows were knit tightly, and he shook his head as if he was giving up that argument.

"The police coming to Berta's tomorrow will cause blowback on you, and I know that situation isn't your fault. But that aside, in your two months of being home, you've done nothing but fan the flames of gossip. I didn't sign up for this, Ariana."

His words stung, and her thoughts were as murky as the rivulets of dirty water that ran across the road as the snow continued to melt. The land still had more white than patches of brown grass, but the smell of spring in mid-March rode on the air.

She hadn't exactly signed up for this either.

"I didn't get everything. I didn't move in with Berta, and I did that for us. But you're right, I'm different. Apparently annoyingly so. I get it. But what did you sign up for, Rudy?"

"Peace and simplicity. The Old Ways. Shutting out the world so we can hold tight to faith. Marriage. Children. The Amish here, especially compared to my home in Indiana, are quite balanced, but that's not good enough for you."

"Balanced? I was preached against, my reputation was ruined, and they used First Samuel 15:23 to say I was full of rebellion, like a witch. That's balanced?"

"No. That was anger, and it was wrong, but you did stir the pot."

Ariana had no idea what to say in response. She crossed her arms and stared out the window.

Rudy slowed the rig. "Don't get mad at me for being honest. I've stood by you through everything, and I'll continue to do so."

"Hopefully without throwing any more hammers across the room."

His face grew hard. "That's not fair. The whole situation has been nothing but stressful since your parents said you weren't their biological child. I've been very patient, Ariana. Still, slinging that hammer was wrong of me. At the same time, you can't provoke men at every turn and then blame us for reacting."

How many different sides did he take just now? *It's your fault. Actually, it's mine. No, I'm wrong; it is your fault.*

She tugged at a loose thread on her thick sweater. "Please tell me I'm wrong, but it sounded as if you just said that when the ministers ruin a good woman's reputation in a matter of minutes and when my fiancé loses control and throws a hammer, it's my fault."

"I said we—the ministers and I—were wrong."

"Wrong. Ya. And I know it was. Before I left here, I thought it was my duty to accept full responsibility for whatever wrong I was told I'd done. Women aren't supposed to hold any man accountable."

In that moment Ariana realized anew what she needed to do to make a difference. Women needed to know more about other cultures and other times in order to balance out what they were being taught. Ignorance wasn't bliss. It made innocent people prey—prey to those who had knowledge, prey to those who knew how to manipulate truth, and prey to their own silly, unbalanced thoughts.

She needed to bring speakers into the café on Friday nights, maybe once or twice a month. Maybe she could get history professors who could open up new worlds of understanding for anyone who chose to come and listen. Despite the frustration over the argument with Rudy, Ariana felt hope and excitement shimmy through her. It would cause a lot of frowning and gossip in the thirty-and-over crowd. One advantage of having her reputation mutilated from the pulpit is that she couldn't go much lower in people's eyes. That brought an odd sort of freedom.

"Rudy, our people need fresh knowledge coming in. We need historians to share about cultures and events that have taken place across the centuries. It'd open minds and free the spirit to see God beyond our tiny town on its tiny dot in the time line of history. That happened to me at the planetarium I told you about. I listened to facts, and I saw God inside it, Rudy. I envisioned this huge, amazing ball of energy that is love. Did you know that in some ancient societies, women were highly esteemed and considered good leaders?" She held up her hands and shook them. "Sorry, rabbit trail. But I wouldn't ever let the teachers discuss the Old Ways or teach the Word, although they could share about the culture. Learning history in that way would open our hearts to something bigger and stronger than the Ordnung, something more valid than man-made laws and rules."

"What?"

She repeated it.

"How?"

"The café. I could open it on Friday nights, have a speaker, serve free refreshments."

"You know some history professors?"

"No, but—"

"Never mind. I know the rest of that sentence. Nicholas. Do you realize you would bring more trouble onto your head? Our heads?"

"But if good is accomplished, who cares?"

He stared out the front window. "You're ruining the surprise I mentioned."

She was ruining it? Just her?

His shoulders were square, taut with anger. "Could you sit back and settle down? This ongoing argument isn't us, Ariana. We need something fun, and I have the answer." He pulled onto a long dirt driveway.

"The Steele place?"

"Oh, so you know it?"

"Ya." It was a small home, maybe a hundred years old. A foreman or maybe a sharecropper probably lived there originally, and her Daed said the main house burned to the ground forty years ago.

"I didn't realize there was a house out this way until my uncle said the last renters just moved out and it's up for rent again."

She knew it well. For years Quill would saddle two horses, and they would explore every inch of Summer Grove, often beyond it. One time when the house was between renters, they were out this way, and Quill asked the painters if they could walk through the house. Her insides had knotted at the idea of asking for permission, but Quill assured her it'd be a mistake to miss the opportunity.

As adventurous as he was, he had a healthy fear when it came to keeping people safe. Maybe that particular point of concern was a gift from God so he would be very careful with those entrusted to him, but his personal sense of adventure seemed limitless. He'd texted her once since returning to his normal life and told her that while helping Gia and the children get acclimated, he'd taken a day off to go deep-sea fishing and had reeled in a five-foot barracuda.

"Hallo?" Rudy sounded annoyed.

What had he just said? "Ya, it is a long driveway."

"I like that. We'll have privacy galore. If we don't grab it, someone else will. I could go ahead and move into it, but I don't really see a reason to. I mean, a man on his own. What am I supposed to do? Go hungry?"

She chuckled. "I'm sure your aunt would have food waiting for you when you arrived at work."

"Ya, that solves that problem, but it doesn't fix the rest. No, I'm not one to live on my own. I like people around me."

The idea of living alone didn't sound so bad anymore, although her first weeks of sleeping in a room by herself at Brandi's house and then at Nicholas's place had been unsettling.

The house came into view, and Rudy stopped in front of it. "The property manager isn't here yet." He set the brake. "I'll rent it now, and it'll be ready and waiting when we marry."

Suddenly she understood. She saw what was happening as clearly as if it were a movie playing out in front of her. He wasn't only looking for a place to rent. He was looking for ways to shore up her commitment to him. Whether he was consciously aware of it or not, he was testing to see if he'd corralled her into the right cattle chute. Since she'd returned, she had felt as if he were using a cattle prod to move her in the direction he wanted. But it had started last fall before they knew she wasn't a Brenneman. He'd asked Ariana to marry him, and she hadn't responded as he'd hoped, which led to their first argument. So the issues between them right now weren't solely from her time away.

A desire to fight for them lunged forward, like a woman trying to snatch her child from oncoming traffic. But why was it so important that she marry him as soon as possible? She was twenty and he was twenty-one. What was the rush? Before she could gather her thoughts well enough to voice them, the sound of car tires on the gravel let them know the property manager was pulling up behind them.

Rudy got out of the rig, all smiles as he waved at the approaching vehicle.

She slid across the seat, getting out on the driver's side.

The car stopped and a man got out. He smiled and said his name was Stuart, and Rudy introduced Ariana to him.

Stuart went up the porch stairs and put a key in the lock. "On the phone you sounded pretty sure of wanting this place. How soon would you be able to move in?"

Rudy started up the stairs behind Stuart, but then he stopped, held out his hand, and waited for her. She slid her hand into his, and he winked, trying to assure her everything would be fine.

She wasn't convinced. Her stomach muscles were taut and trembling.

"Focus," Rudy whispered.

She nodded, knowing this should be exciting, but it felt out of place.

Rudy held the screen door open. "It could be a while before we move in. We're not married yet, but I'd be willing to pay rent between now and then."

"Yeah? But how long? An empty house doesn't fare as well as one that's lived in. It's sort of strange, but normal wear and tear on a house is necessary to keep the infrastructure sound."

"Six months."

They had to go through instruction and be baptized into the faith, so mid-September was the earliest they would be allowed to marry. But the bishop could easily refuse to let them marry. He would probably allow her to go through instruction classes and be baptized into the faith, perhaps to show her God's grace or maybe because if she joined, he'd have the power to shun her if she stepped out of line. But he could refuse to let them marry if he felt she wasn't lining up as he deemed fit.

"I'd have to talk to the owners about that. Neither of you wants to live here during that time?" Stuart walked past the foyer and into the open space.

Ariana tugged on Rudy's hand. "What if we can't marry that soon?"

"Of course we can." He sounded sure. "You just have to play nice, as I've said before." His eyes moved over her face. "Kumm on, Ari. For me. For us."

She pondered the idea. "I . . . I guess I could prepare a meal for the ministers, and we could talk to them together, trying to open understanding on both sides." But she wasn't fond of the idea. The ministers had been unfairly difficult. Still, she could be contrite toward them for . . . something. She felt as if she were digging in the dark, hoping to find some nugget that would satisfy Rudy.

"The bedrooms are pretty small." Stuart's voice echoed from somewhere inside.

Rudy peered down at her, looking pleased for the first time in weeks. It wasn't his fault everything about her had changed. But if she could change back for him, would she?

Stuart came back to the foyer. "Problem?"

"No." Rudy walked into the open space. "Just hammering out our quickest path to moving in here." He turned to her. "Right?"

Quill's voice from ten years ago echoed off the walls as he called her to move away from the front door and look around. *"It's okay, Ari. We were given permission. Now let's enjoy it."*

She'd followed him that day, trusting him despite her anxiety. But now she remained in place by the front door, looking around. "How soon would you need a deposit and the first month's rent?"

"If you want this to stay off the market, I'd need you to sign papers tonight and pay the money by tomorrow night."

She looked at Rudy, trying to convey it was too fast.

He strode through the one-story house, peeking into the bedroom without leaving the open area. "I'm ready to sign."

"I . . . I think we need a little time." Ariana chuckled, trying to soften the fact that she'd spoken against what he was saying to Stuart.

Rudy's face drained of emotion.

She tried to shrug, but her muscles seemed frozen in place. "Couldn't we sleep on it one night?"

Stuart nodded and went toward the front door. "I'll lock up, but you two are welcome to stay here for a bit. Enjoy that nice front porch, walk around the property, and talk things over."

The three of them stepped out of the house. Stuart locked the door and put the keys in his pocket. "Just give me a call when you know what you'd like to do. Maybe it'll still be on the market." He waved, and in no time he was leaving in his car.

"What just happened?" Rudy asked. "Tonight was supposed to be fun, and we should be floating on a cloud."

"You said you don't want to live here alone, so it makes no sense to sign a contract." She needed to be more honest than that, because it seemed as if she was blaming him. "My head is spinning. I . . . I'm not ready to sign a rental agreement. I'm not ready to commit to a home we don't need yet."

"But you were ready to go with Quill to rescue some stranger, ready to borrow money from Nicholas for the sake of the café, and you stand ready to resist the ministers at every turn. It's just too much for you to sign your name under mine on a rental agreement. Do I have that right, Ariana?"

His words were heavy, his sarcasm pointed, and she again struggled to breathe. He loved her, but he wanted to mold her. "It feels as if you're in a hurry to marry me, always have been, but I'm starting to wonder why. Is it because I'll take a vow to obey you?"

His eyes bore into her, distaste easily seen on his face. "I . . . I'm not even sure who you are anymore."

As she stood there studying him, the fog in her mind about what needed to happen began to clear. "Ya, I returned feeling the same way about myself, but I've discovered I'm still me, Rudy. My views of what's right and wrong have changed, but my desire to do good and to make a difference wherever I can hasn't." She didn't want to lose him, even if she had to lose a little of herself. But how much would he require?

"How long do you intend to keep up your peaceful, stubborn resistance against the ministers? Will you brand our children with that stubbornness too?"

He'd once been proud of who she was, but he was embarrassed by her now. He was holding on to the hope of her vow to obey him so he could insist she undo the damage to her reputation.

A dagger pierced her heart as she realized what was happening, what had been happening since the night she returned home from the Englisch world. How had she not seen it before today? Was she out of control, a fool destroying her future because she needed to think outside the Amish box?

"I'm sorry." Tears filled her eyes.

Rudy came close and put his hands on her arms. "Ariana." His tender voice tugged at her, and she again heard Quill asking how Rudy was handling all that was going on with her.

The answer broke her heart. Rudy was tired of it. He wanted the old Ariana back, the one he knew he could mold to his will after they were married. But that Ari was gone, and of all the people who bore fault in that, Rudy had none. She was dragging him places he didn't want to go, and she couldn't give him the one thing he wanted—the girl she used to be.

"You're right," she whispered, unable to speak any louder.

He'd been waiting for her to come back around to him, and excitement lit up his eyes. "Ya?"

"You didn't sign up for this," she whispered and drew a deep breath, hoping to speak loud enough to be heard. "But somewhere along the line, I did, and"—she prayed for the strength to say it—"*we* aren't going to work out. I'm sor—"

"Nee." He squeezed her shoulders, gently pulling her more upright. "I waited for you."

"I know."

"You love me."

"I absolutely do. But it's not enough." He was already tired, already growing resentful, and she'd just begun this journey. She wanted professors to speak at her café. She wanted to hire older teens and have open conversations about knowing themselves and not letting anyone corner them into something against their will simply because they're female. She wanted to expand her café because it suited her. She was twenty, and she wanted to live free of the constraints he wanted to put on her.

He released her. "You promised me! I asked you months ago if I was waiting for nothing, and you promised, Ariana."

"I'm sorry. I thought . . . I believed—"

"Stop." His fist came within inches of her as he slammed it into the column of the porch, and the building shook.

She flinched and took a few steps back. His eyes, face, and body gave off differing emotions—raw, unfiltered hurt; uncontrollable anger; and humiliation. It was beyond what he could cope with.

He cradled his injured hand, flinching in pain, and she wondered if he'd broken it. "Just get in the rig, Ariana."

"Rudy, I—"

He pointed at the rig. "Don't say another word to me. Just get in the rig!"

Thirty-Four

Quill eased his car off the main road and onto the hidden path on his Mamm's property. The police would consider his presence legitimate, but he doubted that would keep the ministers off his Mamm's back if his car was parked in the open in broad daylight.

This afternoon would be hard on his Mamm. She lost so much when Daed died, and recalling all the pieces that were woven into the stress during that time would be tough. Quill wasn't here just to answer questions. He'd come to support his Mamm on behalf of all five sons.

He got out of his car, opened the double-wide shed doors, pulled in, turned off the car, and closed the doors from the inside. He grabbed two brown bags from the car and then went out the small side door of the shed and followed the trail that kept him mostly hidden as he made his way to the house.

He knew this path well. Two hundred steps to the end of the bramble and woods. Ten steps of open space before he was behind the long barn. At the end of the barn, he took another hundred steps until he was behind the cooperage. Once he was on the far side of that building, the back of the house hid him from view as he crossed the yard, climbed over the back of the wraparound porch, and tapped on his bedroom window before opening it and climbing inside.

Good thing his Mamm wasn't jumpy. It didn't bother her to live alone, although she would be happier if Ariana moved in. But year in and year out, Mamm tended her laying hens, gardened, sewed, and turned a nice profit from each task. Like him, her energy and sense of balance were restored through solitude.

"Quill?" Mamm opened the bedroom door. "I thought you'd come through the front door this time."

"I considered it." He set the bags on his bed.

"You're still watching out for me." She smiled and wrapped her arms around him. Her head came to the middle of his chest. Funny how tall and strong she'd felt to him when he was a kid, and now she seemed small and vulnerable.

"My brothers and I feel we've caused you enough trouble to last a lifetime. It's not a problem to be careful even today."

When she released him, he picked up the bags. "Food." He grinned, and they went down the hall to the kitchen. "I'll make dinner for us. Grilled pork chops, roasted potatoes, salad, and garlic bread." He set the bags on the table and noticed her kitchen was messy and her hair wasn't pinned up properly. Neither of those things were like her. "How are you holding up?"

"What do you think they want?"

He pulled the items out of one bag and set them on the counter. "All I know is what Ariana texted. The original report Daed filed about Frieda was lost when the agency went to a new computer system. The police were alerted to that recently, and a detective is following up. I know less than nothing when it comes to police matters, so anything I could tell you would be speculation. But he'll ask some questions, and we'll answer."

"How do you think they were alerted to it?"

"I'm wondering the same thing." He began emptying the second bag.

"Maybe they want to know why no one followed up after filing the complaint. Is that our responsibility?"

"I don't think so."

"Your Daed died and we . . . coped."

"It'll be fine, Mamm." At least he thought it would. Only time would tell for sure. He pulled two jigsaw puzzles out of the bag and shook them.

"Monet. Your favorite. I've got *Garden at Giverny* and *A Pathway in Monet's Garden.* A thousand pieces each." He held them out. "Which one will you open first?" Whichever one she chose, they would just start it today. She would only work on it with one of her sons or Ariana. It could be a month or even several months before it was completed, but when it was done, she'd frame it and hang it in the attic as a visual reminder of the time she had with her family.

She took them and looked at the pictures. "This one."

"Exactly the one I thought you'd choose. I expect it to be done by tomorrow morning."

She tapped the box against his shoulder. "You're funny." She removed a knife from the block and opened the box.

He put the potatoes in the sink and turned on the water. "Frieda hopes she doesn't need to answer anything tonight, but she's keeping her phone close in case I call her."

"Good idea." She dumped out the pieces and spread them across the table.

"What about Ariana? Big plans on a Saturday afternoon? Or do you think she'll drop by?"

Mamm began turning all the pieces face up. "She came by this morning. Seemed a bit out of sorts."

He turned off the water. "Is she under the weather or under stress?"

"She didn't say. Acted fine. Smiled. Talked normally. Maybe she had a headache."

"You say that as if she's prone to headaches. She never has been. Has she been having them since that tree fell and she was hit with some limbs?"

"Not that I know of."

Mamm was being vague. He wanted to text Ariana, but he wouldn't. They hadn't shared a text in nearly a month—until she asked for the Millers' address. And he doubted she would check on his Mamm about the detective's visit until Quill was gone. It's the way things were, the way they would be from here on out. No texting. No talking. No accidentally bumping into each other at Mamm's.

He prepared dinner, and they chatted about nothing until the meal was over. When Mamm rose to clean up, he decided to text Nicholas to see how he was. It'd been very helpful for Nicholas to turn in the rental and take Ariana home. Quill hadn't texted him since the night Ariana arrived at Nicholas's.

Nicholas immediately responded.

> Good. Still driving a rental. Looking at new cars, but the check from the insurance company hasn't arrived yet. How's Ariana feeling? You're back now, right? Make sure she takes it easy. Concussions aren't to be messed with.

Quill looked at his Mamm. "Ariana has a concussion?"

Mamm paused. "She didn't want you to know about that."

He held up his phone. "But now I do. Apparently she and Nicholas were in a wreck."

"Ya, on the highway not more than ten miles from home."

His heart ached for what this meant. "So everyone in the community knows she was with Nicholas?"

"They do now. No one saw them together, but things happened in a way that caused the ministers to ask questions."

"What else do the ministers know?"

"They don't know she was with you. The only people who know are the ones she told—her parents and Rudy."

"That'll help some. On a scale of one to ten, how bad has the backlash been?"

"Isaac has had a change of heart, and he is standing between her and the ministers. Last I heard he's trying to mediate and find peace without giving in to them or coming down on Ariana."

"That may be the most surprising thing I hear today. Hasn't he heeded everything the ministers have wanted his whole life?"

"Every single thing, his whole life. But something odd happened to him that Sunday. He and Lovina were restless during the service. I could see it on their faces. Then he walked out of the Sunday meeting and was out of sight. Not too much time passed before Lovina left too. Then, maybe ten or fifteen minutes later, I saw him running down the road while we were singing the last hymn, with Lovina lagging behind. They went out of sight for a bit. Next I saw, he and Lovina had Ariana with them, and they got in their rig and left, didn't come back in or have the meal. No one saw any more than the back of Ariana, so I didn't know her face was bruised until the next day."

This was great news. Her Daed being on her side would mean so much to Ariana. She'd be encouraged and strengthened in every way. "And she wanted to keep the accident from me?"

"If the tables were turned, you would've wanted the same."

"I don't disagree." He didn't like that it'd happened, but Ari had spared him being worried, and he appreciated that. Getting Gia and the children settled had taken almost two weeks, and he'd been working overtime since flying back home.

"You're calmer about this than I would've expected."

"I agree. It just feels as if Ariana was where she needed to be, doing what she needed to do in helping with Gia, and I can't try to protect her from that. But maybe you or she could tell me when things happen. Not knowing kept me from worrying this time, but now I'll wonder what all is going on that I'm not being told about."

"You and I have zero leverage for the rest of our lives to lecture her about keeping secrets to protect someone and zero right to insist she tell us if she doesn't want to."

"But she's fully okay?"

"Nicholas had her checked at a hospital, so, ya. And she's healing quickly."

"Then I'm sure she's fine."

While he washed dishes, Mamm got a shower and fixed her hair. Then they settled in front of the puzzle and began piecing the frame together.

"Knock, knock, knock," Ari called out.

She'd come, and Quill was glad, regardless of how Rudy would feel about it.

Mamm moved to the front door and unlocked it.

Ariana stepped in. "A new recipe for fudge and an old one for chocolate croissants."

Quill's heart palpitated, and two things hit immediately. He was lying to himself that he could be cool with the fact that she'd been in a wreck. It would nag at him for a very long time. And Ariana's presence felt heavy, a kind of dark weight he hadn't sensed in years. She hugged Mamm.

She glanced his way and held up the plate. "Knowing you'd be here was the perfect time to try a new recipe. Unlike Mikey, whoever he is, you'll eat anything I make."

"You trained me. It was my only way to keep you from tattling to Mamm that I was mean to you," he teased.

"Ya, ya, ya." She plunked the plate on the puzzle pieces in front of him.

"Do I have to?" he asked.

"Nee." She swooped up the plate.

"Wait." He stood. "It was just a question." He held out his hand. "I'll take that."

She gave it to him, but he shifted to catch a glimpse of her eyes. Immediately she turned, removing her satchel and peeling out of her coat.

She had waltzed in talking and acting as if everything was normal, but Mamm was right. Something was off.

Quill picked up a puzzle piece.

Ariana pulled something out of the satchel. "I brought decaf. Should I make a pot?"

"Please." Mamm tugged at her apron. "I'm not sure the apron I put on was a clean one. I'll be back."

Was Mamm giving them a minute to talk? Ariana went to the kitchen counter.

Quill ate a small piece of fudge and leaned against the counter beside her, facing out as she faced in. There were yellow patches on her face where the bruises were healing. "You're healing well."

She nodded. "I am."

"No surprise that I know?"

"It was bound to happen. Have I ever managed to keep a secret from you?"

"I'm not sure I'd know the answer to that."

She prepared the percolator, set it on the stove, and turned on the eye before returning to wipe coffee grounds off the counter.

"No chuckle at my humor?"

She laughed, and he was surprised how real it sounded when it clearly wasn't.

"You okay?" he asked.

"Sure. Absolutely." She looked up, a smile in place. "How are you?"

"Is this how it goes?"

Her forced smile melted, and she came within a few inches of him. "Ya, it is." Underneath her effort to signal she was fine, he saw raw pain. "Please," she whispered.

And just like that, his heart ached for no other reason than hers did. "Sure." He returned to the puzzle table and sat down. "Mamm,"—he raised his voice—"you have a few pieces still left to put in this puzzle."

"Ya, about nine hundred and ninety-five," Mamm called back. "Be there in a minute."

Ariana eased into a chair across from him and began searching for pieces. It was all he could do to keep himself from asking the reason for her sadness and how he could help.

Something moving outside caught his eye through the kitchen window, and he expected it to be the detective, but it was a horse and carriage.

"Rudy's here." Quill searched her face for concern, but instead he saw sadness etched across her beautiful face.

Thirty-Five

Ariana rose and grabbed her coat from the closet. Rudy was getting out of his carriage when she came out the front door. His shoulders were slumped, and he had a cast on his right hand.

He looked like she felt—broken.

They had been so in love that they dreamed of uniting in a lifelong bond, of being each other's world for the rest of their lives. They'd wanted to have children together. And now . . .

What had happened? Whatever took place yesterday evening at the Steele place wasn't what broke them. He wanted peace to reign in his home through obedience to the Old Ways, and she wanted freedom according to Galatians: "It is for freedom that Christ has set us free. Stand firm, then, and do not let yourselves be burdened again by a yoke of slavery." Somehow for them in this Old Order time and place, those two needs were opposed to each other, and they could not pursue both simultaneously.

She stood in front of him, but he could hardly look at her. "Ariana," he whispered. His eyes filled with tears, and he removed his hat.

"How's your hand?"

He lifted his arm, staring at it. "As it should be, useless and hurting." He lowered it. "I'm going home, Ari. Probably Monday. There's nothing left for me here, and I . . . I need to think." His eyes filled with tears. "I'm so sorry."

She touched his soft reddish-brown curls one last time. "I know."

The front door slammed, and Ariana turned. Berta was coming down the steps, apparently heading for the mailbox. She seemed to notice them for the first time. "Rudy?" Berta called. "Hi. We've got desserts and coffee inside."

Rudy seemed perplexed. "Denki,"—he put on his hat—"but I just have a minute."

She pointed at his arm. "You're in a cast."

"It's hard to miss, isn't it?" Ariana hoped Berta would drop it.

"Ya." Berta grabbed the mail and hurried back to the house.

Rudy thumped his cast. "Clearly she doesn't know yet."

"I've told no one. But considering what the community thinks of me, I'm pretty confident everyone has been expecting a breakup."

"Only because they don't know what we have or who we are to each other."

That was sweet, and memories of their good times flooded her, and she knew they would for a long time to come. "What did you tell your aunt and uncle?"

"You know me. I made a joke. I said I fell down and stepped on it. They think I slipped on an icy patch."

She nodded.

"I'm just putting off the inevitable. I have to tell them the truth."

"You need to tell someone you can trust, someone who can help you get perspective on what happens to you when you're angry and why. But you don't have to tell your aunt and uncle. She loves you, but she talks a lot, and there's no need for the whole town, Amish and Englisch, to know. Not here or in Indiana."

"I've had a temper since I was twelve. It doesn't show up often, but when it does . . ."

"Will you find someone who can help you? You can get a hold on this. You are a good man. Don't doubt it."

He stared at her. "That's very kind."

"And true. Will you?"

"Ya."

"If we had remained together, we would've had to address the anger outbursts, but, Rudy, that's not what ended us. I'm no longer the right woman for you, and that means you're not the right man for me."

"What you're proposing—having historians come to the café—will mean constant displeasure and disapproval from the ministers. Maybe decades of it. I'm not cut out for that."

"I know. It's okay. We had no idea where life would take us when we fell in love."

"You did love me, then?"

"I do love you."

He inhaled sharply and nodded. "Me too." He started to touch her cheek. "May I?"

She nodded.

He caressed her face. "You're a treasure, Ariana Brenneman." He smiled. "I don't care what the others are saying."

She laughed. It was an old joke, something he'd said to her before their first date. She hugged him. "Bye, Rudy."

He held her for a long moment and then strode to his rig without another glance her way.

Thirty-Six

Quill sat on the floor of the attic, looking through his Daed's old journals. The detective was late, and Ariana was steeped in grief. Quill needed a distraction. It'd been a while since he'd read through these. Maybe they held some information he'd forgotten about or not realized could be important. Mamm had some by her bedside, but those were personal notes between his parents. Daed wrote to her in those, and she responded, and Quill had never read them.

Ten journals were stacked on the floor near him, but only two mentioned anything about Frieda. Most of them had the date, weather, orders to fill for the cooperage, and a few thoughts that'd been on his Daed's mind that day.

Missing his Daed washed over him. If only he hadn't died . . .

Like all those who'd lost a young parent, Quill had a list of life-changing situations that would have been better if his Daed had lived. Maybe he would've stayed Amish. Maybe not. But whatever the case, Quill would have felt the support of his Daed, and they could have talked.

"Quill," Mamm called, "the detective is here."

"Coming." Quill picked up the journals and stood. The small attic window was more than ample to spot a young woman leaning against the far side of the barn, a view that couldn't have been seen downstairs. Rudy was gone. Ariana was in an out-of-the-way place, looking heavenward.

"Quill?" Mamm called again.

He went down the stairs.

A broad-shouldered man a few inches shorter than Quill was sitting at the kitchen table, his laptop open and a field notebook beside him. He stood. "Detective Torres."

"Quill Schlabach." He shook the man's hand.

They made small talk while Mamm poured three cups of coffee and set them on the table along with the cream and sugar and the baked goods Ariana had brought.

Detective Torres put a little sugar in his coffee. "I have most of the information now from the original complaint. The file was corrupted and sitting in an odd folder. Most of it was restored but not all. I need to ask some questions I already know the answer to, but I have to verify your answers with what's in the file, and then we'll go from there. First, what relation was Eli Schlabach to each of you?"

The man asked his simple questions and moved to harder ones, and Quill sensed he would arrive at an intelligent conclusion. In some ways it was a relief that he was acknowledging the realness of what they'd been through. But as the man talked, Quill grappled to accept that he'd had more choices than it seemed at the time. What did a twenty-year-old know about such matters? Besides, one thing would not have changed: Frieda had to get away from everyone who knew her and start fresh. No amount of police intervention would've altered that.

Twenty minutes had passed by the time Ariana opened the door. She eased into a chair at the table. "Sorry," she whispered.

"Not a problem," Detective Torres said.

Ariana left her coat on and crossed her arms tightly as if she were cold. It was a sure sign of her repressing emotions and feeling stressed. Her capacity to feel so deeply was hard on her, probably a trait she'd give up if it were within her power. But if he knew anything about the amazing young woman sitting across from him, it was that she was resilient.

The detective's phone rang, and he pulled it out of its holder on his belt and turned it off. "This is just an informal Q and A, and I appreciate you folks' time. So let me see if I understand this correctly. Frieda lived in Ohio when you and your husband began to realize something was wrong."

"Ya. Frieda's Mamm, Thelma, is my cousin, and we were good friends. For about a year she constantly talked about how sick Frieda was and how odd her symptoms were. She said that John, her husband, wanted to trust God." Without pausing in her dialogue, Mamm rose, poured another cup of coffee, and set it in front of Ariana. "We went to visit them, and over the course of a week, Eli managed to talk John into letting Frieda be seen by a specialist who was known for dealing with unique medical symptoms. Eli went with them to the initial visit, and the doctor arranged for Frieda to go to a lab to have blood drawn the next day. The doctor was positive they could uncover the issue and get her some relief. But he said it would take weeks to get the results, and we had to return home."

"What did the test results show?"

"Nothing. But Frieda was getting worse, and John kept saying she just needed prayer. Eli was concerned that John was being flippant, so he returned to Ohio a few weeks later. He sweet-talked and cajoled until John agreed that Frieda could be seen again. The three of them returned to the doctor's office. The doctor looked through her charts, did a quick physical, and suggested Frieda see a mental health specialist."

"He thought the symptoms were psychosomatic?" the detective asked.

"Ya, and John agreed with the doctor. But Eli pushed back, asking for more blood work to be done. John said he was being ridiculous and left with Frieda."

"You stayed here while your husband went for the second visit, right? So everything you're telling me is what your husband told you?"

"He told me, but so did Thelma. John wanted to accept the prognosis and drop the matter. Eli didn't, but he had no parental rights. The long and short of it is Eli pestered them, calling and visiting until John agreed to take Frieda to a different specialist. The new doctor ordered a CT scan and said it revealed a possibly enlarged liver. The doctor wanted to do more blood work, this time looking for the possibility that Frieda had been exposed to a poison. And that testing would take two to three weeks. Eli said the moment the doctor mentioned *poison,* the look on John's face changed, and Eli had a gut feeling he needed to get Frieda away from there. It took him a few days, but he talked John and Thelma into letting her come here, saying they needed a break from caring for her. Eli was persuasive when he needed to be."

Mamm looked at Quill, her expression one of sadness seemingly mixed with pride. "Of all the boys, you're the most like your Daed. He was intuitive, persuasive, and solid as the Rock of Gibraltar."

Quill reached over, gripped her hand, and winked. "Can I take the good parts and give back the rest?"

Mamm grinned, shaking her head. "I wouldn't have changed one thing about your Daed, not one."

Ariana nodded. "I wouldn't have changed anything about Eli either." She looked at Quill. "You, my friend, are an entirely different matter."

Mamm laughed, which he imagined was Ariana's goal. He chuckled.

Detective Torres smiled, seeming to enjoy the break in the seriousness. "So Eli brought Frieda here."

"Ya. Getting her out of that house seemed to help a lot. She and Ariana became fast friends. That helped Frieda too. I made sure she ate well and got plenty of rest. We took her to see our local doctor, and he gave her some medication for her nerves while we waited on the blood work to come back in Ohio. But she wasn't here long before her ministers contacted ours, saying she needed to return home. That's when the real battle began. Eli had no proof of what was taking place, and she was only thirteen or fourteen at the time. It was a tug-of-war, and the ministers in both districts were furious with Eli, saying he'd overstepped his bounds. For all we knew, he had. But Frieda was feeling a little better physically and doing much better emotionally, and she didn't want to go home. Eli stood his ground against her parents and the ministers of both districts."

"But the test results eventually came in, right?"

"John said they did. Thelma said she never saw them. Either way, Eli had no rights to see them."

"But if the doctor saw she had poison in her system, he should've intervened."

"Maybe he tried. Eli called the doctor's office. They couldn't tell him anything, but they asked him some interesting questions. They had the wrong address for John, and John is the one who filled out the papers. The test results never arrived at Frieda's house, and since John didn't have insurance and there are a lot of John Millers, the doctor's office had no way of getting the right address until Eli called. By the time Eli hung up, he knew they'd found poison in Frieda's system, although they never said so directly."

"Did your husband ever get his hands on the test results?"

"He did, but I'm not sure how."

"Do you have those results?"

"Ya."

"Could I have them? It is a piece of evidence that corroborates your story."

"I'll get the report." Mamm rose.

"May I use your bathroom?"

"Ya. Down the hall, on your right."

Mamm and the detective disappeared down the hallway, and Ariana seemed lost in her thoughts. Quill had come early, hoping to help his Mamm navigate today, but clearly he would need to talk to someone about all this, maybe a brother or a counselor. His heart beat mercilessly as old wounds opened. But how was Ariana holding up? He dumped a little sugar and cream into her untouched cup of coffee and stirred it.

She didn't look up, but she grasped the cup. "I . . . I thought she had some rare illness and the ministers stood in the way of getting her help. I didn't know her Daed had poisoned her," she mumbled. "What father would do that to his own child!"

"It's called 'Munchausen syndrome by proxy' or medical child abuse. It's a disorder where the caregiver either makes up fake symptoms or causes real symptoms so the child appears truly ill."

Ari's face revealed how distressed she felt. "Her Daed deliberately caused her sickness? For what, to get sympathy or to be mean?"

"He's sick, Ari, or maybe just plain evil. Either way, she's free of him."

"Ya, I . . . I never imagined someone had injured her on purpose."

"Whatever we thought, whatever we've gone through, we've weathered the worst of it, all of us," he whispered.

She nodded. "And yet this will do nothing to change the battle that needs to be fought—to change the deeply ingrained beliefs of total submission to the head of the household and total submission to the ministers or go to hell. It will take a lifetime to begin changing minds and hearts about those things, but I'd like to be a part of bringing that change about, starting with the women."

"If that's where you want to put your energy, I have no doubts you'll accomplish a lot. You can draw women to you and open their eyes."

Ariana didn't respond, and as she brought the coffee to her lips, he wondered if she'd even heard him.

The detective came back and sat down. A minute later Mamm returned, carrying a manila envelope.

The detective opened the envelope and pulled out the report. "So Eli had the results, but how did he know it was John who gave her the poison?"

"He didn't have any evidence, that's for sure," Mamm said. "But he felt confident it was John, so he went to Frieda's ministers with the test results and asked them to take the matter to the police. But John had already convinced the ministers that Frieda was troubled and had taken the poison herself. So Eli went to our ministers here in Summer Grove, but they'd been fed the same story."

"So his hands were tied as far as anyone listening to him?"

"With Frieda safe here, Eli gave the ministers a little time to see what needed to be seen. John said something to the bishop, whether by way of confiding in a man of God or by a slip of the tongue I don't know. But soon after that, the ministers said he was guilty. Still, they didn't want outsiders involved. They wanted to discipline him through shunning and to get help for him through the Amish counseling one another. They also wanted Frieda to forgive him and return home to live under her Daed's roof again. Pressure kept escalating against Eli to send Frieda home, and it was clear the bishops weren't going to budge, so my husband went to the police."

Quill cleared his throat. "The Old Ways say all matters should be taken care of within the community. The Amish aim to be God sufficient and self-sufficient in everything. It's considered a serious betrayal to step outside of the ordinances and go to the world for answers. So Daed's hope of getting the bishops to agree before he went to the police would've benefited the community at large. It would have helped usher in some of the reform he wanted."

Mamm wiped a tear. "He kept trying to find ways to make it all work, to bring unity and reform and to keep us from being shunned."

"And where do you think John Miller is now?"

"Gone." Mamm raised her hands outward. "Fled the moment he caught wind of Eli going to the police."

"How did he hear of it?"

"I don't know for sure, but one of Frieda's sisters called me and said their bishop told John, and he gathered his belongings and disappeared."

"It sounds as if someone was keeping an eye on Mr. Schlabach, and when he went to the police station, that person notified someone in Ohio, maybe the bishop."

"No one would've done that without the bishop directing it. He didn't start out a difficult man. But over the years he has become convinced that he knows when people are telling the truth or lying. He believes God has given him the ability to judge a man's heart." Mamm reached over and grasped Quill's hand.

"Our world was torn apart when my husband died, and for a while I tried to keep as much as possible from Quill, but Frieda's anxiety was out of control. Serious anxiety issues are common if poison has been ingested. I know that, but I don't know if it's psychological because a parent has broken all trust or a physical reaction to the damage the poison did or both. But she was terrified the ministers would make her go back home, and she wasn't holding up well under the stress of the ministers coming by here, trying to talk her into leaving." Mamm squeezed Quill's hand. "Quill took her away one night, telling no one where they were going or why. If no one could find them, no one could pressure her to do as they thought best. Quill got her to a hospital where she could be treated for anxiety and illness."

The detective pointed his pen at Quill. "How old are you?"

"Twenty-five."

"So you snuck away to do what none of the men in this community would do."

"When people don't know what to believe, they often do nothing." Quill had seen it happen firsthand. It was human nature. "Everyone was told lies about Frieda's illness. They said she was looking for attention and using Daed as her shield so she could disobey her father. Our community stopped trying to sort out the truth from the lies. They focused on what they did have power over—tending to their families—and they put their trust in the leaders to administer justice."

"Talking about this makes the Amish sound awful, and we're not," Berta said. "A horrid situation arose, and a few men in power let their need to control the situation block out everything else."

"And absolute power corrupts absolutely." The detective tapped the envelope with Frieda's test results on the kitchen table. "I'll need the name and address of each minister."

"What happens now?" Ariana asked.

"A few more interviews. A detective will interview Mrs. Miller, Frieda, and the siblings. If there's enough evidence, they will issue an arrest warrant for John Miller. If it is as Quill was telling me before you came in—if there's not a picture of John Miller anywhere, no vehicle registration, credit cards, and such—we aren't likely to find him. So the arrest warrant would be just a formality. But we don't need evidence on who gave Frieda Miller the poison to deal with those who were involved in obstruction of justice. The test results prove she was poisoned, and obstruction of justice is a very serious charge. But everything is hazy and convoluted at this point. If Frieda had died, the two bishops—hers and yours—and perhaps the other ministers would be facing involuntary manslaughter charges."

"The bishop still believes we were in rebellion by not yielding to his authority," Berta said.

"Your bishop is free to judge people on spiritual matters, but crimes *must* be reported."

"Could he say that since Eli reported it, he's in the clear?" Ariana asked.

"Sure. He can *say* anything, but evidence and eyewitnesses may say otherwise. According to my notes, the ministers came to this house and tried to get Frieda to return home after they had proof she'd been poisoned. If she was clear that she hadn't taken poison for attention, it was their responsibility to go to the police. Instead, after Mr. Schlabach passed, they pressured her to behave as if nothing had happened to her." The detective focused on Ariana. "I notice you have bruises. How did you get them?"

"I was in a car accident a few weeks ago."

He nodded. "To your knowledge, have any other crimes been committed against any Amish you know?"

"No." Ariana shook her head. "I have nine siblings, four are married, and none have mentioned witnessing or hearing of any abuse. They would've talked about it if they knew of it. But you can ask them directly." She fidgeted with the cup. "I recently spent a few months living outside the Amish community, and until then I didn't understand the concept of adult bullying. Amish women are so fully taught to submit that we believe surrendering to male authority is the answer to everything. In this community a minister or father isn't bullying us. He's exercising his God-given rights." She looked at Quill. "It wasn't until you helped me navigate the issues I was having with Nicholas that I began to see bullying for what it really is."

"Nicholas had no idea he was bullying you. To his credit, once he was called on it, he saw it for what it was and changed."

"He did." Ariana nodded. "Became a likable man. But it's harder to discern bullying when your whole life you've been submersed in the teachings of a few men who all agree about God's will. I used to look into the bishop's eyes and believe the same thing he did—that he was acting out of love because he felt God had given him the responsibility of saving our souls from sin." She shook her head, eyes on the table. "As I see this bullying issue more clearly, this misuse of influence over the flock through the position of leadership, I feel really stupid."

Mamm closed her eyes, tears running down her face. "Me too."

"You shouldn't," the detective said. "Bullies are sneaky and manipulative. Often they're passive-aggressive, acting like a friend, winning people's trust, and then using that power against their victim. Pennsylvania has antibullying laws."

"There are laws against bullying?" Mamm asked.

"Absolutely. The issue runs deep in our society as a whole, and the statistics are staggering. Control is the key thing bullies want, and their main way of getting that control is through fear. Fear of being humiliated publicly and fear of being physically hurt are two of the main ways."

"Or fear of going to hell," Ariana said. "That's what has been held over our heads for far too long." She sighed.

"Look, I think I can help you," the detective said. "An investigation itself usually shifts the balance of power and brings bullies in line while opening people's eyes to recognize controlling behavior. And I shouldn't ask this, but off the record, if you had one thing you'd like to see come out of this meeting today, what would it be?"

Ariana sat up. "For Berta to be allowed to see her sons, daughters-in-law, and grandchildren without negative consequences from the community. And for Frieda to know that people believe her and that the Amish recognize she was done wrong, very wrong."

Quill nodded. "That would be really nice. The ministers have been particularly hard on this family. My four brothers and I didn't join the church, so we couldn't be officially shunned, which should've meant, according to the Old Ways, that we could visit Mamm at will as long as she was okay with it."

"Off the record, I'll see what I can do to make that a part of the outcome." The detective closed his laptop and set his notebook on top of it. "I could be wrong, but personally I believe that by the time I'm finished with the interviews and town hall–type meetings to inform people how badly this situation was handled—without revealing any names, of course—and how many charges could have been brought against those ministers if Frieda had died, I think you could have the red carpet rolled out for you when you visit."

Mamm burst into tears. "It sounds as if I could see my grandchildren without fear of being shunned. Without disobeying my spiritual head."

"It does, Mamm. I agree." Quill hoped the detective was right.

Thirty-Seven

Ariana remained in her chair, still wearing her coat as if the house were cold. But it was her heart that felt the cold winds of fresh loss. Berta grabbed her coat and walked out with the detective. Maybe she had a few questions she didn't want to ask in front of Ariana or Quill. Exhaustion pounded her, and she longed to get into her rig. She would eventually go home and crawl into bed, but right now she wanted to go for a long walk and cry.

Her grief over losing Rudy weighed on her, but how could she leave right now? Berta had a lot to process too. Maybe she'd finally be able to see her family freely and in the open. Ariana hoped that was true.

Quill fiddled with the lid on the sugar bowl. "I didn't think to ask the detective how he knew the case file had been lost."

"Daed called the police station to inquire." Ariana picked up the mugs and took them to the sink. "He said he's had enough believing what he's told and it's time to seek truth outside of what the bishop has to say. I guess it's a new day in Summer Grove."

"This could make a lot of difference for you."

Ariana left the mugs in the sink. "Do you think it will?" She turned.

"When it comes to light how wrong the bishop has been, how spiteful and manipulative, people will see his stance against you as hypocrisy or mental illness. Either way, I think they'll let go of their views on your so-called rebellion."

"Ya. I guess so."

"Frieda is talking more and more often about wanting to come back.

People who've been through what she has have a lot of anxiety, maybe from the whole ordeal, but I think the poison wrecks the system. If things go as the detective expects, it will help her a lot . . . eventually. And maybe she'll be able to push through and return to Summer Grove for occasional visits."

"You tell her I would love to see her anytime, and if she's ever interested in a job, she can have one in the café with as many or as few hours as she'd like. Or if she wants to start that cake and cupcake business she used to talk about, I'll carry them in my café and help her find other places to sell them, like nonfranchised restaurants."

"These last few weeks have been particularly hard on you and Rudy. But this news is going to make a huge difference and fairly fast. Probably within the next few weeks, attitudes in the community will begin to shift."

Ariana slunk into a chair, her body too heavy for her to stay on her feet. "Rudy is going home to live." She couldn't look up from the table for fear she'd break into tears, but she could feel Quill's eyes on her.

"You two have weathered so much. The storm is all but over."

"It's not about that."

Berta walked back inside. "You two look glum, and yet we were given very hopeful news. The detective believes I'll soon be able to see my sons, daughters-in-law, and grandchildren without it causing any trouble. That's amazing." She snapped her fingers. "So explain all this glumness."

Since Ariana was the reason for the sadness, she needed to be the one to respond. "I am very happy for you, Berta. My joy runs deep for the justice that will unfold."

"And yet you sound very sad, so what gives?"

"I'll try to sound better and look less sad." She wasn't going to walk around with her hurt shining for all to see, but it was just too new to hide right now. "Rudy and I are no longer together."

"But he was just here a couple of hours ago."

"He was here to say good-bye."

"I knew you two didn't look happy." Berta's eyes narrowed. "When I saw the cast on his hand, I thought maybe that was the cause. Now, looking back on the strain I saw between you, I'm wondering *how* he hurt his hand."

"He broke it." Ariana stood. "Let's change the subject. I'm really very glad for your good news." She hugged Berta. "It's like we've finally received the miracle we've been praying for all these years."

Berta gently released Ariana and clutched her hands. "Honey, is there something you need to tell us about Rudy?"

"Nee." Ariana moved to the cabinet and got a glass. "Would either of you like some water?"

"My question seems fair, Ari," Berta said.

"But it's not." Ariana filled the glass from the faucet.

Berta clicked her tongue. "Maybe I should talk to his aunt about this."

"Berta," Ariana snapped, "stop." She couldn't let Berta slip off to see Rudy's aunt. "Look, Rudy and I somehow found each other, and the relationship worked." She took a drink, trying to settle her nerves and shore up her strength. "Months later, when he learned things about me that I could hardly tolerate, he never batted an eye. Didn't care that my parents were Englisch or that I'm the result of an affair."

Berta's expression intensified, and she glanced at Quill. Clearly she hadn't known that about Ariana. Very few did. Ariana wasn't sure her Mamm and Daed knew.

She would regret saying these things. She knew she would. But she couldn't stop. "He loved me, not the face or the figure or the hype of me being a twin who survived the fire at the clinic the night I was born or any esteem I had in the community. When I went from a position of respect to one of disdain in this community, he took it in stride." She picked up her coat. "I was in the world with you"—she gestured at Quill—"and he remained patient, trusting, and faithful. I wouldn't have been that person to him if he'd been out there with some female equivalent of who you are to me." She went to the door. "But all of that aside, what really irks me, Berta, is that you're making me defend him. I should be free to rail and complain if I want to, but I should not have to defend him." She reached to open the door.

Berta moved in, flattening her back against the door and facing her. "You're right. We got hopeful news tonight, but I'm furious with myself, with this whole Frieda scenario. I'm angry that I never once got in the bishop's face about it. After Quill got Frieda out and she felt safe, I should've gone to the police and checked on the complaint Eli filed. But I accepted what the bishop dished out as God's lot for me, for this family. So just then the thought of any man being out of line with you angered me."

Berta had targeted what was going on. Each of them was feeling guilty and angry for the blind spots and weaknesses that had allowed the ministers to do them and others so very wrong. Berta and Ariana were openly airing their emotions, and Quill was keeping his under wraps, but the negative energy in the room had a grip on all of them.

Ariana drew a deep breath. "Conversations about Rudy are off-limits."

"Ya." Berta nodded. "I'll say nothing to no one, including you."

"Gut." Ariana drew another deep breath, refusing to cry.

Berta embraced her. "We've been through harsh times before, you and me."

"I'm so very ready to heal and have fun again." Ariana released her. "It seems as if it's been forever since times were light and airy and my heart sang like birds in spring."

Berta cupped her chin. "But it will happen. I promise."

Ariana nodded. "Ya, it will."

"I need to ride for a bit." Berta grabbed her coat. "To get in a rig by myself and think and cry and sing and rail in bitterness at all I've handled wrong. Do you mind?"

Quill shook his head. "I don't mind. I think it's a good idea. I run to get things in perspective, Ariana takes long walks, and you ride in a carriage."

Berta looked to Ariana.

"Nee. I don't mind. Go. I'm leaving in a bit too."

"This revelation about the ministers is tempting me to refuse to attend church for a while, at least until they are openly remorseful or removed."

"You and I feel the same, Berta, but we should go anyway. Our faith is stronger than any lies or any mistreatment by man. In the coming weeks, when the investigation is complete and others learn how wrong the ministers have been, they'll be hurt and confused and laden with guilt for their complacency and loyalty to the bishop's leadership. I think they'll need to see that we were not and are not broken or bitter."

Berta nodded, sighing. "You're right." She left, and the house had never seemed so quiet. Ariana should go, but she wasn't ready, and the dishes in the sink were calling to her. She removed her coat and turned on the hot water.

"You're good and kind to Mamm." Quill set another mug in the sink and then leaned back against the counter and looked at her.

"It's easy to understand women, Berta in particular, and to know what to say." Ariana squirted dish detergent under the running faucet. "It's men I'm weary of." Her words reverberated inside her, and she put a wet, sudsy hand on Quill's shirt collar, turning that spot from light to dark blue. "That was rude. Not you. The more I understand, the more I'm glad you're a friend. And Daed's had a change of heart. I . . . I'm just wrung out right now."

"This thing with Rudy will take a long time, but many other parts of your life will get easier soon."

Tears welled from deep within. "My heart is broken."

"I know." The empathy in his tone implied a deep understanding. "We have the keys to surviving, and we've used them often: faith, family, and staying very, very busy. Be excessively busy, Ari, and one day, maybe years from now, you'll realize you're breathing easy again."

"I didn't lose myself this time." She washed a mug for far too long. "Rudy and I were coming undone—voices raised, anger flowing like lava—but I knew what I wanted to do going forward, and I realized that my views of what is right and wrong will continue to change throughout life. My view of God and myself will continue to change. But my heart that longs to do good for others wherever I can will remain true and filled with love as long as I'm true to God and myself." She dropped the mug into the water. "Look." She dried her hands and pulled out of her hidden pocket a torn piece of paper with handwriting on it.

Quill smiled. "I like this."

"Excellent, isn't it? Of course the given is that the relationship with God is in order first. But then . . . 'This above all—to thine own self be true, and it must follow, as the night the day, thou canst not then be false to any man.' "

Quill continued to look at the note.

Ariana fished the clean mug from the water and rinsed it. "I have a new plan. I don't know how good it is, but it feels right. I'm going to try to have historians come to the café to speak on Friday nights, hopefully at least once a month. I want people to understand this world."

"That's a great idea."

"Do you think so?"

"I do."

"Maybe I should also try to bring in archaeologists and meteorologists and physicists and astronomers and—"

"So scientists, then."

"Sh." She washed another mug. "Scientists have a worse reputation around here than both of us combined. But if I keep the person's title specific, maybe it will take the edge off for most. A few people might be interested."

"Every fire starts with a spark of some kind. But your plan will come with a price, even if the current situation with the ministers causes us to get all new ministers."

"Maybe the pain of that war will help me not feel the loss of Rudy so acutely."

"It seems we've each found our way of being who we are where we are—you among the Amish and me among the Englisch."

"Ya, seems so."

"Could you . . . would you mind sending a text every once in a while to keep me posted on how your plan is going?"

"I can do that, say once a month?"

"Deal. Your plan about speakers is good one, Ari. But remember that it took fifteen years for the civil rights movement in the sixties to accomplish its basic goals, and that was just the beginning. Breaking prejudice and misconceptions is an ongoing thing even today. I expect the time line of reform within the Amish to be much the same."

"I'm in no hurry." Her time was God's, and she might never be willing to yield that limited resource to another man.

Thirty-Eight

Inside her empty café at the end of the day, Ariana pulled her cell from her apron pocket, ready to text Quill. It would be the first time to message him since they'd met with the detective at Berta's home. More than a month had passed, and her head wasn't as foggy or her heart as shattered over the breakup. The fogginess and pain were still there in copious amounts but nothing like the first weeks.

Hey, Quill. End of April, so it's update time.

Detective Torres thinks he's finished interviewing people in Summer Grove. People wanted to know what the questions were about, so there was a gathering at Daed's home.

He answered what he could, doing his best not to assume any missing information or exaggerate the facts. It's a contentious mess—anger and disbelief over the truth. Many feel I've led Daed astray and that's why he called the police and why he now believes the bishop is wrong.

The bishop hasn't said much since he was questioned, which is refreshing.

First district meeting, what the detective called a town hall meeting, will be held later today at the schoolhouse, and police will discuss spiritual church matters versus criminal behavior.

With this much confusion and interest, I expect it to be standing room only. We'll see.

Daed gave his blessing to me moving in with your Mamm. I've been there for five nights now, and even without much in the way of conversations between your Mamm and me right now, there is something very encouraging about sharing a home with someone who also has respected loved ones on the outside.

How's Frieda? She's not responding to texts.

Ariana moved to the back steps and sat, waiting for his reply. The April breeze carried the sweet scents of spring coming to life.

Bubbles showed up on her texting screen, and she waited. He was quick to respond, but if she didn't text him first, would he text her?

Hi, Ari. So good to hear from you. I was beginning to wonder if you'd forgotten to send an update. I didn't know you'd moved in. Good for both of you!

The rumble of what's happening between the police and ministers in Summer Grove has spread far and wide. It's a sad thing but not a bad thing. Every Amish district needs to know where the boundaries are between personal beliefs and people's rights. It's been rough for Frieda. She's been interviewed twice. Once before her Mamm and siblings were interviewed and once after. Some of her siblings want to reestablish a connection with her. She's miserably leery.

Too many still believe what their Daed had told them—that she was faking the symptoms etc.

Some waver, wanting to believe her, or at least saying they do, but they want more proof. I've never been one to call someone stupid. We all have our strengths and weaknesses, but I now fully understand the meme:

Stupid is knowing the truth, seeing the truth, and still believing the lie.

This time concerning church matters remains hard for you. I know it does. But it will get better soon. I promise.

She was ready for things to get better.

Give Frieda my love. Bye.

Take care of yourself, Ari.

Quill waited in his car by the curb as the police officer instructed. He had the engine running, not so much for a fast getaway, but for air conditioning. If this was how hot the end of May was, what would the dog days of summer be like? His phone pinged with Ariana's ringtone. He picked it up from his console, hoping she had better things happening in her life of late.

Hi, Quill. End of May. Update time.

I heard from Frieda two weeks ago. We're texting regularly, and it does my heart good.

In an unprecedented move, the bishop, deacon, and preacher have stepped down. Rumors say all three will face legal charges by this time next month.

In news that's actually uplifting, I went to Bellflower Creek to stay for a couple of nights with Brandi, Gabe, and Cameron. The puppy is doing well.

I also had an afternoon with Nicholas while there. It was a good break. A much-needed one. Mom has a way of putting things in perspective and then insisting we do something fun. We went to a hair show, as if those helpful hair techniques are useful for me.☺

The next weekend Skylar went. When she returned, she talked to me about it. All first-rate stuff. I have good parents—all four of them.

Anyway, I'm currently baking croissants and scones, because tonight is the first time a speaker is coming to the café. The professor is an older gentleman, an archaeologist, who's going to share some of the amazing finds in Jerusalem, and he'll have artifacts and talk about the culture of the day.

Nicholas connected me with him and with enough other speakers that I have the next seven months lined up. I think he pulled a lot of favors to make this happen for me. No one besides my Brenneman family may come, but I'm looking forward to learning new things.

The district meeting with the police went well, I think. Very eye opening and humbling for most. There will be another one tomorrow night. The first one was packed with Amish from Summer Grove and neighboring districts. How are you?

Quill read the text a second time. Healing might take years, but it sounded as if she was getting her feet under her. For Ariana, that was step one to embracing her new circumstances with a sense of peace. It sounded as if some of the pressure involving the church leaders was beginning to dissipate, and the thought of it brought him relief. He glanced in his rearview mirror at the house the police had entered ten minutes ago.

That's some amazing stuff going on, Ari. Why do I feel as if your goal is to torture me? Croissants and scones?

Her message had a bit of cheer, and he felt a smile run from his head to his feet. She'd survived the worst of her grief from the breakup.

Yes, for the record, I'm hungry.

I'm currently doing a bit of work for WEDV, getting a young woman out of a situation. No kids. Simple deal. Police are in her home now, keeping the man under control and preventing him from following her. I'm in my car out of the man's line of sight, a few doors down, waiting. I'll drive her six hours south to start life anew, a place without friends or relatives for her, but somewhere he won't know how to find her. Other than that, work is good. I'm good. Frieda has said on numerous occasions how much she appreciates your texts and that you never pressure her to call or visit.☺

I learned that from you. Take care.

Ariana's heart pounded wildly. Was this actually happening, or was she dreaming? She had to tell Quill. She hurried to the side of the house and pulled her phone out of her pocket. She was allowed to have her phone, but to stand in her Daed's yard and text while thirty Amish men were around would be rude. She stumbled before coming to a halt. Her fingers would not move across the screen fast enough.

Quill, it seems God in heaven has done the unbelievable! End of June update. I know it's a few days early. Deal with it! The Amish of Summer Grove and beyond have come together to bless my Daed with heads of cattle! Dairy farmers have given up one cow each. I'm in the yard watching them being unloaded. When they learned how unfair the bishop's decree was toward my Daed and that it put him in financial straits all these years, they decided to do this! Thirty head, I think. Some cows look to be excellent milk cows. Some will just be okay until Daed works with them for a while. But I'm going to say this gift is worth about $60,000!

All the Amish people who stood silently by and let the bishop convince them of someone's great sin against God helped the bishop bully his victims, and the Amish are coming together to bless the victims, not just Daed. They have arranged a frolic to paint your Mamm's house and anything else she needs. The women float in and out of her home, bringing her small tokens and an abundance of humility and love. They want her to know how sorry they are, and I can't stop crying.

It seems all of them are determined never to let something like this happen again and to make it a point to walk in love, not apathy, confusion, or judgment.

I knew my people had this in them. I knew they did. I've never been more pleased to be Amish.

Hi, Ari. This is an update to beat all updates! It's amazing news, and I'm thanking God with you. Mamm called me a few hours ago and said the new bishop came to see her, and he's removed all restraints on us visiting her.

I didn't know that, Quill. I'd hoped it would happen. I'm in awe at what's taking place. The truth does set us free. Not judgment. Not rules.

With all Schlabachs able to visit their Mamm at will, we'll need to come up with a plan that works for

> everyone so this single Amish girl doesn't get in trouble for fraternizing overnight. How about if you text me when any Schlabach plans to visit, and I'll go to my Brenneman home, leaving all rooms available for your family?

> Good plan. We'll probably keep our overnight stays limited to the weekends, but I imagine there will be lots of visits for the next few months. Mamm will want to make up for lost time with the grandkids.☺

"Ariana," Daed called.

"Coming." Ariana dashed a final text to Quill.

> Gotta go. Daed is calling.
>
> He probably needs help milking all those cows! Bye.

She slid the phone into her pocket and hurried around the side of the house. The phone buzzed, but she'd have to read the text later.

Sweat dripped down Quill's face as he entered his third mile of running. Lexi was by his side, panting but keeping pace. His phone chirped Ariana's ringtone. He smiled and stopped running. He patted Lexi while pulling the phone from his shorts pocket.

> Quill, this is so sad. I knew it was coming, I guess. I just . . .
>
> Oh, wait. Hi. Update time. Mid-July. The sad news:

charges have been filed against all three ministers. They've been taken to jail and will see a judge to set bail sometime this week, maybe tomorrow. Because they helped Frieda's Daed get away by notifying him when your Daed went to the police, as well as other things they've done, they are charged with aiding and abetting and obstruction of justice.

The detective told them that if Frieda had died, they also would have been charged with involuntary manslaughter. That has shaken the community out of its apathy and into vigilance to be kind and gentle inside of church business, like they are when dealing with Englisch folk. I didn't understand all the police jargon, and I'm grateful for justice, but I hurt that this is happening to them. I can't imagine a night in jail for those men. It seems it would be terrifying.

Quill had less empathy for the men than Ariana did, in part because he was a less empathic person. She could hurt for a grasshopper that died between the window and the screen. Still, he didn't wish ill on the men, but he was good with justice having its day. If he'd known six years ago that what they were doing was illegal, he still would've needed to get Frieda out for her sake, but he wouldn't have had to hide for years or sneak into his Mamm's house for visits. Maybe he and Ariana would be dating right now. But he'd been young and inexperienced, and he paid a price for that. Apparently the ministers had a price to pay too.

Hi, Ari. It is disturbing to watch, I'm sure. No one is rejoicing. But don't take on emotionally what's happening to them as if it's happening to you. The concern and fear and upset in their lives are not yours to carry. Okay?

Keep telling yourself: This is not my monkey. This is not mine to carry.

The detective called Frieda several days ago and said that if this goes to trial, she may have to testify. He expects all three men to plead guilty rather than go on trial, because the Word says to agree with an adversary quickly.

However it goes, they could get anything from twenty years in jail to a long probation.

Remember: it's not your emotional baggage to carry.

I feel better already. Thank you! I need to go. New help coming into the café that I have to start training. Bye.

Thirty-Nine

Lovina wiped the back of her wrist across her forehead and then pulled more weeds out of the garden.

"Lovina." Skylar hurried across the yard. "I got cleared!" Skylar waved a paper in the air.

"That's great, honey!" From her crouched position, Lovina held out her hand, and Skylar took it, helping her stand. Lovina's knees weren't what they used to be. "So should I just hug you and be very excited, or should you tell me which great thing took place that we are now celebrating?"

Skylar wagged her finger. "Very funny. Jokes from a woman crouching in the July heat, weeding a garden at noon." She folded the paper and tucked it into the pocket of her jeans. "Why are you out here at this time of day?" Skylar bent and pulled a wad of weeds out of the garden.

"My morning got off schedule."

"You were baby-sitting grandkids again, weren't you?"

"Maybe." Lovina grinned. "So what's going on?"

"I am officially a part of the Big Sister program, *and* I've been cleared to teach music in group foster homes. How cool is that?"

"I couldn't be more proud, but I don't know how you're going to keep up with all you're taking on."

"Ha. Once you learn to work and live like the Amish, everything else is easy." Skylar checked her phone, smiled, and tapped her fingers across the screen. Lovina knew that look. Skylar was texting with Jax. She shoved the phone back into her jeans. "Where's Isaac?"

"Here." Isaac walked toward them, carrying two glasses of lemonade.

"I was in the kitchen fixing Lovina a drink when I saw you arrive. Decided to be nice and fix two."

"Thanks." Skylar reached for the glass.

Isaac held one out to Lovina and took a drink of the other.

"Daed!"

Isaac laughed and gave her the one he'd been holding out to Lovina. He then gave Lovina the one he'd drunk out of as they moved to the lawn chairs under the shade trees. Skylar was one very busy young woman. She worked at the café part-time, attended school, practiced music a lot, and did some volunteer work with Jax. But the most exciting part to Lovina and Isaac was she and Jax had been going to church together for the last few months.

While Isaac and Skylar chatted, Lovina breathed in the delicious aroma of freedom in Christ and allowed her mind to reminisce.

It seemed odd, but as much as Skylar had changed since coming to their home nine months ago, it often felt as if Lovina and Isaac had changed more. Who had been more set in their ways—a twenty-year-old girl on drugs or a fifty-something couple who'd sat under the same cloistered teachings their whole lives?

She didn't know. Only God knew, and He'd known how to bring about changes for everyone.

When had it become natural to give up thinking and just accept that the bishop was in power because God had put him there? But as Ariana had pointed out a few months back, just because God put someone in authority, it didn't mean those under him had to mindlessly yield. She'd explained many things about the Amish that Lovina and Isaac had never considered. The Amish hadn't yielded to the government powers in Europe, which is how they ended up in America. Once here, they hadn't yielded to the US government on numerous topics. They'd stood their ground to be exempted from personal Social Security taxes, and they went to court and some went to jail to fight for the right for education to go only through the eighth grade. So the whole concept of accepting all authority as God's will had to be balanced through deep thinking and a willingness to admit a person is not God and can be wrong. Their forefathers in Europe certainly fought back against the church at that time, confident that the church leaders, who weren't Amish, were not following God's Word.

How had the Amish of Summer Grove become so comfortable giving up all power and opinion that they'd been cavalier and apathetic to what was going on around them?

However it had happened, the detective broke the hold of any person setting himself up as judge and jury. Ariana added to the detective's revelations by bringing in teachers to the café. The once-a-month Friday night events were packed with Englisch and Amish alike.

Because of those evenings and free refreshments, Ariana's café was bursting at the seams, and in a few months she would close for a few weeks and expand the café. When she wasn't working, she spent long days at the public library and had established good communication with Nicholas, who actually attended church. Nicholas said he went so he could cross-reference the different academic approaches to numerous scriptures.

Maybe. But even if that was true, Lovina was praying he would see the truth while searching for facts, just as she prayed that she would see facts while accepting God's truth.

Skylar laughed, and Lovina focused on her daughter. Skylar took another sip of her drink. "I'm planning a big birthday party at the café for the trips' twenty-first birthday. That's four Saturdays from today. I'm inviting family on both sides, Amish and Englisch. You'll come, right?"

"Trips?" Isaac asked.

Lovina leaned forward. "Forgive him. He's getting old."

Skylar chuckled. "We explained this to you. It stands for triplets, because Abram, Ariana, and I have decided that's what we are—triplets from different mothers."

"No wonder I forgot. That's confusing. And impossible."

"Yeah, well, nonetheless, the trips, which, by the way, are a trip, are having a blow-out birthday on Saturday, four weeks from today, starting at five. We'll provide the food."

"You're cooking for everyone?"

"Who do you think I am? No, of course not. We're ordering pizza."

"You do your best to confuse me at times, don't you?" Isaac asked.

"Sometimes. It's fun. You should try it." She jiggled the glass, making the ice rattle. "I just have this pent-up energy all the time lately. I'm like Scrooge at the end of the movie. Giddy. The more I give and do for others, the happier I feel. And foster children are amazing." She held out the drink to Isaac, offering him some of her lemonade.

He took the glass. "Just remember, emotions are like circumstances." He took a sip of the drink. "We can and should do our best to live in a way that doesn't wreak havoc on either, but when tough times hit, and they will, our foundation isn't built on how we feel. We have to keep moving forward in as many positive ways as possible, regardless of circumstances and emotions."

In one fluid movement Skylar rose, put her hands on the armrest of Isaac's chair, and kissed him on the cheek. "You're a smart man." With her thumb she wiped the spot she'd kissed. "But you're messing with my excitement."

With one exception, Lovina and Isaac's children—oldest to the youngest—were faring well, and she was thrilled to see it. She and Isaac were doing really well too. It was amazing what it did to the soul to set aside worry over their children not following the Ordnung closely enough and to use all that energy to simply love and trust God.

But Ariana . . . Her sweet girl still had times of being steeped in grief. She went through her days looking and responding as if she were happy, but Lovina could tell by Ariana's eyes when she was having a bad day or week.

Still, her girl had faith in the value of her work and faith that God would see her through whatever was before her. Ariana was determined to be peaceful and productive.

"Any way you'd be okay with music being a part of the party?" Skylar clasped her hands together, looking as if she was begging. "I'll keep it clean and respectful, but what's a party without music?"

"Can we think on it?"

Forty

The noise of the café rang loudly in Ariana's ears. Between the music and the number of people, it was a very busy place. Pizza had been eaten. Cake had been served. The event was winding down, but it would carry warm memories for the rest of her life.

Twenty-one years old.

Maybe that part wasn't as important as the fact that everyone had survived this past year and was better for it. Her phone buzzed. She hoped it would be Quill assuring her everything had gone fine with his latest rescue. She'd expected to hear from him a few hours ago. He'd left yesterday to help a thirty-something widow with a ten-year-old son. Out of the blue, some man had been stalking her, and she hadn't been able to shake him.

Between the busyness of Schlabach Home Builders and his willingness to help women and children out of dangerous situations, she hadn't seen him in three weeks, but they texted regularly. Actually, Quill, Frieda, and she texted all the time, often with all three included in the messages. She'd received birthday wishes from Frieda on Wednesday, her actual birthday.

Ariana went to the far end of the counter so she could discreetly check her phone. Her screen exploded with colorful balloons and streamers. Then letters appeared on the screen, one by one, looking as if he was handwriting them.

HAPPY BIRTHDAY!

She laughed, and her fingers flew across the screen.

Thank you! Don't know how to be fancy with texts, but here you go☺.

Hahaha. That'll do. I wish I could be there! Are you drinking now that you're 21, or did you get that out of your system during our one night at that bar?

She thought a moment about that strange night last October. She'd been really upset that night at the bar. Now they joked about it. She had a grin on her face as she wrote.

Very funny. It's MY birthday! Be nice.

He sent a GIF of an adorable kitten up close and shaking its head really fast, as if it was saying *no*.

Apparently I need lessons on how to up my texting game.

Apparently so. Too bad you don't know anyone who'd be willing to show you some tips and tricks.

He'd turned twenty-six a few days ago. The Schlabach siblings and spouses had an annual birthday celebration each May. Since the ban against the Schlabachs visiting their Mamm hadn't lifted until the end of July, Berta didn't get to be a part of that again this year. So everyone came in on Quill's birthday, just for this one time. They would return to having only annual parties next May, with the exception that they would have them at Berta's. Ariana had stayed for Quill's party, and it'd been a treat to see Berta surrounded by her family, with grandchildren hanging all over her.

On your birthday next year, I will hide behind texts and be mean.

Okay. I'd like to see that. I think hiding behind these tiny letters or even a cell phone would be really hard, but probably the hardest part for you is BEING MEAN.

We'll see, won't we?

You'll see. I already know the answer.

Oh, did you know your Mamm is here?

Me, being good now. Don't tattle on me.

She cackled, but what retort could she give? It seemed that Quill had stopped putting distance between them, and their camaraderie reminded her of the fun, carefree days before his Daed died and Quill started keeping secrets from her so he could get Frieda safely out of Summer Grove.

"Mom, Dad, Gabe." Skylar's voice poured through the speaker system. "I know we've talked about everything, and we're in a great place, but

I left Bellflower Creek a wreck, and I wanted everyone in this room to know that wasn't your fault. It was mine. My choices. My anger with you that life wasn't easier." She moved to the keyboard. "So this song is for you." Her hands moved across the keys. "It's a song by Chicago called 'Hard to Say I'm Sorry.'"

Her voice was clear, and her eyes moved from one parent to the other as she sang. The words were touching, every apology seemingly heartfelt, but Ariana's favorite lines were "After all that we've been through I will make it up to you."

As the song ended, even Skylar seemed overwhelmed with emotion.

"Ariana Brenneman." Skylar started playing another song. "To the stage please."

Ariana laid the phone on the bar and cupped her hands around her mouth. "Not happening!"

The families laughed. Their brother Mark had put together a small stage in the café—ironic since Mark first saw Skylar on a stage, which began the whole journey of their parents learning Skylar and Ariana had been swapped at birth.

"Abram Brenneman," Skylar said. "To the stage."

"What she said!" Abram pointed at Ariana.

"What is wrong with you people? The way you avoid the spotlight, one would think you're Amish or something."

The room filled with laughter. Skylar had done a fantastic job with everything tonight, the music most of all. She'd found a perfect blend of respect and fun and even had on a dress. The first three songs had been Amish hymns, sung in German by all the siblings just like the *Ausbund* had it, except Skylar accompanied on the keyboard. Then the Brennemans sang the last verse of each song in English so Skylar and her stepsister, Cameron, could sing with them. Every parent had at least a hint of tears before that was done. Mamm was sobbing.

Ariana wasn't sure how many people were here. Mamm, Daed, all the

Brenneman siblings, their spouses, and children. Cilla. Jax. Nicholas. Even his wife, Lynn, and her two teenage sons, Trent and Zachary, came. Brandi and Gabe. Berta. And Levi, a nice young man from several districts away that Susie was dating. Then there were several Amish friends of the family.

This twenty-first birthday had everything these milestones were supposed to have except alcohol and a boyfriend for Ariana. She'd never miss the alcohol, and she and God had hashed through the boyfriend angst.

She'd had to lay that down, because she needed to stay focused and be content right where she was. There was work to be done. Changing minds and attitudes was a slow process.

"Ariana Brenneman," Skylar elongated the words in a deep voice. "It's time to do the closing song."

Ariana shook her head, telling Skylar no.

"Okay, fine. But this shindig is supposed to end about now. It's inching toward bedtime for our nieces and nephews, and it doesn't end until there's a song by the birthday trips."

But they hadn't practiced a song. All the siblings had practiced the songs they'd sung earlier from the Ausbund and the Englisch version.

Salome hugged Ariana. "You sing for us. Make it a celebration of celebrations, because no one in the room would be the same person if it hadn't been for you three."

"That's true of all of you for us."

"Then sing it for that reason too."

Ariana nodded and walked toward the small stage. Family ties were worth fighting for—because when everything was said and done, family mattered, whether they were blood relatives, adopted ones, or, like her and Berta, a choice because there was a connection that defied reason.

Ariana hurried up the two steps. "Skylar." She turned the microphone off. "What are you thinking? We haven't practiced anything."

"Really?" Skylar lifted a brow. "You sure about that?" Skylar looked very pleased with herself. Months ago she had been playing some music after the café closed, and Ariana discovered a delightful song she wanted to learn the lyrics to. Apparently Skylar had used that to nonchalantly teach her and Abram how to sing all the different parts while she played the keyboard.

Abram stepped onto the stage.

Skylar immediately began the lead-in to Ariana's new favorite song, "California Dreamin'," by the Mamas and the Papas, which, according to Skylar, had been a huge hit in the sixties.

The words to the song moved Ariana, the visual of brown leaves and gray skies and going for a walk during the winter. But it wasn't an easy song to sing. One sang, one echoed, while the other started the next verse. She and Abram stepped up to the microphone, and they sang as they had dozens of times while simply enjoying the music. Their version changed a couple of the words in the lyrics, making it a perfect song if one wanted to sing to their family that they were going to stay.

When they finished the song, the room cheered, clearly hearing what they were singing from their hearts. It was the same message they'd been giving, but somehow the flow of the music made it more powerful, and singing it together in celebration of their birthdays seemed to add to the impact.

"The Trips, ladies and gentlemen." Skylar took the microphone with her and moved to stand beside them. "We have talent that will never be heard around the world or much of anywhere except on our birthdays in this café." She pointed out in the crowd of family, evidently searching for someone. "There you are. So Mamm and Daed, can we have a birthday party here every year and have music?"

Mamm lowered her head shaking it. Leave it to Skylar not to consider that she was putting them on the spot. But Daed grinned. "We'll get back to you on that in a couple of years."

Her magnificent, crazy family—some in cape dresses and head

coverings and some in jeans and bangles—hugged and laughed and talked. It took nearly forty minutes for the group to thin to the usual gang of five on a Saturday night—Ariana, Skylar, Jax, Abram, and Cilla.

They cleaned up the mess and talked, but then Ariana shooed them out the door. "I've got this. Go do something else on your Saturday night." She walked outside with them.

Abram opened the carriage door for Cilla. Jax started his truck and backed out, taking Skylar with him. Abram returned to where Ariana stood on the stoop, waving to Skylar and Jax.

"This came for you." He pulled a letter from his pocket. "It arrived this morning, and I was afraid it might make you sad during the birthday gathering. But to keep it any longer seemed wrong."

She took it and read the return address. *Rudy.* "Good decisions." She kissed his cheek. "Denki."

"Happy birthday, Sis."

"Back at you, Bro."

While they drove off, Ariana went back inside the café. She slid the letter into her pocket and gathered cups and plates. She filled the sink with hot water and detergent, but rather than washing the dishes, she dried her hands and pulled the letter from her pocket.

She hadn't heard from Rudy since he left Summer Grove five months ago, almost to the day. Walking to the wide set of stairs that led to Skylar's loft, Ariana opened the letter. She sat and removed it from the envelope.

Dear Ariana,

I hope you're well. My hand is healed, but it took time and physical therapy. I heard of the upset in Summer Grove, and about two months ago the police had meetings here too. I understand they've held them in Pennsylvania, Ohio, and Indiana, telling everyone that crimes must be reported to the police. I think people will listen. Amish in these parts feel that the consequences of hiding a crime are terrifying.

As I listened to a man in uniform explain the law's take on matters, I realized that even though I don't agree with your headstrong ways, you might be right to want to usher in broader thinking and change how people view blind obedience. As for all that went on with Frieda, I'm grateful Quill stood up for what was right. I don't know anyone else who would've made that sacrifice.

I thought about us on the bench in central Ohio when each of us came halfway so we could visit for a few hours when you were living Englisch. I had wanted to meet you halfway in everything. I thought that was very good and progressive of me to feel that way. Looking back, I realize that what I really wanted was for you to be impressed and grateful that I was sacrificing so much for you. But after you returned to Summer Grove, I grew angry because halfway was too far, and I was angry at what was happening to us, but most of all I was angry with you for having changed while away.

You were right to end the relationship. We had become too different to be equally yoked. But lately I wonder if you became that different or if you simply experienced something that set free the real Ariana—the one who always looked at difficult situations and believed it could be better, if only . . .

You hold on to that, Ariana. That is good.

It's time for me to end this now, but I did want you to hear this from me first—I started seeing someone a few months ago, and we will go public with it soon.

Rudy

Ariana stared at the letter. It seemed as if he would marry someone else and have children before she went on another date. Yet contentment and peace welled within her.

Someone knocked on the front door, but she didn't budge. Who had left what behind before leaving the party? "Kumm."

Quill walked in. "Surprise!" He waved his hands in the air. "Am I the only one who came to your party? You should try being friendly once in a while."

"You're very funny."

He didn't shut the door all the way before he walked over to sit next to her. "Is there a reason we're sitting on the steps? Do you not trust the chairs?"

"It seemed a good place to rest, neither going up nor down." She tugged on the edge of the letter, and it fluttered in the air. "Rudy." She folded it. "He's seeing someone."

"You want to talk?"

"Always. Just not about Rudy." They didn't talk about Rudy much. They focused on what was ahead and memories of a gazillion things they'd done together or apart, events that didn't include Rudy. But she didn't avoid talking about him on purpose as if wanting to wipe Rudy from her mind. It was just natural to talk about other things.

"So you're okay?" Quill leaned back on his elbows, looking as if he had all night to talk if that's what she wanted.

"About him seeing someone? Ya, I'm surprisingly good, which shocks me." One day she would share with Quill some of the nice things Rudy wrote.

"I'm glad you're fine, because I have a gift for you." He went to the front door and opened it. Lexi came strolling in, wagging her tail.

"Aww. Come here, girl." Ariana moved to her and knelt. "Are you my gift?" She rubbed Lexi's ears. "Ya?" she teased.

"Uh, yeah," Quill said. "That's a great gift and all—a used dog I'm unwilling to give up, but, uh, this was more what I had in mind."

Ariana looked up to see a young woman inside her café. It took a moment for it to compute. "Frieda!" Ariana leaped to her feet. "You're here."

"Finally found the courage." Frieda looked self-conscious and uncomfortable, but her smile was sincere. "Happy birthday." She held out her arms.

Ariana hugged her, and the two broke into sobs. A moment later they looked in each other's eyes and began talking so fast it sounded as if they'd invented a new language.

As they moved to a table toward the back of the café, Quill went behind the counter and started a pot of coffee. This was the best birthday present she could imagine, and it'd happened through the quiet patience of the best friend she had.

How many times had she longed for this moment? No secrets between them. No judgment or unforgiveness or angst. Only love and hope for a smoother road ahead.

Frieda rushed through a lengthy overview of why she'd felt unable to return to Summer Grove before now, as if she owed Ariana an apology.

Ariana put her hands over Frieda's. "I understand, and what I don't understand, I accept as your right to live as you needed to. It's all okay." Ariana gently squeezed her hands. "All okay."

Quill brought over two cups of coffee. "Ari, will you drop her off at Mamm's house when you're ready?" He chuckled. "Maybe by noon tomorrow?"

As he set the mugs down, Ariana grabbed his wrist. "Don't go."

His eyes studied hers, and she was sure he was calculating dozens of reasons whether to do as she was asking.

"Yeah, please stay," Frieda said. "It'll be like old times."

Quill seemed hesitant, but slowly a mischievous grin appeared. "You mean where you two girls talk, and I poke fun at it?"

That wasn't exactly how it went, but he did have a way of adding dry wit and a man's view that often put all three of them in stitches. But Ariana could fire back humor against his man logic these days. She was sure of it.

"Ya." Ariana motioned to a chair. "Give it your best shot. Make my day." She winked at him before turning to Frieda. "What's your favorite thing about your life in Kentucky of late?"

Forty-One

Abram sat in the theater at Shippensburg University, lights dim as he watched the stage.

The lyrics were about a person's changing and moving on and yet still depending on who she used to be. He listened to the pleasant voice of the actress, watching her sing and emote while holding the hands of her on-stage father.

Abram, Cilla, Ariana, and Jax had all been told by Skylar that they were going to the play *Beauty and the Beast,* performed by a local theater group. Skylar had put her hands on her hips. "It's *not* a request. You've not joined the church yet, and you have to do it." Apparently this was the musical theater version of one of Skylar's favorite movies as a child.

Cilla leaned in close. "It's not our usual date, but this is pretty fun, ya?" she whispered.

Abram nodded and slid his hand into hers. She leaned against his shoulder and squeezed his hand.

Abram squeezed back and bent down to kiss her forehead. "Definitely. We won't be attending plays if we go through instruction this spring and join the church."

The unspoken part was their intention to marry, but that wasn't official. He'd not directly asked, but they'd talked in general terms. Before he asked, he needed to tell her something, and the thought of it caused another rush of nervousness to hit his stomach. How would he word it? Would his conditions be too much for her? They'd been dating for eight months, and he didn't want to lose her.

"I don't mind." Cilla snuggled into his arm.

Ignoring the anxiety of a conversation yet to come, Abram let the pleasant melodies from the singer and the accompanying instruments wash over him, and he fully enjoyed the moment.

He cherished his time with Cilla throughout the rest of the show, although parts of the play seemed rather silly to him. After the musical was over, the audience, including their group, stood up to clap. Skylar had told him that standing and applauding indicated a job well done to the actors, musicians, sound crew, and director.

Following the other theatergoers, they filed out of the row of seats into the loud, echoing lobby.

"Aren't you glad you all came?" Skylar asked over the dull roar of voices, her face beaming. "Wasn't it so, so good?"

Jax put an arm around her shoulders and squeezed. "I'm not sure we can appreciate it as much as you, but, yes, it was a lot of fun. Certainly a lot better than some of the mandatory concerts you've dragged me to." He shuddered.

Skylar laughed. "He's still sore that I made him go to an atonal twentieth-century art music concert a few weeks back. Even I have to admit that pushed the limits of my ear, but I have to attend at least fifteen recitals or concerts per year for my college."

"It was the musical equivalent of a kid coloring on the wall with a crayon." Jax raised an eyebrow at Skylar.

"Come on, if it's intentionally dissonant, that's different than playing a wrong note."

"You catching any of this, Ari?" Abram asked.

She chuckled. "Not very much." She had her phone in hand, texting. "During intermission I called an Uber driver, and she's here. So I'm going to head back to Berta's. I've hardly had time to say hello to her all week, and I live there." She shook her head, looking dismayed by how little time she'd had with Berta the past several days. "Thanks for the invite and the ticket, Skylar. All you lovebirds enjoy the rest of your evening."

They waved and watched as she exited. Last October Ariana and Skylar were backed into corners, both having to leave the home they grew up in and spend time with biological parents they'd never met. Other than God, who was the same yesterday, today, and forever, Abram couldn't think of one thing in the Brenneman lives that resembled what life had been like just one year ago.

Skylar was happy, and everything about her life radiated. Ariana seemed to be doing really well, but she wasn't interested in dating yet. It couldn't be easy to be the fifth wheel on their double dates, but when asked, she went, and they all had a good time. She and Skylar sharpened their wit on each other, and at least once or twice a month their stepsister, Cameron, joined them, which made for lots of laughs. On the weekends when Cameron stayed over, she would stay with Ariana at Berta's place or with Skylar in the loft. If there were Amish who disagreed with those arrangements, they were keeping it to themselves.

"Care for a walk, Cilla?" He hoped she would be receptive to what he needed to tell her.

"Sure, then maybe a piece of cake at the diner?"

"Ooh, traitors," Skylar teased with a wink.

"You"—Cilla pointed at Skylar—"just think of it as studying the competition."

Skylar laughed. "Fine. Be that way."

"Thanks for the outing, Skylar. We'll call for an Uber driver too when we're ready to go home. See *you* tomorrow morning before daylight. See you much later in the day, Jax." Waving to Skylar and Jax, Abram took Cilla's hand and walked out the front door. The October evening was mild and smelled delicious. The air held a pleasant briskness that offset the still-warm Indian summer days.

Nervousness skittered through his stomach. "I'm glad we went to the play tonight."

"Me too." Cilla put on her sweater. Leaves crackled under their feet as they walked toward downtown Shippensburg. The rest of the crowd either got into cars or fell farther behind, so finally they could talk privately.

"Sometimes life requires parting ways with the things we dreamed would happen when we grew up."

Cilla nodded. "Like in the play we just watched. Belle had to adjust to living at the castle instead of going on the far-off adventure she thought she would have. But she still ended up having an adventure."

"Ya."

"Something's on your mind, isn't it, Abram?"

He took a deep breath. "Our conversations have sort of eased into talking about marriage, but we've never really discussed what that would need to look like."

Cilla's brows knit together. "This sounds a little worrisome."

"Ya, it is. See, Cilla, I . . . I have a provision I need you to agree to before we can seriously plan to marry." He was right to bring this up now, wasn't he, if they were going to begin instruction this spring?

"Abram, just tell me. We'll work it out." She slowed her pace and gazed up at him. "Won't we?"

"That's my hope."

"Enough suspense, okay? Please just say it already."

"I don't think we should have children." He forced the words out quickly, and they sounded wrong as soon as they left his lips. "I . . . I *know* we shouldn't have children."

Cilla dropped his hand and recoiled. "Wh-what do you mean?"

"No, I phrased that badly. I think we should have as many children as God allows us to, but I don't think *you* should carry them."

"Oh." She looked at the ground.

He took her hand again and cupped her face with his other hand. "You are my beautiful, kind, compassionate girlfriend. I want us to marry. You'll be an amazing mother and raise our children in the most loving way possible. But your health is too precious for me to risk. *You* are too precious for me to risk."

Tears welled in her eyes. "Things have been going so well that sometimes I forget about the CF, even if just for a few hours. And then it's back to steal the joy other people take for granted."

"I'm so sorry. I wish I could take away that burden."

"But plenty of people with CF *do* have their own children."

"I know, but"—Abram shook his head, hating to tell her no on this when he would give so much to make things different—"they do so at great risk. Many things can go wrong during pregnancy, especially if the mother has CF. You would be prone to lung infections and could easily develop pregnancy-related diabetes, which could turn chronic. Maintaining adequate nutrition would be a struggle."

He'd had Skylar and Ariana help him research this extensively online over the past few months. He had been dreading bringing it up with Cilla, but it was time.

"My doctor said as much too."

"Fertility can easily be an issue with CF patients, and I don't want us on that roller coaster either. And if those aren't enough reasons, I could be a carrier too. The Amish have a much higher rate of carrying a CF gene than the general population. If I'm a carrier, then each child would have a fifty percent chance of being born with CF, and the condition could be a much more severe version than yours."

"Those are a lot of ifs, Abram." She pulled away from him. "Having children is a risk, but everything in life is a risk. Think of what we could gain by trying."

"I know," he whispered. "I've wrestled with this issue and prayed about it for months. I really feel that God is trying to tell us to take another path. That our children are out there, maybe not born yet, but they are out there and waiting for us to find them. Would you love a child any less if he or she wasn't blood related to us?"

"No." She turned and started walking again. "Of course I wouldn't love an adopted child any less."

"Me either." He grabbed her hand. "Look at me, Cilla." He tried to speak in the gentlest voice he could. She turned her face back to him, and he hated to see more tears in her eyes. "I promise, if we get married, I will always make sure you have the best doctors and the best medicines, and I'll be the best spouse I possibly can. I will give you the very best life I know how, throughout all the stages, including raising children. But, please, I have to ask you to do this for me. Let me have surgery before we marry so I never have to worry about losing you because you accidentally became pregnant. I couldn't bear watching your health decline or losing you."

"All my secret dreams as a child . . . although I never thought I'd get them. But I dreamed of finding a husband, then having a child that looked like both of us . . . To permanently give that up is a lot."

"I know. I wish I could change it for you, but life isn't made of dreams. It's made of decisions. Sometimes really hard decisions." He rubbed her hand with his thumb. "You don't have to decide right now. You can take some time. I understand."

"But if I don't agree, you won't marry me?"

A small group of people was coming up behind them. "Let's keep walking and get you that cake."

She pulled away, folded her arms, and stepped aside. They let the group pass them.

"You're willing for us not to marry over this?"

"That's not what I want, Cilla. I want to spend the rest of my life with you, and I'm not willing to shorten the length of that time for biological babies. If you died, my desire to have you back would equal any feelings you have about this. Look at my wild family. We are proof of great love, no matter how we are connected."

She was keeping so much distance a bicycler could've ridden between them. The walk from the campus to the diner was about half a mile, and he was fairly sure she'd walk the rest of it in silence. He wouldn't try to convince her further. The decision was hers. There were Amish men who would jump at the chance to marry her and have children with her. It was hard to think about her breaking up with him and finding someone else, but he'd watched Ariana walk that path, and she was surviving just fine. Ariana saw that Rudy would never be at peace with her activist thinking. And Abram would never be at peace with Cilla taking the chance that she'd do serious, long-term damage to her body in order to carry a baby, let alone more than one.

All Abram could do now was give her time to decide.

Forty-Two

Quill was on the floor in a bedroom-turned-playroom, enjoying time with his nieces and nephews. Lexi lay nearby, her head on her paws as she dozed. His Mamm's home smelled and sounded like Christmas Eve—the best Christmas Eve they'd had as a family in nearly two decades. Dan, the eldest, had left home for the Englisch world almost eighteen years ago, and since he couldn't return for visits, that was the beginning of Christmases starting to feel less full. But today felt like a miracle—Mamm's five sons, four daughters-in-law, Frieda, and eight grandchildren were here. Boldly. Loudly. Here. Oh, and Mamm had another grandchild due mid-January, a boy, and this time she would be there to hold the newborn on the day of its birth.

Quill passed a truck to his oldest nephew. "You guys continue without me."

"Noooo." The moans were pitiful.

"Yeeeees." He winked at ten-year-old Logan and put his hand on seven-year-old Kylie Peyton's head. "You can do it." He fisted his hands, showing enthusiasm as if cheering for them.

Lexi raised her head.

"You stay too."

She stretched and moaned slightly before she rested her head on the floor again, looking content to stay put. Two-and-a-half-year-old Gavin ran to him. "Picky up. I go. I go."

"Okay, buddy." He picked him up and then made a circle with his hand toward the others. "You stay and play. Your parents are busy getting ready for the Christmas Eve feast."

"*Mammi* Bertie says we each get to open one gift tonight after dinner." Eight-year-old Jenna's eyes radiated excitement, and her younger brother, Ethan, stared at Quill, clearly hoping for confirmation.

"That's right. One gift each. That's like a hundred gifts, right?"

The four oldest children laughed at his joke, and the younger ones laughed and squealed because the older ones did. Well, not Gavin. He was tenderhearted and whip smart, but he was the serious child of the group. He watched and listened when the others were rowdy.

Quill turned to him. "You ready?"

Gavin pointed at the playroom door. "We go."

Quill walked down the long hall, thinking of the hundreds of times he'd slipped in through a window and padded down this ghostly quiet, dimly lit passageway. But tonight the hall was lit with kerosene pole lamps at each end. Voices rumbled through the place, a half-dozen conversations taking place at once. The Christmas Eve bustle in his Mamm's house hadn't ever been this busy, even when all five boys were living at home.

Quill stopped by the kitchen and spoke with his family.

Regina, Gavin's mom, reached for him. "I bet you're hungry, aren't you?"

Gavin grabbed hold of Quill's shirt, clinging tightly. "No! Stay Kill. Stay Kill."

Regina laughed. "Fine. Stay with Quill."

"Otay. I eat." He reached for his mom.

Quill gently tousled the boy's hair. The need to be able to say *no* began young. Testing the waters of having power over oneself was important. Quill saw that more clearly now than ever before. It was important from the start for little ones to feel a sense of control over their lives and for adults to pick their battles wisely, neither giving in too much nor demanding their way too often. Would he be a dad one day to put into practice the many things he'd learned as the uncle of eight? He hoped so, but it was best not to think about it.

He passed Gavin to his mom, knowing the little boy would return to his lap as soon as he was full. Quill went to the living room. He wasn't sure where the rest of his brothers were, maybe still fixing the broken shelving in Mamm's closet, but the room was empty. He drew a deep breath, ready for a few moments of solitude. He sat in an armchair in front of the hearth and watched the fire.

He checked his phone, but it told him what he already knew. He hadn't received any new messages from Ari since early that morning.

Dan eased into the room. "Can I join you?"

"Sure." Quill slowly slid his finger down the screen, rereading strings of texts between Ari and him. This is what he did when he wanted to interact with her and it wasn't possible. Reading her texts was like hearing her voice inside his head.

"Will she stop by tonight?" Dan sat in a matching armchair across from Quill.

Quill looked up. "Maybe. I hope so. Tomorrow night for sure."

Mamm walked into the room, carrying two mugs. "Hot chocolate. Ari's recipe. I think she's taught me how to get this right."

"Thanks, Mamm." Quill lifted a mug from her hands.

Dan took the other. "I was just broaching the subject of Ari. She's quite the girl. We all love her. I mean, seriously, what's not to love about her?"

Mamm nodded. "We do. I'm glad she's relaxed her concerns about the trouble it could cause if she is with us while Quill is here. My favorite times are when everyone comes for a visit and she's part of our family meals."

Quill wasn't fooled. There was a point to this topic. "You two gonna say it or keep dancing around it?"

Dan set his mug on the coffee table and leaned in. "Is there a chance for a future with her?"

Quill had expected this to come up. Actually his family had been very patient. Ariana and he had slowly become closer since Rudy left Summer Grove nine months ago, and now Quill's family wanted answers.

Quill sipped the drink. "It's very good, Mamm."

"Denki. Would you answer your brother?"

He nodded. "We have a definite future together, just probably not one that includes marriage and children."

They stared at him, and Mamm looked wounded and worried.

"Probably?" she asked.

"Anything is possible. This past year and a half has proven that, but there's a great divide between us, Mamm. It seems to me that after everything is said and done, she could no more leave the Amish than I could deal with joining them."

Dan rubbed his hands together, a sign he was thinking hard. "You need a woman you can build a solid relationship and life with."

The brothers, all of Quill's sisters-in-law, and Frieda eased into the room and dispersed themselves throughout but focused on this one conversation as if they needed to hear it more than anything else this Christmas Eve.

"Let me get this straight, Dan. You think I can ignore how I feel about Ariana and pursue finding someone I can marry? I'm in love with her. That's the truth. And I believe she loves me, but I don't think she's *in* love with me. That aside, it's a wonderful, rock-solid friendship."

Dan stood and walked to the fireplace. "So you'll be her best friend until the right man comes along and she falls in love again?"

"That's about the gist of it. Look, I never expected the future with her to be easy. And I'll say this one last time, so hear me: after everything is said and done, I don't believe she could leave the Amish any more than I could cope with joining them."

"Have you asked her? Have you told her how you feel?"

"No, and I won't. Our volunteer work is valuable. Her contributions to the Amish are not any less important than me getting women and children out of violent situations. The strides she's making to open minds and hearts to truths the people in Summer Grove have never known or considered are incredible. If she leaves for any reason, but maybe especially if she left to be with me, an iron door will close."

Mamm knelt beside him, looking deep into his eyes. "Quill, you getting a chance to build a life with Ariana is why I've stayed. It would've been so much easier to move back to live with my relatives in Indiana or even to leave the Amish and join you boys in Kentucky. But when you left with Frieda, and I was silently nudging you to do so, I came to realize how deeply Ariana loved you. She was young, and I thought that at fifteen she was only capable of a crush and she'd be over it in a few months. But I was wrong. She grieved hard for two years. When she came of dating age, she couldn't stomach the idea of going out with anyone for a while, and then she started dating a lot in order to put behind her what she felt for you. So when I saw how much you loved her, I decided to stay. Not interfering or nudging you two together in any way. Just being here so you could run into each other. But you're not even going to ask her out or anything?"

"I knew you were the best Mamm in the world." Quill plunked his mug on the table and looked at Dan. "*Finally* we know why Mamm wouldn't leave. What you've given Ari and me is incredible. The healing of past hurts I caused her is complete. She respects why I left. You did that, Mamm. Your sacrifice gave me the incredible friendship I have with her. But, Mamm, we can't let all these wonderful freedoms the new bishop is allowing cause us to forget that in her heart she's Amish and in my heart I'm not."

Mamm nodded. "I wanted to do more. I wanted to make up for wrong steps, wrong—"

"You know what, Mamm?" Quill clutched his hands around hers. "We love you so much for all you've done. Look around this room and absorb it. Please don't dip regret out of yesteryear's pool based on what we know today. If only we'd known this, we could've done that. I felt the same way after talking to the detective. But we didn't know. We can't rewind the clock. What we can do is stand in faith, trusting we have the strength for each new day. All of us are here, in your home together on Christmas Eve. That is an act of God, so let's celebrate that miraculous gift."

Mamm smiled, nodding. "Okay."

Quill helped her stand. He offered her his chair, but she didn't sit.

"I have food to fix and presents to wrap." She walked toward the kitchen but stopped.

Quill sat again.

Dan scratched his head. "Then what can we do to help if this no-win love affair continues across the decades?"

"Dan, stop," Regina scoffed while shifting Gavin on her hip. "All this endless talk of how things might go, and you, dear husband, are ignoring the fact that every concern you've expressed over Quill's future could unravel with one strong tug by the gatherer of threads herself—Ariana."

Quill's heart thudded at the thought. He couldn't ask her to leave the Amish for him, but at the same time, he knew his will to leave her Amish life intact would come undone if Ariana fell in love with him. "You understand that even under the new ministers, her leaving would cause a difficult division between her and her family. They love her, and that won't change, but their contact with her would be considered a bad influence on the family and the community as a whole."

"But they allow Skylar to come and go," Regina said.

"That's different. She was raised Englisch and came to them as a drug-addicted mess. They helped her. The Amish ways got her on the right path for her. That's a positive story. Skylar was an outsider from the start, but Ariana was raised Amish. If she turns away, she won't be invited to weddings or births or birthday parties or holidays or even to a meal or to sit by the fire in the backyard and visit. They would have no choice but to consider her lifestyle as a poison she could pass on to others, especially those who haven't joined the faith. The adults would come to her place to visit, bring a dish, and stay for coffee, but she'd never again be welcome to join at will any family event. Come on, Regina, you know how this works. It's a divorce, and Ariana would lose custody of everyone who's Amish. We are all back in Mamm's house after years of battling, in part because she has no young Amish relatives that we could have a bad influence on. But could we go into any other Amish home to visit?"

She shook her head. "No. But love doesn't yield to facts. It doesn't fade because of obstacles or because there's pain that will have to be carried for a lifetime. Love bears all things and keeps thriving."

Quill didn't want that kind of loss for Ariana. But if she offered to leave the Amish for him, he would accept it. Still, it was too much for her to give up, even for a man who loved her more than life itself. His hope was that love would bear them remaining friends and nothing more. That's what was best for everyone involved, especially her.

"Knock, knock, knock." Ariana's voice echoed through the house, and a moment later she was standing in the doorway of the living room, her arms filled with presents. "Merry Christmas!"

His family welcomed her, and Dan lifted the gifts from her arms. Her eyes met Quill's, and she raised an eyebrow while grinning. "That's your deep-in-thought position."

He lifted his arms from the chair, looking at how he was sitting. "Is it?"

The sound of thunder rumbled through the house, and he knew the children were running. A moment later they hurried into the living room, laughing. Lexi was bouncing along with them as if she was part of the pack.

Ariana pulled a pair of ice skates off her shoulder and passed them to Quill. "You needed new skates. These are used, but they'll fit and work. Midnight. At the pond. Ya?"

Before he could answer, she melted to the floor, talking to his nieces and nephews about what they hoped to get for Christmas.

She didn't need for him to respond. There was no other answer but *yes.*

He knew they would skate and laugh and talk until he would barely be able to keep from pulling her into his arms.

Forty-Three

April

Steam rose in Abram's face as he stood over the grill, bacon sizzling on one side and six buttermilk pancakes cooking on the other. Martha was beside him, scrambling eggs and making toast. He glanced out the pass-through, seeing the new help as well as three of his sisters—Ariana, Skylar, and Susie—hustling to keep up with the Saturday crowd. Cilla was somewhere nearby, but he couldn't see her.

It was hard to believe that Ariana and Rudy had broken up more than a year ago. But after a couple of months, she'd seemed perfectly fine with it.

The low rumble of the café made him smile. It had closed for a week last month while a construction crew tore down a wall to the building next door and connected the two spaces. Ariana had bought that building too. That area now had seven couches, eight love seats, and three coffee tables scattered throughout, along with a dozen regular café tables with four chairs each.

He worked only on Saturdays now and on snowy or rainy days when roofing was at a standstill. Other than that, he and Jax were a team again, working long, productive hours on construction sites.

The café had become like an extension of the family's home, a place where they gathered to have special meals or to sample Ariana's newest recipes. Sometimes Ariana made anniversary dinners for their siblings and served only that one couple. Tonight she was serving Mamm and Daed a special meal here, but since it wasn't their anniversary or either of their birthdays, Abram wasn't sure why.

Cilla came through the swinging door, giggling about something. "Is the newest batch of chocolate croissants almost done?"

Martha put scrambled eggs on two plates that already had toast and bacon. She set them on the line. "Table two, please." She seized the pot holders. "I'll check the croissants, but the timer says they need three more minutes."

Cilla grabbed the plates, paused in front of Abram, and winked. September, the month they would marry, could not come soon enough for them. Every person who intended to join the faith would begin instruction classes next month. Abram returned the wink, and Cilla left the kitchen, causing the swinging door to swoosh back and forth.

He gripped two warm plates and set them on the counter and then stacked three pancakes and three pieces of bacon on each. "Table four. Order up." He moved the plates to the line.

Susie came into the kitchen, looking content and confident. She was still seeing Levi, the young Amish man she'd begun dating about nine months ago. He was really nice, two years older than Susie, and lived a few districts outside of Summer Grove. "Denki." She wasted no time taking the plates to table four.

All the café work would draw to a close for Abram and Cilla come fall. Once they were married, they would spend their Saturdays going through the process to become foster parents, and after they were licensed, they'd be busy caring for the foster children given to them. It had taken Cilla only a few weeks to be absolutely sure that she and Abram were meant to marry and, after talking with a nearby foster family, that they were meant to provide a home for foster children. Maybe one day God would allow them to become the forever parents to a few of those children.

Skylar's understanding of the foster-care system had been very helpful in getting them started.

Ariana swooshed into the kitchen just as the timer rang.

"How do you do that?" Abram asked. "You always waltz into the kitchen the moment the timer is going off for the croissants."

She grabbed pot holders. "Could be because it takes two days of prep to get them just right, and every part of me knows when they're ready." She removed the large pan from the oven and set it on the cooling counter. "Or it could be because I keep a timer in my apron pocket set one minute earlier than this one." She held up the timer from her pocket, chuckling.

"How did I not know that?" Abram looked at the orders on the rail to see what he needed to fix next.

"Guys." Skylar walked into the kitchen, hair in a ponytail, wearing jeans and a lacey pink tunic and holding a pot of coffee. "The hot plate for the coffee is cold. The generator seems to have cut out again."

Abram passed Skylar his white apron. "I'll see what's going on."

Skylar put the apron on and took over his place behind the grill. He grabbed his toolbox and went outside.

Ariana put on a sweater and walked out with him. "I refilled the tank before we opened."

"Ya, I know." Abram jiggled things, checked the tank, and tried to start it. The engine didn't turn. He got a Phillips screwdriver out of the toolbox. "There is no reason for this thing to act up. It's April, decent weather and everything," he mumbled while removing screws. "You know what you need, Ari? An Englisch partner so we can get approval to have electricity in the café. Skylar would agree to be that person, so why not ask her?"

Ariana moved to the small set of steps that led to the back door of the café. "I don't want to put her in an awkward position. She's here now, living in the loft and working at will, but if she becomes a partner, it would come with responsibilities and some weird dynamics to be DNA Amish and lifestyle Englisch. Besides, I . . . I have a plan to solve the issue. I just need a little more time."

"Ya?" He removed the cover. "Sounds good. What kind of plan?"

When she didn't answer, he set the cover aside and took a seat next to her. "Want to talk about it?"

"Ya. I've wanted to for a while, but it seemed right to talk to Mamm and Daed first."

"Ah, the reason you've made plans for just them to come here for dinner tonight, a private place to talk openly."

She stared out across the field. "Everyone did so much to get this café running while I was away, and you've never wavered in your love and respect, but . . ."

"You aren't joining the faith."

"I'm sorry."

He put his arm around her shoulders. He'd been fairly sure this was coming, but there weren't any words to describe the feeling. He was both disappointed for the loss it would mean and elated that she would be true to her heart and not follow the expectations others placed on her. "Mamm and Daed won't be as shocked or as hurt as you think."

She turned to look at him, and her eyes reflected hope that he was right. "I thought it was the right thing, the only thing, to remain Amish. I've been convinced God's purpose for me is that I use my knowledge of the worlds I know—Englisch and Amish, atheists and believers—to open minds and usher in truth and faith on all sides. But . . ."

"Now you're choosing not to go through instruction to join the faith."

She nodded.

Abram rubbed her shoulder. "I'm behind you, Ari. No one can fix all the ramifications of your decision, but I think with some time most of the Brennemans will learn to respect your decision, and I know Mamm and Daed will."

Forty-Four

May

Ariana put the finishing touches on the oversize birthday cake, staying on task when what she longed to do was walk across the Schlabach kitchen, cradle Quill's face, and kiss him. It was fully possible she'd accomplish more if she grabbed him by the shoulders and shook him. He was steadfast in friendship and stubbornly pretending there was nothing else between them.

Kerosene lamps burned as voices echoed off the walls. For the first time since Christmas, the whole gang of Schlabachs was at Berta's again, as well as Frieda and the young Mennonite man she was dating, Ryan. It was an evening set aside to celebrate every adult birthday. The Schlabachs and Frieda drew names and would exchange gifts after dinner. It was both a practical and memorable way of doing adult birthdays.

Ariana wasn't part of the family gift exchange, but Berta had asked her to help fix the meal and cake. Even if Berta hadn't asked, Ariana would still be here rather than with her Brenneman family. This was where she wanted to be. The more time she spent with Quill, the more time she wanted. Her feelings for him were driving her crazy. There was something so deep between them that it defied description.

"Hey." Quill's soft voice came from behind her, startling her. "Where are you?"

She realized then that Berta had called to her moments earlier. "Oh." Ariana glanced at the set table filled with food and surrounded by people. "We need to talk."

Last month when she'd told her parents she wasn't joining the faith, they had taken the news much better than she'd expected. But Daed had asked her to wait before officially coupling with Quill, not that they'd used the term *coupling*. He felt the family needed time to adjust, to talk about it openly. Her Daed asking for time to embrace the concept wasn't something he'd have done or even known he needed a year ago, so she'd agreed. Today was a month later, and her Daed had given her a gift to bring to Quill.

Quill's eyes were glued to her face. "A good talk or a bad one?"

"Good." She longed to grab him by the collar, pull him close, and tell him how she felt. "Really good."

Quill's smile warmed her heart. "Then what are you waiting for?"

"Hey, guys?" Regina called. "Very restless kids. Let's eat, please."

Ariana winked at Quill. "It's time to eat."

"I don't want to."

"That's a first." She set the decorating bag on the counter. "We'll talk later, after cake and presents and cleaning up the kitchen."

"Just torture a man, Ariana Brenneman." He talked while making his way toward his chair. "Anything else you need us to do first. Maybe milk the big herd at your Daed's place or something?"

She chuckled and took a seat. As Quill moved to the opposite side of the table, she could feel his eyes on her. After the prayer they passed the food around, and conversations flowed easily.

"So,"—Frieda passed her a bowl of mashed potatoes—"we think we've found a solution for where to live . . . after our July wedding, of course. I'd like to move within easy driving distance of here."

Schlabach Home Builders had a huge construction site not too far away, and the brothers had their homes in Kentucky up for sale. They intended to move about twenty miles outside of Summer Grove, far enough away they weren't bumping into Amish constantly, but close enough to visit Mamm more easily. Quill had yet to decide what to do. It made little sense to keep a place in Kentucky when their work for the next five years or more would be in Pennsylvania.

"About fifteen miles north of here, we found a cute home to rent that would work nicely. It's about halfway between Berta's place and Ryan's parents. I would just need to learn to drive."

The Schlabachs rumbled with approval. She'd met Ryan at a Mennonite multichurch event, and they seemed perfect for each other. And Quill, his brothers, and sisters-in-law had wanted her to get up the courage to learn to drive for quite a while now.

Ryan held out the bread to Frieda. "And I'm not teaching her. Apparently I make her nervous." He smiled at her in a way that was clearly flirting.

Dan cut a piece of steak. "Ariana picked up on driving pretty quickly, right? Maybe she could take you for a spin and show you a few things. You'd have to jump on that fast, though. Mamm, didn't you say that instruction begins during church tomorrow?"

"Is that how Amish instruction works?" Ryan asked. "You have to submit to all standards from the first day of instruction forward?"

"There's some leeway during that time period." Ariana grinned at Frieda. "But I'd be happy to teach you how to drive."

"Our new ministers are kind and caring," Berta said, "but don't invite trouble, Ari."

"I wouldn't. They know my intention."

"Your intention?" Dan asked.

"Dan, stay out of it." Quill shook his head as if annoyed, but Ariana saw the humor flicker in his eyes. Quill turned to Ari. "Your intention?"

The room rippled with laughter.

"I . . . I have a gift for you. From Daed." Ariana hurried to her satchel and pulled out a silvery box with a burgundy ribbon around it.

While Daed was trying to wrap his heart around the fact that Ariana wouldn't join the faith, he was in a furniture outlet store and stumbled onto a framed quote. He said the quote hit him so hard his knees almost buckled. It was exciting that her parents had the money to buy new furniture, but for Daed to see this quote in a remote corner of the store and for it to warm his heart meant so much to her.

She returned to the table. Everyone was quiet, watching Quill and eating in slow motion.

"From Isaac?" Quill untied the ribbon around it.

"Daed saw it and bought it, but it's as if the message is from me to you or you to me."

Quill lifted the lid. He saw the words and looked up at Ariana. Candlelight sparkled off the tears in his eyes. A moment later he was out of his chair. "Excuse us. Keep eating."

He took Ariana by the hand, and they went down the dimly lit hallway. Maybe she should've grabbed a candle or lantern.

"Your Daed believes the universe conspired to help me find you?" he asked.

"Or vice versa." She leaned against the door frame to his bedroom, taking in the man in front of her. She didn't need to ask if he loved her. She could feel it as clearly as if it were a physical object between them, as warm as a blazing fire on a winter's night, as vibrant as a garden in summer.

Quill rubbed his forehead, looking a bit unsure of what was happening. "This is how you feel?"

"You don't know?"

"I . . . I'd . . . dreamed, but reality has a gulf between us that I didn't expect . . ." He cradled her face. "You won't be able to be a part of everything going on in your Brenneman family. You'll be like a distant neighbor who gets the news after the fact and not the family invite."

"I will miss the freedom to come and go. But Mamm and Daed have promised to visit often. They'll keep the grandchildren so my siblings can do the same. There will be plenty of drop-ins by my older siblings at the café, without their little ones, and Susie and Martha can continue working there. But, ya, I'll grieve at times over the locked gate between them and me that only they hold the key to. But I know you'll help me through it. I know our joy will exceed that grief. And I know I will never regret us or choosing a lifetime with you. I promise. The real question is, can you trust me on that?"

He exhaled, leaning his forehead against hers. "I want to." He brushed his lips against her cheek. "God is my witness, I want to." He put a few inches between them.

She lifted his hand, turning his palm upward. "When I had to leave Summer Grove to live with my Englisch family, I was so angry with you I wouldn't allow contact between us."

"I remember."

"You knew I needed you, so no matter how difficult I was, you kept making yourself available to me. And the day came when my world crashed around me, and no amount of resolve could carry me through. I needed *you.* I needed you in order to survive in that chaos, but you can't see that I need you for everything? We are two people the universe has conspired to bring together, ya?"

"Ari," he whispered. He put her hand on the center of his chest, where his heart was pounding like mad. "Is this really happening?"

She tugged on the three-strand leather cord around his neck until she was holding the necklace, the one she had made for him when she was just a kid. Each cord had a meaning—one represented God, one her, and one Quill. The medallion had been forged from a silver spoon, and she'd drilled a hole in the center and carved angled braid marks across the round surface. He'd worn it ever since, almost as a prayer that it would be true—God, Ariana, and himself united forever.

She tugged gently on the tattered necklace. "It seems we've been in the process of happening since the day I was mistakenly brought into an Amish home from a burned-down clinic or maybe before that day."

He drew her hand to his lips and kissed it. "I think it'll take a lifetime to reveal to you how much I adore you."

"I'll take that deal. Is there something you want to ask me?"

"There is, but my question skips right past the all-important first date we've never had."

"It'll be a good story to share with our children and grandchildren."

"Will you marry me?"

"My heart on the topic is the same as it has been all my life, but my opinions about marriage and children have changed." She shook her index finger at him. "We'll write our own vows, and I want time with just us, no children. When we have children, I want to limit the number so that all our time and energy don't go only to us and ours but we have time and resources to give to others."

"Good grief, Ariana Brenneman." Quill kissed her face all over. "Tell me yes already."

She was tempted to say "yes already," but there would be time for reflecting on this moment and teasing about it later. It would be a good marriage, a fun one that each would be grateful for every day. "Ya, I'll marry you. Anytime. Anywhere."

"Somewhere neutral"—Quill hugged her, holding her gently in his warm embrace as he spoke—"so Mamm and your Amish family will feel comfortable attending . . . if they will."

"They will." She took a step back and cradled his handsome face. "I know we can find the perfect venue for us and our Amish and Englisch families. I know we can."

"Me too."

"Gut." She touched her lips with her finger. "Now kiss me."

Quill gazed into her eyes, seeming to absorb the beautiful, life-altering shock of the last few minutes.

He lowered his lips to hers.

Epilogue

Five years later

Standing inside the warmth of her own home, Ariana relaxed as Quill rubbed her shoulders, easing the discomfort from her achy body. Music drifted softly through their living room, and she turned to face her husband.

He slowly leaned in and put his forehead against hers. "Would you like to get off your feet? Jasmine cream and a foot rub await."

Ariana kissed his lips. "I'm fine right where I am, but thank you." She rested her head on his chest, her rounded belly not yet large enough to keep her from snuggling in Quill's arms. Often as he held her, she felt as if she were melting into him. If love were a tangible object, she was sure this home would burst at the seams. But love always served a purpose. Love felt good and gave energy, but its purpose reached far beyond that, and Ariana was fulfilled beyond her wildest imagination to be a part of all that love wanted to accomplish.

Quill oversaw all things electrical for Schlabach Home Builders, but his heart was more invested in helping women and their children who were in dangerous situations get to safety. Schlabach Home Builders and J&A Roofing, Jax's and Abram's business, had built a home for her and Quill, a small one with a beautiful craftsman breezeway that connected to Berta's home. After that they'd built a few homes as temporary housing for women and their children who'd been rescued.

Ariana had bought an additional building and now had expanded

Brennemans' Perks twice since the original purchase. The café was open eight to eight, six days a week, and there was always at least one Brenneman on duty during that time. She'd trained all of her sisters and her Mamm how to be the manager on site. She currently had forty other Amish women working for her. The café was a hub of the community. People—Englisch and Amish alike—filled the place to capacity regularly. Speakers still came once a month, and a permanent small stage had been added for them and for the live entertainment, which could be a local church band, karaoke, or even a cappella singing by Plain people, all of which happened on Saturday evenings.

Lexi was sprawled on the couch, seeming to doze, and yet her tail was slowly wagging.

Ariana's thoughts moved to her family. She and Quill visited with her Englisch family regularly—most often Brandi, Gabe, Cameron, and Nicholas. There were church traditions they kept with them, and they took turns going on trips with her mom's family and then her dad's. But the people she saw the most were her Amish family.

The dairy farm ran smoothly and at a good profit, so Daed and Mamm were doing really well. Salome and Emanuel still lived with Mamm and Daed, not because they had money issues or needed to save for future surgeries for Esther, but because the situation benefited both families. It freed Salome and Mamm to alternate working at the café while the other one kept things running smoothly at home. Esther had undergone a successful cosmetic surgery, which had been paid for, and the money for a second surgery, which should be the last one, was already saved.

Abram and Cilla had wed, but before they did, he'd informed the church leaders and both his family and hers that due to Cilla's cystic fibrosis, they'd decided they wouldn't have children of their own. The church leaders said the decision fell under the category of physical health, and they wouldn't express an opinion, and they expected the church members to follow suit. Cilla's family, her mom in particular, was very grateful to

Abram for making that difficult decision. They had adopted two precious little ones and had hopes of adopting at least two more.

As soon as Skylar finished college, she and Jax married. They continued to do volunteer work with the poor and homeless. Skylar's life was also immersed in teaching music—from private lessons for the underprivileged, to working with foster children and group homes, to helping Nicholas with charity events.

Susie was married, and she and Levi had a precious little boy.

Martha worked full time at the café. She seemed disinterested in getting married. Maybe she would be like Mark, who hadn't found *the* one until he was in his late twenties.

The baby made several rapid moves, and Ariana moved Quill's hand to her belly. His deep blue eyes gazed into hers, and her heart raced. Every day for five years he had let her know how grateful he was they were together. The baby seemed to ball up and shift to where Quill's hand was. They laughed softly. "You seem to have powers to move more than just me."

Quill grinned, and when the baby jolted, as if kicking a soccer ball, Quill startled and then laughed.

They didn't know the gender. It didn't matter. They were together, and this was their child. They'd held off starting their family for a lot of reasons, and now they hoped they would be blessed with three or four little ones, about two years apart. They were looking forward to the love and chaos that would fill this home, but Berta seemed even more excited than they were.

Ariana and Quill had ample time with his brothers, sisters-in-law, nieces, and nephews. She was blessed by her sisters working at the café, which allowed them to steal coffee breaks to visit. But as former Amish now living in the world, she had very limited time with many of her siblings' children. The parents had to make that decision, and Ariana did her best not to let that hurt her. Some of her siblings seemed to have resigned themselves to their reality—the Brenneman family would forever intermingle with their Englisch family in influential ways, and regardless of how respectful and careful Ariana, Quill, Skylar, and Jax were, the ongoing effect could not be undone or ignored.

Life and love were messy, and relationships were often hard, but through the upheaval that had almost broken her, she'd figured out who she was and what she wanted. Even in the best family situations, life was about walking in love and finding one's place.

Ariana had found hers.

Glossary

ach—oh

Ach, Daed, Ich lieb du.—Oh, Dad, I love you.

Ach, du liewi Bobbeli!—Oh, you dear baby!

Aenti—aunt

As gut—That's good

Ausbund—a hymnal

Bischt du allrecht?—Are you all right?

Daed—father or dad; pronounced "dat"

denki—thank you

des iss—this is

draus in da Welt—out in the world

Du kannscht.—You can't.

Englisch—non-Plain person, a term used by the Amish and Plain Mennonites

fehlerfrei—perfect

Gern gschehne.—You're welcome.

Grossmammi—grandmother

Guder Marye—Good morning

gut—good

hallo—hello

Ich bin hungerich.—I am hungry.

Ich denk du bischt verhuddelt. Du schwetze wunnerlich.—I think you are confused. You talk strange.

Iss es allrecht?—Is everything all right?

Iss es heiss?—Is it hot?

Kann Ich kumm rei?—Can I come in?

Kapp—prayer cap or covering

kumm—come

liewer Brudder—dear brother

Mamm—mom or mother

Mammi—grandmother

nee—no

Ordnung—order; set of rules

Sell iss wunderbaar, Daed.—That is wonderful, Dad.

Was iss geh uff?—What is going on?

wilkum—welcome

ya—yes

Main Characters

Ariana Brenneman—A dedicated but inexperienced twenty-year-old who was raised Amish. The truth surrounding her birth and the threat of a lawsuit against the midwife who delivered her has ripped Ariana from her beloved Amish roots.

Abram Brenneman—A loyal and supportive brother to Ariana who grew up believing she was his twin.

Isaac and **Lovina Brenneman**—A poor Amish couple that are dairy farmers. They have ten children, some grown and some minors. They raised Ariana, believing she was theirs.

Salome Brenneman Glick—The eldest Brenneman daughter, who is indecisive but loyal. She's married to **Emanuel,** and they have five children, including **Esther** and **Katie Ann.** They live in the same home as Isaac and Lovina.

Susie Brenneman—The eighteen-year-old daughter, who is sassy and determined.

Martha Brenneman—The fifteen-year-old daughter, who is sweet and maternal in nature.

Abner, Ivan, Mark, and **John Brenneman**—Along with Abram, the sons of Isaac and Lovina.

Brandi Nash—The Englisch mom who twenty years ago gave birth to Ariana in an Amish birthing center a few minutes before Lovina Brenneman gave birth to twins, a girl and then a boy. She is now a sincere, trendy, and fit mom who has raised Skylar as well as a stepdaughter, Cameron.

Skylar Nash—The talented but once-addicted young woman who was raised by Brandi Nash in a non-Amish home. She is the biological child of Lovina and Isaac, and the Brenneman children are her biological siblings.

Gabe Crespo—Brandi's husband and Cameron's father.

Cameron Crespo—Gabe's fifteen-year-old daughter, who befriends Ariana.

Nicholas Jenkins—Ariana's biological father, who helped raise Skylar Nash.

Lynn Jenkins—Nicholas's wife and mother of two sons, **Trent** and **Zachary.**

Quill Schlabach—A twenty-five-year-old man who grew up in Summer Grove with Ariana and was a close friend. But he has left the Amish.

Berta Schlabach—The mother of Quill and his four brothers—**Dan, Erastus, Leon,** and **Elam**—who have also left the Amish. She is also a matronly friend of Ariana's.

Frieda Miller—A friend of Ariana's who disappeared with Quill several years ago under mysterious circumstances.

Cilla Yoder—A young Amish woman who has cystic fibrosis. She helps out at Brennemans' Perks and has feelings for Abram. Her Mamm is **Emma,** and her sister is **Barbie.**

Noah Stoltzfoos—The bishop for Summer Grove.

Gia Rice—An abused woman with three children.

Yvonne—The cashier who passes messages to Gia.

Melanie—A woman who helps women escape bad or dangerous relationships.

Blake Torres—The detective who follows up on the case against Frieda's father.

Acknowledgments

To my Amish friends, as always, thank you.

To my wonderful family, you make my life all I want it to be.

A special thanks to my daughter-in-law Erin for all the help—from office work to powerful brainstorming sessions to endless encouragement. Also special thanks to my youngest son, Tyler, for putting your life on pause, leaving New York, and meeting me at my writing hideout to help as needed, especially by updating notes and charts for editors so I could focus on the creative side of writing. Thank you to Catherine King, reader-turned-brainstorming-partner, for your help.

A very special thank-you to Common Grounds Coffee Shoppe and Mocha Moe's Coffee House—two very special cafés right here in Flowery Branch, Georgia. The atmosphere and character of each are quite different, and between the two I found the inspiration I needed throughout this three-book series—and as a bonus, many great cups of coffee, tasty foods, and lovely conversations with owners and managers!

I have dear memories of Gene Burch, manager of Common Grounds Coffee Shoppe, who passed away and is deeply missed by countless people. Contrary to normal store hours, Gene opened this coffee shop one beautiful Sunday afternoon in 2009 and helped us hang lights and tulle, and then he served food so I could host a bridal shower in that charming spot. It was then that Common Grounds kindled in me a desire to make that endearing café an integral part of a story line.

Thank you to its owner, Randy Dill, for being a rock in the community and for navigating the changes at the coffee house while supporting Gene through the toughest of times. And a warm thank-you to Susanne McManus, who now runs this lovely coffee shop.

Thank you to Mary Ann, Sameh, Moe, and Samantha Behiry, owners and operators of Mocha Moe's Coffee House. The ingenuity and resourcefulness of your café are too endearing not to become a part of my heart and therefore a part of the series as Ariana bought adjoining buildings and updated her café.